NO HONOR
IN DEATH

Siobhan Dunmoore Book 1

Eric Thomson

No Honor in Death
Copyright 2014 Eric Thomson
Third paperback edition October 2018

Published in Canada
By Sanddiver Books
ISBN: 978-1-5060877-3-3

Sanddiver
Books

— One —

Tortured metal screeched as the ship shook under the pounding of another broadside.

"Commander Dunmoore!"

Not just a shout but also a plea, a panicked entreaty. The voice drilled through pain and wormed its way into Siobhan Dunmoore's concussed brain, driving back the blessed darkness that had cocooned her momentarily. A strong arm shook her right shoulder and she gradually, unwillingly, reacquainted herself with her surroundings. The acrid stench of burned polymers and superheated metal assailed her nostrils. She grunted in distaste, reflexively, almost instinctively. The universe shook, and her body shifted abruptly. Something hard bit into her lower back and sent fresh waves of agony coursing through her.

She opened her eyes and closed them immediately, stung by the gray fumes filling the ship's bridge. Dunmoore's mind took a few seconds to reconnect with reality, and she immediately wished it had not. The worst nightmare was hundred times preferable to the pulsing horror around her. But this was war, and she was a commissioned officer of the Commonwealth Navy. Had been since... since too long.

"Commander, please wake up." The young ensign's voice tugged at her, fighting the part of her soul that craved darkness. Her memory of the last moments before the plunge into unconsciousness came back mercilessly nonetheless.

Blinding salvos had hit the crippled ship's remaining shields, collapsing them with a spectacular bloom of warring energies. In another place and another time, it would have been a beautiful, surreal sight: distorted auroras of green and blue, beacons in the night. But beneath shimmering curtains of light, the backlash from competing waves of radiation had burned through the hull, eating metal, plastic and flesh indiscriminately, cutting a wide swath of death through the already damaged battleship. The captain...

"Commander Dunmoore, please, you've got to wake up. The captain's dead. The CIC was destroyed by the last hit." Siobhan bit back a yelp of pain as the ship shuddered again. "You're in command."

The ensign was close to tears, his words half smothered by the insistent scream of the sirens. "They're coming back for another run. Please!" His naked, heart-rending plea finally broke through. Something within her knew that hiding from reality meant imminent death unless she did something. Though it might not make an iota of a difference. Her eyes focused on the smudged face hovering a few inches above hers.

Ye gods, he can't be old enough to shave yet. Are we so desperate that we take children into battle? The sudden weight of responsibility threatened to crush the air out of her struggling lungs, and full consciousness returned, unmercifully. *The ship, the crew, mine now, by default.*

Her eyes met Ensign Hernett's and she saw the terror fighting for dominance within them. He *was* a child, his gold rank stripe still shiny and new. Academy Class of '65, his commission a few weeks old and this, his first battle. Most likely his last, too.

With an effort of will Commander Siobhan Dunmoore, first officer of the battleship *Victoria Regina* pulled herself up on the twisted command chair, gasping at the surge of pain flaring through her battered body. She took the ensign's proffered hand, blinking away tears. Her eyes met Hernett's again, and she saw his need for reassurance, for someone to tell him what to do. It steadied her.

Dunmoore's head throbbed from the blow that had knocked her out. Nausea rose in her throat, and she barely suppressed a retch as the acid taste of bile filled her mouth.

She grimaced, turning her bruised, soot-smeared face into a mask of death. For a second or so, the image of another ruined bridge superimposed itself on her vision, and she made the mistake of shaking her head to clear away the mirage. Dunmoore nearly passed out again from the incredible pain.

Unsteadily, she braced herself on the jagged remains of the chair and glanced around at the damaged, smoking consoles, the shattered screens and dislocated bodies. Red battle lights, diffused by smoke, gave the ship's nerve center a hellish cast. Conduits had broken free and hung in tatters over the helm. The main view screen flickered and sparks flew as overloaded damage control systems gave up the fight. Dante's Inferno had nothing on *Victoria Regina*'s bridge. Satan and all his demons could be capering around and not look out of place. An automatic extinguisher hissed dully behind her, dampening an electric fire, one of many. Too many. She recognized a starship's death throes only too well.

Ashes to ashes...

"Status," Dunmoore croaked, still dizzy. She tried to raise her left hand to grasp the ensign by the shoulder, to steady herself but found her arm would not respond. A glance down told her why. It hung at an unnatural angle, the bones broken. Somehow, the injury did not register on her overloaded nervous system, though whatever had broken it had also torn open the sturdy, vacuum resistant material of her tunic. The flesh between the tattered strips of black material had more in common with raw liver than human skin.

Unreal. Like I'm not connected to that arm anymore. Severe nerve damage?

A blackened face appeared in front of her eyes, like some jinn from an ancient eastern fairy tale, complete with beard and turban.

No, that was a bandage. Too bad. A jinn would be damned useful right now.

"Number Two and Three shields have collapsed, sir." The apparition said, spitting out every word in a raspy, tortured voice. Gunnery Chief Sen was steadier than

Hernett, though his eyes had the same wild, frightened spark. Nobody ever got used to the carnage of a losing battle, not even after years of war. Some just learned how to ignore it for a short while. Others vanished into a permanent fugue. "The lower forward battery is out of commission, as are all the starboard guns."

Starboard... The word connected the last of the shaken synapses in Dunmoore's brain. The Imperial Shrehari cruiser *Tol Vakash*. Captain Brakal. He had ambushed *Victoria Regina* with a small task force five light years from enemy-occupied Cimmeria. A glance at the flickering tactical display confirmed what her memory dredged up: the old lady was selling her life dearly. Of Brakal's four-vessel force, only his ship remained. The smaller escorts were now nothing more than debris. But *Victoria Regina* was no longer in any condition to stop *Tol Vakash*. The Shrehari had struck her hard on the starboard side. Not quite a killing blow, but her lifeblood was draining away just as inexorably.

The human battleship hung in space like a punch-drunk boxer waiting for the knockout blow. Only there would not be a referee to stop the match or a manager to pick up the loser and nurse him back to health. The Imperial Deep Space Fleet bred killers, and it was *Victoria Regina's* misfortune to fall victim to one of the best.

Dunmoore's churning guts clenched into a tight knot, threatening another bout of nausea. Her brain did not want to believe what her eyes saw very clearly. Brakal was coming about to finish off *Victoria Regina* and kill what remained of her seven hundred and fifty strong crew. His attack had been masterful, unexpected and completely un-Shrehari, almost human in its unconventional daring and reckless disregard of imperial doctrine. It had worked. So far. But the fight was not quite over yet. The thought of all those lives hanging on her next order steadied Siobhan. A final, desperate gambit slowly formed in her mind.

Commander Dunmoore, acting captain of *Victoria Regina,* would have her say, and give Brakal a final lesson in human tactics. Even wrecked, the battleship remained a dangerous weapon. In the right hands.

A sudden wave of coughing racked Dunmoore's battered body, and she felt, for the first time, the full agony of her broken arm, bruised back and the hundreds of hot stabs where minuscule metal pieces had sliced through her battledress.

Damn! No nerve damage after all.

She clamped down on the pain, forcing herself to ignore everything but the Shrehari cruiser. Her eyes found the ship's status board, with a gaping black hole on the schematic where the Combat Information Center used to be. Gone, her friend and mentor, the captain of the ship, incinerated by a plasma bolt that had punched through armor and layers of decking. Dunmoore cleared her throat, blinking away the tears in her eyes. Bile rose again, burning like fire and added to the rage building within. Adnan had taught her well. His ship would go down fighting, as he would have wanted it. With an astonishing coldness, Siobhan Dunmoore knew what to do.

"Helm, bring her about — ninety degrees starboard — increase speed to one-half and stand by for further course changes." Siobhan's voice was uncharacteristically hoarse, deep, unfeminine, damaged by the toxic fumes and the stress of battle, but it carried a firmness that steadied the helmsman, though his fear was still very real and all too visible in his wide-eyed stare. Another kid caught in the implacable meat grinder of war.

"Ninety degrees to starboard, increase to one-half and stand by for further course changes, aye, sir." At least his voice remained steady. Navy training prevailed. Siobhan felt a sudden flash of pride in her crew. There would be commendations for everyone when this was over.

Provided the afterlife has a subspace link to 3rd Fleet.

"Engage. Guns, bring all remaining firepower to bear forward, ready at my command."

"Aye," the chief growled from his console, visibly relieved that Dunmoore had taken control and was giving orders, any orders. "You've got the upper forward battery, the port guns, and the secondary forward guns. And one missile launcher."

He could have added, 'less than half of *Victoria Regina's* full armament,' but Dunmoore knew that. As first officer, she knew the battleship intimately and experienced the pain of her death throes. The *VR* had been — *was* — a good ship.

The massive vessel slowly came about and accelerated, her abused hull creaking ominously. All eyes remained fixed on the flickering screen, the dazed and shocked survivors oblivious to the ship's death rattle. A small bright speck grew steadily against the backdrop of stars: *Tol Vakash* on a collision course.

Learn, you Shrehari bastard, that unpredictability and surprise is mine to use at will.

A surge of viciousness, driven by pain and despair, filled her. "Helm, come to mark sixty, rotate on central axis one-hundred and eighty. Now!"

To his credit, the terrorized young petty officer at the starship's controls reacted promptly. *Victoria Regina* rose above *Tol Vakash's* course, her hull groaning so loudly that several of the bridge crew exchanged worried looks as if fear of the ship breaking up added anything more to the general terror of fighting a losing battle, lightyears from home. Maneuvering thrusters firing along her hull, the Empress Class battleship turned slowly in a maneuver that owed more to pre-spaceflight barnstormers than wet navy tactics.

Dunmoore steadied herself and gave the crew a final glance. The old gunnery chief met her eyes. He had figured out what she was about to do and nodded minutely in approval before turning his attention back to his weapons. None of the others had an inkling of her intentions. But then, chief petty officer second class Sen and she were the only veterans left alive on the bridge. The rest were mere kids. Kids about to join the millions already ground up by the Shrehari war machine. The Empire had a lot to answer for. So did her own government.

"Helm, zee minus one-hundred at my mark; prepare to increase to full."

"Zee minus one-hundred."

"MARK!"

With a sound of rending metal, the battleship *Victoria Regina*, almost a kilometer long and a third of a kilometer wide, plunged to spear *Tol Vakash* in a last, desperate attempt to salvage at least a pyrrhic victory from this disastrous encounter. A panel tore loose as the internal gravity wavered, the generators stressed beyond specs. No one paid the falling debris any attention.

Somehow, as if she had a window into Brakal's mind, Dunmoore could sense his surprise, his sudden hesitation at the unexpected maneuver. Battleships were not designed to move like fighters, and battleship captains were not known for kamikaze attacks. *Tol Vakash* filled the center of the screen, looking like a butterfly about to be pinned down by a collector's needle. Part of Dunmoore's mind screamed at her to change course, avoid the collision, but she, like the others, stared at the screen with sick fascination, hypnotized by the onrush of death. Theirs and the hated Imperials'. Lord Tennyson's words, dimly remembered, came back to her.

...Into the valley of death...

"Optimum range, sir," Chief Sen called out.

"Wait for it," Siobhan replied, her voice rising above the noise of a ship at the limits of endurance. "At point-blank."

Victoria Regina shook under the thrust of her sublight drive, beginning to disintegrate on her own, well before she struck her opponent. Ensign Hernett turned to stare at her, a pleading, puppy-like look in his eyes. He did not want to die. None of them wanted to die. Siobhan gave him a tight, brief smile. For a shavetail, the kid had held up splendidly. He would have made a good line officer with a bit more experience. Too bad.

"Guns, at my mark..."

*

Siobhan Dunmoore woke, bathed in sweat, her heart beating a loud, disjointed tattoo that filled her ears with the dull roar of rushing blood. She knew she had yelled out the order. Again. Her left arm hurt like crazy, though the multiple fractures had been healed by *Victoria*

Regina's skillful surgeon weeks earlier. It still looked like hell and the cellular memory of pain remained all too vivid.

The cabin was quiet. Only the hint of a hum disturbed the monastic silence. The absence of sound was shocking after the deafening pressure of her nightmare, the same nightmare she had most nights. But she was no longer on *Victoria Regina*. She was on Starbase 31, in the transient officers' quarters, and the old battleship was nothing more than orbiting scrap, awaiting final disposal in a star system many light years away, her bell already in a navy museum, awaiting the birth of a new ship with the same name. The way this war was going, the bell might not wait too long.

As for the Grim Reaper...

The nightmares were slowly sapping Dunmoore's sanity. The *VR* was the fourth ship she had shot out from under her in less than five years. Two of them had been her own commands. What made this one worse was Adnan's death. He had been one of the few people in the Fleet whom she could truly call her friend, and whom she would trust with her life. Now she felt utterly alone again, vulnerable and open to the petty politics that had pursued her for years. Or maybe it was all paranoia. She no longer knew.

They say even paranoids have enemies.

She rose and ran a long, slender hand through short hair the color of burnished copper. The timepiece by her bed showed it was nearly three bells in the morning watch. There was no point in trying to sleep again, though her body and her soul craved rest, it was not the kind of rest she could get during an interstellar war. She had seen more than her share of action and bore the scars to prove it. Yet the Fleet would give her no respite. Experienced officers were a precious commodity, even officers like Siobhan, who teetered on the edge of burnout.

With the last tendrils of her all too vivid dream slowly dissipating, she stepped into the shower and washed off the restless night. Standing under the warm air jets, Siobhan glanced at herself in the mirror and sighed. She looked thinner than ever, drawn, and pale, with sunken, dark rimmed eyes.

Though Dunmoore's handsome, angular face was but a pale shadow of itself, where even the smattering of freckles had faded with fatigue, her large brown eyes still radiated an intensity that could silence the most insubordinate spacer. Now, though, they also had that strange spark people usually associated with nut cases. They were the eyes of someone who heard voices and had an irresistible urge to obey them.

And what are my voices saying today?

Those eyes had stared down Captain Brakal of the Imperial Shrehari Deep Space Fleet moments before he broke off a fight that had suddenly become uneven. No sane commander risked a good ship against a madwoman with nothing left to lose and the full bulk of a dying battleship at her command. Brakal had been outmatched by despair, and he had known it. Yet in his parting call, he had honored the humans in the ritual Shrehari way. No wonder the imperial commander was fast becoming a legend among his Commonwealth opponents. The kind of legend to make human commanders envious. Especially commanders like Siobhan Dunmoore. With her record, the only thing she was fast becoming was a three-striped jinx. Which made the new assignment all too fitting. And if Fate continued to fuck Siobhan Dunmoore with her fickle finger, this could just as well become her final assignment, let alone her final command.

Shaking off the early morning blue devils with an irritated shake of the head, Siobhan finished washing and pulled on a clean, well-pressed service uniform. The dark blue, high-collared tunic with the three gold stripes of her rank on the cuffs of both sleeves, hung loosely on her tall, slender, almost rangy frame. She bore a long pale scar running from behind her right ear along her jaw line and down the side of her neck, disappearing under the tunic's collar, a souvenir of the battle of Antae Carina, where she had lost the corvette *Shenzen*. It was only one of many such marks of a hard career etched on a tough body.

As a final touch, she slipped on thin, black, leather gloves, to hide the ugly scarring on her left hand, burned by reactor coolant on the cruiser *Sala-Ad-Din* as the crew fought to keep it from exploding. At least the hand still worked, mostly. When this war was over, maybe she would be able to get reconstructive plastic surgery. *When...* Maybe by then she would not care anymore. Or she would be dead, like so many of the Academy class of '53.

At thirty-four, Siobhan Dunmoore looked like a woman ten years older. Crow's feet at the corner of the eyes from too much squinting, lines around the mouth from too much worrying and a dusting of gray hair at the temples from too many sleepless nights. But she did look every inch the veteran starship captain she would be again in a few hours, right down to the impressive rows of ribbons on her left breast. Veteran, at thirty-four. She shook her head in a mixture of amusement and despair. She had reached the rank of commander in just under twelve years, as fast, if not faster than her youthful ambition had once desired. But nobody had told her it would be this hard, this wrenching, this utterly draining. No wonder so many starship captains either burned out or went mad. Right now it was an even bet which way she would go. Maybe she should get herself a pair of steel marbles to play with, just in case.

A few minutes before six in the morning, Commander Dunmoore left her temporary accommodations and made her way to the officer's mess for breakfast. The rest of her meager personal belongings were already on board. Or should be. Shifting from ship to ship, a few times in nothing more than a lifeboat had whittled down her luggage considerably. But she had long ago learned to save sentimentality for human beings, not objects, and her spare personal life reflected her spare turn of mind. Unattached, unburdened and, she thought with a wry grin, unhinged. Fortunately, no one was around to see the sudden, manic twist on her thin lips.

*

The spartan mess hall was empty save for a navy steward who promptly seated her by the huge bay windows and poured her a large mug of coffee. While she sipped the scalding liquid and waited for her meal, Siobhan Dunmoore let her eyes roam the cavernous inner space dock. Five of the 31st Battle Group's ships were docked for repairs and refit after a brutal tour on the line. But only one ship interested her, an old missile frigate close to retirement, the last of her class afloat. Whether that retirement would be honorable or not would depend on one Commander Siobhan Dunmoore, soon to be the captain of the missile frigate *Stingray*.

An unlucky captain for an unlucky ship.

From a distance, the frigate retained her graceful beauty, with the elongated sweep of her main hull, the slant of the two-tier superstructure on her top and the single tier on her keel, and the main hull framed by long hyperdrive nacelles. She had the elegance of a bygone age when the slow pace of peacetime naval construction gave shipwrights and architects the time and desire to create not merely functional ships, but beautiful, efficient designs. *Stingray* was all that, and much more. But she was also worn out, one of a dying breed, surpassed by the quickly designed and built wartime products of thirty shipyards working around the clock.

Stingray was supposed to be in refit after her last cruise, but Dunmoore could not see any activity around her. A frown creased her forehead. The 31st, like any other Battle Group, was hard pressed and could not afford to keep its ships in the dock for any length of time. Starship engineers worked watch after watch to keep them in space. Why could she see no evidence of that on her new command?

It was a question that could have many reasonable answers, yet her mind found only one. And that answer did not bode well for the crew. Admiral Nagira had warned her, and he was a fair man, able to stay above all the petty intrigues that had followed Dunmoore for most of her career. She replayed the interview with the commander of the 3rd Fleet again in her mind.

*

"The investigation into the loss of *Victoria Regina* has determined that a Court of Inquiry will be unnecessary. Captain Prighte and you acted with the highest professionalism and competence. I have recommended Captain Prighte for a posthumous Navy Cross, which means he shall probably get a Distinguished Service Medal," Nagira shrugged at the navy's idiosyncrasies. Personally, he would have given Prighte the Commonwealth Medal of Honor for his leadership, but the politics of the Service had long ago placed the dead captain among the outsiders. Insisting on Dunmoore as first officer had made him no friends among the privileged and incompetent of what Nagira privately thought of as the officer caste, the wealthy, indolent drones who advanced through patronage, not ability. Fortunately, the war was weeding them out through courts martial and deaths. Not fast enough, in his opinion, but in a few more years, the officer corps as a whole should be a whole lot healthier, provided the Empire did not win.

"We have lost a good captain, and a strong ship. *Victoria Regina* is to be scrapped. She is beyond repair."

This time, it was Dunmoore's turn to shrug. She found it difficult to care for much. It had taken her seven days to bring the dying battleship home. Then, she dealt with the aftermath, writing to the families of the two hundred and thirteen killed crewmembers, answering the investigators' questions, visiting the injured in the base hospital, and all the other tasks that came with decommissioning a ship. She had no energy left and no time to regenerate her depleted reserves. The nightmares also gave her little rest when she did have some down time. Most of *Victoria Regina*'s senior officers were either dead or in sickbay, and she had to apportion the work among young, mostly shell-shocked lieutenants and ensigns, as well as bitter old chiefs. The *VR* had died hard, but it had been a lingering, painful death.

Vice-Admiral Nagira's comfortable office made an eerie contrast to *Victoria Regina*'s ruined compartments. Her eyes took in the richly tinted mahogany furniture, the leather-covered chairs, the cabinets with their intricate scrollwork, the Japanese silk prints on the walls, the sound-dampening wall-to-wall carpet, and the magnificent view of the planet below. But she did not really *see* any of it. Just as she could not bring herself to care much for the admiral's words.

"For what it's worth," Nagira continued, all too conscious of Dunmoore's state of mind, and worried for her more than he cared to admit, "the crew will all get commendations for their performance. Losing *Victoria Regina* might hurt us, but losing three escort cruisers will hurt the Shrehari more, as will the blow to Captain Brakal's prestige in the eyes of the Imperial High Command."

Dunmoore did not comment, and Vice-Admiral Nagira resumed his monologue after a quick sip of coffee. Siobhan too had a mug of the admiral's excellent brew in her hand, yet she had not given it any attention. Nagira's black eyes studied her weary face with concern.

"Your own actions after Captain Prighte's death will go far in removing any official doubts about your ability," he continued, "and I have directed that a special citation be included in your file. I know it will not do much in the short run." Dunmoore shrugged again, too tired to care about Nagira's sympathy. "But coupled with your actions at the Sigma Noctae Depot last year, it will go some way in protecting your career. You know I have always believed you to be a superior commander, and my faith remains unshaken."

Even though I wonder whether you did not lose too much of yourself on Victoria Regina.

Siobhan Dunmoore acknowledged the compliment with a nod, but her face remained set in its weary lines.

"Thank you, sir." It came out strangled and hoarse. Nagira examined her face, wondering whether it was emotion or remaining damage to her vocal cords. He needed her strength and her clear mind.

"I have been looking for a suitable command for you ever since *Victoria Regina* limped in, held together only by the force of your will and the strength of your crew. I will not hide the fact that your name still brings up considerable opposition from certain quarters, but I was insistent and ultimately successful. However, I fear your new command will be a double-edged sword." This time, Admiral Nagira was rewarded with a slight raising of Dunmoore's eyebrows.

"I suspect I obtained that command for you because no one else wanted it, which probably commended it to the enemies of Siobhan Dunmoore." Nagira shook his head minutely. That was not exactly the whole truth, but close enough. The same could be said for his next words. "I need every ship I can put on the border, and I don't believe in superstition. As far as I am concerned, you are getting that command because you are probably the one officer in the 3rd Fleet who stands a good chance of rehabilitating her. My other option is to disperse her ship's company and start from scratch. Which would be a waste of a potentially decent crew."

"What ship, sir?" Siobhan asked, a sick kind of interest now animating her pale face. She heard the gossip of the Fleet as much as any other officer and the worm of suspicion raised its ugly head. This was the moment most officers dreamed about, getting a major starship of their own. Not a small auxiliary or escort, but a rated ship. It should have been her moment of personal glory. But the sick feeling only intensified and Siobhan took a deep breath, setting the coffee aside as if the strong, bitter scent nauseated her.

"The missile frigate *Stingray*."

"I thought so," she whispered. "The unlucky ship. The jinx."

"As I said, commander," Nagira replied with more sharpness in his voice than he had intended to use, "I do not believe in superstition. However, I do believe in bad leadership, and *Stingray* is a sad example of the worst kind. Her previous captain is now facing a Disciplinary Board and will probably be dismissed from the Service."

"Who is he?"

"She." He paused for a few heartbeats. "Commander Helen Forenza." When he saw Dunmoore's face tighten, hc gently continued, "I told you this assignment was a double-edged sword, Siobhan. I would rather try to rehabilitate *Stingray* than take her out of service, and you are the one officer I believe can do it."

"Because I've got little left to lose?" Dunmoore asked bitterly, showing real emotion for the first time.

Nagira sighed mentally. It was not a reaction he liked. She had more than enough reason for bitterness, but sinking into self-pity was something that did not suit her. Yet he could not tell her everything.

"No, Siobhan. Because I have faith in you. And whether you believe it or not, you have more to lose than you think. You *do* have friends."

Dunmoore looked away, embarrassed at her conflicting emotions. She had always hated people who wallowed in self-pity. Now, she was guilty of that sin herself and despised her own weakness. Nagira sipped his coffee in silence, letting her sort out her feelings. If the old combative spark was still there, somewhere, she would take up the challenge and win, or go down trying. If it was not, then she was lost to the Fleet no matter what.

After a few moments, Siobhan looked up at him, face set in an implacable mask.

"When do I take command, sir?"

Nagira repressed a smile of pleasure, conscious that Siobhan, in her present state, would have interpreted it as a smirk of victory. She had a volatile character, and that made her a top-notch fighting captain, but when she was down, that trait turned against her and those around her at the most awkward times. And this was as awkward as it got.

"In four days, Commander Dunmoore. That will give you enough time to take the courier run to Starbase 31. There will be no formal change of command. Commander Forenza has already been shipped planet side and is currently awaiting the board's pleasure."

"Thank you, sir. Will that be all, sir?" She was suddenly impatient to leave and drown her misery in work.

"Yes, commander." Nagira rose, followed by Dunmoore. "Your orders will be delivered to your quarters by this afternoon. Good luck." He held out his hand. Siobhan took it and gave him a perfunctory shake. Then she straightened up and saluted with just a touch of the old rebellious, insubordinate and self-confident Siobhan. The spark he had seen in a young, bright, and aggressive lieutenant long ago was still there.

As she turned to leave, Nagira softly said, "Just remember to trust your instincts, Siobhan. You are a good officer, and spacers respect that. And," he smiled briefly, "stay away from windmills."

Then, she was gone.

Nagira stared at the closed door for a long time, wondering whether he had condemned her to career oblivion, or worse, and deprived the navy of the services of a good commander. But there was no painless escape from this one. Dispersing *Stingray*'s crew was the coward's way out, and Hoko Nagira had prided himself on never taking the easy route. Yet he wondered whether Siobhan, already teetering on the edge, would be able to salvage the ship, its company, and its reputation, without utterly ruining what was left of hers, or worse, destroying her sanity.

*

Siobhan drained her mug, the coffee's bitter tang mirroring the residual bitterness in her soul. Her interview with the 31st Battle Group's flag captain, an hour after arriving the previous day, had only reinforced the fears raised by words Admiral Nagira *had not* spoken.

As prescribed by naval tradition, Dunmoore had immediately gone from the docking port to the command deck, intending to report to Rear Admiral Kaleri, her new commander.

An officious senior clerk informed her Kaleri was not available, and she was to report to Flag Captain Jadin. Seething at the man's manners, but unwilling to cause a scene the moment she arrived at a new duty station, Siobhan beat a quick retreat to Jadin's office suite. The flag captain kept her waiting for an hour, while clerks and junior officers streamed in and out of his office at a constant rate. It did not bode well for a pleasant meeting.

Finally, an acne-scarred lieutenant poked his head into the antechamber.

"Captain Jadin will see you now." After a brief pause, he added, "Sir."

Siobhan took a deep breath to flush her resentment away and marched in, coming to a halt the prescribed three paces in front of Jadin's desk. She saluted. The flag captain, gazing out the window at the distant field of stars, did not turn or otherwise acknowledge her existence. Angry, Siobhan dropped her hand and assumed the parade rest position. After nearly a minute, Jadin turned around and examined her much as a biologist examines a new species of bacteria. Stung, Siobhan returned the favor.

Flag Captain Jadin was thin, elderly and carried himself with almost artificial erectness. His weak, receding chin, beaked nose, and bulging eyes gave him the kind of pop-eyed appearance that had been fodder for caricaturists for centuries. The eyes held a disdainful, detached look. He sniffed.

"Commander Dunmoore. I see you are not quite recovered from your ordeal on *Victoria Regina*. Well publicized, that was." His enunciation was excruciatingly perfect, pedantic even, and his tone left no doubt that he believed the publicity surrounding Siobhan's actions was at her instigation, for self-promotion.

"Admiral Kaleri is on the planet right now, and will not be able to receive you. I shall not disguise the fact that your arrival is unwanted by the admiral. In her opinion, which I share..." *You probably do not have a bloody opinion of your own,* Siobhan savagely retorted in her mind. "...*Stingray* should be decommissioned without delay. The ship is old and the crew — well you shall see for yourself. It distresses Admiral Kaleri that her recommendations were not considered. Nevertheless, you are here, though I have serious doubts about your competence to command a frigate. You have a questionable record of accomplishment with your previous commands. I suppose being one of Admiral Nagira's favorites makes that irrelevant."

Siobhan did not reply for a few moments, but her anger dissipated, replaced by a coldness that matched Jadin's. *Very well. This is how it's to be, then.* "Thank you for making my position clear, sir. I shall endeavor to prove you wrong."

"Or die trying?" Jadin mockingly asked, not at all put out by his inability to provoke her into an insubordinate response. "We shall soon see. I wish you to familiarize yourself with this Battle Group's standing orders, operating procedures and signals. You will sail in one week from now. Make sure your ship is ready, or suffer the consequences. I will have your orders sent over in the next few days."

Jadin turned his back toward Siobhan and gazed out the window again, signaling the end of the interview. Dunmoore snapped to attention, saluted and turned on her heels. His voice checked her step.

"One piece of advice, commander. Keep your energies confined to your ship or yours might be one of the shortest commands in naval history."

*

"Excuse me, sir," the steward had reappeared at her elbow, carrying her breakfast. Siobhan's attention returned to the officers' mess, and she gazed up at the man in surprise. He was a veteran, too disabled by combat injuries to continue serving on a warship and his white tunic bore a broad wound stripe. A badge of honor. He placed the plate in front of her and deftly refilled her coffee mug.

"Thank you, spacer."

"Be my pleasure, sir." His voice had a deep growl as if his vocal cords too had suffered the outrage of the Shrehari broadside that had beached him. She felt a sudden kinship with the man. They both bore the marks of their service like proud badges. He hovered near Dunmoore for a few moments, evidently wishing to speak, but unable to form the words.

"Begging your pardon, sir," he finally said, "you be takin' *Stingray* then?"

His eyes met hers without shame or fear.

"Aye."

His head bobbed. "Don't take no notice of her bein' a jinx then, sir. She's a good 'un an' she's got good spacers aboard. All they needs is a good skipper. One they can trust."

His words shocked Siobhan into momentary silence. Before she could recover, the steward had left.

Gazing thoughtfully at her ship, she ate her breakfast, wondering about Vice-Admiral Nagira's double-edged sword. When she took command of her previous ships, she had felt a buzz of excitement that made her whole body tingle with anticipation. Not this time. It was as if something vital within her had snapped, or simply worn out. Maybe it was the memories. Or maybe Siobhan Dunmoore was simply past it. Washed-out at thirty-four. She shrugged and finished eating, her eyes slipping back into the long-distance stare that alarmed spacers who had never experienced the losing side of a battle.

By the time she finished her meal, the mess had filled. Most of the other officers ignored her. She did not care. There was not a spacer on the station who did not know that the tall, redheaded commander with the tired eyes was the unlucky ship's new skipper.

She toyed with her mug until her chrono read fifteen minutes to the start of the forenoon watch, a quarter to eight in the morning. Dunmoore had sent a message to *Stingray* advising them she would come aboard at eight. There had been no reply, and she assumed that meant they were ready and waiting. If not, then God help them.

As she left the mess, she felt the eyes of many an officer on her receding back. And the eyes of a disfigured leading spacer in an immaculate white steward's tunic.

"Good luck," he whispered as the doors closed behind Siobhan, "because you're gonna need it, cap'n."

— Two —

The missile frigate *Stingray* was berthed at Dock 37, well below the station's habitat levels, down at the bottom of the central well. It seemed like the admiral wanted to keep her crew as far as possible from the others, to avoid contamination as if bad luck was contagious. Perhaps it was.

Siobhan ignored the glances, both curious and speculative, of spacers from other ships as she walked to her ship. She wore the silver and black stingray insignia on her left sleeve and a ship's captain's star on her right breast, leaving passers-by in no doubt of her identity. But the scrutiny did not actually register, and she absently returned salutes.

The station's side of Dock 37 was empty, abandoned as if no one wanted to approach the jinx. A thin layer of dust covered almost everything. The floor was deeply scarred and scuffed by generations of spacers and their gear. Through thick windows, Siobhan saw huge grappling arms holding the frigate tightly in her berth. *Stingray*'s white hull seemed as tired as her new skipper, her metal tarnished and aged under the dock's uncompromising lights. Close up, the frigate was huge, but even that was an illusion. The old *Victoria Regina* could have swallowed her for lunch without as much as a belch.

A transparent gangway tube led from the dock to *Stingray*'s main airlock, like a thick umbilical cord joining an unwanted child to an unwilling mother. An empty sentry post stood forlorn at its mouth, abandoned like the rest of the dock.

Dunmoore's footsteps echoed through the long, empty gangway. She kept her eyes fixed ahead, building up a head of steam. The ship's pitted and scarred main airlock was closed, but lights on the control panel showed green. It was not locked from the inside, contrary to standing regulations. Siobhan's face tightened as anger began to bubble up from within. Patience was not one of her virtues and this morning, it had vanished entirely. She breathed in deeply before touching the keypad, her nostrils filling with the acrid tang of lubricants, reactor coolant, and recycled station air. Kicking ass was a bad way to start a new command.

The airlock opened with the weary groan of lousy maintenance. Just inside, a petty officer second class, his service dress tunic unbuttoned, beret casually tucked under a shoulder strap, sat in a cheap chair balanced on its back legs, reading something no doubt pornographic. His erection was painfully visible under his tight uniform trousers.

At the noise, the man's head swiveled toward the gangway, a look of annoyance crossing his features. Then, his brain caught up with what his eyes saw, and he struggled to rise, overbalancing on the chair. He fell backward with a clatter, head striking the bulkhead with a dull thud while the reader went flying across the airlock, landing at Dunmoore's feet.

After a few stunned moments, he managed to untangle his thick limbs and awkwardly got to his feet, still dazed, struggling to regain some semblance of dignity. Fury tightened Commander Dunmoore's features. Her nostrils flared whitely as she stepped aboard her ship and saluted toward the bow, where in the days of wet navies, the national flag used to fly. Then, she turned her attention on the petty officer, examining him from head to toes with blazing, contemptuous eyes. He was a short, stocky man, with a red face covered by a fine tracery of broken veins. Small, piggish eyes framed a thick, oft-broken nose beneath a mop of dark, greasy hair.

Bleary-eyed, disheveled and unshaven, his breath and body odor were distinctly stale. The dark blue tunic had seen better days and bore evidence of food and drink stains. He was the sorriest picture of a non-commissioned officer Siobhan Dunmoore had ever seen.

She locked eyes with the PO and read the emotions passing through them. His initial annoyance had been replaced by fear, but that was in turn, giving way to a sly craftiness. Siobhan came to the instinctive conclusion that the man was a bully. Maybe even a coward, but definitely someone to watch. A good ship shone through her non-commissioned officers, and *Stingray* was looking shabbier by the second.

"Commander Dunmoore. Permission to come aboard?"

"Sir?" He attempted a smile, which faded the moment it appeared, killed by Siobhan's scornful stare.

"You are?"

"Petty Officer Second Class Zavaleta, sir. Bosun's mate."

"Tell me, *Petty Officer* Zavaleta, do you usually look like a bag of shit or is today a special occasion?" Siobhan kept her voice deliberately low. Zavaleta seemed to lean toward her as if to better understand her words. The slyness gave way to fear again at the lack of emotion in her expression.

"Sir?" He glanced down at his tunic and, fingers trembling, hastily buttoned it up. Then, he put his beret on and came to attention again.

"Pick up your bloody reader, PO Zavaleta."

"Aye, aye, sir."

Straightening up again, eyes narrowed in an unconscious display of rancor, Zavaleta truculently held out the reader, its screen gray and scuffed. "Palm print, please, sir."

Dunmoore placed her hand on the cool screen, but not without a twinge of revulsion at what it had shown moments earlier. "Commander Siobhan Dunmoore, captain, CSS *Stingray*."

The reader flashed as it acknowledged her identity.

"Permission to come aboard granted, sir," Zavaleta replied, his tone taking on more than a hint of nauseating oiliness. A bully, then. Someone who would have thrived under Commander Forenza.

Not under me, boyo. Nor, if you continue like this, will you keep those stripes for very long.

"Thank you," Dunmoore automatically responded. Then, her voice took on its earlier edge. "Zavaleta, you will not, under any circumstances, inform anyone on this ship that I have come aboard. Do you understand me?"

Zavaleta looked at her for a few heartbeats, digesting his new captain's order and then nodded as understanding filled his face. Understanding and a look of pure malice that disturbed Siobhan. She was repelled by the intensity of the naked emotion.

"Aye, aye, sir."

"And Zavaleta..."

"Sir?"

"Find someone to relieve you so you can get cleaned up and put on a proper uniform. And lose that porno crap you've got loaded on the reader. You've just used up your one chance with me. Next time I find you in this state, I will put you up on charges."

Leaving a stunned Zavaleta behind, Dunmoore stepped out of the airlock and into the main hull. The corridor was wide and well lit. Though free of litter and clean, it felt grungy. Siobhan could not explain the feeling as she walked toward the lift bank at the heart of the frigate. She did not meet any crewmembers along the way, and even though the ship's environmental systems hummed along, *Stingray* could just as well have been abandoned. She certainly felt that way. If starships had a soul, then this frigate was a very lonely one.

A poorly maintained lift whisked her up to the bridge deck. Moments later the door opened with a tired whisper, revealing a darkened compartment empty save for a single officer sitting in the command chair, playing a game on a small computer screen. At the sound of Dunmoore's entry, the officer, a lieutenant, looked up. More alert than the duty petty officer at the entry port, he immediately jumped to attention, his right hand quickly fastening his tunic.

"Lieutenant Devall, sir, officer of the watch, and ship's gunnery officer," he introduced himself in precise, clipped tones with only a hint of an accent. "Welcome aboard, captain."

Siobhan nodded. "Thank you, Mister Devall. At ease."

Devall relaxed minutely as she examined him in much the same way she had inspected Zavaleta. He was a good-looking man in his late twenties, with a handsome, chiseled face, intense blue eyes and impeccably styled blond hair. His uniform was superbly tailored and would have passed muster on any admiral's guard, or in any aristocratic salon. He had the look that spoke of a privileged upbringing, much like her predecessor, Helen Forenza.

The lieutenant's languid, almost nonchalant gaze, as he met Siobhan's eyes, was nevertheless guarded, wary, as he waited.

He examined Dunmoore in the same manner she examined him, and came to the conclusion that, exhausted as she seemed, *Stingray*'s new captain was probably as dangerous as an overloaded gun capacitor. He knew someone was going to taste the lash of her coiled anger before the watch was over.

"Stand easy, lieutenant," Siobhan finally said, her damaged vocal cords transforming the matter-of-fact words into a harsh order. He adopted the parade rest position, eyes staring over her right shoulder. "Where is the first officer?"

"Shore leave, sir."

Siobhan raised her eyebrows in astonishment. "Didn't you get my message that I'd be on board this morning?"

"Aye, sir. It's been logged in. But the first officer was already ashore. He didn't get the word." Malicious enjoyment briefly flashed across Devall's eyes.

No love lost there. "And the crew?" Her voice took on a dangerous edge.

"Half are on shore leave; the remainder is either at harbor watch stations or off duty." There was a barely perceptible pause. "Sir"

"I see," Siobhan replied abruptly, choosing to ignore Devall's manner. "Is it standard procedure on *Stingray* to have only the OOW on the bridge during harbor watch?"

Devall shrugged as if the question was irrelevant. The gesture annoyed Siobhan immensely. "There's not enough to do to bother with more than one person at a time."

"I see," Siobhan repeated, eyes narrowing. If it was standing procedure, she had no cause to tear into him until she established her own ways. *But if you do not get rid of your world-weary act soon, you'll find out what* my *ways are.*

"Open the ship's log, lieutenant."

"Sir." Devall nodded, his face losing all traces of his earlier disdain as he correctly read the captain's mood. He walked over to the first officer's station and touched the keypad. "Ready, sir."

Siobhan joined him, inhaling a brief whiff of expensive after-shave. She pulled a small data wafer out of her pocket and shoved it into the reader. Then, she placed her hand on the screen.

"Computer, I am Commander Siobhan Alaina Dunmoore, NO199235."

"Acknowledged," the computer's impersonal voice replied. At least this one sounded female. On *Victoria Regina,* the computer had always sounded like a muscle-bound bruiser. Some misguided soul had programmed it to flirt with her a few weeks after she took over as first officer, thinking it would be a splendid joke. A month of back-to-back watches had cured that particular sense of humor.

"I hereby take command of the frigate *Stingray.*"

"It has been so logged."

"Mister Devall," she turned to the lieutenant, "you will not post my taking command for another hour, nor will you advise anybody that I'm aboard."

"Aye, aye, sir," he replied, sudden amusement dancing in his pale eyes. He was quick on the uptake, usually a good trait in a gunnery officer. "Do you need someone to guide you around the ship?"

"No, lieutenant. I'm quite familiar with Type 203 frigates."

"Anything else then, sir?" The hint of disdain returned.

"No." Face set in a hard mask, Siobhan Dunmoore left the bridge. When she was gone, Devall shook his head and whistled softly. Many people were going to be in for one hell of a shock. Especially the first officer. He sat down in the command chair again, this time without loosening his tunic, and smiled. Dunmoore looked like someone who ran a tight ship. Good thing he had not taken Kowalski up on her bet.

*

The door to the wardroom automatically opened at her approach, exposing a sight that added fuel to Dunmoore's anger. Used plates, utensils, and cups littered the tables, the coffee urn was cold and empty, its traditional shine dulled by a lack of care. Like the ship itself. But what actually made Siobhan's blood boil was the sight of three officers sprawled around a littered table, their tunics unfastened and rumpled. The three, clearly worse for wear, were playing cards for money, in contravention of regulations.

It took them a few moments to realize their privacy had been invaded, and the oldest of the three, a woman, quickly got up and closed her jacket. The two younger men were up and getting dressed seconds later, their movements as unsteady as the focus of their bloodshot eyes.

Not trusting herself to speak Siobhan Dunmoore merely glared at the trio while they arranged their uniforms. When they finally came to attention, eyes staring straight ahead, the captain of *Stingray* took a deep breath and turned her blazing anger on the senior of the group. She was a hard-faced lieutenant of average height who appeared to be several years older than Siobhan. Her short dark hair was shot with gray, and lines marked the corners of her green eyes. Her bloodless lips were tightly pressed against each other. Siobhan read no shame or resentment on her face. She saw nothing at all.

"You are?" Dunmoore asked her.

"Luttrell, ship's surgeon," she replied in a surprisingly deep alto, "Sir."

For some reason, Siobhan got the impression that Luttrell dearly wanted to continue her sentence by asking, "And you?" She could almost see the surgeon bite her tongue. Turning toward the youngest man, an ensign who looked like he was fresh out of the Academy, almost young enough to be Luttrell's son, Siobhan asked, "You?"

"Ensign Sanghvi, sir, junior navigator." His face was red with shame, and he looked like he'd rather be reaming out plasma conduits under full sail than stand here explaining why he was gambling with his seniors. He was handsome, in a boyish way, with his mop of chestnut hair, and large, sensitive brown eyes.

The third officer, a large, bald, swarthy man who kept licking his thick lips was perspiring heavily.

"You?"

He bobbed his shiny, bullet-shaped head several times, lips working furiously. "Lieutenant Rossum, sir. Purser."

Dunmoore let the silence deepen as she stared at them.

"For some reason I cannot begin to identify," she growled, "I thought this was a warship, not some cheap, rat-infested floating casino. In all my years of service, I have *never* seen such a disgusting, filthy wardroom. If I didn't know better, I'd have you all imprisoned for impersonating commissioned officers of the Commonwealth Navy. Right now, I'm not sure whether to arrest you or make you clean this pig sty with a toothbrush." Before she lost what remained of her temper, Siobhan growled, "Clean this place up. Do it yourselves. Do not make the wardroom steward do it. Then get yourselves cleaned up. I will decide what to do with your sorry asses later." Then she turned on her heels and stomped out.

Luttrell glanced at her companions and grunted. "We've got a live one, laddies, and no mistake. Something tells me she subscribes to the hard-assed school of command, and doesn't give a shit what anyone thinks. It'll be an interesting change if nothing else."

"Gods above," Rossum wiped his forehead with a thick handkerchief, "hard-assed could get us all in deep trouble, Viv."

"I wouldn't worry too much, chums. She'll be wanting to look good, like all skippers. Turning over rocks to see what's wiggling underneath ain't gonna do it. So long as we keep the past as buried as it gets."

*

The door to the captain's cabin opened at Siobhan's touch, and she stepped gingerly over the threshold. It was bare save for the permanent fixtures: bed, desk, computer terminal, closet, and washroom. And the two small boxes containing her personal effects. At least those had made it to their proper destination. But bare as the cabin was, she could still feel the traces of Commander Forenza's occupation, a dampening presence just like the dullness she felt in every other part of the ship.

Siobhan and Forenza had been classmates at the Academy, and lifelong enemies. That Forenza had finally met her downfall was small consolation to Siobhan. Most likely her family connections would ensure she did not suffer for her misdeeds. The real story of her dismissal would probably never be known. Earthers protected each other. The only thing Siobhan knew for sure was if she failed to pick up the pieces left by Forenza's habitual self-indulgence and scheming, she would be the one paying the price.

*

Engineering was as silent as the proverbial grave. The main fusion reactor pulsed dully, its energies damped with the ship at anchor. She knew the matter/antimatter reactors in the nacelles would be dark and silent, dead without the highly volatile fuel.

A short, stocky woman wearing coveralls stamped with a lieutenant commander's two and a half stripes emerged from the chief engineer's office. She glanced at Dunmoore in surprise and came to attention.

"Chief Engineer Tiner, sir." Her small dark eyes darted around the engine room, looking everywhere except at Siobhan. Tiner had a seamed, weathered face topped by an unruly thatch of iron gray hair.

"Commander Dunmoore," Siobhan replied.

"Yes, sir. New captain, sir."

"Ah, finally someone who knew that I was expected aboard," Dunmoore replied with more than a hint of sarcasm in her voice. She immediately regretted her tone when she saw the engineer flinch. Siobhan forced herself to smile and took a gentler tone. "Why don't we tour the engine room, Mister Tiner? You can brief me on the ship's status."

Within minutes, Siobhan's heart began to sink. *Stingray* was in bad shape and deteriorating fast.

"Why the long list of repairs, Mister Tiner.?" The captain's voice was loud in the silent engine room. Before she could reply, Siobhan continued, her volatile temper gaining the upper hand. "Most of these problems you can fix yourself. All you need is to request the necessary parts. The ship has been in port for some time now. Did you do *anything* to put her back to rights?"

"Ah," Tiner floundered under the intense stare, "yes sir, we did a few minor fixes, but there – ah – was some question whether we would be decommissioned, sir."

"As you can deduce, this ship will remain in service. Therefore, I suggest you start work, and the sooner, the better. I expect my chief engineer to keep the ship running, not running for excuses."

"Ah, yes sir, but –"

"That will be all, Mister Tiner."

When the chief engineer returned to the privacy of her office, she found herself shaking uncontrollably, as if Dunmoore had jolted her with a live feed from the reactor. It did not matter that she had no choice under Captain Forenza. The ship was in a lousy state, and Tiner knew it. She ran a thick, callused hand through her hair and sighed. How she was going to get out of this mess with her career intact, she did not know.

*

By the time Siobhan returned to her cabin, she felt a pounding migraine grow behind her eyes. Pushing it aside as best she could, she turned on the intercom.

"Captain to bridge."

"Bridge," Devall's languid voice replied, "OOW."

"Mister Devall, send out an immediate recall for all crewmembers currently ashore. Leave is cancelled as of this moment. No one is to leave the ship unless it's on business. And track down the first officer."

"Aye, aye, sir."

"I want a status report in two hours. Captain out."

Without bothering to unpack her bags, Siobhan Dunmoore carefully lay down on the bed and closed her eyes. But wishing did not make the migraine disappear, no more than it made *Stingray* disappear.

On any other vessel, the arrival of a new captain meant a masthead to keel scrubbing, the full manning of the harbor watch and a proper side party to greet her. Instead, she saw a warship all but abandoned by people who had stopped caring. Whoever had logged her message had kept the information a closely guarded secret, knowing the blame would fall elsewhere.

— Three —

The intercom woke Dunmoore from a restless nap. She sat up too quickly, triggering a wave of nausea and she retched miserably, fighting to keep down the bitter, half-digested remains of her breakfast.

"Captain, the first officer has reported aboard. He's on his way to your quarters. Seven crew members are still unaccounted for."

"Good. Advise the shore patrol to arrest the missing people and deliver them to our airlock. Let me know when they've been handed over. And ask the cox'n to stand by. I'll see him after I speak with the first officer."

"Aye, aye, sir."

"Captain, out."

With an effort of will, Siobhan arranged her uniform. Then, she carefully sat behind the desk and waited. The wait was not very long.

"Come," she called out when the doorbell chimed.

A stocky, powerful looking man in his late thirties stepped into her cabin and came to attention in front of her desk. His square face was dominated by dark, hooded eyes that stared at her warily. He seemed older than Siobhan, and as tired and discouraged as she felt.

"Lieutenant Commander Pushkin reporting to the captain as ordered." The first officer saluted stiffly. His tone was clipped, his words precise, but he sounded strained. "I apologize I wasn't aboard when you arrived."

Dunmoore returned the salute. "Sit down, Mister Pushkin."

"I wasn't aware you'd be arriving this morning, sir," he replied defensively as he sat in the hard chair facing Siobhan.

"I sent a message to the ship yesterday when the courier docked. It has been logged in."

"The message wasn't passed on to me, sir." Pushkin's eyes held a dangerous glint. *Bingo*, Dunmoore thought. "But I'll make sure whoever forgot to tell me, won't forget again."

"I hope you enjoyed your shore leave," Siobhan replied, her voice still controlled, but nonetheless hard. "From what I've seen, it'll be a long time before anyone steps off the ship again."

Pushkin's nostrils flared. "It wasn't much of a leave, sir."

Siobhan arched her eyebrows. "Oh?"

"I was on ship's business, sir."

Dunmoore's voice took on a honey-sweet tone that masked her growing irritation. "Then pray tell why were you logged out as being on leave?"

"It was nothing." Pushkin looked past her shoulder at the porthole, his jaw working furiously.

"Nothing," she replied in a soft tone, eyes narrowed, "kept my first officer from carrying out his duties aboard this ship?"

Pushkin suddenly rose and turned angrily toward the door. "If you must know, captain, I was getting one of our crew out of jail dirtside. I logged it as leave so my movements didn't come to the attention of the Provost Marshall."

For a moment, Siobhan was speechless, robbed of her anger by his words and the intense bitterness in his voice. "Why?"

He whirled around to face her. "One of ours was about to get shafted by the local cops. They don't exactly adore the navy dirtside, war or no war. If I hadn't gone down myself, Able Spacer Bertram would be facing two to five for assault and battery."

"Did he do it?"

Pushkin laughed bitterly. "Does it matter, captain? But you wouldn't understand, would you? Simple spacers being pegged as fall guys for whatever crime they can pin on him. Just as long as it doesn't touch your precious reputation."

"Dammit!" Siobhan's voice lashed out, "that was uncalled for, Mister Pushkin, and as much of an insubordinate attitude as I'll tolerate on my ship now or ever. I'm as concerned for the welfare of my crew as you are. Judging by what I've seen so far, probably more." Red spots danced in front of her eyes. She breathed in deeply and sat down, eyes blazing.

"I'll let the matter pass. How you dealt with problems before now was your privilege as first officer. What concerns me more is this run down, damn near unserviceable ship with what looks like an unserviceable crew sitting at anchor, doing nothing whatsoever to regain space worthiness."

To Siobhan's surprise, Pushkin shrugged, his clenched fists loosening their death grip. "This ship hasn't exactly been a priority with Battle Group staff, captain. Nobody told us what was going to happen, and rumors of decommissioning her were in the air. Until Command decided what to do with the ship, there wasn't any point in wasting effort." He sounded almost defiant.

Siobhan did not know what angered her more. Pushkin's dismissal of his responsibilities, or his implicit admission that no one gave a damn for *Stingray*, not even her first officer.

"Mister Pushkin, rumors of decommissioning do not excuse the lack of care I've seen. Spacers who don't give a damn anymore are evidence of a lack of proper *leadership*, notwithstanding your commendable efforts to protect one of ours from rough justice dirtside."

"With all due respect, *sir*," Pushkin interrupted, his tone bordering again on insolence and contempt, "you know nothing about *Stingray*."

Siobhan slammed her hand on the desk's smooth surface, the sound echoing like the report of a gun. She ignored the pain coursing up her arm.

"Mister Pushkin, you will not interrupt me." Face white with anger at her loss of control, she breathed in deeply, struggling to recover her composure. Her eyes met Pushkin's again. The first officer, in his agitation, had let his guard slip, and Siobhan read his bitterness, a living, writhing thing, fighting to take over. The venom in his expression shook her enough to bring back her self-control.

"Very well, Mister Pushkin." Her voice was calm, relaxed, though her eyes still held his with the full force of her will. "Let's start this over again. I've been given command of *Stingray,* and my brief is to get her back into the war, notwithstanding anything that may have happened up to the moment I stepped aboard. This ship will sail in one week. I am prepared to do what I must to make this happen. You, the first officer, will be part of the solution, or you will find other employment. Understood?"

Face tight, Pushkin replied, "Aye, aye, sir."

"I wish to speak with all the officers in the wardroom, which had better be clean by now, in half an hour."

"Aye, aye, sir. Will that be all?"

"For now, Mister Pushkin. Dismissed."

He saluted Dunmoore with stiff precision, eyes filled with anger and humiliation. When he was gone, she sighed and slumped back in her chair, massaging her temples. The interview had gone as badly as she had feared. Though he deserved her anger, he was also, until she relieved him, her right hand, and the man who would turn her orders into action. One thing was clear by now. This was the unhappiest ship she had ever seen. Siobhan touched her desk terminal's screen.

"Computer, access authorization Dunmoore, captain's logs for the last six months."

"The captain's logs are unavailable," the computer's soothing, dull voice replied.

"Why?"

"Under Article 115.1, the captain's logs have been impounded by the Disciplinary Board, pending resolution of charges against Commander Forenza."

"Damn!"

"Please rephrase the question."

"Disregard," Siobhan smiled briefly at the computer's mistake. "Display ship's logs for the last cruise."

"Under Article 115.1, the ship's logs have been impounded by the Disciplinary Board, pending resolution of charges against Commander Forenza."

In frustration, Siobhan hit the keypad, switching the terminal off. If the Forenza family still had as many connections within the navy, those logs would vanish forever, no matter the outcome of Helen Forenza's hearing. The only way she would discover why her ship was in such a lousy state and why the crew's morale and pride were in tatters, was through her crew.

Siobhan got up, intending to work off her frustration by pacing the small cabin, but she forgot her migraine. She reached the toilet just in time.

In her misery, she did not hear the first ring of the door chime. When the sound finally registered, she climbed to her feet and glanced at herself in the mirror. If she had looked bad this morning, she looked ghastly now. Quickly rinsing out her mouth with water, she adjusted her uniform and returned to her desk.

"Come."

The door whispered open, and a thickset slab of a man stepped in. His close-cropped blond hair contrasted neatly with the short gray beard surrounding a battered, homely face. Intelligent, pale brown eyes shone under thick brows, framing a flattened nose. His shipboard uniform was clean and well-pressed, but the short tunic strained over a muscular chest. The sleeves of the tunic bore the starburst and crossed anchors of a chief petty officer second class.

Five years had wrought many changes on the man, but his coarse features still registered the smug satisfaction Siobhan knew so well. She rose, a smile breaking through her gloom.

There is a God after all.

"Cox'n reporting to the captain as ordered, sir," Chief Guthren saluted, a tentative grin emerging from the beard.

"It's been a long time, chief."

Siobhan felt unexpected warmth in the pit of her stomach. Five years and a whole lifetime ago, a younger woman, not yet worn out by strain and fatigue, had taken

command of a small scout ship. The powers that had
decreed a maverick lieutenant named Siobhan Dunmoore
would take her first step up the ladder of command had
also given her a senior petty officer under a suspended
threat of court-martial as cox'n: Guthren.

"Aye," Guthren relaxed, smiling with genuine affection
now, "a long time. You're looking well, skipper. An' your
stripes suit you. Not before time, either."

"Still a silver-tongued bastard." Guthren, dependable,
loyal and a true friend. Someone to watch her back aboard
this treacherous ship. "Sit, chief. Sorry, I can't offer you a
celebratory libation."

Guthren shrugged. "All ye have to do is breathe in
deeply. With the booze sloshing around this tub, I figure
a body could get a real hangover without the joy of
oblivion."

"That bad?"

The chief's eyes roamed the cabin, briefly touching the
ancient ship's clock on the sideboard, one of the captain's
few personal belongings that had survived all these years.
Its face bore the outline sketch of a gaunt knight on
horseback, holding a long, thin lance. The clock was a gift
from the crew of that scout ship, presented by Petty Officer
Guthren to the skipper on the day the old *Don Quixote* was
decommissioned and sent to a fiery grave. The *Don* had
been a happy ship, a family. He grimaced, facing Siobhan
again.

"Bad ain't the word, skipper. I came aboard last week,
the day the old skipper walked down the gangplank, to
replace a drunken idiot of a cox'n. With any luck, he'll
finish the war in a psych ward dirtside. The man had many
ghosts riding him, not least the ghost of Captain Forenza.
The whole ship is filled with those ghosts. What crew ain't
drunk is catatonic. Tried to kick some sense into the non-
coms, but they were past the point of caring. Just waiting
for a transfer, waiting for the crew to be broken up.
Officers, well..." he shrugged. "Spent the last few days
getting settled and digging up some dirt on this here tub.
No joy on the grapevine. People don't want to talk. When
I found out you were coming in as skipper, I figured I'd

better wait before really tearing into things. No point in sorting out the non-coms if the officers aren't gonna play."

His smile came back. "Though now that you're aboard, skipper, we can turn this thing back into a warship."

Siobhan tried to match his smile. Guthren's presence aboard did much to lift her spirits, but his words dampened most of that. The cox'n was a man of the old school. Tough, hard-nosed, brutal if necessary, but honest. And loyal, she reminded herself. That counted for so much.

"We will, chief," she sighed, "we will."

Guthren frowned briefly. He remembered Dunmoore as a fire-breathing damn-the-torpedoes kind of officer, one of those who would win the war for the Commonwealth. There was little of the old Dunmoore in the face of the tired, worn-out woman sitting across from him. Except in the eyes. They still burned somewhere deep within.

"What have you been up to lately?" Siobhan asked, massaging her temples, wanting to discuss anything but *Stingray*.

"This and that, skipper. I got my chief third stripes thanks to you after we left *Don Quixote*," they did not exactly leave the scout ship, more like scuttled it into a star, "and spent two years as cox'n on the *Shantung* corvette. Then they had me posted as company commander at boot camp, Fleet School Wyvern. Not exactly my first choice. I tried for Special Ops and made it through training. Spent six months with a team out on -" he paused, suddenly embarrassed. "Anyways, from there it was a quick jump to chief second and a posting here."

"A good way to spend a war, chief."

"Aye. Heard that you had a good run too, especially with the Sigma Noctae Depot. Spec Ops Command uses that one as a training problem," he beamed proudly. "A one-woman strike."

His face hardened quickly, however. "Anyways, I figure we both learned enough in the last while to take this bunch on and kick some serious butt. I'm ready to start the moment I walk out of here."

Siobhan nodded. "I've started already. Have you met Petty Officer Zavaleta?" She went on to describe her encounter with the man in excruciating detail.

Guthren grunted. "Zavaleta is a waste of rations from what I've seen and heard, skipper. A bully who should never have worn stripes. He must do his job somehow to survive, but for the rest…"

Dunmoore slumped back into her chair, massaging her temples again. "I'd really like to know what's wrong with the people on this frigate. I've seen garbage scows where the crew had more pride. My predecessor obviously had a different way of doing things. Different, hell! If the non-commissioned officers can run around looking and acting like Zavaleta…"

"Like I said, skipper, the crew's either drunk or staring out at a black hole. They'll need more'n a little shock treatment."

"Go ahead and do it. Hit 'em hard, chief and tell 'em how it is."

"Before the end of the watch, skipper," he nodded. "Begging' your pardon, sir, but Zavaleta was bloody lucky this morning, I'm thinking. Just let me sort 'em out, skipper. Like old times. We'll put this ship under navy discipline again." He briefly studied her exhausted face. "You just take care of yourself, sir."

"Aye, chief. And thank you."

Guthren rose, grinning. "Old times, skipper. *Don Quixote* was a good ship, with a good skipper. This one will be too, or I'm hanging up my starbursts."

*

"Ten-SHUN!"

Pushkin's bark silenced the assembled officers of *Stingray* as Dunmoore entered the wardroom. The buzz of animated conversation that Siobhan had heard from the passage died down, and seventeen pairs of eyes turned toward the captain. Many of them were bloodshot from lack of sleep or overindulgence of alcohol, or both.

A fine lot they were. Most wore shipboard dress, rumpled in many cases, except for the engineers, who seemed to wear their worn-out coveralls with a moody defiance. The eyes that met Dunmoore's showed a combination of wariness and fear when they betrayed any emotion at all. It was evident they had been discussing her.

They would be the usual mixture of average officers, incompetents and shining stars, with most falling into the first category. She would have to figure out who was what soon, and without Pushkin's help. If Devall's attitude was any indication of the wardroom's dislike for the first officer, then she was sure those feelings were reciprocated.

Repressing an overwhelming urge to clear her throat, a sure sign of nervousness, she let the silence live on for a few more heartbeats. Then, her voice cracked out loudly in the small room.

"At ease."

Like Lieutenant Devall had, earlier on the bridge, they assumed the more formal parade rest and did not stir. So they knew already she was a very pissed-off woman. Good.

"I am Commander Siobhan Dunmoore and as of eight bells in the morning watch, captain of *Stingray*. Under the circumstances, I'll dispense with the customary bullshit speech a new skipper usually gives. I am not at all sure I'm going to like being your captain, nor do I even for a moment think I've inherited a fine crew and ship."

Her tone was hard, her words sharp and she saw several of the younger officers take a sudden interest in what she had to say.

"It is my considered opinion, after spending the forenoon watch aboard this ship, that *Stingray* has more in common with a whorehouse than a Commonwealth warship."

The resentment was almost palpable, as were the undercurrents of humiliation and fear. But none made the fatal mistake of speaking out. The look of disgust on Siobhan's face, made harsher by her barely repressed pain, was too much for anyone to challenge.

"I don't really give a damn, about what happened under my predecessor. The state of the ship and crew speaks for itself. The navy and Admiral Nagira have given serious thought to dispersing this crew and starting from scratch.

You all know what that would mean to your careers." She paused and let her eyes rest on each of them in turn.

"Well, by the grace of God and the Grand Admiral, you've been given a chance to clean up your act, and I am the instrument of the Lord and the Admiralty. This ship will sail in one week, repaired and resupplied. Once we are out in interstellar space, I will retrain this crew to bring it back up to navy standards."

"Ladies and Gentlemen, the Commonwealth is at war and cannot spare a single ship, no matter how old. If you cannot or will not perform your duties by the standards I will set, I will rid myself of your presence so fast your lousy performance report will take *years* to catch up."

Her words cracked over the silent officers like a bullwhip.

"The enlisted spacers aboard this frigate look to you, the officers, for leadership and example, and by God, you will give it to them, or I will know the reason why. I have seen too many good officers, petty officers, and ratings die under the guns of the Shrehari to have any mercy for slackers, incompetents, and feather merchants."

"My orders on how this ship will be run are simple: by the book, as per navy discipline and without stinting any effort. There will be no more liberty during this stay in port, and you will be working back-to-back watches until I am satisfied that your individual departments and divisions are up to snuff."

"The cox'n will be informing the chiefs and petty officers of what I expect, and you will reinforce that by making sure the crew understands what I want. You will not get another warning, and I expect nothing less than exemplary discipline, conduct and work from this moment on. Department heads' meeting in the conference room *now*."

"Ten-SHUN!" Pushkin's order rang out, carrying with it the full weight of his resentment. When Dunmoore had vanished down the hallway, he speared the assembled officers with his cold eyes.

"You heard the captain," he growled, "and you will make damn sure her wishes are carried out, or I'll personally make your lives a living hell. The next officer who crosses me or stabs me in the back," he stared significantly at Devall, "will regret the day he or she was born."

Where the officers had been wary of meeting the captain's eyes or showing emotion, they had no such restraint for the first officer. Contempt, disgust, and anger challenged Pushkin and mocked his words. His face twisted into a cruel grin.

"Yes, hate me all you want," he growled, "but do as you're told. That woman," he pointed over his shoulder, "is no clown like the high-and-mighty Captain Forenza, and you'd do well to remember that."

He turned on his heels and escaped the wardroom for the bridge, leaving a low buzz of conversation in his wake. Word of the captain's tongue lashing would be around the ship before the end of the watch, no doubt feeding the hands' long-standing contempt for their officers. It would make Dunmoore's job that much harder, but if that is what she wanted, so be it. The contempt was richly deserved.

*

Siobhan looked around the table at the department heads. "To repeat what I told all the officers in the wardroom, this ship will sail in one week, repaired and ready. There will be no letup of work until all systems, and all departments meet the navy standards set out in the relevant publications and orders. And that, of course, includes individual discipline, dress and deportment, as well as the general cleanliness of personal quarters and common areas. I will not threaten you with reprisals for failure to meet the standards in the time allotted, nor will I accept excuses for such failure. If your departments fail to meet standards in one week, I will beach you, and you will never be employed aboard a ship again. Period. All of you know your jobs. Do them, or find another line of work."

She paused and gauged their reactions, reading their body language. Lieutenant Drex, the second officer, met her eyes openly, his expressionless face nevertheless hinting at approval. Luttrell, unsurprisingly, met Siobhan's gaze with the same lack of concern or emotion as before. Lieutenant Kowalski's stare challenged the captain while Devall's sardonic smile appeared to have become a permanent fixture since Siobhan had taken command of *Stingray*. Rossum, the purser, and Tiner, the engineer, avoided her eyes and looked down at the table.

"From now until we sail, no one will go ashore unless it's on business. All visits ashore will be in service dress, as will sentry duty at the entry port and the watch post on the station end of the gangway. Personnel on board ship will wear properly pressed and cleaned shipboard dress at all times unless their duties require wearing of coveralls or other work uniforms. Dress and deportment had better be up to Mister Guthren's exacting standards, or he will know why, officers included. No civilian clothing will be worn. No alcohol will be consumed aboard ship until further notice. Anyone smelling of booze gets a ticket to the brig. Those with stripes will lose them."

"Begging your pardon, cap'n, but the crew won't like that. It could spell trouble," Pushkin growled.

"Mister Pushkin, the day I run my ship according to the wishes of the crew isn't going to come in this eternity or the next," Siobhan replied, a dangerous edge in her tone. "No booze or recreation for anyone until it's deserved, understood?"

The first officer slowly nodded, "Aye, aye, sir."

"By the end of the first dogwatch, each of you will provide me with a list of everything that needs to be done to get your department back up to navy standards, and I mean everything. I want your estimate on how long it will take, what resources you need, especially resources from outside the ship and how you intend to go about it. In brief, I want your complete plan. If this sounds like I'm teaching you to suck eggs and aim to breathe over your shoulder, you're right. You will prove to me that you know what you're doing. And once you've completed each step, I will personally inspect the work. This ship is not my first command. I know all the tricks and dodges. Try them and pack your bags." Siobhan met the dark looks with an arrogantly raised eyebrow.

"You may resent my orders, and you may resent me," she said, "But if you wanted my trust, you should have made sure I found a proper warship when I signed on this morning, not a reject from the Fleet's junkyard. Now, you'll have to earn that trust the hard way, and believe me, I'm as hard as they come. By the time this week is over, you'll be fantasizing about beating the living crap out of me. Take your aggressions out in the gym. Many people have tried to do away with me these last few years, and none have succeeded. Keep me happy, that's the best advice I can give you."

Siobhan could sense the ill feeling in the room like a living presence. But the words had to be spoken.

"If you've got a problem you can't solve, see the first officer, but make sure you've got some options to give him. And before you call in the station engineers, make sure it really is something that can't be done with our own resources. I don't want to hear of any problems unless it's something I *should* get involved in. Learn to make the difference."

She breathed in deeply and looked around the small room again.

"Any questions or things you disagree with? This is the only opportunity I'll give you to speak your mind before we start. Once this meeting breaks up, you will carry out my instructions as given."

Utter silence greeted her challenge.

"Very well then. Just one last point. On my ship, I expect everyone to lend a hand and get dirty, including the officers and chiefs. We sail in one week. That's how much time you have to get your act together."

She rose, and Pushkin called the officers to attention.

Siobhan could feel another bout of nausea coming on and wanted to return to her cabin as fast as she could before she got sick in front of everybody. Leaving the room, she briefly caught Luttrell's eye and read a flash of concern, the first emotion the surgeon had shown.

The crewmembers she met quickly moved out of her way, but many stared at her with hostile or sullen eyes, when they did not look down at the deck or carefully studied the bulkheads. None snapped to attention, as was customary on better-disciplined ships, but all conversation ceased. Siobhan felt like she was emanating a dampening field.

The ratings and petty officers looked like any other bunch of spacers in the navy, except for a certain seediness in their personal appearance. It matched the feel of the ship, and Siobhan wondered again how Helen Forenza had managed to screw up a navy frigate so thoroughly.

The moment the cabin door closed behind her, Siobhan sighed and rubbed her temples. Now that her iron control was slipping, her vision began to blur, and bile rose in her throat. She spent an agonizing few minutes retching over the toilet, her empty stomach contracting painfully. Then, she lay down on the bed and turned off the lights, grateful the first ordeal was over.

Hopefully, she had managed to convince her officers that she would break their careers without remorse if they crossed her. Instinct told Siobhan that it was the only approach that would get their complete attention. They were too dispirited and suspicious of one another to respond to anything less than shock treatment.

— Four —

At two bells into the first dogwatch her computer terminal beeped loudly. Cursing, Siobhan reached up and acknowledged the message. Then, slowly, she sat up, wincing, and glanced at the terminal's screen.

Ship's surgeon reporting the sickbay ready? This I have to see for myself.

A glance in the mirror to adjust her uniform stopped her momentarily, and she groaned. Her pale, tired face now had startling black smudges beneath shiny, bloodshot eyes, but it was the state of her service uniform that gave her pause. She had napped on and off all afternoon wearing the high-collared tunic, and it showed.

Quickly, Siobhan unpacked her bags and changed into the shipboard dress of black trousers tucked into calf-high boots and short blue jacket, cinched at the waist, over a white, high-collared sweater. The three stripes of her rank gleamed dully on the tunic's shoulder boards, as did the gold fighter pilot's wings on her left breast.

On the short walk to the sickbay, two decks down, she was grimly satisfied to see frantic activity spiced by loud curses from angry petty officers. Those crewmembers not occupied with some delicate task straightened to attention as she passed, and the POs in charge of the work details saluted, their expressions carefully guarded. While their movements had an awkwardness that spoke of a continued lack of practice, Guthren's efforts to restore discipline were beginning to show, and activity, no matter how chaotic, was better than the dead calm she had seen when she came aboard.

The door to the sickbay whooshed open as she neared. Lieutenant Luttrell, who was discussing something with a medic petty officer, broke off the conversation and snapped to something like attention. Siobhan's face must have shown her relief when the doors closed, shutting off the noise from the passageways because Luttrell suddenly looked at her with professional concern.

"Welcome to sickbay, captain." The older woman, having experienced a brief touch of Dunmoore's steel, was determined to tread carefully. After lying low for so long under Forenza, it would be easy to continue keeping her own counsel under Dunmoore. And probably just as appropriate. This one could be as much trouble as the other, only of a worse kind. The legal kind.

"You reported your department ready in record time, Doctor. I'm here to inspect." Siobhan deliberately sounded skeptical and saw her tone rattle Luttrell. Professional pride?

"Aye, sir. We didn't have much to do to bring it up to navy standards, sir." Luttrell's expression verged on what used to be called 'silent insolence.' They used to flog sailors for less than that, in the old days of sailing ships.

But the surgeon had a right to feel resentful this time, as she proved to her new captain. The operating theater, recovery room, and ward were spotlessly clean and had obviously been so before Dunmoore's arrival.

Luttrell demonstrated that all her gear was serviceable. The sickbay staff, while not exactly the image of naval discipline, were nonetheless no different in appearance from any other group of medics. Sure, their hair was a tad too long, their uniforms a tad rumpled and their attitude leaned toward the relaxed end of the spectrum, but their medical smocks were spotless, and their answers were professional when Siobhan questioned them.

Only the long list of patients in the medical log disturbed Siobhan. In her experience, the number of sickbay visits rose as morale dropped. Judging by the size of Luttrell's practice before Forenza's relief, there was no morale to speak of on this ship, and too many 'accidents' that left marks strangely similar to those inflicted by human feet and fists. Luttrell shrugged, apparently unwilling to discuss her cases and Siobhan did not have the energy to fish for information.

After the tour, Luttrell invited Dunmoore into her small office. When the door closed behind them, Siobhan sat on a corner of the doctor's desk and looked at her speculatively. The look was returned with defiance.

"Well, Doctor, I must say I'm impressed. My initial opinion of you was lousy. But I can't fault your sickbay and medical staff, even if they don't have that perfect navy look."

Luttrell, momentarily checked by Siobhan's mild tone and words, looked away. "I've got my faults, captain, but where doctoring is concerned, I don't screw around." The rueful tone briefly softened Siobhan's face, and she suddenly felt that she could learn to like the hard-faced surgeon.

"As for the navy look," Luttrell continued, this time with a small smile, "a lot of us medical people are draftees, and we try to keep some shred of our civilian identity."

Siobhan's eyebrows rose, and she was about to ask a question when Luttrell spoke again, cutting her off. Whether Dunmoore would react badly or not, the doctor had her duty and her oath to uphold. And it would end the questions before they became too personal and pointed. She raised her strong chin at Siobhan.

"Now that you've inspected me, captain, it's my turn to inspect you. A migraine?" Luttrell whipped out a medical sensor and pointed it at Dunmoore. When she saw the readout, she grimaced. "Bad, eh? Since when have you had it?"

"Since I reported aboard," Siobhan replied, fascinated by Luttrell's sudden transformation from a closed and sullen officer into a concerned and professional doctor.

"And you didn't come and see me," the surgeon tsked, shaking her head, unsure whether to be angry or amused at the captain's stubbornness. "Mind you, I can understand why. I wouldn't want to see the ship's surgeon if my first impression was the one you had. I'm surprised you're still functioning." She shut the sensor off and dropped it on her desk. "But I can understand that too, strangely enough."

Luttrell opened a small cabinet behind her desk and took a thumbnail-sized gray patch from a box. Then, she walked up to Siobhan, and without asking, pushed up the hair lying over the nape of her neck and slapped the patch on her skin. Almost immediately, the pounding and migraine receded as the nerve inducer took effect. Siobhan sighed.

"Feels better, doesn't it, captain?" Luttrell asked, with a pleasant bedside smile.

"It does," Siobhan smiled back.

"Next time, don't wait so long."

"I won't, Doctor."

"When you have a spare half-hour, I'd like to run a full physical on you. You have more problems than just the migraine. I'd say you're courting a burnout, on top of suffering from borderline malnutrition and unhealed wounds."

Siobhan looked at Luttrell in surprise. Her assessment was more accurate than she expected a surgeon to learn from a brief sensor scan.

"How can you tell?"

"Good, traditional frontier medicine, captain. I practiced on the outer colonies before the war, before being drafted into the Service. You learn to make your diagnostics on instinct and observation. Few colonies have a full medical suite like we have here."

Siobhan nodded, eyebrows raised. "I'm impressed. And you're right. I still haven't fully recovered from the wounds I took when my previous ship was all but wrecked. And the aftermath, decommissioning her, writing to the next of kin, making sure the wounded get the best treatment and now getting a problem ship..."

"That'd do it, sir. Guess your sleep's not too good either. Nightmares and such," the doctor shrugged. "I'd tell you to relax, and plan for a few days leave, but I'd be whistling in an ion storm. What I will say is to try and get at least eight uninterrupted hours of sleep a night, see me whenever you feel a migraine or some other problem start, and get some decent food."

Siobhan shrugged. "I'll try, but under the circumstances..."

"Tell you what," Luttrell held up her hand and returned to the cabinet. She pulled out a carton of nerve inducers. "Take the whole box. Slap one of these on your neck before going to bed, and the nightmares will be manageable. It's not something you'll find in medical texts, but believe me, it helps."

"Personal experience?"

"Yeah. A long time ago. And don't worry, it's not addictive."

Siobhan took the box. At that moment, her stomach rumbled loudly. Luttrell gave her a mock surprised look.

"See," she said accusingly, "I was right. You are undernourished. Now that the migraine's gone, your body wants some food. When's the last time you ate?"

"Breakfast, but I upchucked it a few hours later."

Luttrell turned on her intercom. "Sickbay to captain's clerk."

"Kery here," the clerk's voice replied a few moments later.

"The captain has asked me to order her some grub. Get a tray from the galley to her ready room in fifteen minutes. And make sure it's heaped high." Luttrell briefly glanced at Siobhan, muting the transmission. "Anything in particular, skipper?"

"Yes." She stared at the surgeon, eyes narrowed in thought. "I want the food to come from the lower deck galley, not the wardroom."

The doctor looked at her for a moment, and then nodded her understanding.

"Kery, make sure the food comes from the main galley, not the wardroom."

"Aye, aye, Doctor."

"Sickbay, out."

"I think this ship's in for quite a change," Luttrell softly said, looking at Siobhan, "more than I expected."

"It is, Doctor, you can bank on it," Siobhan replied, in the same tone. Then she turned to leave, saying over her shoulder, "Thanks for the doctoring."

"Don't mention it, sir. It's my job – something I'm damned good at." As Siobhan crossed the threshold, Luttrell added, "There's still a lot of good on this ship too, captain. They just need the right hand at the wheel."

Dunmoore did not reply. She merely nodded, without looking back, and let the door close behind her. Just then, Pushkin walked down the passage, face dark with anger. Upon seeing the captain, he stopped and came to attention.

"I'm sorry, sir, I wasn't aware you'd be inspecting sickbay now. I just read Lieutenant Luttrell's report." His voice was tense, his words clipped.

Siobhan repressed a curse and a sigh, realizing she had accidentally snubbed her first officer again. *Behind every positive aspect, there's a cloud.*

By custom, the first officer always accompanied the captain on an inspection. *After* making sure everything was ship-shape.

"I'm sorry, Mister Pushkin," she replied, trying to sound contrite, though she doubted that he was in any mood to be mollified. "I didn't think when I decided to come down and inspect sickbay. I'm afraid I not only left you out but also surprised Lieutenant Luttrell."

Hopefully, her last comment would prevent Pushkin from taking out his frustration and humiliation on the doctor. Paranoia was an ugly thing, but she was not exactly helping her first officer.

"However, be that as it may, the sickbay passed muster."

"Very well, captain," Pushkin replied, angrily entering her comments into his personal computer, for the ship's logs. "I'll return to engineering then."

"Problems?"

"Nothing that can't be fixed, sir," he replied a touch savagely.

"I'll be in my ready room. Please advise me when the next department is prepared for inspection."

For a moment, Pushkin looked at her, as if gauging the sincerity behind her peace offering. Then he replied, in a slightly calmer tone, "Aye, sir. I will."

*

A tray of hot food was waiting when she got to her ready room. She took a sip of the scalding hot coffee and grimaced. It was bitter and burned, very different from what the shiny urns on *Victoria Regina* had chugged out watch after watch.

The food, when she took her first bite, was not much better. Siobhan had eaten worse, but never aboard a warship. She was pleased with her decision to sample the lower deck galley's food. Now she knew there was another problem to deal with, one which had a direct impact on the crew's day to day morale. All she needed to bring the food question to its inglorious but all too logical conclusion was to discover that the grub in the petty officers mess and the wardroom was better than this. Somehow, it would fit with Helen Forenza's instinctive snobbery. But hunger was robust enough to make Siobhan eat every bit.

She slumped back in the chair and closed her eyes, relishing the freedom from pain and starvation. Her enjoyment lasted but a few minutes, until the ship demanded her undivided attention again. *No wonder I'm starting to look like the Crone of Chronos. No rest for the wicked.*

"First officer to captain."

Siobhan sighed and sat up, touching the intercom pad.

"Go ahead, Mister Pushkin."

"Second officer reports the security division ready for inspection, sir."

"Good," Siobhan nodded. She had been wondering whether her initial impression of Lieutenant Drex would bear out. Now she would see. "I'll meet you down there."

"Aye, aye, sir."

*

Pushkin was waiting by the door leading to the ship's small brig and security office. He still wore his dark scowl but was beginning to look frazzled. Dunmoore was ironically pleased by his overworked appearance. It made a satisfying contrast to his bitter demeanor when they first met.

As she approached, Pushkin touched the door's keypad and came to attention. Siobhan nodded at him and stepped through. Drex, in immaculate shipboard uniform, like the four bosun's mates standing behind him, called his spacers to attention.

"Security division ready for the captain's inspection, sir."

"Any problems to report, Mister Drex?"

The second officer's angular features remained impassive. "None, sir. All small arms and battlesuits are operational, ammunition stocks are full, and security systems are functioning. I suggest the captain visits the brig and security center first, then the arms locker."

"Very well, Mister Drex. Lead on."

He was true to his word. The facilities were spotless, his bosun's mates sharply turned out, and it was clear that he took great pride in showing her that he had not let his department go slack.

The ship's bosun, a chief petty officer third class, waited for them at the arms locker with another group of mates. Chief Petty Officer Third Class Foste was a tall, thin woman with closely cropped hair, intense black eyes, and hawk-like features. For a moment, Siobhan was struck by her resemblance to Drex, even though they differed physically in every respect. Then, it occurred to her that the resemblance was due to the same hard-nosed attitude toward their jobs. Nevertheless, it was an interesting observation, and it was heartening to see that Helen Forenza had not been able to break everyone's spirit.

The small arms she presented for inspection showed signs of wear, but as advertised, were fully functional, just like the armored suits. Pushkin followed her everywhere, taking notes on his personal computer, never dropping his scowl, but never making a comment. When the tour was complete, Siobhan turned toward Drex.

"Excellent turn-out, lieutenant." She deliberately said the compliment loud enough for the bosun and her mates to hear.

"Thank you, sir. The rest of my department will be ready within two days, sir. I wanted to present the security division now so I can assign the bosun's mates to other tasks after your inspection. My full report is in the ship's log."

Siobhan nodded. "Very well, Mister Drex."

The second officer, Pushkin, and Dunmoore left the weapons' locker and Pushkin excused himself. Engineering still needed his undivided attention. Eventually, Siobhan was going to have to ask him exactly what was going on that required his constant presence. Alone with Drex in the passage, she glanced at him sideways, eyes narrowed.

"Tell me, Mister Drex, you're a mustang, aren't you?"

"Aye, sir. Used to be cox'n in the *Baikal*. Heavy cruiser."

"How long since you got your commission?"

"Three years, sir. Captain made me an officer when she was paid off. The old *Baikal* took it bad at the battle of Torrinos and had to be scrapped. I came straight to *Stingray*. She was a good ship, the *Baikal*. Damn shame it is."

"I know the feeling. I was second on the *Sala-Ad-Din* at Torrinos."

"One hell of a battle, sir," Drex nodded. "Lost a lot of good ships and spacers then."

"You came aboard *Stingray* before Commander Forenza?"

"Aye, sir. Cap'n Yuan back then. He got his fourth stripe and went on to command the cruiser *Nairobi*. After that..." He shrugged.

Siobhan sensed a reticence to speak about the more recent past and decided not to push, yet. But she was disappointed. She thought Drex might have been the one officer on board whom she could ask about Forenza's time in command, but it appeared not. It could not be misplaced loyalty to her predecessor. Not a former chief like him. The 'why' was beginning to gnaw at her, and she repressed her frustrated curiosity with difficulty.

"If you'll excuse me, sir," Drex came to attention and saluted.

"Carry on, lieutenant."

As soon as she was alone in the bare corridor, Siobhan felt the fatigue of the long day seep into every muscle, and a ghostly throbbing in her skull reminded her of Luttrell's words. The second dogwatch was almost over, and she still had a pile of reports to sort through before going to bed.

When she entered her cabin, she was surprised to find the bed made, her clothes put away, and a small coffee urn chugging in the corner. She had not ordered anyone to do her housekeeping and felt a momentary stab of irritation. Then, she frowned and turned the computer terminal toward her. A few queries answered the question of who. Her clerk, Kery, had taken it upon herself to play captain's steward. Was it an attempt to curry favor, or something entirely different?

Siobhan spent the next two hours reading reports and making notes in her personal log. Judging by what she had seen and read so far, it appeared that only Luttrell and Drex had maintained their particular departments up to a decent standard under Forenza. As Dunmoore already knew, engineering was a disaster in the making, with navigation and supply not far behind. Signals and gunnery she could not tell from the reports, and left a note for the first officer to have Devall and Kowalski redo them.

At six bells in the evening watch, Siobhan gratefully stripped off her uniform and slipped between the sheets, wearing nothing but her birthday suit and a neural inducer. It was to be her first night without reliving those terrible haunting hours on *Victoria Regina*.

She fell asleep almost immediately in the peace and solitude of her quarters. But throughout the ship, cursing and swearing spacers worked to meet her exacting standards under the supervision of hard-faced, angry petty officers, who in turn labored under Chief Guthren's biting tongue. It was not the most glorious way of starting a new command.

*

She woke eight hours later, after the first night of real sleep in weeks, feeling surprisingly refreshed and at ease. Doctor Luttrell's prescription had been extraordinarily useful, though the woman herself remained a closed book. For all that she made a lousy first impression, Luttrell certainly knew her business, at least as far as migraines were concerned.

Siobhan noticed the 'message waiting' light blinking on the computer terminal. The reminder of her ship's problems put a damper on her mood. After a quick shower, she slipped back into her uniform and called the galley for a breakfast tray. With the migraine's disappearance, her appetite had returned, though it could vanish just as fast after she read the messages.

Leading Spacer Kery delivered breakfast a few minutes later. She did not speak, apart from acknowledging Siobhan's thanks, and set about making the captain's bed. When she was done, Kery slipped out of the cabin, silent as a ghost, and left Dunmoore to her solitude.

Kery was a strange fish, Siobhan thought. Quiet and unassuming, but her dark, inquisitive eyes missed little. Twice yesterday, she had caught Kery examining her when the clerk thought she was not looking.

Both times, Dunmoore had felt acutely uneasy without quite understanding why. She wondered, not for the first time, what the relationship between Forenza and the clerk had been like. Captain's clerks held a great deal of informal power aboard ship, power that was all too easily abused.

Guthren had taken an instant dislike to Kery and suggested to Siobhan the she transfer her off *Stingray*. Not only did Kery know too much, Guthren believed, but if lower deck gossip was accurate, used what she knew. Without Forenza's protection, the short, dark-featured woman could easily become the target of revenge. One more question mark and one more problem.

Siobhan wolfed down the bland meal, fueling her body without enjoyment. Her clothes hung loosely on her lean frame these days. The ordeal on the battleship had melted away several kilograms from a body that had no fat to spare. The captain was grimly satisfied the wardroom food was no better than that from the lower deck galley.

The ship's cooks needed some re-training or proper motivation.

The migraine's disappearance had brought the previous day's events into clearer focus, and Siobhan, never a woman to tolerate inefficiency or weakness, felt a renewed determination to clean up *Stingray*.

Admiral Nagira had given her a job to do, and she would see it through. If her crew thought yesterday was bad, they had not seen anything yet. She turned to her computer and opened the first message. It was from HQ, and it was not exactly a 'welcome, fellow warrior' note. Warriors, in Siobhan's estimation, did not sound this pompous and self-important.

"Dunmoore, this is Commander Sones, Battle Group Supply Officer. Call my aide to arrange a meeting soonest. I must speak to you about your purser, Lieutenant Rossum. His behavior is really intolerable: bullying, attempting to bribe and suborn the supply staff. There is an established procedure to request stores. Your people must adhere to it. I cannot accept anything less. Further behavior of that nature will be reported to the flag captain. I expect to hear from you today. Sones, out."

A dark grin of amusement twisted Siobhan's thin lips. She wondered exactly how Rossum had 'subverted' supply personnel. In her experience, a little *baksheesh* went a long way when one had to bypass the bureaucratic bullshit that made every request for toilet paper, antiship missiles or tungsten rivets an exercise in creative writing. Every supply petty officer in the Fleet was open to a bit of profitable subversion.

I must see what Rossum is doing to piss-off our friend Sones, and find out if he is actually getting somewhere.

Having been deputy commander of a notoriously corrupt Fleet Depot herself, Siobhan knew more than most about what could and could not be done. But at least, Rossum was doing *something*, which was better than twenty-four hours ago, when the ship's stores had been empty with no plan to fill them.

The next message was a short written note from the Battle Group Personnel Officer. With regrets, he was unable to fill *Stingray*'s empty slots for the foreseeable future. She would have to make do with her current complement. Curious, Siobhan called up a ship's roster.

Hmmm, we're missing the third engineering officer, two bosun's mates and one supply petty officer. Since when, and for what reasons, I wonder.

She touched the keypad. "Third engineering officer's slot, open since the 2nd of March of this year," she read, "after Sub-Lieutenant Byrn was dismissed from the Service." Siobhan frowned. *Dismissed from the Service? Why?*

The computer's answer was quick and short. "That information is not on record."

"Leading Spacer Savarin was transferred to Starbase 31 on the twelfth of January of this year, after contracting a chronic illness," Siobhan smiled, wondering if the chronic illness had a sexual origin. Even five hundred years after the discovery of penicillin, the human race still found ways to contract new sexually transmitted diseases with alarming frequency.

"Able Spacer Vasser and Petty Officer Melchor died in a shipboard accident on the 16th of February of this year."

"Cause of the accident?"

"That information is not on record."

Siobhan sat back, eyes narrowed in speculation. Sub-Lieutenant Byrn's reason for dismissal not being on record, she could understand, especially if he appealed the decision and won. But two crewmembers dying in an accident aboard ship, that had to be investigated and the report published.

"Two crewmembers die of an accident. No record on file," Siobhan softly spoke to herself, eyes staring at the bare bulkhead beyond the desk. "A short while later, an engineering officer is dismissed from the Service. No record on file. Not long after that, the ship's captain is relieved and ordered before a Disciplinary Board which, if it finds enough evidence, is empowered to order a general court-martial. No record on file. Coincidence or related chain of events?"

Without the logs, the only ones who could tell her about those incidents were her officers and crew, and if yesterday was anything to go by, she was not going to learn much about Forenza's days as captain of *Stingray*. It was not a case of misplaced loyalty, she was sure of that. A dispirited crew had no loyalty to give.

Bottling her sudden frustration, Siobhan re-routed the message to Pushkin's terminal and turned to the next one in the queue. It was another written note from the personnel officer and informed her that all transfer requests from *Stingray* were denied, as there were no available replacements. All returned transfer requests were attached to the present message.

Well, that certainly made sense. No point in approving transfers if he could not even fill the existing vacant slots. Though why did he return the requests? Why bother? For a moment, Siobhan stared at the screen, frowning. Then, out of curiosity, she took a look at the application forms.

The day after Forenza had left *Stingray*, it seemed that half the crew, including officers, had asked to be posted to another ship. She glanced at the message again and for the first time noticed the signature at the bottom. Usually, she did not care much for navy bureaucrats, but this message made her curious. Siobhan's eyes briefly widened in surprise at the name.

"Ezekiel Holt," she whispered. "What an interesting coincidence. I wonder..."

Her gloved hand shot out to stroke the com, and then it stopped in mid-air as doubts made her hesitate. Siobhan had not seen Ezekiel since shortly after wrecking *Shenzen* at Antae Carina. He had been her first officer on the corvette, an officer of great promise until her pigheaded recklessness deprived him of the chance for a career.

Apparently, the navy had decided they could overlook his horrible wounds and subsequent disability, at a time when they needed every decent officer who could think straight. And a cripple in a staff job would free up another officer fit for warship duty. At least, the navy had shown the decency to promote Ezekiel to lieutenant commander.

Shenzen's former first officer did not testify in person at Siobhan's court-martial. He had been too busy recuperating in a regen tank at the naval hospital on Wyvern. But he had given recorded testimony, and Siobhan had been surprised that Ezekiel had shown no bitterness or anger. He had supported every one of her decisions, but that had been in the weeks following the battle when even Siobhan had not been able to think straight. Two years living as a cripple, knowing that admiral's stars were forever beyond his reach, might have embittered him. Siobhan was sure she would have soured on the skipper whose impulsive behavior had ruined her.

Undecided, she turned to the next message: new orders from Battle Group. Siobhan cursed under her breath when she read them. *Stingray* had to sail in three days, cutting her refit time in half. No reason for the early departure was given, and the latest intelligence reports, which she digested on her way from 3rd Fleet Headquarters, did not hint at any change in the stalemate with the Imperial Navy.

Siobhan switched on the intercom. "Captain to first officer."

After a few seconds, Pushkin's somber face filled the vidscreen.

"Aye, sir."

"Bad news, Mister Pushkin. Battle Group HQ has ordered us to sail in seventy-two hours. Concentrate on getting the ship supplied and taking all necessary spare parts aboard. We'll complete only the most urgent repairs in the dock. The rest will have to wait until we're under way."

It was evident from his expression that Pushkin did not like the change in plans any more than she did, and was biting back choice curses, but he nodded.

"Aye, aye, captain. The crew will have to work two watches out of every three, but we'll sail, even if the tugs have to take us all the way to the hyper limit."

"Good. Captain, out."

At least Pushkin seemed to be taking an interest in running the ship again, or more likely was focusing his frustration on his work. Either way, she preferred sullen action to sullen inaction.

Siobhan stared at the blank vidscreen for nearly a minute. The more she thought about the sudden change in orders, the more she wondered. Rear Admiral Kaleri knew about *Stingray*'s condition. Why give the frigate less than four days to get back into space? For a moment, Siobhan felt tempted to call Kaleri. Then, remembering Jadin's sneering manner, she had a better idea. And anyway, she had to know.

"Bridge, this is the captain. Get me a link to the Battle Group Personnel Officer."

"Aye, aye, sir. One moment please."

The screen blanked out, then, a few seconds later, it lit up again.

"Personnel, Holt."

"Hello, Ezekiel. It's Siobhan Dunmoore."

Ezekiel Holt had been one hell of a good-looking young man, once: clear blue eyes, short blond hair, and devil-may-care smile, a silver-tongued rogue if there ever was one. That was gone now. She had destroyed that handsome man. His left cheek bore a large red splotch, where super-hot lubricants had burned away the skin. A black patch covered his left eye, and those were only the injuries she could see. She knew he bore many more marks from her handling of *Shenzen*. Volatile, they called her, and it seemed only the people around her suffered for it, never Siobhan Dunmoore. At least not physically, though the memories still plagued her.

Siobhan had expected anger, bitterness or at least a cold reception. She was not prepared for Holt's reaction. His mangled face softened as pleasure lit up his single eye and he smiled with a warmth she had not felt in a long time.

"You're looking damned good, skipper. I'm glad to see you back on your own ship."

Nonplussed, Siobhan searched his face for signs of sarcasm or mockery, but found only genuine delight at seeing her, as if the old friendship they enjoyed on *Shenzen* had never vanished. The way he called her skipper brought back fond memories of their time together and the less pleasant memories of the battle where she lost her second ship. It also brought unexpected moisture to her eyes.

"You-" she cleared her throat, "you're looking good too, Ezekiel."

He grinned and pointed at the patch. "You like the pirate look, skipper?"

Siobhan smiled lamely. "Yeah. Must work wonders with the ladies."

"You don't know the half of it." Before Antae Carina, Holt's exploits on shore leave had been legendary. "Wounded war hero and all. And thanks to you, I can show off my Navy Cross too." He pointed to a striped ribbon on top of all the other ribbons he wore on his tunic.

Siobhan blinked back her emotions. And thanks to me, she thought, you're not even going to be able to make a decent career out of that Navy Cross.

"I'm glad the navy decorated you. You deserved it."

"Hey, so did you, Skipper. But I guess you didn't have a good boss to write up the commendation."

Siobhan must have lost her iron control over her expression because suddenly Ezekiel screwed up his face and frowned.

"What's wrong?"

She shrugged. "Many things, Ezekiel. Too many." Siobhan hesitated, unused to discussing her troubles with others. But this was Ezekiel. She owed him absolute honesty, and so much more. "To tell you the truth, I didn't know how you felt about me. I nearly didn't call."

Holt sighed and shook his head in mock exasperation, a gesture he would often make to tease her when they were on *Shenzen*.

"You thought I blamed you? Damn, skipper, if I remember well, we were all behind you when you decided to disregard orders and go after that Imperial Task Force. There isn't an old crewmate alive who doesn't still think you took the right decision, and that the court-martial was a bloody joke. C'mon, smile a little, skipper. You're so much cuter when you show your pearly whites."

His cajoling tone finally drew a small grin and Siobhan visibly relaxed.

"That's a lot better," Ezekiel smiled broadly. "Hey, things have been good for me. I'm a general staff officer now, fully qualified thanks to a painful stint at the Naval War College. When this shindig is over, I'll be so bloody invaluable that the navy will keep me around until I keel over from old age. And seeing what commanding starships has done to you, maybe I'm better off playing puppet master behind an admiral's skirts."

That last was not entirely accurate, and Siobhan knew it, but obviously Ezekiel was well on his way to convincing himself that it was what he wanted out of life. It hardly surprised her. Holt had always shown a more levelheaded attitude than she had. That was why they made such a good team on *Shenzen*. Her hotheaded drive and his ability to temper her worst excesses with cool, well thought-out advice.

"I'm glad for you, Ezekiel." She smiled. "Even if you have joined the ranks of the real enemy."

Holt laughed with delight. "Now that's the Siobhan Dunmoore I remember and love. And contrary to popular belief, the staff is on your side."

Dunmoore snorted.

Ezekiel's single eye took on a sly cast. "Tell me, Skipper, since you thought I hated your guts, it had to be more than a desire for auld lang syne that made you give me a ring."

Siobhan looked away, feeling cheap and transparent. "Guilty as charged."

Holt laughed again. She had not changed much. Aged a little, but it only made her more handsome. "There are a lot of people out there who wish you'd say that to a general court-martial."

Dunmoore grinned wryly. Trust Ezekiel to bring a smile on her face every time. He had not changed a bit over the years. If anything, his ordeal seemed to have given him a cheerier outlook on life, something Siobhan could not match.

"Don't worry, skipper," he continued, pleased that he was still able to make her smile. "Since you didn't call when you got here, I figured you were still feeling guilty about my injuries, so I made sure I gave you a reason to ring me up me on official business. Otherwise, you'd have avoided me altogether."

Siobhan shook her head. "You know me too well, Ezekiel."

"Hey," his voice lost its bantering tone, "you're like the older sister I never had. I missed you."

Siobhan felt a surge of emotion rising once more and did not trust herself to reply. When Holt spoke again, his manner was all business.

"If you've got time, I suggest we meet face-to-face. How about lunch at the officers' mess?"

There was something in Ezekiel's tone and the look in his eye that urged her to accept. All of her earlier misgivings about *Stingray* came flooding back.

"Eight bells in the officers' mess then, Ezekiel."

"Right, skipper. 'Till noon. Cheerio." His smiling face vanished as he cut the link.

Siobhan remained lost in her thoughts for what seemed a long time.

*

"All hands, prepare for static reactor test in one minute." The chief engineer's voice echoed throughout the ship, repeating the message.

Exactly sixty seconds later, Siobhan felt a rise in the subliminal vibrations that pulsed through a living ship. But something was wrong. She could not put her finger on it, yet after years in space, she had developed a sensitivity to every nuance of a starship's moods. As she was about to call engineering, all lights went out, the environmental systems stopped humming, and the computer screen turned blank. In the few heartbeats between a total system failure and backup power from the station kicking in, *Stingray* was dead.

Just like *Shenzen* immediately before she ordered her crew to abandon ship. She shivered at the memory. Too many memories this morning. Five years of war had scarred more than just her body. Slowly, Siobhan counted to twenty, curbing her own impatience, giving her chief engineer or first officer time to report. At the count of nineteen, the intercom screen blinked insistently.

"First officer to captain."

Siobhan touched the darkened vidscreen. "Dunmoore."

Pushkin's face was, if anything, grimmer than before. Rage and disgust filled his eyes. Behind him, engineering was in pandemonium. Sparks flew off in all directions, hazy smoke slowly rose, stirred by the resurgent air cycler, and loud, angry shouts echoed in the background.

"The main reactor is offline, captain. Something in the plasma interlink control shorted out catastrophically. If we'd had any antimatter fuel on board..." He shrugged, leaving the rest unsaid.

Siobhan's face tightened. "Just as well this happened during a static test, then. I want a full report before the end of the watch. And I want to know how long this is going to take to fix."

"Aye, aye, sir," Pushkin replied savagely, though his anger was clearly directed at the engineers behind him, not Siobhan. "But we'll sail on time, I guarantee you that."

Dunmoore nodded. "Captain, out."

*

She busied herself with ship's business for the next few hours, reading endless reports, authorizing more requests in that one sitting than she had in six months on *Shenzen*. *Stingray* was short of just about everything, except problems. The work, however, failed to keep her mind from dwelling on the order to sail earlier than planned. She finally switched off her computer with a sigh of relief and changed into her service dress uniform in preparation for her meeting with Ezekiel.

When Siobhan neared the entry port, the petty officer on duty, smartly turned out this time, snapped to attention and saluted.

"Good morning, sir."

"Good morning, PO...?"

"Fesal, sir. Bosun's mate." Siobhan nodded, memorizing the face and name. Fesal held out the datapad. "If you'd please sign out, sir."

The captain pressed her palm against the matte screen.

"Thank you, sir." He saluted again and touched the keypad to unlock the entry port.

As Siobhan walked down the gangway, she saw a pair of sentries at the duty station on the dock end of the tube and let a small smile play on her lips. This was already much better than yesterday. The sentries snapped to attention as she approached and the senior rating saluted. Siobhan wordlessly returned the salute and continued toward the bank of lifts without breaking stride. Chief Guthren was as good as his word. But she already knew that.

When she entered the officers' mess, a few minutes before noon, the same invalid steward as before greeted her and took her to a secluded alcove at the far side of the large dining room.

"Mister Holt ought to be along shortly, cap'n," he rasped. "Can I get you anything while you wait?"

"Coffee, please." What Dunmoore really wanted was a stiff drink, but her orders against booze applied to the captain too. If she started off her command by disregarding her own rules, she would lose the fight before it started. The coffee in the mess was a damn sight better than that aboard her ship, and she badly needed a good brew.

Moments after the steward delivered her cup, she saw a tall, blond officer walk into the mess, limping slightly and leaning on a black, silver-trimmed cane. Siobhan watched Ezekiel approach with the same anguish she felt before calling him earlier that morning. A born athlete, he used to have an energetic, healthy stride. Now, he was a cripple.

She rose as he got near and looked into his smiling face. The image on the vidscreen had not lied. Ezekiel was delighted to see her. They almost embraced, but propriety reduced the effusiveness of the reunion to a simple handshake.

"You're a sight for a one-eyed pirate, skipper," he said, holding her gloved hand in his own, "and getting lovelier all the time. If I didn't think of you like the older sister I never had, I'd try working the old Holt charm on you."

Siobhan could not help but smile at his ebullience. She knew she looked half-starved and driven, and Ezekiel's compliment touched her deeply.

"Don't change, ever, Ezekiel," Siobhan replied, smiling with delight.

"Why change a winning formula, skipper. After the war, when the medics have finished rebuilding all those kids who took it worse than me, I'll be just as good as new."

He sat down with a wince, and Siobhan's look of concern returned. But Ezekiel waved it away.

"Substandard bionic leg. Nerve connections constantly on the fritz. On bad days, it's as if I have arthritis. But most of the time, I can't feel it. As I said, when this shindig is over, I'll get myself fixed properly. At least the hand works fine." He flexed his gloved left hand experimentally a few times. Then, he pointed at Siobhan's own hands. "I see you're waiting to get yours fixed too. Maybe you should wear those things after the war anyways. Gives you a dangerous look."

"Just like that eye patch."

Ezekiel sighed theatrically. "War is hell. Hey, in a room full of airbrushed aristo officers, guess who gets the ladies' attention first, and keeps it? I kinda like the patch by now."

Siobhan shook her head. "You're a real marvel, Ezekiel. I wish I could take you on as my Number One, eye patch, bionics and all. I sure could use you right now."

His face became serious all of a sudden. "So I hear, skipper. Sorry, I can't oblige. One-eye gimps get permanent shore billets." There was no rancor or bitterness in his tone. Only acceptance and a hint of regret.

Ezekiel had been speaking the utter truth when he compared Siobhan to an older sister. He had a deep affection for her, and a lot of respect. Hotheaded and stubborn she may be, but as a warship captain, she had few equals. And all too many enemies.

"So," he continued, "I hear you've been doing grand deeds since we rescued Task Force 301."

"Depends who's talking, Ezekiel. But yeah, I did have a bit of action at the Sigma Noctae Fleet Depot."

"Way I hear it, you saved the goddamn place single-handed, after cleaning up the rot and putting a dozen shady operations out of business."

"Always take space tales with a grain of salt, Ezekiel."

He shrugged, ignoring the edge of cynicism in her voice. Under the circumstances, she was entitled to take a darker view. But it saddened him nonetheless. Siobhan had been more spirited, cheerful and defiant the last time he saw her.

"I know you, skipper, and you never do things by half. It endears you to us good guys, but we don't have a monopoly on the Fleet. Shall we order?"

They caught up on each other's lives while they ate, Ezekiel passing lightly over his time at the Wyvern Fleet Hospital, with its weeks of regen therapy and the subsequent fitting of bionics and rehabilitation. But he kept her laughing with his stories about the War College, which Siobhan had not attended, and probably never would.

Dunmoore, in return, talked mainly about the happy days aboard *Victoria Regina*, or some of the more outrageous stunts she pulled at the Sigma Noctae Depot. The old friendship was still there and for Siobhan, it was a blessed relief to be with someone she liked and trusted. Since Adnan Prighte's death, she felt alone and in her loneliness, often fell into the trap of self-pity. With Ezekiel, it was impossible to remain morose. They had grown close a long time ago, and that closeness came back with frightening ease as if the intervening years had never happened.

Once coffee was served, Ezekiel lit a small herbal cigar, grinning apologetically at Siobhan. "Little habit I picked up. It helps on my bad days. Some active ingredient in the weed."

He puffed contentedly for a few minutes, comfortable in the silence, and Siobhan saw his features relax as the herbal mixture temporarily covered his pain. Things were not quite as rosy as Ezekiel had let on, but she decided not to touch the subject again. Her old friend had gone to some lengths to make sure she did not feel guilty about his injuries, and if he wanted to hide his true condition, then so be it. At least one of them could have some peace of mind. She owed him that.

"I'm glad you called me," he finally said, "and not only to catch up on old times. I guess my returning every one of those transfer requests gave you the bug to check out who signed the damn memo."

"And you waited until I was on board to send that, and the regrets about replacements."

"Yeah. What I've got to tell you isn't something you discuss over an open comlink."

"Hence the officers' mess."

"Right again. In my spare time, I also took some counterintelligence training, so I know a bit about covering my tracks." For a moment, Siobhan did not know whether to take him seriously, and then she saw the hard glint in his single blue eye.

"I hate to say this, skipper, but you've taken on an ugly can of trouble. Since I know a few things I shouldn't, I figured it was only fair that you know them too. I presume you know who your predecessor was?"

"Helen Forenza. We were classmates at the Academy." Siobhan's lips compressed into a thin line as her face hardened. "She's living proof that the Commonwealth is sinking into the biggest rot since the demise of the Roman Empire."

"Yeah, a real sweetheart. The day someone decides to stop passing assholes through the Academy because they come from well-connected families, the quality of the officer corps is going to go up substantially. We might even win the war for a change. Anyway, that's the heart of your problem. Forenza. Do you know why she was relieved of command?"

"No. There's a conspiracy of silence when I'm around. But I can guess, seeing the state of the ship."

"Partially right. I've been here for the last six months, and in that time, *Stingray* hasn't brought a single imperial ship to task. Not one. And God knows frigates get every bloody chance there is. The real story is buried so far I can't get my hands on it, but it's more than just incompetence on Forenza's part. Some say she's yellow from tip to tail."

"And they'd be right. She was one hell of a bully at the Academy."

"Yeah, well hold on to your hat, skipper. It's supposed to be a big secret, some sort of judicial gag, but the story is, on her last cruise, she failed to answer the calls for assistance from a battleship under attack by the Shrehari's biggest hot dog, a guy named Brakal."

When he saw Siobhan's face blanch, Ezekiel nodded. "Yeah, that was your ship, *Victoria Regina*. It rather confirms the stories that Forenza ran whenever there was an enemy bigger than a gunboat in the offing. When the official report on *Victoria Regina*'s fight came back to Battle Group, with a question from Admiral Nagira why *Stingray*, which was in the area, did not respond, Rear Admiral Kaleri called the frigate home. The moment she reached port, Kaleri impounded all her logs, had all the principal officers questioned, and Forenza vanished planet side, without so much as a bosun's whistle for a farewell. For your general fund of knowledge, the Kaleris and the Forenzas both hail from Mother Earth, have enough money to buy a couple of colonies cash on the barrel and probably belong to the same country clubs."

"So that's why the crew doesn't want to talk to me. They know I was aboard *Victoria Regina*."

"Hell, your face was plastered all over the Fleet News after you brought her home. They know all right. Probably damned scared that you'll find out and take Forenza's cowardice out on their hides."

"And with reason," Siobhan replied, anger coloring her cheeks.

"Easy, skipper." Ezekiel placed his good hand on her forearm. He knew her hot temper intimately, and wanted, no *needed* her to remain calm. "Your crew's got a bad case of the beaten dog syndrome. From what I hear, Kaleri's been closing her eyes on many things. If Nagira hadn't given the order, Forenza would still be in command."

"Closing her eyes on what, Ezekiel?" Siobhan's tone brooked no evasions. Holt saw in her face that same determination and fire that had driven her to sail *Shenzen* headlong into an Imperial Task Force and sure destruction.

"This is only rumors, you understand. But stories go around that Forenza's been going through the crew like a whore at a convention. And not just the guys, either."

Siobhan nodded. "Not surprising, and not exactly news. She did the same at the Academy. I turned her down. She's hated me ever since."

Ezekiel raised his eyebrows but did not ask any questions. "Story's also that the ship's split into half a dozen factions who couldn't work together in a pickle even if the legendary Admiral Raskolnikov was on the bridge."

"Not surprising either. By dividing the crew and officers against each other, they won't band together and work up the guts to relieve her. It worked if the crew let a distress call go without acting."

Ezekiel looked at his former captain with renewed respect. She had always possessed a quick mind, and her troubles had not dimmed it a bit. Good. Admiral Nagira was going to get what he wanted; he was willing to bet his life on it.

"Then," he continued, "there's the accident that resulted in the death of a rating and a petty officer. There's another beauty that vanished into the bureaucratic maze, never to be heard of again."

"Wasn't it an accident?"

"You tell me. The investigating officer, a Sub-Lieutenant Byrn, was formally charged for impropriety two weeks later and, thanks to Admiral Kaleri, given a chance to resign for the good of the Service."

"But the computer said he was dismissed."

"Yeah, once the kid signed on the dotted line, they changed the voluntary resignation to an other than honorable dismissal."

"Didn't he protest?"

"He didn't have time. Privateers attacked the civilian courier carrying him home. All the patrol ship found was exceedingly small debris. With his death, his personal records are sealed, and I don't know what the substance of the charges was." *Or, to be accurate, I don't officially know.*

"Ye gods," Siobhan suddenly shivered, "what the hell is going on, Ezekiel?"

"I could venture a dozen explanations, Skipper, but there comes a point where it just gets too damn dangerous to speak certain things out loud."

Somehow, Ezekiel's last comment worried Siobhan a lot more than anything else he had said so far. But she nodded slowly, a grim look spreading over her lean features.

"That would explain a hell of a lot of things, and it makes me wonder whether I shouldn't tell Nagira that the crew is beyond saving, that he should start from scratch."

"Not a good idea, Skipper." Ezekiel shook his head. "That would please Kaleri to no end. She recommended the ship be put in long-term refit or decommissioned immediately. Our good admiral is not exactly pleased by your appointment, but she figures you'll fail and be discredited, which is second best. And the crew will be dispersed anyways."

"So what is Kaleri afraid of?"

Ezekiel shrugged. "Dunno, but there again, I can speculate dangerously. Mind you, it was high time Forenza was pulled in front of a board, even if she'll get off. I can't see her ever getting another command either way. Too many people in high places have had to take notice of her poor record, and Nagira is one of them. *Victoria Regina* broke the elephant's spine, and there's no turning back."

"Coming back to Kaleri's desire to see the crew of *Stingray* dispersed, and by the same token isolated, this wouldn't perchance have anything to do with the fact that my time in space dock was cut in half this morning?"

"Yup." Holt ground out his cigar. "That and the fact that Forenza's board meets the day after you sail. By the time the high-ranking gentlebeings of the board will wish to hear the witnesses in person, *Stingray* will be back on active duty, and oh so sorry, cannot be spared, but we have their recorded testimony."

"Machiavellian."

"No, not Kaleri. An understudy of Machiavelli's understudy, maybe, but if a crippled lieutenant commander figured out so much for himself, definitely not Machiavellian."

"Crippled in body, Ezekiel, not in mind. You always had a flair for ferreting out deep dark muck. This has to be a lot more than a case of a lousy crew under an abysmally incompetent commander. For some reason, I feel I have to warn you to watch yourself. If there really is more to it than meets the eye, you could be at risk."

Thank you for that, skipper. But this time, the shoe's on the other foot.

"Even if I were, skipper, I couldn't let you go without telling you what I'd found. It's all because of that strange little thing called loyalty. You know what I'm talking about: one of humanity's nobler characteristics? Somehow you have an uncanny ability to bring it out in the most unlikely people."

Touched, Siobhan reached out to squeeze Ezekiel's good hand. She did not know what to say, but let her eyes express her gratitude. Holt broke the spell and looked at the antique naval clock dominating the dining lounge.

"Listen, skipper, I know you've got a hell of a lot of crap to handle. Believe it or not, so does Ezekiel Holt, Esquire, of the general staff. If you can, I'd like to see you again before you sail. If not, good luck. I'll try to watch out for you on this end."

"Thanks, Ezekiel. It was good to see you again."

"And you." Holt rose, and they shook hands.

He watched her leave, worry creasing his brow. Siobhan Dunmoore taking command of *Stingray* was the best, the only way out other than to let it all slide. He did not like what it might do to her, and he did not like being less than truthful with her. But needs must when the rot was spreading faster than it could be cut out.

Siobhan was as exhausted and dispirited as he had ever seen her. Vulnerable. He wished again that he could be aboard the frigate as first officer to protect her, most of all from herself. But he had a job to do here, and intellectually, he knew he would be of better help to Siobhan this way.

Yet it still hurt to see her like this, and to know that she faced so much more than just a crew with a morale problem. At least he had been able to get her old cox'n from *Don Quixote*. A bit hard to extract him from a Special Ops team, but necessary. Guthren was one of the disciples who would die before betraying Dunmoore. One of the small, select brotherhood to whom loyalty was akin to religious faith.

"A friend of yours, Holt?" A voice behind him asked tonelessly.

He turned to face Captain Darius Jadin, Flag Captain of the 31st Battle Group and Admiral Kaleri's familiar. Holt heartily detested Jadin, and he knew that dislike was mutual. Jadin's haughty manners and his reputation as a martinet on board ship put him firmly on Holt's hate list. Respectfully, but with a distinct 'none of your business tone,' he replied, "My former skipper, sir. On *Shenzen*. Haven't seen her in years."

Jadin grunted dismissively and turned to leave. Then he stopped and speared Ezekiel with his dark stare. "A piece of advice, Holt. Keep your nose in your own business and we'll all be happier."

Ezekiel watched the flag captain leave, his single eye narrowed. Jadin's turn would come soon enough. His hands might not be as dirty as some, but dirty enough.

— Five —

The citizens of Shredar's lower town quickly moved out of the way when they saw the tall Imperial Navy officer striding down the narrow, twisting alley. Sons of the Warrior caste were an uncommon sight among the poor plebeians, except for tyros searching out whores, cheap taverns, and blood fights.

But this one was no tyro. He wore the insignia of a ship commander on his black uniform, and the long, curved dagger of his caste thrust into the broad green sash around his waist. He took the uneven steps and cobblestone alleys with a confidence born of many victories, ignoring the stench and filth around him.

Though the hunched beggars, thieving pedlars, and diseased whores watched the commander pass by with narrowed eyes, they wisely chose to ignore him. Even if he were not scowling enough to promise instant death, annoying one of his caste was very dangerous. If a Warrior decided to visit the capital's slums, that was his affair, and no one else's, except maybe the *Tai Kan*'s, the Council's secret police.

There was little on Shrehari Prime, or anywhere else in the Empire, that escaped the *Tai Kan*, including those fingered by the Council for swift execution. After the events of the last few hours, the commander well knew that he could die at any moment, and it was a perverse sense of defiance that had brought him to cross the lower town on his way to the tavern where his second waited. If the Council had set the *Tai Kan* on him, then let those mutant sons of diseased carrion eaters act swiftly and take him now, where his murder would not raise an eyebrow. In these parts, his body would disappear within moments.

There were many who used the dead for ritual purposes, mere amusement, or even profit among the lower orders, especially the bodies of the highborn.

As he passed beneath a flickering street lamp, those who cared to look would have seen an arrogant imperial officer of pure race, but one who had lived a hard life, unlike that of most aristocrats in the capital.

His head was shaved in the Warrior caste fashion, leaving a strip of black, stiff hair running from his forehead over the top of his shiny, olive skull down to the back of his thick neck. The tonsure exposed a bony ridge and elongated predator's ears that twitched and moved as the commander unconsciously listened for threats. His face had the cruel features common of his species, but black eyes deeply recessed below thick eyebrows held a gleam of violence that eclipsed even the commonplace ferocity of the average fighter.

A young prostitute's eyes met the commander's, and she turned away in fear, shivering for a long time after he was gone. She had seen many violent males in her short, grinding years on the street, but never one like this.

The commander ignored her, as he ignored the low caste soldiers who gave him drunken salutes as they stumbled across his path, more often than not on the arm of a sober whore who would take the remainder of their month's pay in a few hours. He also ignored the snatches of bawdy and oft-treasonable drinking songs that floated on the night air as merry-makers went in and out of the numerous inns, taverns, and brothels.

After five years of stalemated war, he felt little charity for the shit-brained incompetents who ruled the Empire. The excrement on the Council deserved the mockery of the people and the Imperial Forces, as did the mother of the child-Emperor, a real whore if there ever was one.

After a while, the worst of the slums vanished behind him in a haze of wood smoke and darkness as he finally reached the district surrounding the imperial barracks and the spaceport. Turning right, he took a narrow and dark alley barely wider than a one man ground speeder, a block before the bright lights and shore patrols on the main boulevard. At the bottom of a seeming dead end, a discreet sign advertised his destination.

The commander opened the door, letting a wave of loud conversation, smoke and ethanol fumes wash over him. The harsh, guttural tones of the imperial tongue spoken by drunk army and navy officers were grating, but he ignored that too and scanned the room through narrowed eyes.

Most of the other patrons had given him one brief glance and had returned to their affairs. Not all imperial uniforms were welcome at the *Khorak*, and an Imperial Security or *Tai Kan* uniform would have found a cold reception. But not a Deep Space Fleet uniform.

Only one officer did not return to his solitary affairs: the commander's second. He raised his silver mug to signal the commander, who quickly made his way through the hard drinking crowd to the corner table, far from indiscreet ears.

Ignoring the scowl on his superior's dark, leathery face, the second asked, "How fare the Lords of the Imperial Council?"

"Those motherless turd hatchlings of a syphilitic human have displayed their courage and desire to win this war in its full glory."

"And you told them your real thoughts," the second nodded knowingly, though without disapproval on his angular face. Like the commander, he wore his hair in the Warrior caste manner, and had an imperial's cruel features, but he was younger, less burned by the interstellar radiation that penetrated the imperfect shielding of imperial warships.

"That I did, Jhar," he took a gulp of the ale a silent server had placed before him, "hoping to remind them of our glorious past and put some backbone into those old women. I am surprised the *Tai Kan* has not seen fit to kill me as I crossed the slums on my way here. But then, the Council no longer even has the courage to impose proper punishment on an officer of the Warrior caste. We have fallen far as a race, Jhar, and will fall even further if we let the humans win the war. Then, we might as well adopt their soft ways for we will never again find the spirit to conquer."

"Too true, commander," Jhar grimaced, displaying sharp, yellowing teeth. "So your suggestions were not accepted."

"Hah," the commander barked loudly, slamming his massive fist on the scarred table, "not accepted? I was ordered to cease using irregular, human-style tactics and return to our tried and true imperial ways. The ways which have brought us to this stalemate." He spat on the floor's granite flagstones in disgust.

"The humans have stopped our mighty Fleet because their ship commanders and admirals have learned to think, to use their weapons and warships to maximum advantage, and to adapt at every turn. We can only execute beautifully choreographed and ineffective actions because we have replaced clear thinking and initiative with unthinking aggression and unquestioning obedience. Meanwhile, the humans build better ships, and their commanders learn new tricks. If we do not change our ways, this war is lost." He laughed humorlessly. *Bach*! It was lost the moment they managed to stop our invasion in its tracks."

"Did you use such defeatist talk before the Council?"

"I may be a bitter, overaged warship commander, Jhar, but I am not that stupid, or suicidal. No, I spoke to the Council of initiative, of small-scale action and local victory. Of fighting magic with magic. And it was as if I talked to a granite wall, but with even less intelligence than the dumbest stones. The end result is that I shall no longer be given an assault force to, in the words of Admiral Trage, waste in senseless attacks. We shall sail alone, and at the end of a short tether. I am no longer to be trusted. So be it, then!" He drank deeply again and wiped his mouth with the back of his hand. "Still, I have won more victories than those vacuum brains can even dream about, and they lecture me on winning and losing."

"Especially Trage."

"Yes, especially Trage. That maggot-eaten product of a human's intestine has the temerity to lecture me, the most experienced commander in the Deep Space Fleet! And he has only commanded a ship for two turns, in peacetime, before climbing into the cesspit of intrigue at the Admiralty. I wish I could slice open his belly, slowly pull out his intestines, and garrote him with them."

"You would get much help, commander. Trage remains on the Council only because he has friends in the *Tai Kan*. But it is enough."

The commander shrugged. He cared nothing for admirals and their fancies. Yes, he was old for his rank, but he much preferred his duties to the higher glories of an admiral's robes. At least on his ship, he knew who the *Tai Kan* agents were, and they, in turn, knew the crew would ensure they died horribly if anything happened to him. There was no loyalty beyond that which a commander wins on his own warship. And no honor.

"May Trage and the rest of the Council die of an internal rotting disease passed on by their poxed concubines." He drank again.

Jhar sensed his commander was becoming morose, and that alarmed him for it could lead to a sudden fight with the first man to look at him or say something offensive within earshot. But he had just the thing to fire up the anger again.

"I fear, commander, I have further bad news for you," Jhar growled.

"Speak."

"The Council's displeasure appears to have been more public than you might expect. Our ship's turn in dry dock has been set back again."

The older man swore as he pounded his thick fist on the scarred table again. "They go too far. How long the delay?"

"Fourteen days."

"Argh! More time to wallow in the slime of the home world. I long for the day we return to the war, and I can turn my anger on humans."

"And I, commander. But fourteen days before we enter dry dock it shall be. Do you wish to hear what the noble Yard Master said when I told him you would object?" Jhar smiled evilly as he asked the question, for he knew his commander would find a way to damage the Yard Master permanently for his insolence, even if he came from a family which claimed greater nobility.

"What are the mutterings of a REMF to me?"

"REMF, commander?" Jhar looked at him in surprise, for the word sounded suspiciously like something in the human tongue. Thanks to his study of humans and their tactics, his superior had picked up a surprising amount of expressions that gave Jhar and the rest of the crew a fascinating and oft-amusing insight into the humans' ways.

"Rear echelon motherfuckers," the commander intoned in Anglic, causing a few surprised heads to turn in his direction. When they saw who had spoken, they quickly ignored him again. News of the Council's displeasure traveled fast indeed.

"In the Noble Tongue, it means 'Incestuous fornicators who hide from battle.' The home world is filled with them. But tell me anyway, Jhar. It might amuse me."

"As you wish, commander. He said honorless sons of turds who ape weakling humans have no business on a warship, much less claiming membership in the Warrior caste, and he did not care a maggot's fart for whatever words you chose to yell at his closed door."

The commander looked at his second with apparent fury for a few heartbeats, and then burst out laughing. He pounded the table with murderous amusement.

"Ah, Jhar," he said, when he had drowned his laughter in the remainder of his ale, "you know how to cheer me up. Yard Master Hralk, having the courage of a diseased pimp, will regret his words before the sun rises and will sleep in fear for a long time, waiting for my revenge. A revenge that will never come. Letting him squirm is revenge enough."

This time, Jhar joined his commander in laughter.

"Enough," the commander finally said. "We must plan, for I do not intend to let the Empire fail in its noble task through the stupidity and cowardice of the Council. They cannot see the hurt we have inflicted on the humans by our assault on the battleship, for they see only three ships lost against one. But where we can afford to lose paltry escorts with questionable crews, the humans cannot afford to lose a single capital ship. Destroy enough of theirs, even if we lose three small vessels for each, and we are still ahead. We can produce six cruisers for every one of theirs. And the humans will have learned to fear us. Cause and effect, Jhar. Soon, the humans will give each heavy warship a large number of consorts which can no longer be used elsewhere, and which will cease to be available to fight, since we will not attack where they are strong. In that, there is an opportunity to recapture the initiative."

"Your crew is behind you, commander," Jhar said, fierceness glowing in his deep-set black eyes.

"Yes, except for the *Tai Kan* spies."

"Accidents happen, commander."

"That they do," he mused, stroking his thick jaw. "There is opportunity and glory out there, Jhar. We will get it and may the Council choke on their whores' teats. Come. Let us return to *Tol Vakash*. I long to pace my bridge again."

With those words, Commander Brakal rose to his impressive height, staring down the few officers who had the temerity to glance at him, and strode out of the tavern, proud and arrogant. Let the Council and their stupidity go to hell. Brakal knew he was right, and so did a growing number of young firebrands waiting to take their first commands. A following was easy to build when the cowardly excrescences wearing the fine robes of admirals failed to bring glory to the Empire.

Out in the alley, Brakal took a deep breath of the city's fetid air and waited for Jhar to catch up.

"Tell me, my friend," he asked his second, "what is the word among the officers of Shrehari Prime?"

"Divided, commander," Jhar replied. "Those who were elevated to the Warrior caste stand behind you, though they do not, as yet, feel strong enough to challenge the ones who wish to remain uncommitted or those who want to see you fail."

"My distinguished colleagues," Brakal spat dismissively, "enfeebled by generations of inbreeding and indolence."

During the long peace before the present war, imperial officers had all been born into the Warrior caste. Preferment, corruption, intrigue, and nepotism had replaced merit and honor. Brakal however, born into the Warrior Clan Makkar, second son of the Clan Lord, had earned his advancement and owed nothing to anyone. Which was why he remained a commander and was not in admiral's robes.

"Your distinguished colleagues who hate you for preferring those raised to the Warrior caste over those born to it," Jhar countered.

The war, initially successful thanks to the humans' fecklessness, had gone well despite the incompetence of most of the High Command. Brakal regretted that his father had died less than two turns before the Council contemplated the folly of attacking the Commonwealth. As lord and admiral, he had a voice in the *Kraal*, the assembly of Lords that advised the Emperor, and a voice in the Admiralty. But he died of a cowardly murder two days after the old Emperor passed on to join his ancestors. Had he lived, he would have tried to dissuade the Emperor from authorizing the war. Failing that, he would have led the Fleet to victory. Admiral Maranth, Lord of Clan Makkar had been a superb warlord, and old spacers still spoke of him with awe in their voices.

"Hate me they can, but they dare not touch a Clan Lord."

Less than one turn into the war, Brakal's elder brother Mharak, then Clan Lord, died in the battle of Ybarrina Prime. A glorious death, which brought honor to the clan, but which also left Brakal as Clan Lord. It was an empty honor. The *Kraal* no longer sat because it contained too many Lords who were openly critical of the Council's handling of the war. But the Fleet was embarrassed that it employed a clan lord who was less than an admiral.

"They touched your father."

"A cowardly murder, Jhar, for which payment has not yet been extracted in full."

"Trage?"

"He and others. Their day will come. One day there will be more men in the Warrior caste raised there by merit than those who landed there, on their fat arses, due to an accident of birth."

Jhar grunted. Of humble birth, he had distinguished himself early, and when the Imperial Fleet expanded, the ancient right of elevation was restored, by need, not choice. He had been one of the first lower caste spacers to shave his head and receive the blessing of the infant Emperor. Many of the hereditary Warriors deeply resented those who were elevated and hated with a passion those of noble blood who supported elevation.

The two officers passed the guard post at the entrance of the military spaceport, Brakal absently returning the crisp salute of the sentry.

"No," Brakal, said, returning to Jhar's earlier comment, "they dare not cut me down now. It would be too dangerous, too obvious. Once Trage and the others retire, that will be the time of greatest peril. For now, they pray to their ancestors that a human warship will do their dirty work for them."

"They nearly had their wishes granted, commander."

"Hah," Brakal snorted, "the flame-haired she-wolf on the human battleship? She surprised me. That is all. I had always believed humans placed a premium on their own lives. Their writings are full of it and other incomprehensible muck. But it appears desperation gives some of them suicidal courage."

"Imagine, though, commander, if you'd been killed by a female, a ship's second at that."

"Do not," Brakal snarled back, "make the mistake of underestimating human females. That one is more worthy than a dozen of my brother hereditary Warriors."

Jhar saved his reply for another time as they rounded the corner and came within sight of Brakal's shuttle. Upon seeing them, Toralk, Brakal's bodyguard, standing by the open door to the cockpit, snapped to attention. His right hand slapped the hilt of his dagger, re-affirming his oath to die for his commander.

"To the ship, Lord?"

"To the ship, Toralk, and stop calling me Lord," Brakal replied irritably.

Ever since Mharak died, and Brakal became head of the clan, Toralk had insisted on calling him lord instead of commander. He was the only one aboard the cruiser who dared do so, but then, Toralk and Brakal had grown up together on the family estates. Toralk's family had served Brakal's for more generations than either cared to remember and when Brakal joined the Fleet, so did Toralk, the one as an officer, the other as low caste spacer. Toralk had been watching Brakal's back for over twenty turns, and neither could imagine living without the other.

Toralk slid into the right hand seat and strapped in. When Brakal had joined him, taking the left-hand seat, the bodyguard looked to his commander.

"Do you wish to pilot, Lord?"

"I do, Toralk, but it would be unwise. In my present state, I am liable to buzz Admiral Trage's residence at an altitude low enough to remove his putrid head from his weak shoulders."

"Treasonous talk, Lord," Toralk chided his master, and friend, a faint smile playing on his thin lips. Behind them, Jhar burst out laughing at Toralk's impudence, because the old chief petty officer was absolutely right, and Brakal would absolutely ignore the advice.

"What is treasonable," Brakal replied, in a mock angry voice, "is a ship's Second and a commander's bodyguard daring to remonstrate their beloved leader."

"...and Lord," Toralk added, unwilling to let his master have the last word.

"Fly the machine, excrescence, and cease trying to prove your wit to all and sundry, or I will have you retired to the estate, to harvest tubers."

Toralk snorted softly, "Yes, Lord," and gunned the shuttle's thrusters, taking them away from Shredar's unhealthy miasma of physical and moral pollution.

*

Tol Vakash still bore gaping evidence of the human she-wolf's desperate battle run, but the cruiser retained her sleek beauty and dangerous aura. Brakal loved his ship and crew, even though love was a concept he could not visualize. The nearest the Imperial tongue came to love, was honor. And that sentiment motivated Brakal in everything he did.

A quarter guard, as well turned out and as fierce-looking as any of the Emperor's household troops, greeted him on the pressurized shuttle deck. Brakal inspected them with grim satisfaction. They too were the best in the Fleet, veterans of more battles than any could remember, and they would cheerfully die for their commander, if not for the Emperor.

But his interview with the Council never left his thoughts, and he felt the earlier anger return as he walked down the bare passageways, his eyes absently noting the irreproachable cleanliness of the ship. He knew that all compartments would pass even the most rigorous inspection. His crew's pride would not let it be otherwise.

When he passed the wardroom, he heard the faint rush of loud voices roaring at each other. The doors suddenly opened on his gun master, Lieutenant Urag, who came to attention and grinned, showing a mouthful of yellowing, fang-like teeth. His breath stank of strong ale and would have knocked down a charging *barloi*.

Behind Urag, most of the ship's officers were seated around the wardroom's single table, drinking and telling each other stories that brought on gales of raucous laughter and backslapping fierce enough to fell all but the strongest Warriors.

"Commander," Urag roared, to cover the voices of his friends, "I was about to come looking for you. We received word you were back. The ale is particularly bitter tonight as if brewed by the gods themselves. Come join us."

Brakal grinned back, his earlier bad mood slipping away. A night with his officers was always an excellent occasion. As he and Urag approached the table, the others made room for their commander. The chief engineer, an ugly, massive, troll-like Warrior, handed him a brimming mug of foaming purple ale. Brakal downed the spicy drink in a single gulp, to the cheers of his officers, who immediately gave him a refill, to sip this time.

Soon, Brakal was laughing and shouting with the rest of them as officer after officer told tall tales, usually involving bawdiness, jokes at the expense of the Council, and feats of battle that could not possibly be done by anyone short of the gods.

Life aboard *Tol Vakash* was good, better than any reward of rank or position.

— Six —

"We've got a serious problem, captain." Pushkin, a face like thunder, was waiting for Siobhan at the entry port, his pad tucked under his arm. "The base supply people claim they don't have the parts we need to fix the reactor flux regulators that blew this morning, and even if they did have some, they don't have the available personnel to swap them out."

"And without those parts, we're not moving." Siobhan's good humor at seeing Ezekiel evaporated like dew in the morning sun. "Damn!" She stopped and faced Pushkin, anger hardening her lean face.

"What do you think, Mister Pushkin?"

"The fuckers are lying, captain," he replied with surprising candor. "Flow regulators wear out regularly. An engineering supply store that doesn't carry spares should be spaced."

Siobhan raised an ironic eyebrow as she locked eyes with her XO. "It seems that you and I agree on something, at last, Mister Pushkin. Does Tiner think she can do the job without the Starbase engineers if we get her the parts?"

Pushkin did not reply for a moment, neither did he look away. Then, he slowly said, "She's got experienced people in her department, captain. They'll manage the job, or I'll know the reason why."

Satisfied at his tone, she nodded. "Then let's see about getting the parts. Anything else critical while we're at it?"

They started walking toward the bridge again, absently returning the salutes of crewmembers as they went along.

"Critical, no. Non-critical, plenty. I sometimes think we'd get better service at an imperial supply depot. Hell, the Imps probably love *Stingray*. We're more of a hindrance to the Fleet than a threat to the Empire, and that's worth a full load of stores, especially Shrehari Ale."

Siobhan, surprised at Pushkin's remark, stopped again and looked at him, grinning mischievously. "Why Mister Pushkin, gallows humor? I'm both surprised and pleased. I had you marked down as a puritan."

To her annoyance, the first officer kept a dark expression his face, eyes remaining carefully neutral. He did not return Siobhan's smile and the momentary crack in his shell, if it ever had been there, was gone, leaving the same angry, disillusioned man she had met the day before.

Siobhan shrugged, fighting her own frustration. "As you wish. Join me in my ready room and we'll see if we can't shake those parts loose. Someone's trying very hard to make us fail, and I don't like it one bit."

Pushkin grunted but did not challenge her.

Once in the privacy of her small office, she tossed her beret on the desk and sat down, motioning Pushkin to take the other seat. He ignored the invitation and remained standing, hands clasped in the small of his back in a perfect rendition of the parade rest as if he were a cadet at the Academy waiting for his Tactical Officer to chew him out. Siobhan stared at Pushkin for a few heartbeats, willing him to unbend, but to no visible effect.

"You spoke to Commander Sones?"

"Aye, sir. All oiliness and sincere regrets. He promised to look into it, but assured me that nothing could be done for six or seven days."

Siobhan snorted. "And when I ask Admiral Kaleri for a delay in sailing, the parts will suddenly appear, and we'll look like asses."

Pushkin's eyes registered surprise at the notion that Battle Group staff would conspire to make them fail, and Siobhan suddenly realized that he'd probably been completely out of his depth with Forenza, who was born into a world of double-dealing and intrigue. That would explain a lot of his simmering anger and bitterness. Forenza probably kept it that way on purpose too, to preserve her authority. No wonder Pushkin had a scowl permanently etched into his features.

"As they say, Mister Pushkin, one fights plasma best with plasma. I think I have an idea to get around the staff's pettiness, even if it is deliberate obstruction ordered by someone higher on the totem pole. Fortunately for us, I have an old friend in a good position to help." She turned to her terminal. "Bridge, get me the Battle Group Personnel Officer."

A few seconds later, Ezekiel's craggy face filled the screen. "Holt. Oh, hi captain. What can the staff do for you?"

"Hello, Ezekiel. Sorry to ask this again, but is there really nothing you can do about those replacements I asked for? I know you told me at lunch that it was quite impossible, but..."

Holt hid his surprise well, but Siobhan knew he had realized this call was not about replacement personnel at all.

"I'm sorry, captain," he slowly replied, his single blue eye watching Siobhan carefully for clues, "but I can't accommodate you."

"Damn!" Siobhan swore, screwing up her face in mock disgust. "It seems I can't get anything out of the staff these days. No personnel, no stores, not even critical spare parts. Well, thank you anyway, Mister Holt."

"Sorry, captain." Ezekiel shrugged, but Siobhan had seen understanding light up his face. "Maybe after my watch ends, I can come by and show you why I can't get those replacements. It might put your mind at rest that the staff is doing all it can."

"Oh, all right, Mister Holt. I'll even buy you a cup of coffee for your troubles. Dunmoore, out."

Pushkin looked at her uncomprehending when she sat back in the padded chair. "I fail to see..." He started.

"Ah," Siobhan raised her hand, smiling, "wait until Lieutenant Commander Holt visits us. If he's successful, you'll understand. Ezekiel was my first officer in *Shenzen* and is pretty quick on the uptake."

Pushkin did not exactly shrug, but it was evident he still did not understand. Siobhan was tempted to leave it until Ezekiel showed up, but remembered just in time that

Forenza had probably treated the first officer in such a manner. If she was ever going to develop a decent working relationship, she had to break him away from the past.

Patiently, Siobhan explained what she had in mind, and the nuances of deception that flowed around every hierarchy. When the first officer finally left the ready room, he understood, but she caught him shaking his head just before the door closed on his retreating back.

Alone in the corridor, the first officer brooded as he made his way to his cabin. He did not know what to make of Captain Dunmoore and the ambivalence gnawed away at his insides. On the one hand, Pushkin hated her for taking the job that he considered his alone, the only chance he might have had for promotion. At thirty-eight, he was long in the tooth for a lieutenant commander and had never been given the opportunity to prove himself. The war was five years old, and most of his classmates were either dead or had commands of their own. When Forenza was relieved, he had desperately hoped to take the step and replace her. He felt he'd earned it, believing, not incorrectly, that he had kept the ship from plunging into a worse state. But the hope had been naïve, and he hated himself for that.

On the other hand, Dunmoore had been right to come down on him for *Stingray*'s condition when she came aboard. He was enough of a realist to know that he had failed in his duty. But his bitterness, when he learned he'd been passed over again, had overwhelmed his judgment. By then, he no longer gave a damn. Yet Pushkin had to admit that Dunmoore had been more lenient than she could have been, and seemed prepared to give him a chance to wipe away the initial bad impression.

No, he did not know what to make of her and did not really want to like her either. But keeping his bitterness and anger stoked twenty-four hours a day was taking its toll, and it was not getting him anywhere. Though he wanted to tell her to go to hell and get the ship back into shape on her own, somehow, he could not deviate from the duty he had carried out for many years. Then, there was the unspoken hope that if she got what she wanted from the crew and the officers, Dunmoore would not delve too deeply into a recent past Pushkin would rather keep buried.

*

"Captain, there's a Lieutenant Commander Holt at the entry port, asking to see you."

Siobhan turned toward the intercom. "Have him brought up to my ready room, and ask the first officer to join us."

Maybe Pushkin would learn something in the art of deviousness. And maybe he would lose some of that bitterness by being included in the discussion, though there were moments when she was ready to give up and let events take their course.

Pushkin was there a few moments before Ezekiel arrived. He stood silently in the parade rest position in front of her desk, waiting. When Ezekiel stepped into her office grinning, she introduced them.

"Mister Pushkin, this is Lieutenant Commander Ezekiel Holt, in charge of Battle Group Personnel. He and I were in *Shenzen* together. Ezekiel, my first officer, Gregor Pushkin."

The two men sized each other up as they shook hands perfunctorily. From Ezekiel's expression, Siobhan could see that he held a low opinion of Pushkin. She hoped her first officer did not realize this. A vain hope, judging by Pushkin's expression.

"Sit down, Ezekiel, Mister Pushkin. Let's see what you've got."

To her relief, this time, Pushkin consented to take a seat, though he remained stiff and unyielding.

"Well, Skipper," Ezekiel started, taking off his beret, "from your message, I gathered my colleague running supply wasn't giving you what you needed, and I did some quiet checking. What I found was that Kaleri apparently made it known that no one was to go out of his way to help you. If you're made to look incompetent by not sailing on time, there'll be a lot of happy people around."

Siobhan glanced at Pushkin and noted with satisfaction the sudden interest in his eyes

"I found your requests in the files, which makes me suspect that you'll get the stuff when it is too late to meet your sailing date. Sones has ordered that all supply or engineering requirements from *Stingray* go to him personally, which means his staff doesn't know what's going on. But he's got the parts you need, and in plentiful supply too."

Siobhan smiled. "All that's left then is to find a way to get them out of his grasp."

"I've got something for you, skipper, and it's right up your alley," Ezekiel grinned evilly, looking more piratical than ever. "Sones has gone off duty for the day, and when he's off, he doesn't like to be disturbed short of a Shrehari assault force emerging within gun range. His staff doesn't like him much, except for a few bum lickers, and won't incur his wrath by calling him while he's busy indulging in his preferred forms of recreation. If you show up at the engineering depot with a work party, I'm sure you can charm the duty chief into giving you the parts. Sones'll find out in the morning, but by then, you'll have the stuff, and he's just going to look foolish by making a big thing out of it. Anyway, neither Kaleri nor Sones wants too much attention from 3rd Fleet right now. As for the duty chief, he'll take the lumps, but either he's one of the bum lickers, in which case so fucking what, or he hates Sones and will be all too happy to shaft him."

"Sounds like a plan, Ezekiel," Siobhan smiled. She looked at Pushkin again and saw that he was looking distinctly uncomfortable. Whether it was because of Holt's easy way with Siobhan, because he had not come up with the plan himself, as any good first officer should, or because he lacked the courage to raid the supply stores, she could not tell.

"What do you think, Mister Pushkin?"

The first officer shrugged. "It might work, sir. But..." He left his doubts hanging, unwilling to appear churlish in front of Holt. Siobhan saw her friend's eye flash with contempt.

"Thanks, Ezekiel," she smiled at him again, ignoring Pushkin's distinct lack of enthusiasm. "Your snooping won't get you in trouble, will it?"

"Nothing I can't handle, skipper. Oh, and before you think I'm also in the obstructing game, what with denying you replacements, that's genuine. Unless the vacant position is critical, no ship in the Battle Group is getting anyone for now. The training system isn't producing enough and the Fleet's launching new ships every day."

Siobhan nodded. "I never doubted you, Ezekiel. What do you think the best time for the heist would be?"

"Near eight bells in the evening watch. The duty chief will be looking for the end of his shift, and most daytime personnel will be in bed. Anything else I can do for you, Skipper?"

"You've already done enough, Ezekiel. Any more and I'll really get you in trouble."

Holt shrugged dismissively. "I can't just sit by and watch you get shafted. That being said, I have to get going. No rest for the wicked."

"Or the devious. Thanks, Ezekiel."

"Don't mention it." He rose and put his beret on. "Mister Pushkin," he nodded at the first officer, who had also risen to his feet. Neither offered to shake hands with the other, confirming their mutual dislike. Holt saluted and left.

When Ezekiel was gone, Pushkin, back into his irritatingly stiff parade rest position said, "I'm not sure I like this, captain. It could backfire badly."

"That's why I'll be leading the raiding party, Mister Pushkin."

His disapproving frown deepened, but he did not object, clearly unwilling to put his ass on the line, although this kind of operation was clearly not the captain's job. It annoyed Siobhan just as much as his artificial stiffness did, and she felt tempted to provoke him with a pointed comment, but that would not have helped.

"Have sufficient personnel and grav floats waiting at the cargo airlock at seven bells in the evening watch. Dismissed."

*

At the appointed time, Siobhan, wearing tight-fitting coveralls with metal rank insignia gleaming on the collar points, met the work party under the orders of the fourth engineering officer. The ensign, a petite woman no more than a year out of the Academy, looked distinctly uncomfortable with her orders. The same could not be said about Chief Petty Officer Weekes, the engineering chief, and the other ratings of the work party. They seemed delighted at the idea of raiding base stores in the dead of night as if this was the most fun they had in ages. Which also said a lot about *Stingray's* previous management.

Pushkin too was waiting at the airlock, as disapproving as ever, but he made no attempt to dissuade her. Nor did he wish the party good luck. As they filed out of the large airlock, he watched them leave, his lips compressed in a thin line of worry.

Ezekiel Holt was right, and the corridors of the base's dockyard levels were empty at this time of night. The few people they met ignored them, as they would ignore any work party from one of the docked ships and they reached the engineering stores depot without incident.

The duty chief petty officer was watching a three-vee flick in a cubby to the left of the massive doors guarding the precious starship parts. When Siobhan entered the small office, the chief, a grizzled man in his late forties, with a paunch and a face lined with burst blood vessels, glanced at her in annoyance. Then, his expression changed as he spotted her rank insignia and the hard, slender female body encased in tight coveralls. She smiled at him.

"What, ah, can I do for you, sir," the chief asked. His nametape identified him as Moller, and he was clearly rattled by Siobhan sudden appearance.

"Commander Dunmoore, chief. I've come to pick up the spare parts I ordered." Siobhan's smile widened.

"Yes, sir. Ah, what ship, sir?" Moller picked up a data pad and flicked it on. If he thought it unusual that a ship's captain was leading a work party, he kept the thought to himself.

"*Stingray*, Mister Moller."

He looked at his datapad and frowned. "I'm sorry, sir," he finally said, sounding unhappy. "Your request isn't on any manifest.

"Damn!" Siobhan pouted, an expression she personally found ludicrous, but it seemed to have the required effect on Moller. He looked even more miserable. "My first officer put in the request this morning. Both of our reactor flux regulators blew during a static test, and I have to sail in less than three days. It'll take me most of that just to put the new parts in, let alone test them."

"Well sir, maybe the paperwork didn't make it all the way down. It happens, what with the bureaucracy upstation. Let me see if the central computer has your request." He turned toward his console and began searching.

"Ah, I see, sir," the chief said, a wry smile on his face. "The request got stuck in Commander Sones' office. He hasn't had time to approve it yet." His tone hinted that he did not hold his department head in very high regard.

Siobhan grimaced. "By the time he gets to work tomorrow morning, I'll no longer have enough time before my sailing date."

"Don't worry, sir," the chief grinned like a man about to bestow a favor. "These things happen all the time. Tell you what, I have the list now, and we have everything in stock. With your work party, it won't take long to fill your order and let you get your ship ready in time. I'll just need your thumbprint for my pad, and it'll all be as per regulations."

"Thanks, Mister Moller. You've saved my hide from Admiral Kaleri. You won't get into trouble for this now, will you?" She made a concerned face.

"Don't worry about Mister Sones, sir," the chief grinned. "Let's get going, then."

*

An hour later, grav floats loaded high with crates, Siobhan and her work party made their way back to the ship. Dunmoore felt distinctly pleased with herself.

Pushkin was at the airlock when they arrived. He made no comment and asked no questions about the raid. After greeting his captain, he simply issued orders for the unpacking and installation of the parts, as if this had been a routine matter. But when Siobhan passed him to return to her cabin, she caught him glancing at her, and there was something different in his eyes. It lasted only for a heartbeat, then he went back to work, his harsh voice driving the engineering crew to their tasks.

It took him a long time to accept the grudging respect he felt for Dunmoore and the nagging embarrassment at having let her do a job he should have done. Consciously or not, the new captain was making him feel inadequate as first officer, and Pushkin hated the sensation.

*

The next morning, more by chance than design, Pushkin was with Dunmoore when Sones called. Feeling mischievous, Siobhan connected the vidcom to the briefing screen in her ready room so Pushkin could see Sones without the latter seeing him.

"Good morning, Commander Sones. What can I do for you?" Siobhan's tone was sweet and innocent, and Pushkin's eyes narrowed at her gall.

"Don't act like nothing happened, Dunmoore," Sones' puffy face was red with outrage, heavy jowls quivering as he spoke. "First, your purser, now you suborning my people. You had no right to those parts, and believe me, Admiral Kaleri will know of your pilfering as soon as I finish speaking with you. I could bring you up on charges for this, you know, and you won't be able to weasel out of it like you did before."

Siobhan raised her eyebrows at the threat and the implication that *Shenzen* court-martial two years ago acquitted her on a technicality. When she replied, her voice was hard.

"Can the threats, Sones. You told my first officer you didn't have the parts, yet I found the stores filled to the rafters. That'll look real fine in front of a Disciplinary Board. Battle Group Purser hoards supplies desperately needed by beleaguered warship."

"I told him they weren't available, which is different," he protested, as outrage at being called purser instead of high-and-mighty general staff officer fought with the fear of her counter-threat.

"Bullshit, Sones. I'll take my first officer's word well before yours." Siobhan had the satisfaction of seeing surprise in Pushkin's face. "You complain to Admiral Kaleri if you want, but you'll have to explain why you weren't going to release critical parts and thereby cause my ship to miss its sailing date."

Sones' eyes took on a sly look. "Maybe I don't have to explain myself to the admiral. She knows who she can trust, and an officer who routinely gets ships shot out from under her doesn't qualify."

Siobhan sighed theatrically, biting back an urge to reach down the comm link and choke him. "Make an issue of it, Sones, if you like. Just remember that this will all be recorded in the ship's logs, and they are sent to navy Command through 3rd Fleet every few weeks. Admiral Nagira has taken a particular interest in *Stingray* and will read them, I can assure you of that. Now I can either make a note that you've been most helpful or that you've been obstructive. Your choice."

Sones suddenly became uncertain. He hemmed and hawed for a few moments. It was clear that word about her sponsor had made its way to his ears. Not that Nagira had any time to review logs, but a man of Sones' limited intelligence probably still saw three-star admirals as demi-gods, not harassed and overworked creatures. *Stingray* was but one small frigate among 3rd Fleet's two hundred warships. And then there was Ezekiel's comment that neither Sones nor Kaleri wished closer attention from 3rd Fleet right now.

"Very well," Sones wrapped himself in a cloak of wounded dignity by replying in a tone that attempted to be condescending but failed miserably. "I will overlook your irregular actions this time. However, I warn you. Try this again, and you will pay dearly. Sones, out."

Siobhan had no doubt Admiral Kaleri would hear of the incident, and would somehow make sure the captain of *Stingray* regretted it, sooner or later. That was part of the price for playing devious games. She who held the rank held the power. Kaleri was known not only to carry a grudge but also to take subtle and deadly revenge. Deadly for a career, that is. No one had ever proven she had done anything worse.

Siobhan looked at Pushkin, and this time, she was sure she saw a glimmer of respect in his dark eyes, even if the ever-present scowl was as deep as ever.

"There you are, Mister Pushkin. Sometimes a captain has to play distasteful games for her ship's welfare. I don't like doing it any more than you like seeing me do it." Siobhan smiled when she saw her comment hit home. "And I don't expect you to do this kind of stuff at every turn. Just be aware that when events require, you and I have to work out some alternate means. For the good of the ship."

"Aye, aye, sir," he nodded. "For the good of the ship." Whether he agreed or not was open to debate. "Was there anything else?"

"No. I just hope those parts were the only critical supplies we needed because I've shot my broadside."

"We're still short of a lot of stores, sir, but nothing that'll keep us from sailing."

Siobhan nodded and was about to dismiss her first officer when he surprised her with an unexpected question.

"Begging your pardon, sir, what's going to happen now? I mean with Commander Sones?"

"He'll tell Kaleri, and then wait for an opportunity to extract his revenge, with interest." She shrugged. "Nothing we can do about that, except keep our eyes open and make sure it doesn't hurt the crew."

"Aye, sir." He saluted and left, his habitual bitterness struggling with respect, and a growing realization that she was getting on with the job a lot better than he could ever have done under the circumstances.

Alone once more, Siobhan decided to scan the list of shortages, but not because she mistrusted Pushkin. He had not taken a single wrong step since the department heads' meeting on the first day. Which did not mean he shone as a first officer, but he showed grudging promise.

That made her wonder even more why he had left the ship in such a desperate state after Forenza was relieved.

What the captain really wanted to see was what, if anything, she could obtain by other means. Though she told Pushkin she had fired her broadside, there were always other swindles she could pull. And after speaking with Sones, it had become personal: Siobhan Dunmoore against the staff of 31st Battle Group.

Pushkin had been right. There were no critical shortages. Ammunition, food, and consumable parts were in sufficient supply. But there were little if any of the luxuries that made a long patrol bearable: no new entertainment chips, canteen supplies and the like. It was not something she could complain about, yet it would affect the morale of the crew in a very direct manner. And Sones knew it. Siobhan frowned deeply when she spotted one shortfall she considered critical.

There was not enough coffee aboard to last a week.

On every ship in the Fleet, the big, shiny coffee urns were kept chugging watch after watch in each of the messes, and wherever enterprising spacers found room to install one. Real navy coffee was as vital to spacers as oxygen. She would have a real morale problem if she sailed without it. *Damn Sones for being so bloody unfair!*

She pressed the intercom. "Captain to purser."

Rossum's perspiring face appeared on the screen moments later. He looked worried, like a man about to receive a tongue lashing. Siobhan briefly wondered whether he had a guilty conscience, or whether it was a typical response after two years of Helen Forenza's 'gentle' leadership.

"I note that the base is unable to provide us with sufficient coffee, Mister Rossum."

"Ah, yes, sir. Sorry, sir but there's none to be had at supply. A general shortage, I understand."

"You did manage to get other supplies that were supposedly in short supply."

"Ah, you heard, sir." Rossum pulled out his white handkerchief and patted his bald, shiny head. "Yes. I got enough of the basics to last, but when I returned for the coffee and other commissariat things, the doors had unfortunately closed. Sorry, sir."

Siobhan shook her head. "No matter, Mister Rossum. At least you got more than they intended to give us. Commander Sones' opinion of your methods matters little to me, especially after this morning. Results are the only things that count."

Rossum looked distinctly relieved, though he never stopped sponging the sweat from his face.

"Now, I'm sure there is coffee to be had on the station," Siobhan continued, "just as I was sure the parts for the regulators were there." The plump purser nodded, grinning. Evidently, the story about her liberating engineering stores had already made the rounds and had met with approval. "But we'll try a different approach for this. What have we for barter, Mister Rossum?"

"Not much, I'm afraid, captain. Not for coffee." He seemed genuinely apologetic.

Siobhan scrolled through the ship's stores list. A vague entry caught her attention.

"Mister Rossum, what does the manifest mean by captain's stores?"

"Ah, sir. Those are Captain Forenza's own supplies. She has not yet given us any instructions for sending them on."

"What are they?"

"If memory serves, sir, three cases of VSOP cognac from Dordogne, a few crates of claret, also from Dordogne, and some other things of, ah, questionable interest..."

Siobhan grinned evilly. "Now there's something that would interest people who have coffee to spare. Not the questionable items, mind you." She could well imagine what those were. "But the booze."

"Sir," Rossum suddenly looked distressed, "those are Captain Forenza's own stocks. We can't just take them."

"Sure we can," Siobhan nodded, eyebrows raised. "I think it's about time Commander Forenza did something nice for the crew, and what could be nicer than ensuring we have an adequate supply of coffee?"

"But what do I tell her when she asks for the cognac and wine?"

"You've searched the ship high and low, and regrettably, the booze has vanished without a trace. Or if you don't want to do it yourself, I can tell her." Judging by how she treated the crew, Forenza probably believed that her stores had been pilfered the moment she left the ship.

"No, no, sir," he shook his head, fat cheeks shaking, "I'll do it. No problem there."

Siobhan smiled crookedly. She would have never pegged the soft-looking purser as having enough guts to tell Forenza her stash of booze, worth thousands of credits, was gone. Then again, maybe he was a born liar and obfuscator, like many pursers in the Fleet. It seemed to be a requirement of the job.

"I'll leave you to it then, Mister Rossum. There are enough ships in port for some serious trading, and I doubt *they* have any problems getting more from the commissariat. If you can't get enough out of them, try the messes and clubs. There isn't a mess manager born who'd pass up a chance to get cheap booze for the bar."

"Aye, aye, sir!" The purser's eyes seemed to shine at the prospect of hard haggling.

"Mind that you don't let on how much we have. Barter bottle by bottle. Otherwise, we won't get a decent trade."

"Never you mind, sir," Rossum grinned, "I'll get enough coffee and still have some cognac left over to spike it with."

"Carry on, then, Mister Rossum."

*

The purser was as good as his word, and Siobhan raised her opinion of him a few notches. At first glance, he might look shifty, overfed, and soft, but he produced results.

By the end of the first dogwatch, he had not only managed to horse trade for enough fresh coffee beans to last two whole months, but he had a case of cognac left to spare. As he told Siobhan, he would keep it in reserve for future needs.

Dunmoore left her ready room in a good mood, but she should have realized it was not going to last on a ship loaded with enough ill-will to re-start the Thirty Years War. She chose to pass through the bridge instead of using her private door and came face-to-face with an incident that confirmed her fears about the real depth of her problems. As she stepped through the door, the irritating, nasal voice of her sailing master assaulted her ears, setting her nerves on edge.

"Well, I'm so sorry, Mister Pushkin, but the intelligence staff have told me the new star charts aren't available, and I'm not about to start questioning their word. I don't see why we don't make do with the old charts. There's no reason to get all huffy about it."

Siobhan felt her blood pressure rise at the insolence of Shara's tone and nearly stepped in, but then thought better of it. Neither had noticed her and though the remaining bridge crew threw furtive glances in her direction, they remained silent. Which was interesting. It proved they had little liking for either Pushkin or the sailing master.

"Lieutenant, you damn well know that space hazards appear and vanish all the time. How do you expect to do your job properly without current charts?"

Anybody else would have backed off at Pushkin's apparent fury, but Shara seemed untouched as if she felt immune to his authority. Siobhan frowned. Shara and Forenza came from the same planet and social background. Had the sailing master been part of her predecessor's clique? It would explain her arrogance.

"Well, I can't get them, Mister Pushkin, and that's that." Shara wore a look of furtive satisfaction on her thin, sallow face.

"We shall see," the first officer growled. Then, he suddenly noticed Siobhan standing behind the rear railing, arms crossed. "Captain on the bridge," he snapped, his black look spearing the ratings and petty officers who hadn't warned him of her presence. His gaze bode ill for the defaulters but the crew dutifully came to attention, several hiding snickers, and sneers behind bland facades.

"Carry on," Siobhan said softly when silence had fallen on the bridge. "Report, Mister Pushkin."

"We're having problems getting updated charts, sir," the first officer replied, disgust visible on his hard features as he glanced at the insolent sailing master.

Out of the corner of her eye, Dunmoore saw Kowalski survey the scene with apparent interest. She had not been able to peg the signals officer yet, but it was evident she disliked Pushkin and Shara.

"So I understand. What excuse has the staff given, Mister Shara?"

"They have no updated copy ready for distribution, sir." Shara's voice grated on Siobhan's nerves like sandpaper.

"How old are our current charts?"

"Six months."

"I find it hard to believe, then, that there are no updates available. Fleet procedure is to issue new charts every three months. Why did you not update them three months ago?"

Shara's arrogance suddenly changed to uncertainty as Dunmoore challenged her. She remained silent for a few moments, clearly searching for an acceptable answer. Kowalski's expression shifted to amused malice as she too waited for a reply.

"There, ah, wasn't any occasion, sir," the sailing master finally replied with an embarrassed smile.

"I shan't ask why not, Mister Shara. Mister Pushkin, please join me in the ready room."

Shara looked relieved, thinking the first officer was about to be taken to task for the charts, and her malicious arrogance returned. Siobhan speared her with a glance that could have rivaled a battleship's guns in action, and her expression changed so rapidly that more than one crewmember fought to hide a smile.

Once they were alone, Siobhan sat on the corner of her desk and looked at Pushkin in silence. He, in turn, retreated into his parade-like formality. Siobhan finally sighed.

"As if fighting the staff wasn't enough, I now find my officers arguing in public. On my bridge."

Pushkin started, his eyes filling with anger, and Siobhan realized she had said the wrong thing again. He was a touchy bastard, and his bitterness at the universe was quickly becoming a nova-sized annoyance.

"What I mean," she quickly continued, before he hid behind his wounded pride, "is that I cannot understand why my sailing master has the temerity to gainsay my first officer."

Her words did not visibly mollify Pushkin, but she felt, rather than saw him relax.

"Tell me if I'm wrong, Mister Pushkin," she softly continued, "but Lieutenant Shara was rather close to Commander Forenza." When he did not reply, she became blunter. "In fact, I'd say she was Forenza's bum licker. Only that could explain why she has the nerve to argue with you. Well, Mister Pushkin, you have my permission and my full support to discipline her. I will not have anyone on this ship gainsaying you. You are my executive officer, my right hand, and my voice. And it's about time this was made clear to all."

"Yes, sir," he replied, voice gruff but visibly surprised at her open gesture of support. He was clearly not used to these words from his captain.

"Just one note of caution, Mister Pushkin, before an argument starts, shut the offender up in no uncertain terms and take her, or him, to a private spot and *then* chew them another asshole. Arguing in public does nothing for crew morale, or respect for their officers."

"Yes, sir." His stance stiffened further, but not in anger at Dunmoore's mild rebuke. He was genuinely annoyed at himself for having to be reminded of what he should know but had forgotten.

On a hunch, Siobhan asked, "Commander Forenza had the habit of chastising her officers in public, didn't she? Including you?"

"Aye, sir," he grudgingly acknowledged but did not elaborate. Siobhan felt her earlier frustration at not knowing what had gone on. Before she could ask a question that would ruin the fragile understanding between them, she stood up.

"I'll let you get on, then. Advise me of what you intend to do about getting new charts."

"Sir?" He glanced at her, uncertain.

"You'll find a way, Mister Pushkin, I'm sure. As you now know, there's more than one manner to obtain what we need. Dismissed."

Siobhan retreated to the desk, sat and steepled her fingers beneath her chin. The incident on the bridge, while demonstrating a lack of proper leadership on both sides, had revealed some of the rifts among her officers and crew, the divisions Ezekiel had warned her about.

Pushkin, she had decided to trust for now. His emotions were too close to the surface for any deeper scheming. But Shara was definitely someone to watch. Any friend or sycophant of Helen Forenza was a danger to her, and to her crew. Especially one so stupid. As for Kowalski? Siobhan could not figure out where she stood. According to her file, she was a colonist from Cascadia, and therefore a natural enemy of aristocrats like Shara or Forenza. The chime of the intercom interrupted her thoughts.

"Sickbay to captain."

"Dunmoore."

"Doctor Luttrell, sir. Your medical files have arrived. I would like to give you a complete physical as soon as you can spare me some time. Now if possible."

"Any reason to hurry," Siobhan asked, irritated at the interruption. Before Luttrell could reply, the captain caught herself and softened her tone. "I'll be right there, Doctor."

"Good, Luttrell, out."

Siobhan shook her head as she rose. It would not do to alienate Luttrell out of sheer churlishness. She would have to watch her temper more carefully.

Then, she smiled.

The physical would be a good occasion to ask Luttrell some questions. Maybe the draftee doctor had fewer reasons for avoiding the past than the career officers, had. It was worth a try.

— Seven —

When Siobhan entered sickbay, Luttrell gave her a welcoming grin and shooed out all of her assistants, so that she and Dunmoore were alone in the examining room.

"How's the migraine been behaving, captain?"

"Fine. No more nightmares either." Siobhan smiled, struck again by how much she felt she could like her ship's surgeon.

"I'm going to have to ask you to strip, captain. But it's purely a professional request," Luttrell added with a wry grin. "Oh, and the deck is warmed so you don't have to worry about cold feet. I try to keep my customers as comfortable as possible."

"I guess you're the kind of doctor who takes the hands-on approach when examining patients," Siobhan commented, pulling off her gloves.

"Strangely enough, sir, I've got this urge to determine a person's condition with my own senses, not through fancy machinery. A leftover from my days as a colonial sawbones, when I didn't have all these cute toys. It allows me to see why my patients hide their otherwise functional hands behind stylish gloves."

The doctor nodded at Siobhan's left hand. "Reactor coolant burns look nastier than they are, but I can understand your wanting to keep them hidden. Tends to distract anyone you're talking to. Just like big breasts."

Siobhan laughed at Luttrell's wry, but accurate comment, releasing the tension she had felt earlier and in the process gained a new appreciation for the doctor's bedside manner. Luttrell tsked and clucked when Siobhan finally stood buck naked in front of her. Dunmoore's body was covered with a network of fine white scars.

"You've led a hard life, captain."

Siobhan, feeling embarrassed, shrugged. "Just unlucky, I guess. Or maybe not. At least I'm alive," she added. "It's all stuff that can wait until the war is over."

"Please lie down on the diagnostic bed, captain," Luttrell replied, all business.

Dunmoore complied. "I understand three crewmembers had more bad luck lately than I've had, Doctor."

"Indeed." The surgeon seemed uneasy all of a sudden.

"I wonder what kind of disease put Leading Spacer Savarin on the beach. Was it VD?"

Luttrell glanced up from her scanner and grinned at Siobhan, though the look in her eyes was less amused. "You could say that. Halterian Syphilitic Leprosy. I managed to catch it before his genitals literally dropped off, but there's no real known cure. Although he's been beached, he continues to serve the Commonwealth by puzzling medical researchers at the Wyvern Fleet Hospital to no end. He's only the tenth human to come down with the bug, and scientists from all over are probably fighting each other for a chance at his tissue samples."

"How did you know it was that disease?"

Luttrell shrugged. "I'm insatiably curious and read everything I can get my hands on. The symptoms are pretty characteristic, and I remembered seeing their description in the Commonwealth Medical Journal last summer. Relax, captain."

The doctor began her hands-on examination, feeling and squeezing Siobhan's limbs, abdomen, and breasts. She winced when Luttrell manipulated her left arm.

"Not quite healed yet, eh?"

"There were worse cases ahead of me. *Victoria Regina*'s surgeon did a good job under the circumstances. We had hundreds of casualties after the fight." Siobhan studied Luttrell's face but saw no reaction to the name of the ill-fated battleship. "I guess Savarin can be happy that you've made a virtue out of curiosity. Men have this curious attachment to the things between their legs. What about Vasser and Melchor? Accident, I understand?"

The surgeon busied herself with the medical scanner again and did not reply for a few moments. Then, she looked up, a guarded expression on her hard face. Her earlier good humor was gone.

"Yes, captain, an accident. That's what the inquiry established."

Something in Luttrell's tone and choice of words hinted that she had doubts about the cause of death, but was not prepared to discuss them.

"How did the accident happen? I can't find a copy of the inquiry on file, and the logs have all been impounded."

"I'm not sure I remember, captain." Luttrell looked away, but not before Siobhan decided that the doctor was lying.

"You conducted the autopsy?"

"Yes. Not a pretty sight."

"Why?"

Luttrell's green eyes met Siobhan's again, this time revealing nothing.

"They were crushed by a container weighing more than a ton."

Siobhan nodded. Melchor had been the purser's petty officer, and part of his job would have been to check the stores periodically. Vasser, a bosun's mate and therefore jack-of-all-trades, was a natural choice to help him conduct an inventory audit.

"Any idea how it came to fall on them?"

Every container in a warship's narrow holds was securely clamped down by three different systems, to ensure it did not shift if the artificial gravity flickered, especially during battle maneuvers. For all three systems to fail at once, while an inspection detail was directly in the container's path, stretched the laws of probability to the breaking point.

"Like I said, captain, I don't really remember the details. The person who'd best know is Sub-Lieutenant Byrn. He was the investigating officer."

"I'm afraid Byrn is in no position to tell anyone about the accident anymore." Dunmoore's voice was harsh. "He died when the courier taking him to Wyvern was blown to bits by an unidentified raider."

Luttrell turned her head toward the far bulkhead. "I didn't know," she softly replied. "I'm sorry. He was a good sort. Better than many aboard this ship."

"Then why was he dismissed?"

The doctor shrugged. "Some bullshit about selling parts on the black market. Forenza supposedly got word from the Criminal Investigation Division and put him ashore the last time we touched port."

"You don't believe it, do you, Doctor?"

"After a while on this ship, I'll believe anything. You can get dressed now. I'm done."

"You didn't answer my question, Doctor."

"Yes dammit, captain, I think Byrn was framed," Luttrell turned toward Siobhan, sudden fury lighting up her green eyes. "Don't ask me why. I don't know. But Forenza was willing to ruin anybody just for refusing her, so it could be anything."

Siobhan met the doctor's defiant stare, convinced Luttrell was lying again. Not about Forenza's vengefulness, that was true enough, but about the reasons behind Byrn's sacking. Lieutenant Luttrell believed the third engineering officer's dismissal and the death of two crew members a few weeks earlier were linked. And she was frightened of revealing what she really thought.

"So how's my health?" Dunmoore asked as she stood up and started to get dressed.

"I'd say that apart from a lack of proper nourishment and rest, you're in excellent shape," Luttrell replied, a rough edge to her deep voice. "Not that I expect your general state to improve very fast on this ship. Just make sure you don't overdo the tough captain act. Get your rest regularly, and your recent injuries should heal normally."

Siobhan felt tempted to use the opening for a few probing questions about Ezekiel's story that *Stingray* refused to render assistance to the beleaguered *Victoria Regina* but thought better of it. She had already poked at enough unhealed scabs in one sitting. Luttrell's change in mood had been swift and sudden enough to remind Siobhan that she was still an intruder on *Stingray*, even if she was the sole master on board after God.

"Captain..."

"Yes Doctor," Siobhan glanced up at Luttrell's mischievous grin. The surgeon's mood had apparently swung back, now that the questions had stopped.

"I like the gloves. They give you a dark, sexy kind of look. Very appealing."

Dunmoore could not help but laugh at the comment. Yet though the atmosphere seemed back to where it had been when the examination started, it was not quite the same anymore. The good humor seemed forced.

"As long as you don't fall for me, Doctor."

"Have no fear, captain. I stay strictly with the under-thirty crowd. More vigor. Have a nice day."

"Goodbye."

Luttrell stared at the door for a long time after it closed behind Dunmoore. She suddenly, irrationally, wished she could have been more honest with the captain. Siobhan Dunmoore had a compelling quality that had been lacking in Forenza. And she was likable. Very likable. A quicksilver character and a mind to match.

But the surgeon knew she lacked the courage. All she wanted was for this war to end so she could go back to frontier doctoring, far from the bullshit of the Fleet.

With a sigh, Luttrell returned to her office and wrote the required medical report on the health of one Commander Dunmoore, Siobhan. If only she had the guts to write an honest medical report on Dunmoore's predecessor. It would have saved a lot of grief. And maybe young Byrn would still be alive.

*

"Well, that's it then, the rest will have to wait until we're under way." Siobhan suppressed a yawn. "If you're happy with the watch keeping bill, I say we call it a day and get some sleep for tomorrow."

"Aye," Pushkin nodded, pushing his big shoulders back to relieve tense muscles. "At least we'll be leaving as ordered, no thanks to the staff. The tugs are confirmed for eight bells in the morning watch, and the refueling stop at Thetis Alpha four hours after that."

"Good. Oh yes, I forgot to ask. What about current charts, Mister Pushkin?"

"Sorry, captain. I meant to tell you but with all the crap flying about..."

Siobhan waved his apology aside. "I understand. So you solved the problem."

"Aye, sir. In fact, it was Kowalski who found the solution."

"Kowalski?" Siobhan's eyebrow shot up in surprise. Help from an unexpected source. "How so, Mister Pushkin?"

"She's something of a computer whiz, I've discovered. A hidden talent, as it turns out." There was a hint of criticism in his voice. "Anyways, she came up with an idea to use the open tap into the base's library to hack a path into the navigational data banks. Seems the security on those isn't that great. We've got the new charts downloaded, and it'll be a long time before the staff figures out what happened."

"Excellent. Pass my thanks to Lieutenant Kowalski."

"Sir." He nodded once.

"Any last points. I'm about ready to crash."

"Yes, captain. I understand Mister Rossum found an unexpected source of coffee."

"Several sources, I suspect," Siobhan smiled. "One of these days, I'm going to thank Commander Forenza for her generous gesture in donating her private stock of booze as barter material."

"Sir?"

"When Commander Forenza left *Stingray*, she forgot several cases of cognac and claret," the captain explained, "which were in the hands of the purser. Since she won't need them planetside, I suggested to Mister Rossum that he put them to good use as barter material. He showed commendable diligence in flogging the hoard. We still have a case of cognac left for future needs."

"Commander Forenza knows about this?"

Siobhan grinned broadly. "No. But I'm sure she'll be delighted to have left such a fine gift to a crew she obviously loved. If she ever finds out."

Expressionless as always, Pushkin nodded and rose, oblivious to his captain's ironic tone. "Good night, then, sir."

"Good night, Mister Pushkin."

Out in the passage, Pushkin shook his head. Siobhan would have been amused to see the pleased glint in his eyes. Though he would not admit it, the first officer liked her solution to the coffee problem. It was a subtle and satisfying revenge.

He still was not sure how to take the new captain, but one thing was clear by now. Dunmoore was as different from Forenza as a nova was from a black hole. And for the latter at least, the comparison was apt, though Dunmoore did show all the flash and ebullience of a burning star. All that remained to see was whether Dunmoore would burn them all. But where was the line between self-interest and loyalty?

*

Stripped down to her underwear, Siobhan stretched her tall frame, groaning with relief. *Stingray* would sail on the morning tide, even if she was not completely repaired. Kaleri's attempt to discredit her had failed.

Absently rubbing her left forearm, she glanced around the bare cabin, thinking that she had not even replaced the personal effects lost on *Victoria Regina*. Her quarters were not particularly inviting, but she would get used to them, in time. At least Forenza's presence had faded as her own had asserted itself.

She yawned loudly, relishing the simple act, and padded over to the porthole near her bed. The cavernous docks looked unchanged, even during the Starbase 31's notional night.

The ancient ship's clock sitting alone on the bare shelves across the cabin chimed softly, ringing eight bells in the evening watch. Midnight.

She stared at the outline of the old knight on the clock's face. *Don Quixote*. The clock and half a dozen ancient, leather-bound books printed on real paper were the only things that had survived five years of war and four wrecked ships.

She touched the leather spine of one of the books, remembering. It had been a gift from Admiral Nagira, a token of his respect and affection, and something to ease the pain of losing her first command. Siobhan pulled out the five hundred-year-old copy of Miguel Cervantes' masterpiece and opened it to the flyleaf. There, Nagira had inserted a note inscribed in green ink:

To "Dona Quixote" Dunmoore. Choose your windmills well and never, ever, lose the impossible dream. Hoko Nagira

Siobhan cherished the book as much as the clock. It reminded her of the good times, and of the young officer she had been not so long ago: full of fire and determination, ready to fight the entire Empire, assured of victory. The flames were still there somewhere, as was the pigheaded determination she inherited from her father. But the assurance of victory was gone, shattered by too many deaths. What remained in its stead was a dogged insistence on seeing it out until the end, whatever it may be.

She replaced the massive tome and touched its neighbor unconsciously, a book of nineteenth-century poetry given to her by a distant, but proud father on her graduation day. Siobhan thought of him briefly, out there on his far-away pioneer world, safe from the Shrehari, working like a madman to forget the death of his wife, Siobhan's mother.

With a last glance at the graceful ships surrounding hers, Siobhan slipped between the cool sheets on her bed and switched off the lights. The only sound in the quiet cabin was the soft, hypnotical ticking of the clock, shadowed by the knight of the sorrowful countenance. Once the ship was underway, she would fall asleep to the low hum of the engines, the almost subliminal vibrations of the powerful reactors and would wake the instant anything went amiss, from a minor power surge in the flow tubes to a full-scale battle stations alert.

For now, she enjoyed the unaccustomed peacefulness and let herself drift off, forgetting, for the first night since she came on board, to place a nerve inducer on the back of her neck, just below the skull.

*

"*Now,* chief! All barrels," Siobhan yelled, her voice drowning out the groans of the dying battleship. A chunk of ceiling crashed down, narrowly missing the helmsman, but with his eyes fixed on the screen, the petty officer did not even notice.

Then, the shock waves of the discharging guns reverberated throughout *Victoria Regina*'s battered hull. Almost immediately, bright flowers of pure energy blossomed on *Tol Vakash*'s upper shields. The protective globe around the Shrehari cruiser crackled blue and green with the warring surges of power, like a giant energy sculpture. Suddenly, the dancing lights vanished as the shields collapsed, overcome by the battleship's last broadside.

"Got her," Chief Sen exulted. "Shields are down, direct hits amidships."

"Impact in twenty seconds, sir," Hernett's high pitched voice cut off the old sailor's growl.

"Another salvo, chief."

"Damn!" The old man swore. "No can do, commander. All conduits are down, probably burned out. She's fired her last."

Siobhan nodded calmly, beyond caring. "Brace for impact."

"Power surge on the Shrehari, sir. His primary drives."

"*What?*" The information did not immediately register through the wash of pain and resignation.

Then, before their astonished eyes, *Tol Vakash* jumped to hyperspace. One instant, the imperial cruiser was there, secondary explosions dotting its hull, then their view of space distorted and it was gone.

Energy and radiation shock waves from the precipitous jump buffeted *Victoria Regina*. Seconds later, she passed through the spot occupied a moment earlier by the Shrehari. The bridge crew was silent, unable to grasp that the intended suicide run had failed, and the enemy withdrawn.

Sen broke the eerie stillness, his voice choked with tears of relief. "You did it, commander. You scared the bastard into running. You fucking outwitted the great Captain Brakal."

"Subspace communication, sir," the signals rating called out from the back of the bridge, disbelief filling her voice. "It's from Brakal."

"Speak of the devil," Sen swore. "What does that monster want?"

"Put him on screen." Dunmoore's voice was flat.

A cruel face filled the front viewer. Deep-set, black eyes stared out at Siobhan from beneath an angular skull, bald except for a strip of bristly black hair, like a cock's crest.

"Greetings human. This is Brakal, commanding the imperial cruiser *Tol Vakash*. Your captain?" His Anglic was harsh, guttural, but understandable.

"Dead," Siobhan replied, wanting to hurl insults and more at the murderous barbarian, but unable to show anything other than cold dignity. Adnan would have been proud of her rare restraint.

"A pity. He fought well and was an honorable adversary. I am sorry. You are?" The damnest thing about it, Siobhan realized, was that the bastard *did* appear genuinely sorry.

"Siobhan Dunmoore, first officer."

Brakal nodded, stroking his massive jaw.

"You made the last battle run." It was not a question, and Siobhan did not reply.

"Interesting," Brakal continued. "Whenever I think I understand humans, I am always surprised. You too fight well, Dunmoore. Your captain was a good teacher. May I know his name, so I may honor his memory?"

"Adnan Prighte." Siobhan felt detached from reality as if someone else was having this calm conversation with the man who all but destroyed her ship and killed her best friend.

"*Harkash nedrin rakati* Adnan Prighte," Brakal pronounced solemnly, raising his fist in the Shrehari salute, "your name shall be remembered and honored."

Siobhan was stunned. She understood the imperial tongue, and if she was not mistaken, Brakal had just given her dead friend the highest honor a Shrehari Warrior can give.

"Why?" Her voice was but a whisper.

"The corrupt and greedy direct this war, but men of honor, and women of honor, fight it. I hold no hate for you humans, and were our Empires not at war, I would be honored to meet you as a friend. Your ship is safe for now, Dunmoore. No imperial vessel will come to give you the deathblow. You have earned the right to fight once more. Until we meet again, as honorable foes."

Brakal's face vanished, replaced by the eternal light of the distant stars.

"What was that all about, sir?" Sen finally asked, his voice soft and filled with a kind of awe. Though he did not understand the imperial tongue, he knew something extraordinary just happened. He could read it on Commander Dunmoore's pale, smudged face and in her unnaturally bright eyes.

"Honor, chief," she turned to look at him directly, and Sen, for the first time, saw the tears she was holding back. "It appears that murderous bastard out there has a sense of honor after all. He commended Captain Prighte to the care of his ancestors as a true Warrior, worthy of rebirth."

The old non-com shook his head. "Like the bugger said, just when we thought we understood the bastards, they go and surprise us again. Did he mean it when he said no Imp is going to come and destroy us for good?"

"I think so, chief. Somehow, I get the feeling Brakal will make sure of that. Honor again." She let that sink in for a few heartbeats, then, "Mister Hernett, plot the best course to Starbase 30. Chief, get me a status report, critical damage first. Let's get *Victoria Regina* home."

Then, Siobhan glanced down at the broken body sprawled on the deck below the captain's chair and started to tremble as shock finally set in.

*

Siobhan woke, her body bathed in sweat, the sheets tangled around her long limbs. As she fought to still her rapidly beating heart, the ancient ship's clock across the cabin struck two bells, its soft chimes sounding like death knells. Tears ran down her cheeks, unnoticed, as she felt all the pent-up sorrow break free.

The clock chimed again, four bells, and Siobhan rose from her bed, her grief spent. When she touched that tender spot on her soul, she was surprised to find the wound had begun to scab over. It was as if the tears had removed a great weight.

In two hours, *Stingray* would slip her moorings and head out to war, with *Captain* Dunmoore as her master. It behooved her to look the part.

Grinning at her disheveled appearance, Siobhan stepped into the shower, astonished to hear herself whistling a tuneless drinking song. It was one she had often sung in *Victoria Regina*'s wardroom, and it pleased her to hear its refrain again.

— Eight —

The door to the bridge opened before Siobhan with a tired sigh. A wave of loud voices, each overriding the other, assaulted her ears. She frowned at the chaos on *her* bridge, one hour before sailing. If the crew could not work with calm professionalism in space dock, they would be hopeless in battle. Hopeless, and very quickly dead. As she stepped across the threshold, Lieutenant Commander Pushkin spotted her out of the corner of his eyes. His voice cut through the babble like the roll of thunder.

"Captain on the bridge."

All noise ceased as officers, petty officers and ratings snapped to attention. Only the muted sounds of the space dock's open frequency buzzed from the loudspeaker in the signals alcove. Repressing her anger, Siobhan calmly walked over to her chair behind the helm console and sat down.

"Status report, Mister Pushkin." Her voice was deceptively calm.

"Still some problems with the sensors and one of the reactor control modules has just switched to amber."

"I assume Mister Tiner is giving the control module top priority?"

"Aye, sir."

"Feed a full system status report to my console, Mister Pushkin."

Siobhan scanned the report with one eye only. From beneath half-closed lids, she watched the bridge officers as they prepared for departure. The noise level had considerably diminished, but not the tension. Instead of shouting, Pushkin now growled at any officer or petty officer who attracted his wrath.

It failed to generate the calm, controlled atmosphere Siobhan expected from her crew. Instead of loud chaos, she had quiet chaos. At least before, there had been some form of communication. Now, there was little. Nor was there any of the excitement that usually ran through a ship's company preparing to sail. It was as if the momentous event had declined to a status lower than routine, an annoyance.

Alert to every nuance, Siobhan saw the lines of friction she noticed before begin to split open. Her sailing master was at the center of much of the discord on the bridge. She managed to offend almost everybody.

Chief Guthren, who would con the ship out of spacedock, sat beside her, his massive shoulders almost touching the painfully thin woman. But his body language showed that he wanted to be as far away as possible from her. Preferably on another ship.

In the same glance, Siobhan saw why. Shara leaned over and spoke softly to Guthren, a condescending smirk on her face. Though she did not hear what the sailing master said, Siobhan could guess, just by Guthren's cold, almost icy reaction. Shara was playing dangerous games. The chief petty officer did not take kindly to arrogant or supercilious officers, and the sailing master was both, in spades.

From opposite corners of the bridge Lieutenants Trevane Devall and Kathryn Kowalski observed events with bland expressions on their faces, but with interest sparkling in their eyes. Both looked from the captain to Shara and back at the captain as if expecting Dunmoore to explode in a burst of righteous fury. Siobhan ignored them, as she ignored everything else, preferring to see where the crew's interpersonal dynamics led. It was already clear that she and Guthren were the outsiders, but even among old shipmates, there was little, if any ease.

She had pegged most of her senior officers already, but Devall and Kowalski were still mysteries. The gunnery officer's behavior failed to arouse her prejudices about aristocratic younger sons, and he often surprised her with calm professionalism, even though he never lost his sardonic smile.

Kowalski was a different mystery altogether. There was something strong and willful bubbling just below the carefully studied words and gestures. But whether it was an ambitious sort of professionalism, squashed under Forenza, or an insubordinate and potentially dangerous character, Siobhan could not tell.

What irked Dunmoore about both officers was their watchful reserve as if they were evaluating and judging her. Though she could accept the usual caution officers kept around a new captain, Siobhan felt as if the two lieutenants were hoarding a store of criticism just beyond her reach. The gods only knew what they, and their cronies, discussed when she or Pushkin were not around to listen. One thing was sure, though, the two were allies, even friends, and she suspected they were at the origin of her less than sterling reception the other day. Who better to hide a message than the officer of the watch and the signals officer?

*

Siobhan heard the hail from space dock control over the muted loudspeakers before Kowalski, busy staring at Shara, could react.

"Mister Kowalski," Dunmoore's eyes opened to spear the sardonic young officer, "I'll trouble you to pay attention to your duties. Spacedock control has just signaled that the tugs are on their way. Please acknowledge the message." Though the captain's voice had remained mild, there was no doubting the steel behind it, this time. It cut through the whispered conversation like phase cannon.

Kowalski had the grace to blush as she tore her eyes from the navigation console to carry out her orders. The others pretended to busy themselves, but Siobhan caught a few subdued snickers. Shara was smirking openly at Kowalski's back, happy to see her reprimanded by the captain.

"Stations!" Dunmoore's voice whipped across the bridge, stiffening spines and halting even the softest whispers.

"Ship ready for undocking, sir." The first officer announced a few seconds later. Siobhan glanced at him approvingly. Pushkin was learning.

"Release mechanical moorings; stand by to release energy moorings."

"Release mechanical moorings, aye," Pushkin replied. "Signals, make to space dock, 'Release mechanical moorings.'"

Soon after, dull thunks reverberated through the ship as the great magnetic grappling arms broke free. Now Siobhan felt the first tendrils of excitement course through her body, and her mood improved considerably.

"Spacedock confirms that the tugs have positive tractor beam lock," Kowalski said, her left hand cupped to her ear as she listened to the stream of radio traffic over a small earpiece.

"Release energy moorings."

"Released. We are under the guidance of the tugs."

"Stand by thrusters."

"Thrusters standing by, aye sir." Guthren's deep voice boomed.

"From spacedock control, sir." Kowalski again. "*Stingray* is cleared for departure. They wish us good hunting."

"Acknowledged," Siobhan replied, eyes fixed on the front screen.

Her pulse increased as she felt the blood course through her whipcord-thin body like a stream of supercharged particles. She glanced at Pushkin out of the corner of her eyes, but the dour first officer showed none of the emotions she felt. For Siobhan, hands-on control of a massive warship was as exciting as and even more rewarding than sex. She could feel the throbbing of the reactors through her seat and wallowed in the sensation of power, the rush of command.

Slowly, almost imperceptibly, the view changed as the tugs, one on either beam, pushed and maneuvered the frigate's great mass toward the gaping space doors. Though it had none of the majesty of a nineteenth-century warship leaving harbor under full sail, *Stingray*'s graceful glide thrilled Siobhan nonetheless.

"Rear view, Mister Guthren."

"Aye, sir."

The screen changed to show open space doors and Siobhan relaxed. Her ship was aimed dead center, proof that the tugs were doing their job. But as she glanced at the crew, she found them stiff, almost holding their breaths. It was as if they were afraid of a collision, or remembered another unfortunate departure in the recent past. Then, the screen showed nothing but stars nestled in the velvety black of the universe and they were through.

"Flip view to the front."

Starbase 31's spindle-shape receded as the tugs pushed them out to the regulation safety limit.

"From spacedock, prepare to come under our own power." Kowalski's voice was matter-of-fact, untouched by any sense of awe or joy. In her heightened state, Siobhan felt anger at the signals officer's usual blandness.

"Thrusters ready, sublight drive standing by." Guthren sounded as confident as she ever heard him.

"From space dock, tugs will release the ship in ten seconds."

Typically, Siobhan would have ordered the thrusters to engage with split-second precision the moment they were free of the tugs' embrace. It gave watchers a show of competent ship handling and was just the kind of cocky action for which frigate captains were known. But she was uncertain of her crew, and could not afford a mistake in what was a relatively crowded orbit.

"The ship is at a relative stop from the Starbase, sir," Shara's nasal voice interrupted her thoughts.

"We are floating free."

"Thank you, Mister Pushkin. The undocking process was satisfactory." But Siobhan could see that the first officer knew 'satisfactory' just was not good enough for her. He nodded curtly, his scowl deepening.

"Helm, pivot the ship one-hundred and eighty degrees horizontal."

"One-eighty horizontal, aye," Guthren stared intently at the screen as his hands manipulated the controls. There was no real need to pivot the ship toward their departure vector, apart from a minor concern for traffic security, but it gave Guthren a chance to demonstrate his handling of the big frigate. Yet when she looked at Pushkin again, the first officer's expression clearly showed that he believed her order was a useless waste of time.

Glancing at the attitude readout on her console, Siobhan saw the display slowly rotate through a half-circle. As she was about to warn Guthren to fire the opposite thrusters and stop the rotation, he did just that. *Stingray* came to rest exactly one-hundred and eighty-one degrees from her initial heading. Which was about as good as any ship handling she had seen.

"Heading changed one-hundred and eighty-one degrees, captain," Guthren announced, not even bothering to fudge that extra degree.

"Very well, Mister Guthren. Sailing master, quickest course to refueling station Thetis Alpha at three-quarters speed."

"Laid in, sir," Shara glanced at the cox'n with distaste.

"Engage, Mister Guthren."

The ion drive exhausts glowed dark orange as they pushed the frigate out of orbit and into interplanetary space.

"Ship sailing at three-quarters speed, on course, captain. Arrival in three hours, forty-five minutes." Guthren announced, ten minutes later. Even though she was old, the frigate still had a good rate of acceleration. Siobhan nodded with satisfaction. They had not even felt the increased thrust, which proved that the artificial gravity, at least, was working within specifications.

"Very well, cox'n. Mister Pushkin, bring her to cruising stations and join me in my ready room." Without a glance back, Siobhan left the bridge.

"Sir!" Pushkin barked. He turned to the sailing master, a look of distaste on his angular face. "Mister Shara, I believe you have the watch. Place the ship at cruising stations."

The sailing master slaved her console to the one embedded in the captain's chair and rose from her seat. Under Pushkin's watchful eyes, she slipped into Dunmoore's still warm seat.

"I relieve you, sir." Shara avoided Pushkin's eyes.

"I stand relieved. You have the con."

There was no hint of respect or friendliness in the brief exchange, only the guarded tones of officers who hated each other but were going through the required motions because it was expected of them. The first officer swung around the railing at the rear of the bridge and entered the captain's ready room, all too aware of the covert glances on his receding back. Pushkin was not popular, and few officers or enlisted spacers felt any sympathy at the thought of him being chewed out by the new captain. It only served to increase his bitterness and his sense of being at war with the universe.

He hated the constant reproach in their eyes. But if it had not been for him, things would have been much worse.

"Please sit down, Mister Pushkin. Coffee?" Siobhan spoke loud enough so that her question floated through the closing door and reached the ears of the bridge crew. Devall and Kowalski exchanged looks of surprised interest.

In the ready room, Pushkin, expecting another rebuke from Dunmoore for the way the bridge crew worked, or rather failed to work, had already braced himself, and did not immediately react to Siobhan's question.

"Ah, sure, cap'n," he finally replied, relaxing just a fraction.

"Kery," Siobhan called, "two cups of java, black, and no sugar." She cocked an eyebrow at Pushkin. He nodded.

A few moments later, the other door opened, and the mousy clerk came in, a mug in each hand. She deposited them on Dunmoore's desk and vanished without saying a word. Siobhan took a sip of the scalding liquid and stared at Pushkin over the rim of her cup.

"I sincerely hope I will never again see the sight that greeted me when I entered the bridge this morning. A bridge crew that can't work smoothly together and communicate in tones that don't blow out the decibel meter won't survive a battle. Cool, calm professionalism was the only thing that kept *Victoria Regina* from becoming space debris." Pushkin's hard expression remained unchanged at the mention of the ill-fated battleship. But was there a trace of uneasiness in his posture? "When the imperial broadside punched through her starboard shields and destroyed the CIC, nearly tearing us apart, the bridge crew kept functioning because they'd been trained to never, ever lose their cool, and concentrate on their duties. Only because of that were we able to return effective fire and drive Brakal away."

Pushkin shrugged. "Individually, most of 'em are okay, but..."

"But, Mister Pushkin?"

"They haven't been a tight crew since I've been here."

"Let me guess, Commander Forenza's command techniques on the bridge were of the adversarial kind."

"Yes," Pushkin shrugged again as if it didn't really matter. Yet his eyes said otherwise. The look pleased Siobhan because it proved the first officer had not completely given up, that some things still mattered to him.

"What would you consider the single most disruptive factor among the first watch bridge crew, the varsity team?"

Pushkin hesitated for a few moments as if deciding whether to trust Siobhan or continue their dealings with brooding silence, then spat out one name.

"Shara."

Siobhan slowly nodded. Brooding, but straightforward. And he disliked the sailing master intensely.

"Lieutenant Shara was obviously on good terms with Commander Forenza. How good?"

"Good enough to get away with crap no other captain would tolerate," Pushkin replied, disgust and anger making his voice tremble ever so slightly.

"Captain's pet."

"Yeah."

"The others?"

"All right, I guess. Devall's an arrogant bastard, but he does his job well for someone who hasn't had an enemy ship under his gun sights for over six months. Kowalski? Well, she's hard to place. Knows her stuff, but pretty standoffish. Arrogant too. Neither of the two likes me."

Straightforward again. Siobhan nodded. "And the petty officers and ratings will take their cues from the officers. Are the second watch crew, especially the quarter-masters competent?"

Pushkin grimaced. "I wouldn't give them any complicated maneuvering orders until they've had a lot more training."

"The same probably goes for most of the crew."

The first officer laughed harshly. "An understatement, sir."

"It's pretty obvious we don't dare head straight for the border, with the amount of repairs still outstanding, and the need to retrain the crew." Siobhan was amused to read relief in Pushkin's eyes. "No, Mister Pushkin, I'm not as suicidal or glory seeking as navy gossip makes me out to be. From Thetis Alpha, we're going to jump halfway to the patrol area and spend a week or so drilling the crew in every conceivable maneuver. *Then* we'll head out."

"Your orders leave you that latitude, sir?"

Bold question coming from you, Mister Pushkin, Siobhan thought. "No. But Admiral Kaleri won't find out until it's too late. I'd rather take my lumps with her than with the Imperial Fleet."

Pushkin seemed uncertain at that as if he feared Kaleri more than the Empire, but he did not reply.

"Coming back to my earlier line of thought, we, you and I, will have to turn this crew into something that can withstand anything the Imperials throw at us because I intend to hunt in the manner for which *Stingray* was designed. In my book, that requires a very flexible kind of leadership, one that draws the maximum initiative from each crewmember. Getting angry, growling, and reprimanding at every turn won't do. Not with a crew that shows so many signs of being dysfunctional. Piss the officers off, and they'll turn around and crap on the crew.

But there are exceptions." She smiled at him and turned on the intercom.

"Mister Shara, please join us in my ready room."

The astonished sailing master rose from the command chair and headed for the back of the bridge, her washed-out eyes sweeping the crew. She felt fury rise in her throat on seeing Devall and Kowalski glance at her with guarded amusement. They expected her to come out of Captain Dunmoore's room with a freshly chewed asshole.

"Mister Devall," she croaked, "you have the con."

The doors slid aside at her approach, and the thin navigator stepped into the room, stopping a regulation three paces in front of the captain's desk. But instead of snapping to attention and saluting, she stood legs apart, hands loosely joined in small of her back. Her eyes stared at Dunmoore with defiance, after giving Pushkin a dismissive glance.

"Sir?" She inquired, her tone almost insolent.

"Lieutenant Shara," Pushkin growled unexpectedly, "you bloody well know how to report to your captain. Kindly do it before I give you a quick refresher course. With the tip of my boot."

Shara looked at him, an eyebrow rising lazily then, with deliberate slowness, she came to attention and saluted.

"Sailing master reporting to the captain as ordered. *Sir!*"

"Mister Shara," Siobhan smiled tightly, voice deceptively smooth and soft, something Pushkin had begun to recognize as a danger signal. "Since I took command of this ship, I have found your attitude and behavior toward your superiors, peers, and subordinates to be arrogant, insubordinate, and totally unacceptable for a Commonwealth Navy officer and a sailing master on my ship. I don't really give a damn what kind of relationship you had with Commander Forenza, or how many admirals supped at your father's mansion when you were a cadet. If you don't start acting like a goddamned officer, you will find yourself counting mess tins on a third-rate supply depot for the rest of the war."

"Sir. I resent your insinuations, and your insults to my character," Shara replied, cheeks reddening with anger. "And I –"

"I don't really give a damn what you resent, Lieutenant Shara," Siobhan replied, her voice as calm as before, but with a hard core that hit the sailing master like a slap in the face. "As long as you are on my ship, you will bloody well take whatever I say, and act accordingly. Oh, and don't bother threatening me with a complaint to Admiral Kaleri. By the time I'm through with you, a Disciplinary Board will overrule anything your family friends might try."

Siobhan saw her words hit home and smiled cruelly. But inwardly, she knew that if Shara did complain to Kaleri, she could cause her a lot of trouble. It would probably take an act of mutiny on the sailing master's part before she would be hauled in front of a board. Pushkin knew it too, and while his face showed pleasure at Siobhan's words, his eyes also showed worry at Shara's connections, and what they could mean to him if she complained. However, Siobhan was not done yet.

"For starters, Mister Shara, you will begin to treat the cox'n with the respect he deserves as the senior enlisted man. He *is* the Chief of the Ship, and as far as I'm concerned, he's one of the best damn chiefs and ship handlers in the Fleet. If you cannot bring yourself to respect his experience and ability, you will at least give the appearance of doing so."

As Siobhan paused to draw her breath, Shara attempted to protest again.

"Sir, I res-"

"*Silence*! You will speak when I give you permission." Siobhan's gloved hand hit the desk, cracking like a gunshot. Shara took a step backward as Siobhan's sudden outburst hit her like a gale-force wind. "You may have been Commander Forenza's favorite while she was captain of *Stingray*. Those days are over. She is now facing disciplinary charges for failing in her duties. You'd do well to remember that, or you will most assuredly join her. Dismissed, Mister Shara."

Face red, body shaking with anger and humiliation, Shara saluted and spun on her heels. As the doors closed behind her, Siobhan heard the sailing master snarl at a rating.

"A very dangerous enemy, sir," Pushkin softly said.

Siobhan looked at him in surprise. "Maybe, but she's also a foolish woman, and that, we can deal with. How much of Forenza's friend is she? Or Kaleri's, for that matter?"

Again, Pushkin seemed hesitant before replying, as if still unsure about the wisdom of confiding in a captain he'd known for only a few days.

"Too much for comfort," he finally said. "Shara and Forenza were always meeting behind closed doors, plotting God knows what. The sailing master knew more about ship's business and the captain's intentions than I did. Sometimes, I wondered who the *real* first officer was."

Siobhan was beginning to understand why he carried such a chip on his shoulder. It must have been hard to see his authority undermined at every turn by an officer of Shara's low caliber and rank.

"As for Admiral Kaleri," he continued, "Forenza got away with murder under her command, and if Shara is Forenza's asshole buddy..."

"*Les amis de mes amis sont mes amis,*" Siobhan quoted in French. The friends of my friends are my friends.

Pushkin looked up at her in surprise, and then nodded. "Aye, captain. That's right."

"So I can assume Admiral Kaleri will hear of everything that happens aboard *Stingray*, filtered through Shara's malice."

"You can bet on it, sir."

Siobhan shrugged. "Then let her hear. At this point, I couldn't care less about a sailing master spying on me for the benefit of my Battle Group commander. If I'm to fall, then I will. One way or another. And it wouldn't be the first time."

Pushkin's eyes widened in surprise at Siobhan's raw honesty, and he mentally raised his opinion of her by several orders of magnitude. Maybe, he would also be able to trust her. But after Forenza...

"Tell me, Mister Pushkin," Siobhan suddenly asked, "when you said, a moment ago, that Forenza got away with murder, were you speaking figuratively, or were you being literal."

As if a curtain had been dropped, Pushkin's expression became guarded again and the fragile rapport that she had developed over the last few minutes dissolved. Siobhan cursed herself mentally but kept her expression bland and unconcerned.

"Figurative, captain," he replied, his voice gruff, his eyes refusing to meet hers. "Will that be all, sir?"

Siobhan repressed a sigh of frustration. "For now, Mister Pushkin. After we've fueled, we'll discuss the remedial training plan."

The first officer stood, snapped to attention, and saluted. Then, he turned and left Siobhan to her thoughts. He, like Luttrell, knew more than they would admit and refused to speak about it. Fear, perhaps? But of what or who? And why?

*

"Captain, we're on final approach to Thetis Alpha."

"I'll be right there, Mister Pushkin." Siobhan closed her personal log and rose, adjusting her uniform. The final approach to a refueling station, and the refueling itself were among the most delicate maneuvers a starship could do. It took little to ignite the antimatter and blow both station and ship into another dimension. A captain's worst nightmare was an enemy raider appearing just as the ship was taking on fuel.

Siobhan glanced at the split screen, one-half showing a real-time view of the station, high in orbit around the greenish-blue gas giant that provided the raw matter for the fuel, the other half showing the usual tactical schematic display of their approach.

"One-hundred thousand kilometers and closing," Pushkin announced as she sat down.

Siobhan nodded. Then inspiration struck. "Take her in, Mister Pushkin." She stood up and stepped away from her chair. He looked at her in astonishment, as did Shara, Devall, and Kowalski. Only the cox'n showed no reaction. He knew Dunmoore's ways.

"Aye, sir," the first officer replied a few heartbeats later. He slipped into Siobhan's seat, shoulders squared, while she moved over to his vacant station. "Cox'n, stand by braking thrusters. Prepare to cut sublight drive on my mark." His voice was deep and confident. Shara, for once, kept her eyes firmly on the screen, lips tightened into a thin line of disapproval.

"Take her three points to port; raise the angle of attack by two points." The real-time view of Thetis Alpha shifted minutely as *Stingray*'s course changed to parallel the line of refueling buoys. This far out, the change was minuscule, but over the remaining distance, it would suffice. Siobhan smiled with approval. Pushkin was careful and able to think out his maneuvers far ahead. Too many officers made greater course changes at a distance, only to correct them closer in. As Siobhan knew, Guthren had a light touch on the helm, and he executed Pushkin's orders with deft precision.

"Cut sublight."

Siobhan would have kept the ion drives on for a bit longer, but refrained from commenting. If Pushkin wanted to coast in and conserve power, that was fair enough. The few minutes' difference would not matter.

Thetis Alpha shimmered brightly against the dark turquoise of the planet Thetis. At this distance, they could see the many storms stirring up the thick soupy atmosphere, winds which could tear a warship apart, were its captain foolish enough to brave the crushing gravity well. The unmanned fuel tankers that sucked up the atmospheric gases for transport to Thetis Alpha's refinery were the only ships able to get close enough without damage. And even they stayed at a respectable distance, using a specially adapted tractor beams to fill their large holds.

"Braking thrusters on for ten seconds on my mark."

"Standing by," Guthren replied, all business as his thick fingers danced over the helm console.

The first officer knew he was being tested by Siobhan, and scrutinized by the remainder of the bridge crew. Yet he showed no nervousness. Only natural tension.

"Mark." Faint vibrations ran through the ship as the forward thrusters fired. They lasted exactly ten seconds. Pushkin's eyes narrowed as he studied the tactical display.

"Cox'n prepare to fire the aft starboard thrusters for three seconds on my mark."

"Standing by."

"Mark."

Siobhan could see no immediate effect, but experience told her Pushkin was adjusting the course to pass as close to the buoys as safely possible.

"Port thrusters one second. Mark."

His aim was as good as any Siobhan had seen. She felt her shoulders relax, realizing only now how tense she had been in the last few minutes.

"Braking thrusters for five seconds."

"Standing by."

The line of buoys grew on the screen, close enough to touch. From the first officer's console, Siobhan switched on the starboard secondary screen, to get a side view of their approach.

"Mark."

Slowly, majestically, *Stingray* came to a full stop relative to the orbiting station, a bare four hundred meters from the first refueling buoy, which sat on the end of a kilometer-long pylon connecting it to Thetis Alpha. Siobhan nodded, eyebrows raised and lips pursed as she checked the readout on her console. They were precisely level with the buoy, both horizontally and vertically, which would please the fuel pumpers to no end. They liked a magnetic hose without kinks or curves.

"Excellent, Mister Pushkin," Siobhan said as she stood up. "That was one of the sweetest approaches I've seen in a long time. You too, Mister Guthren. Excellent handling."

And it had been. No excess use of thrusters to correct over corrections, no overt signs of tension. Calm and professional, just the way she liked it.

Her compliments drew approving looks from the others. Even Kowalski nodded. Pushkin's stock had gone up in the last ten minutes, which was all to the good. It was probably the first time in a long time that he'd been allowed to display his ship handling skills. He even allowed himself the hint of a smile, and Siobhan knew she had done the right thing. Trust your instincts, Nagira had counseled. The admiral had been right. Only Shara kept her eyes fixed on the screen, looking as sour as three-week old milk.

"Let's hoist the antimatter on board, Mister Pushkin."

"Aye, aye, sir," he replied crisply, pride gleaming in his dark, hooded eyes. "Engineering, stand by for refueling."

"Standing by," Tiner's voice sounded tinny over the intercom, "all systems green, magnetic integrity confirmed."

"Mister Kowalski, make to Thetis Alpha, '*Stingray* ready for refueling.' And put them on loudspeakers."

"Aye, aye, sir."

"Hello, *Stingray*," a cheerful voice boomed through the speakers, "my compliments for the approach. First time in a long time we didn't have a heart attack watching a ship come in. So, what'll it be? Ordinary or supercharged?"

"We'll take the ordinary, thank you," Pushkin replied, a small grin playing on his lips. "Supercharged gums up the plasma tubes."

"Too true, too true," the controller replied with a mock sigh. "Still, it's sad that nobody wants to ream out tubes anymore nowadays, to get that extra kick only supercharged can give. Are you guys ready?"

"Fuel port open and standing by."

"Okay, folks, here she comes."

A round mating module, pushed by small thrusters, separated from the buoy and headed for the ship, trailing a black hose the diameter of a shuttlecraft, behind it. Within moments, it attached itself to *Stingray*'s lower hull.

"We've got positive contact," the controller announced.

"Confirmed," Tiner replied, without waiting for Pushkin to ask. "Ready to take the fuel on board."

The black tube glowed as the magnetic field lining its interior came to life.

"Comin' through."

"Magnetic bottles are filling," Tiner confirmed.

Five minutes later it was done, and the mating module sailed back to its buoy, the huge black hose vanishing inside the smooth, shiny cylinder. "Anything else Thetis Alpha can do for you folks? Top up your oil, or wash your windscreen?"

Pushkin and Dunmoore looked at each other, uncertain what the controller meant by his last question. Siobhan shrugged.

"No thanks," the first officer replied.

"Okay. That'll be five hundred thousand creds. Cash or charge?" The controller was clearly amused at his own wit, even if it was a bit obscure for *Stingray*'s bridge crew.

"Charge it to my account," Siobhan said, looking at Pushkin with a raised eyebrow, "care of Admiral Kaleri."

"Will do. Have fun on the line. Cheerio, folks."

Siobhan returned to her seat. "Lay in a course for jump point Gamma, Mister Shara. Then calculate a jump to-" she rattled off a series of coordinates.

Shara half-turned in surprise at Siobhan's directions. "Those coordinates are nowhere near the line, sir."

"I know that, Mister Shara." A small smile briefly passed over the sailing master's thin, bloodless lips, then she turned back to her console.

"Course laid in."

No doubt Admiral Kaleri would find out about Siobhan's disregard for her orders, probably as soon as Shara could find a way to send a message without anyone else knowing.

"Engage, Mister Guthren."

— Nine —

Dunmoore finished her log entry and saved it. The ship pulsed with power, her FTL drives pushing *Stingray* across the lightyears. The subliminal vibrations soothed her nerves and she could almost believe the worst of her problems had been left behind. Almost.

Shortly after jumping, the intermix controllers had developed a malfunction, and had to re-emerge. It had taken Tiner the better part of three hours to track down the cause of the problem and replace the defective part. That made it forty-eight end-of-life malfunctions or impending failures since they left port.

The parts in question had been everyday consumables, carried by every ship, and regular maintenance should have seen them replaced by the time they reached ninety percent of their predicted life span. She could understand a dozen or so failures. War had sharply reduced the time a warship spent in dry dock, and no ship's engineering crew could do everything. But forty-eight?

Without the old logs, she had no way of tracking down the under way maintenance schedule or the frequency with which the frigate had been resupplied with spare parts. Neither Tiner nor Pushkin were talking.

When she had pressed the engineer, Tiner had become agitated and had given her disjointed and wholly unbelievable explanations. Even Dunmoore's comment that *Stingray*'s end-of-life failure rate was well beyond average failed to get a straight answer.

Her old ship's clock chimed six bells. One hour before midnight, and watch change. Feeling stiffness in every muscle, Siobhan stretched her arms above her head, wrinkling her nose at the aroma from her armpits. She looked longingly at her shower and bed, but there was one more thing she wanted to do before turning in.

Siobhan called up the watch list on her computer and nodded. Soon, she would not have to look, to know who was on deck and she would know their strengths, weaknesses, ambitions, and fears. She called the bridge.

"OOW, Lieutenant Devall, sir." The elegant gunnery officer's face appeared on the small screen, looking as fresh as if he'd just gone on watch.

"Mister Devall, *Stingray*'s sensors have just picked up a suspicious reading. It looks very much like that of a Shrehari cruiser."

He looked at her uncomprehending for a few heartbeats, then understanding lit up his blue eyes, and he smiled.

"Aye, aye, sir." His head turned away from the pick-up. "PO of the watch, cut out FTL drives; Mister Sanghvi, sound battle stations." Devall looked back at the captain. He opened his mouth to ask if she had any other orders, when the ship emerged from hyperspace, wrenching Siobhan's stomach in the familiar and inevitable nausea. Before the momentary sickness dissipated, the siren sounded throughout the ship. Lights dimmed as the computer re-routed all available power to the weapons' capacitors and the shields. Behind Devall, the bridge glowed red, and Dunmoore briefly had a vision of the hell on *Victoria Regina*'s bridge near the end.

She shook off the feeling. "Advise me when the ship is ready. Dunmoore, out."

Calmly, Siobhan shrugged on her uniform tunic. Then, she stepped out into the corridor. Half-dressed crewmembers were running to their stations, spurred on by the shouts of their petty officers. She flattened herself against the bulkhead to avoid being run down.

Any warship going to battle stations looked like complete chaos to a layman, but in this case, it also looked like total chaos to an experienced naval officer and three-time ship captain. Dunmoore compressed her lips into a thin line and quickly made her way to the bridge.

Most of the primary bridge crew had already arrived, with one glaring exception. When Shara showed up, face flushed and out of breath, Pushkin stared at her and pointed to the navigation console. He did not have to speak. His expression said it all.

"Ship is at battle stations, sir," the first officer announced a few minutes later.

"How long?"

Pushkin grimaced. "Six minutes."

"Lousy."

"Aye, sir." Pushkin nearly shrugged, but thought better of it.

"Mister Kowalski, give me ship-wide." Kowalski nodded, and then gave her a thumbs up signal.

"All hands, this is the captain. You'll no doubt be interested to know that the time it took to get to battle stations was six minutes. Against an experienced Shrehari captain, that means you've been dead for three." Her harsh voice echoed throughout the ship. "On my previous ship, the battleship *Victoria Regina,* we managed to reduce it down to three minutes. *On a battleship*! And this is a frigate, with half the size and a third of the crew. When the Shrehari ambushed us, our speed at changing from cruising to battle stations was the only thing that saved the ship. Even then, over two hundred crew died."

Siobhan glanced around the bridge and found that no one would meet her eyes. It had to be more than just shame at a lousy performance. Maybe Ezekiel was right.

"For the next week or so, until I'm satisfied, this ship will do battle station drills, damage control drills, and any other drills I can think of until we've got it right and fast. Because if we don't, we will never touch port again. The Shrehari don't fuck around, and neither do I. All hands stand fast." Siobhan made a cutting motion, and Kowalski switched off the public address system. "Mister Pushkin, cox'n, it's time we inspect the crew at their stations." Her tone bode ill for everyone.

Alone in the corridor, she stopped and looked at the two men in turn. "I can see why this ship hasn't fired a shot in anger for so long. Maybe Commander Forenza was smart enough to know that she'd never have survived, even if she wasn't smart enough to command this ship properly." The first officer and cox'n had instinctively come to attention and returned Siobhan's angry gaze with impassive stares. It was the first time Siobhan had openly criticized her predecessor, but Pushkin did not so much as twitch, let alone came to Forenza's defense. "Make no mistake. I intend to find and engage the enemy. And touch port again with kill marks on our hull."

"Aye, aye, sir," they replied, almost in unison. Guthren's lips twisted with disgust. "I'm afraid you won't like what you'll find on your inspection, cap'n. This is the first battle stations drill they've had in three months, and spacers will go slack if you don't get at 'em daily."

"Then let's make sure this is the last time they'll be slack."

*

Guthren was right. Half of the crew were not even wearing battledress or carrying their emergency breathing gear, which meant they would die messily if the hull in their section were holed. Many of the ratings were clumsy or unfamiliar with the weapons or damage control gear. Only the petty officers and officers were anywhere near ready, and that was more out of long habit than anything else.

As they inspected each division, Guthren and Pushkin took copious notes. Judging by their scowls, there would be the devil to pay later. Originally, Dunmoore wanted to give the department heads a thorough dressing down but decided to let Pushkin handle it instead. Ensuring the ship was ready for her orders was his responsibility. She said as much when they returned to the bridge.

"All right, Mister Pushkin. It's your show. Stand the ship down and resume original course and speed. I'll be in my quarters."

"Sir."

It was past four bells in the night watch by the time Siobhan slipped into bed. When she finally fell asleep, the nightmares returned. But this time, the faces on the ruined bridge were those of her present crew, a bad omen if there ever was one.

*

Siobhan woke four hours later with a low-grade headache, and a mood to match. She checked the logs of the night watch and saw that Pushkin had talked to the officers already. Guthren had done the same with the chiefs and petty officers. Siobhan grunted, scratching her tousled hair. At least things were happening. Whether it would make a difference, she did not know.

There was more to the problem of *Stingray* than just lousy training, no drills, and bad blood. The fear that had permeated the ship when she came aboard was still there, even though performance had improved.

Siobhan was sure it had something to do with the accidental deaths, and probably more. If those two men had been murdered, it had to be for a damn good reason, more than just Forenza's peccadilloes, repulsive as they were. Could it be related to the ship's poor state of maintenance?

Dammit! Her officers knew a lot more than they were willing to say. Trust. Trust was the key. And her predecessor had already abused their trust in a most horrible fashion. On further thought, she could not blame them for treating her with caution. What if Siobhan Dunmoore turned out to be another Helen Forenza? The two had been classmates at the Academy. Thankfully that was where the resemblance stopped.

She dressed and briefly considered ordering a breakfast tray to her cabin, then thought better of it. Her anger was still simmering, and her appetite suffered as a result. Unable to get Vasser and Melchor's so-called accident out of her mind, she decided to visit the hold in which they were killed, if only to get a better picture of the site. She tapped the intercom.

"Captain to second officer."

"Drex here, sir," the lieutenant replied after a few moments.

"I'd like to visit the hold where those two crewmembers died in February. Preferably now."

"Aye, sir, I'll meet you at the security office if you like." Was there a hint of reticence in his voice? Siobhan could not be sure.

"That'll be okay. Dunmoore, out."

She stepped out of her cabin into a quiet passageway. It turned out to be not so quiet when her ears picked up harsh whispers around the bend. Curious, she rounded the corner, feet silent on the bare metal deck. She came face-to-face with Kery and Shara having a subdued, but vicious argument. The clerk carried a food tray apparently meant for Siobhan and had probably been intercepted by the sailing master as she crossed into officers' territory. They stopped the moment they became aware of her presence and snapped to attention.

Kery mumbled a good morning, while Shara just nodded, her expression verging on open insolence. "A problem, Mister Shara?"

"No, sir," she drawled, her voice grating on Siobhan's nerves. "Just some administrative business."

Dunmoore frowned, clearly showing disbelief. But there was nothing to do, short of interrogating them. She was in no mood for it, even if there was something about the incident gnawing at the back of her mind. There were more important things to worry about.

"I'll be having that breakfast later, Kery." She turned on her heel and walked away. They watched her in silence until she was out of their sight.

Siobhan met Lieutenant Drex by the door to his office. He snapped to attention and saluted, a guarded look in his dark eyes.

"Good morning, sir."

"Mister Drex," Siobhan nodded. "Shall we?"

"Aye, sir. Starboard hold three. If you'll follow me."

"Tell me, Mister Drex," she asked, as they made their way to the lower deck, "why didn't you do the investigation? Why an Engineering Subbie, instead of an experienced second officer?"

Drex shrugged without glancing back at his captain. "Commander Forenza's orders, sir. It might have something to do with the fact that Vasser was in my division. Kept it at arm's length."

Siobhan grunted, unconvinced. "Strange even so. You've had what? Ten, fifteen years' experience as a bosun's mate and bosun, before becoming cox'n, most of that time in the security division. Seems to me that kind of experience shouldn't go to waste."

The second officer shrugged again. "Lots of waste on this ship, sir. We learned not to question Commander Forenza's orders. We're here, sir."

Ah ha! Dunmoore thought, eyebrows going up. The first cracks in Drex's shell of utter propriety.

"What I find strange, Mister Drex is that the investigating officer found himself removed from the ship by the Battle Group CID detachment and charged with black marketeering soon after submitting his report." Drex made to shrug again, but Siobhan added, with a hard edge in her voice, "and he died shortly after that, killed when the ship on which he was traveling was destroyed by an unknown raider, seventy-five light years inside our borders."

Though his face remained impassive, she had the satisfaction of seeing that her words had some effect on the stoic second officer.

Siobhan smiled coldly. "From your point of view, it's just as well that you didn't do the investigation. Who knows? Maybe the CID would have found some peccadillo you'd rather have kept hidden. From there it's a small step to an ill-fated courier." Her smile vanished. "I don't believe in more than two coincidences in a row, Mister Drex. When I see a third on the horizon, I either come about and run or clear for action. Let us visit the hold now." *And let's see you stew in that*, she added to herself.

It proved to be both an educational and a disappointing visit. The starboard hold, as she knew from her study of *Stingray*'s blueprints, was both long and narrow, with full doors on both ends, and a gantry suspended from the ceiling. It contained stacks of standardized containers, piled three or four high, on either side of a narrow inspection passage, like a footpath at the bottom of a small canyon.

"One of the engineer's mates working in a nearby compartment, Able Spacer Bertram, heard the container shift and crash and reported it at the same time as the alarms kicked in. But when the rescue party got there, Vasser and Melchor were dead." Drex stopped halfway down the hold and pointed up. "The container that fell was in the same place as the blue one, with the foodstuff markings."

"I understand the containers are fixed into place with three redundant systems, to prevent just this kind of accident."

"Aye, sir. Three systems. Magnetic clamps, lock-downs and tie-downs."

"Tell me, Mister Drex, what are the odds of all three failing at once? Add to that a massive example of Murphy's Law, the fact that the container had shifted enough to topple over the very instant Vasser and Melchor were beneath it. As I said, two coincidences in a row, I'll take. More than that..." Siobhan let the words hang between them.

"Aye, sir," Drex finally replied, eyes on the stack of containers. "I don't know much about statistical averages, being only a simple mustang, but what I've told you is the way it happened."

Simple mustang? Siobhan's eyebrows shot up. Chiefs were not known for their humility, especially not old sweats who earned a commission.

"Don't sell yourself short, Mister Drex," she replied, studying the older man. "I've seen more than one mustang who had more real life knowledge and brains than half a dozen splendid Academy graduates lumped together. Thank you for the tour." She nodded and turned toward the door, leaving the second officer standing among the towering stacks of containers, a thoughtful frown on his seamed face.

By the time she reached her ready room, the captain's appetite had returned, and she called her clerk for a breakfast tray. The quiet woman appeared a few minutes later and silently placed it on her desk. All the while, until she was gone, Dunmoore watched her, the earlier incident with Shara still ringing false.

Suddenly, she had it. Chewing on a slice of toasted nutbread, Dunmoore nodded to herself, grinning darkly.

For someone as meek as Kery, the clerk had shown surprising nerve in her argument with Shara. Now that she thought of it, Siobhan realized that an outsider would have believed Kery the superior and not Shara. Interesting. Fascinating, even. So why was Kery putting on the quiet mouse act with Siobhan and the others?

Then, Guthren's words on that first day sounded in her ears. "Beach her," the big cox'n had said. Maybe his advice had not only been for Kery's own protection.

There were too many dangerous undercurrents on this ship, and she was discovering more every day. Thoughtfully, Siobhan took a forkful of omelet and began chewing. Her face screwed up in a grimace at the taste, and she remembered that she promised herself to do something about the cooks. This could not go on. Pushing her tray aside, she called the purser.

*

"Mister Rossum, how would you rate the food on this ship?"

"Average, sir," he sounded uncertain and mopped his bald skull with his ever-present handkerchief.

"Wrong. It's bloody awful. Any reasons why?"

"Well, ah," Rossum glanced away, "I guess our cooks aren't the greatest."

"Then it seems the navy has a problem if all cooks on a single ship are lousy. Would you say the Fleet's School of Catering is putting out duds?"

"No sir."

"Well, Mister Rossum?"

"Our cooks haven't been able to produce decent meals for a long time, sir." The words seemed to cost the purser a lot of courage.

"And why is that?" Siobhan asked, her patience rapidly evaporating.

"I think it has something to do with, um, a lack of proper ingredients."

"You think? You're the purser. Are we, or aren't we getting a full supply of foodstuffs?" She had the satisfaction of seeing Rossum flinch.

"We, ah, have, this time, sir."

"Meaning you didn't have before."

"N-no." Now he seemed scared of something. "Not always."

"When didn't you, Mister Rossum?"

"Odd times, sir." He was lying, just as Luttrell, Pushkin, Drex and the others had been lying to her. Dunmoore stared at him in silence, letting the seconds pass. Rossum patted his scalp, face and neck again, the movements jerky and nervous.

"We have a full stock now, right?"

"Aye, sir."

"Then you will inform the cooks that I expect proper food at all meals in all galleys at all times. They will prepare menu number," she thought for a few moments, "two, and will keep on serving menu number two until it comes out to my satisfaction. I will eat the food from all three galleys, just to make sure. Needless to say, if they serve the same menu too often, the lower deck will give them sufficient motivation to improve their skills. Is that understood, Mister Rossum?"

Lower deck justice was often harsh and swift, and the cooks lived there. It should work.

"Aye, aye, sir."

"One more question. Petty Officer Melchor was yours, wasn't he?"

"Aye, my supply PO." His eyes took on a guarded look.

"What was he doing in the starboard hold the day he died?"

Siobhan literally saw the curtain fall, cutting her off from the purser, as his face lost all expression. She had seen the same reaction before, in Pushkin, Luttrell, and to a lesser extent in Drex.

"Routine check, sir, after taking delivery of supplies from the tender."

"That'll be all, Mister Rossum."

Siobhan sat back in her chair. The tender? Now there was a variable she had not considered. Each Battle Group had its own tender, an armed freighter that delivered supplies to the patrolling ships on the line, extending their operational tour length beyond what they could carry themselves. She wondered why some food items had been in short supply and not others, even though food deliveries by the tender were a standard load, based on crew size. Each ship was entitled to a certain quantity of supplies, ranging from rivets to peppercorns, and she had never heard of anyone shorted by their tender. Starbase 31's warehouse was filled to the rafters – she had seen it herself during her raid. There had to be a pattern somewhere, but she was damned if she could see what it was. All she had now were unrelated pieces and a deepening sense of frustration.

*

"So, d'ya think our new cap'n's gonna kick butt any 'arder?"

"Sure she will, shithead," the burly leading spacer replied around a mouthful of bread. "Cap'n Dunmoore's even gonna come and kick your sweet little ass herself."

Able Spacer Bertram made a rude noise. "She don't even know I exist, otherwise, she'da made me chief just on my good looks."

"The day you become a chief, Nosey, is the day I become a fucking beauty contest winner," Rownes said, winking at Able Spacer Vincenzo who was chewing on a tough piece of reconstituted meat with a look of concentration on his swarthy features, "eh, Vince?"

Vincenzo nodded solemnly at the big woman. "And if you become a beauty queen, Banger, I become the Grand Admiral," he replied, the meat finally resting in his stomach where, he was sure, it would give him heartburn for the remainder of the day. "But hey, if our lovely *capitano* wishes to drive us like slaves, I would not mind. I go for the pain and humiliation," Vincenzo leered at Able Spacer Demianova, the fourth and youngest member of their mess table. "Maybe you like some of that too, eh, Demmi? If you ask real nice, maybe Banger will tie you up on her big gun and let you have it."

"Don't frighten the kid, Vince," Banger replied lazily, blowing him a mock kiss. "If you actually go for the domination stuff, how come you never joined Cap'n Forenza in her cabin for fun and games?"

Vincenzo made a rude noise in the back of his throat. "Leave that to the little rats like Kery. Where is the creep anyways? I don't see her since we sail."

"Dunno. Probably keeps to her cubby." Banger replied, chewing on a sour, red apple. "Cox'n wanted to beach the rat, but the cap'n wasn't going for it. Cox'n said no one was to touch her, or anyone else for revenge, and that everybody on the old tub was in for a second chance. Guthren sounded like he meant it too. He ain't the kind I'd wanna get pissed-off. Not like that fucking drunk we had before."

Vincenzo snorted. "Not too difficult to be a better cox'n than Riveroff."

"Yeah, but Guthren ain't just a better edition of Riveroff. For one thing, he fucking *knows* what's going on. It's freaking uncanny if you ask me. Hey Nosey, didn't you say Guthren was the cap'n's cox'n before this?"

The little ferret-faced man shrugged. "So I heard. An' I heard they're tight too. Me, I'm not makin' up my mind 'till I know which way the plasma flow's goin'. Survival, like. Cap'n Dunmoore's a lot different from the old bitch. You're right, Banger. We's gotta watch our step."

Rownes grunted. Despite their differences, for Yvonne 'Banger' Rownes had been an honest merchant spacer, and Nosey Bertram a smuggler and thief who was given the choice of enlisting or jail, they were good buddies and watched out for each other. Just as they watched out for Vincenzo, the group's cynic and all-around conscience, and Demianova, whom Banger had sort of adopted since she became the other half of her gun crew.

"Coming from you, that is a strange endorsement," the fine-featured Russian said, wiping the remains of her meal from her plate with a chunk of bread. The lower deck mess was nearly empty by now, most of the other spacers either drifting off to their quarters for a few hours rest or leisurely heading for their duty stations ahead of the upcoming watch change.

"That's 'cause you ain't been with us when the cap'n high-jacked a load of spare parts for the barky," Nosey replied, straightening his back and looking at the young woman with the air of someone who's in on a great secret. "Downright impressive, she wuz. Scary even. 'Had the chiefy there eatin' right outta her hand. She'd a made one hell of a good smuggler before the war."

"If I didn't know any better," Banger chuckled, "I'd say you had a thing for the cap'n."

"So mebbe I do," Nosey replied, a sly grin spreading across his rodent-like face. "She's a right looker."

"Too skinny and pale," Vince interjected. "Now Banger here, she has the form I like." He leered at the gunner's mate.

"Sorry, Vince," she said, a look of mock disdain on her face, "but you ain't my type. And even if you were, you'd still not be my type." Then her face became serious again. "One thing's for sure, though, this old tub is turning into something different and I, for one, ain't at all unhappy about it. When they drafted me off the *Johnny Reb*, I was expecting to serve in the navy, and now, maybe I will. I'd rather run drills every damned watch for the next month than sit on my duff the moment I'm off duty, 'cause the fucking drills are gonna keep us alive. Goofing off and grabbing our asses sure as shit won't. Yeah, Dunmoore's a lot different from Forenza. At least now we have a cap'n who fucking cares about the ship, and us."

"I have not seen any evidence that she cares about her crew," Vince said, shrugging. "Not that any good work will change a blessed thing aboard this jinx. We are unlucky, and that is that." Like most spacers, Vincenzo had a quiet, if healthy respect for old superstitions. You never knew out here what could help or harm.

"Unlucky!" Banger snorted. "Hell, the only thing wrong with this tub is the previous management. Ain't no such thing as unlucky ships. Only shitty captains. And if you can't see what she's doin' for us now, you never will, asshole," She made a face at Vincenzo. "What d'you want? Free beer at the end of every watch? Ship-sponsored orgies? Shit, you want Forenza to come back, is what you want. You're fucking sick, Vince. A good cap'n, who cares, is one who runs her ship tight and makes sure the crew knows their jobs, so they don't get killed by the first Imp we fucking run across."

Before Vincenzo could reply, Nosey held up his right hand and grinned at his friends, a sly look making his face even more ferret-like. "I've 'eard sumptin' that'll make you all think again 'bout the new cap'n and the way she cares about little us."

Knowing how Bertram liked to draw out his revelations, Rownes make impatient come-on signs. "Spit it out, Nosey. We gotta go on watch soon and don't have time for your screwing around."

Nosey put on a hurt look. "I ain't screwing around. An' if you don't wanna hear the story, let's go on watch now an' forget it."

"Nosey," Banger growled, raising a clenched fist. It had become something of a ritual among their little group.

"Okay, okay, ya big-teated gun-whalloper," Nosey replied, his grin returning. "Cap'n's told the pusser them cooks is gonna be makin' the same menu 'till they get it right. She said mebbe it'll give them buggers 'nuff in-cen-tive," he struggled over the unfamiliar word, "to make sure their cookin' gets better. Said that the crew'll tell 'em right 'nuff if they don't get the message."

"And so we will," Vince said, rubbing his stomach mournfully. "That meat was a real crime against humanity if you ask me."

"You are too soft, Vince," Demmi interjected, "back home, that meat is considered a great luxury."

"*Si*, because back home, you are barbarians. Vodka and cucumber. You have no appreciation of the good cooking. Now where I come from, food is the most important part of life, and -"

The Russian gunner snorted. "Not to waste time on your idiotic comments, Vince," she said, "but I think Banger and Nosey are right. This ship will become better. Captain Dunmoore is okay. She is top-notch."

"How d'you know, Demmi?" Bertram scratched the side of his huge proboscis.

"She was second officer in cruiser *Sala-Ad-Din*, where I served my first tour after Fleet School."

"You never told us," Vince complained accusingly.

Demianova shrugged. "Was not important. I say she is a-okay, do you believe me?" When the others failed to reply, she shrugged again. "So I keep quiet and wait. Maybe she is not as a-okay as captain. But I see no difference until now. Tough and demanding, *da*, but fair too. She keeps us alive on the line, you see."

"Okay, slack-*asses*," an unpleasant voice interrupted the conversation before either of Demmi's comrades could ask any more questions. "Get your butts in gear. Watch change is in a few minutes, and you'll be late by the time you get to your stations. Vincenzo that means I'll be taking care of you personally."

Vince groaned under his breath and turned to look at Petty Officer Zavaleta, his immediate supervisor, who was smirking with barely suppressed glee.

"It is still ten minutes before the change, PO," he replied in a resigned voice, "and I will be on time."

"No, you won't, asshole. When you get to your station, you'll be late because I said so. Now move it, greaseball. I get the feeling you need a fucking counseling session, I do."

"Hey," Banger stood up, "you've got no call to be insulting and threatening Vince, PO."

"Stay out of this, Rownes. If you know what's good for you."

"Listen, PO, if you're pissed off at life, don't take it out on Vincenzo."

"What did you say?" Zavaleta advanced on the bigger woman menacingly. Rownes stood her ground defiantly. He was a bully who had thrived under Forenza, and like all of his kind was a coward. Banger easily outweighed and outreached him, and knew she made the man nervous beneath his bluster.

"Calm down, Banger," Vince laid a restraining arm on Rownes. "It's all right. The PO needs someone to pick on, and these days, it's me."

"Only because you're too fucking placid to defend yourself," Banger growled, eyes never leaving Zavaleta. Vincenzo pushed back his chair, rose and headed for the door, ignoring Zavaleta' dangerous smile as he went around the non-com.

"You're gonna pay for this, Rownes," Zavaleta whispered, before turning to follow Vincenzo. He was scared of the gun captain and knew she knew it.

"I think not," Banger replied, too softly to be heard by anyone but Nosey and Demianova. "I think Cap'n Dunmoore ain't gonna stand for assholes like you. I sure know Chief Guthren won't."

*

Out in the passage, but still within view of the other three, Zavaleta gave Vincenzo a brutal shove. "You and I are gonna have one hell of a little talk about your attitude, greaseball." Rownes knew that was more for her benefit than anything else, and a sick knot of fear for Vincenzo hardened in her gut.

Nosey swore. "You think the cap'n will make Zavaleta change? She doesn't know what happens down here, nor, I bet, does she care, even if ya say she's top-notch, Demmi. Zavaleta and his friends will continue, just as long as she gets her ship into fightin' shape."

Banger shrugged, hiding her concern. "Then we will have to take care of Zavaleta and his friends."

She was about to add something else, when the battle stations siren went off, for the second time in twelve hours. Whatever she wanted to tell Bertram and Demianova was drowned in the strident noise, and the thought lost in a flurry of activity.

*

"Much better, this time, Mister Pushkin," Siobhan nodded, "but not good enough yet."

"Aye, sir. Four and a half minutes, but they're still not prepared by the time they man their stations."

"At least there's progress. I-"

"Excuse me, sir," the cox'n stuck his head into Dunmoore's ready room, "I think you'll want to know about this sooner rather than later."

"Come in, Mister Guthren. As I was telling the first officer, there's been a gain in speed, if not in efficiency."

"Aye, it's a start at least, sir." The cox'n clearly had something else on his mind and was not interested in the results of the drill. "What I came to say, sir is that we've got a discipline problem I have no choice but to report." Siobhan raised her eyebrows questioningly. "One of the ratings struck a petty officer," Guthren continued. "The PO is bringing charges of striking a non-commissioned officer, insubordination, and mutiny."

"Mutiny?" Siobhan sounded incredulous. She glanced at Pushkin, who shrugged. "Who's the PO, and what exactly happened?"

Guthren grimaced. "PO Zavaleta has brought the charges. One of his ratings, Able Spacer Vincenzo, bosun's mate, refused to move as fast as ordered by Zavaleta, and when the PO gave him a push to get him going, Vincenzo turned around and apparently assaulted him."

"Any witnesses?" Siobhan remembered Zavaleta. Somehow, it did not surprise her that he was one to get into a scrap with a rating. He was a born bully.

"No, sir. It happened by the lower port airlock, Vincenzo's station at general quarters. Judging by what I've seen, Zavaleta gave back as good as he got and more. Says he was defending himself and trying to subdue Vincenzo."

"Damn!" The last thing she needed on this ship was a summary trial, especially if it was what she thought it was. It would kill what little progress she had made improving morale on the lower decks. "What's your opinion, cox'n?"

"Frankly, sir? Zavaleta tried some informal counseling, and it backfired. He's a brutal bastard, but a coward. Knows who he can and can't piss around with. I guess he misjudged Vincenzo, for all the good it did the kid." Guthren scratched his beard thoughtfully. "Come to think of it, Vincenzo is a quiet guy. I wouldn't have pegged him for a shit disturber."

"Was informal counseling used often under Commander Forenza?"

Pushkin looked ill at ease. Informal counseling was the euphemism for beating the living shit out of a subordinate in private. It was a court-martial offense, though some commanding officers of questionable competence tolerated it because it was an easy if short-term means to enforce harsh discipline. Siobhan had never believed in the practice, though she did tolerate taking the hard cases to the gym for some remedial martial arts training.

"Unfortunately, yes." Pushkin sounded deflated. "Morale had sunk to the point where the worst among the non-coms were getting better at bullying than leading. Those assholes have ruled the lower decks for a long time. A lot of bosun's mates among them, come to think of it."

Which means our good Mister Drex, under all that hard-assed mustang competence, either closed his eyes on the brutality, actively condoned it or is, in fact, an incompetent who doesn't know what's going on under his nose. So much for relying on him to help. I'll have to watch him too. Dunmoore mentally sighed.

"I hope this incident was the first since I took command, for it will certainly be the last."

"You can count on it, sir." Guthren nodded. "So what do we do about Zavaleta and Vincenzo?"

"I'll see them both in my ready room. Zavaleta first. Now would be best, I think."

*

"Petty Officer Second Class William Zavaleta, reporting to the captain as ordered, sir." He stood ramrod straight, a regulation three paces in front of Dunmoore's desk, his hand at his brow in salute. For once, his uniform was immaculate, he was freshly shaven, and Siobhan could find no obvious fault with the man if she ignored the visible marks of hand-to-hand violence on his face.

"At ease, PO." With precise movements, Zavaleta adopted the parade rest position, his piggish eyes staring at the bulkhead above Siobhan. "What the hell happened with Vincenzo?"

"Well, sir, I —"

"Relax, Zavaleta, and look at me when you're speaking." Siobhan's tone was sharp and biting. When the man's eyes met hers, they kept contact briefly before sliding away to the side. If eyes were indeed the windows of the soul, then

Petty Officer Second Class Zavaleta was none too happy having his captain look in.

"Aye, sir. Anyways, Vincenzo's a slacker with an attitude problem. He's been giving me trouble ever since he joined my division. And it's been getting worse since we sailed." Zavaleta smiled ingratiatingly. "The man can't get his mind back to proper navy discipline, sir, now that you're our skipper. Always a few assholes like that in any crew."

Siobhan felt her stomach contract at the man's gross hypocrisy and blatant attempt at flattery. She particularly resented his using the word 'skipper'. Her crews on *Shenzen* and *Don Quixote* before that had started calling her 'skipper' once they had become a tight, efficient group, where such affectionate familiarity denoted respect.

Guthren had seen his captain's face change and knew the reason why. He growled into Zavaleta' ear, "You call Captain Dunmoore 'captain' or 'sir.' You ain't earned the right to call the skipper 'skipper.' And stick to the facts."

"Aye, cox'n." Zavaleta replied, anxious to keep his superiors' good will. "Like I said, Vincenzo's attitude's going downhill. He started giving me lip even in the mess when I went round to make sure the slackers came on watch on time. Then, the battle stations siren went off, and I sent him to his station. When I went down to inspect, as is my job," Zavaleta drew himself even straighter with self-righteousness, "I found Vincenzo slacking off at his post. He weren't with the proper kit, or in the proper position to defend the airlock from boarders. So I gave him the order to straighten up and get going. When he did not move fast enough, being an insolent bastard, I gave him a shove, to get him moving, like and that's when it happened. He turned around and tried to punch me out, calling me all sorts of names in that bastard language of his."

"You mean Italian," Siobhan asked coldly, her voice soft and menacing. Though Pushkin and Guthren recognized her rising fury, Zavaleta seemed oblivious.

"Oh, aye, sir," Zavaleta grinned. "Gibbered away in it as he jumped me. Landed a few before I could stop him. Man's a bleedin' demon. Dangerous, sir." The PO pointed at his face. "Good thing he dropped his weapon before he attacked. Otherwise, he might just have used it to break my skull open."

He's lying. Siobhan looked briefly at Guthren and saw her conclusion reflected in his eyes.

"Mister Guthren, march PO Zavaleta out and Able Spacer Vincenzo in. Have the PO stand by."

For a moment, Siobhan read confusion and worry in Zavaleta' eyes. Her tone and manner had finally registered with him, and he felt the first tendrils of fear worming through his gut. The feeling increased when he saw Guthren's broad, unsmiling face.

Vincenzo, when he marched in between two armed bosun's mates, looked terrible. Contrary to Zavaleta, he had not been given time to change and get his appearance in order. His face also showed far more damage than Zavaleta's, and he walked with a limp. If the spacer had indeed instigated the assault, he had certainly suffered the worst of it. Was Zavaleta so stupid as to think she could see the state of his alleged attacker and still believe his version of events? Most likely Forenza had swallowed any story fed to her, as long as she did not have to make too much of an intellectual effort.

"Able Spacer Vincenzo brought before the captain, as ordered, sir," the senior of the two bosun's mates, a rough leading spacer, announced.

"At ease."

The two escorts adopted the parade rest position, like Zavaleta, had done before them, but Vincenzo took the opportunity to relax with a silent sigh of relief as if he was in pain and did not want to show it.

"Able Spacer Vincenzo, you have been charged by Petty Officer Zavaleta with assaulting him while he was performing his duties. A very serious charge indeed. I'd like to hear your side of the story."

Vincenzo glanced left and right, at his two escorts, in an involuntary movement, before aiming his gaze at the bulkhead behind Siobhan. The action was not lost on the captain, who knew enough to realize the man was wary, if not scared, of the bosun's mates at his side. His tongue gingerly probed his swollen lips as he formulated a reply. Vincenzo's left eye was already swelling shut, and would completely vanish behind the puffy, blackened flesh before the interview was over.

"Well, sir," Vincenzo's tone was hoarse, probably from a blow to the larynx, and his words were slurred. "What PO Zavaleta said is true, sir."

Siobhan was caught unprepared by his answer, even though she should have seen it coming.

"How do you know what PO Zavaleta said, Vincenzo?" Siobhan's tone was brittle as she felt her face flush with anger.

"He told me what he would say to you before he marched in, sir."

Siobhan glanced at Guthren, standing behind and to one side of Vincenzo and his escorts. The big cox'n shrugged, a look of disgust on his flattened features. That was it, then. No complaint, no case against Zavaleta. The bastard wins. At least officially. Guthren's expression promised something entirely different, however.

"Very well, Able Spacer Vincenzo. I now advise you that I will proceed with Petty Officer Zavaleta' charges against you. The cox'n will deliver a copy of the charge sheets to you within the next twenty-four hours. In that time, you will decide on an assisting officer and so inform the cox'n. Mister Guthren, have Able Spacer Vincenzo examined by the surgeon, and if she declares him fit, have him brought to the brig."

"Sir." The cox'n snapped to attention and rattled out a series of orders to the senior of the two escorts.

"Oh, and cox'n," Siobhan said, as Vincenzo and the bosun's mates turned to march out, "have PO Zavaleta report to the surgeon also."

When the doors closed, Siobhan sat back and looked speculatively at the first officer, who remained silent.

"What do you think, Mister Pushkin?"

He shrugged, his eyes fixed on the door. "Vincenzo's been told to stay silent, and he's cooperating. Typical in cases of informal counseling. If he accuses Zavaleta of beating him up, Zavaleta' friends and supporters, like the two bosun's mates of the escort, are going to make sure he regrets it. We're not going to get the truth out of Vincenzo. He'll take his lumps, and like it."

Siobhan nodded. It confirmed what she thought. But it infuriated her because it was damned unfair, and lousy for morale. Yet if Vincenzo played along with Zavaleta, there was nothing she could do.

"If you'll excuse me, sir," Pushkin rose. "I've still got to see to the aft damage control team. They fucked-up royally during the drill."

Left alone, Siobhan fumed, but she could not see a way around Vincenzo's silence and Zavaleta' lies. When the lower deck decided to keep things to themselves, no officer in the Fleet could pry the truth from their closed ranks.

*

An hour later, Luttrell called Siobhan, asking for an interview. She was visibly outraged, and it was not hard to divine why.

"Sit, Doctor," She watched Luttrell with narrowed eyes while the surgeon sat down, and waited for her to speak.

"That kid you sent down to be examined -"

"Vincenzo."

"Right. I hope you're going to give that asshole Zavaleta what he deserves for beating the living shit out of a fucking defenseless rating." Her voice was trembling with rage.

"Vincenzo admitted that he assaulted Zavaleta, without provocation." Siobhan kept a flat, unemotional tone.

"Bullshit!" Luttrell's cheeks turned scarlet. "I examined both of them. Zavaleta has a few bruises, nothing to crow about, but Vincenzo? Hell, the kid's closer to fucking hamburger meat than human. He has a mild concussion, three cracked ribs, severe bruising on the legs, torso and face. Half of his teeth are loose, and he's damned lucky he didn't lose an eye. He sure as shit won't be seeing the inside of the brig for a while, *captain*! I've kept him in the sickbay, under observation, and he'll stay there until I say he can go."

The doctor's blazing eyes challenged Dunmoore to contradict her.

"Not that your opinion will make much difference at Vincenzo's trial," the captain replied, as calm and emotionless as before, "but how do you think he suffered his injuries?"

"Trial? You're going to try the kid for having defended himself against Zavaleta? And I figured you were different."

"Doctor! You forget yourself. If Vincenzo doesn't speak up, there is nothing I can do. Now, I asked you a question. Answer me."

"Sure, captain," her face twisted into a mask of disgust. "The only way that kid could have sustained those injuries is by being knocked down on the deck and literally having the shit kicked out of him. He's fortunate to have escaped any internal bleeding. Oh, and his arms are more bruised than anywhere else, which means he was trying to protect his head and face. Make of that what you will."

"As I said, Doctor, I cannot do anything unless Vincenzo decides to contradict Zavaleta' story. Now if there's nothing else, I have pressing matters to attend."

"No, sir," Luttrell spat, "there is nothing else, sir."

"You are dismissed, Doctor."

"You know, captain," she said standing up, "when you came on board, I naively believed the bullying would be a thing of the past." The surgeon laughed humorlessly. "We officers never learn the realities of life, do we? Under Commander Forenza, I got a steady stream of kids who'd fallen down access tubes, stumbled over thresholds, slipped on a piece of soap in the showers or injured themselves during supposedly consensual sex, and always it was kids working for the Zavaletas on this ship. Forenza didn't give a damn when I tried to make her see the pattern. The bullies kept the lower deck quiet, and that's all she cared for. Hasn't been a beating or a rape since Forenza left the ship. Until today. Goodbye, captain."

One step forward, two steps back, Siobhan thought humorlessly when she was alone again. Whatever she had gained with the doctor was gone. It was useless to rail against the unfairness of life or Admiral Nagira for dropping her into this fucking mess right after *Victoria Regina.* This was her problem, and she had to solve it.

— Ten —

"Fuckin' asshole Zavaleta," Nosey growled as he, Rownes and Demianova met in a corner of the depressingly austere mess after watch change. The mood on the lower decks was ugly, a throwback to the bad old days.

"So," he looked at Demmi, disgust twisting his rodent-like face, "your precious a-okay Cap'n Dunmoore ain't so fuckin' hot after all. She's gonna put Vince in the brig, even though the poor bugger only defended himself. Ain't no justice if you ask me? Poor fuckin' Vince is all fuckin' beat ta shit, and Zavaleta is struttin' around like a bleedin' peacock who's just screwed a lady peacock. I say we take care of Zavaleta ourselves, 'cause ain't no one else gonna do it."

"Dangerous talk, Bertram," a soft voice said from the shadow of a half-height divider. "Anyone would think you're planning a mutiny."

"What do you want, Jallaba?"

"Just a word to the wise, Rownes. Keep you little buddy here from saying stupid things and it'll be just fine. Vincenzo didn't want to play ball, and now he's got the fucking bat stuck up his ass."

"More like Zavaleta kicked the living shit out of him to get his jollies," Banger replied, eyes narrowed, a dangerous edge to her voice.

"That's not what Vincenzo told the captain," Jallaba smirked. "I was there. He admitted to the charges. It's open and shut. Summary trial's gonna last all of two minutes, then its thirty days in the brig for the little twit. That's what happens when you fuck around with PO Zavaleta, and you'd do well to remember, Rownes. The PO don't carry you in his heart these days either." He laughed softly and walked away to join his friends in the far corner.

"Whaddaya think, Banger?"

"I think Vince's been told to shut up and play along, otherwise, things will be a lot worse for him."

"Would not be the first time on this ship," Demianova growled. "But that does not solve the problem."

"Bloody hell, Demmi, it looks like your precious cap'n ain't doing much to help Vince. Fuckin' Jallaba wouldn't come here pissin' on us if she was wise to Zavaleta."

"Ain't that simple, Nosey," Rownes raised her hand to silence Bertram. "Zavaleta lays the charges, and Vince gets a chance to explain himself. If he doesn't, then the cap'n can't do nothing but work on what the asshole says."

"Then we gotta get Vince to talk!"

"If Zavaleta and his buddies scared Vince into keeping mum, Nosey, d'you think we're gonna get him to speak up? There's more of them than there is of us, and Vince'll pay for it, sooner or later."

"So we give up?" Nosey sounded disgusted.

"No," Rownes replied, a thoughtful look on her face. "Tell me, Demmi, you said Dunmoore was all right as second on the *Sala-Ad-Din*. D'you think she's gonna listen to a rating who tells her a PO's been counseling another rating, even if no one saw the shit-kicking? Tell you why I ask, love. If I go up and tell Dunmoore what we think has happened, and she doesn't believe me or take me seriously, and Zavaleta still gets away with what he did to Vince, I'm next on the list, and so are you two."

Demianova considered the question seriously. "I think Captain Dunmoore will listen. Will she believe?" The young woman shrugged, "God only knows. It is a risk."

"Damn right it's a fuckin' risk," Nosey vehemently replied, "but Vince is our buddy, an' I ain't gonna let him go down for something he didn't do."

"Relax, both of you," Banger held up both hands. "I've already made up my mind to tell Lieutenant Devall. He'll listen, that much I know, and he'll probably believe me. If it backfires, so what. At least we'll have tried something. If it works, then maybe the bullshit will be over on this ship, and we'll have done everyone a favor. I'm getting real tired, you know."

From his vantage point across the room, Leading Spacer Jallaba watched Rownes leave, determination written large on her broad features. She did not spare him a glance, though when Jallaba's eyes drifted toward her table, he saw Bertram and Demianova look at him with open hostility.

The bosun's mate briefly wondered whether he should warn Zavaleta there was trouble in the air, then shrugged, deciding Rownes and her friends did not have the guts to run to the officers with their stories. No one had done so before, and every rating knew that it was still damned dangerous to do so now. A starship had a lot of dark corners and dangerous places where a body could lose her step and take a long fall onto a waiting fist.

*

The door chimes interrupted Siobhan as she and Pushkin were planning the training schedule for the next week. She looked up, a flash of irritation crossing her eyes. Dunmoore's meeting with Luttrell had soured her temper further, and even Pushkin was treading carefully.

"Come."

Lieutenant Devall stepped in and came to attention, as precise as a cadet. "Pardon the intrusion, sir, but I have some new information relating to the incident involving Able Spacer Vincenzo."

Siobhan looked at the gunnery officer with raised eyebrows, surprised that the aloof aristocrat cared about a simple rating, especially one who was not in his division. Her irritation vanished in a flash.

"Speak, Mister Devall."

"Sir. One of my gun captains has brought information to my attention which might shed some light on the events during the battle stations drill. She overheard PO Zavaleta threaten Spacer Vincenzo with counseling."

Devall spoke in a matter-of-fact tone, but the interest in his dark blue eyes was unmistakable. Siobhan leaned forward and steepled her gloved fingers under her chin, ignoring the sudden roiling of acid in her stomach.

"This gun captain, is she reliable?"

"Aye, sir. Leading Spacer Rownes is in charge of the Number Two portside one-oh-fives, and her performance has always been beyond reproach. I consider her one of my best."

Siobhan did not immediately reply. She did not know the gunnery officer well yet, and could not judge what he considered beyond reproach, not in this ship.

"What's her background?"

"Leading Spacer Rownes was a merchant gunner before the war. She was drafted when her ship became a casualty, and after Fleet School was assigned to *Stingray*. Her gun crew is well-trained, and she has never caused a disciplinary problem. I consider her fit for promotion to petty officer third class."

Siobhan thought for a moment, trying to remember the gun crews she had seen during her inspection at general quarters.

"Is she a big boned woman, older than the rest?"

"Aye, sir. Nicknamed Banger." Devall seemed both pleased and impressed that Dunmoore could remember a junior rating after only a short time aboard.

"Yes." Siobhan nodded. She could see the Number Two portside one-oh-five turret in her mind's eye. Whatever else might be wrong with her, Siobhan's memory retained its voracious efficiency. Rownes' gun crew had indeed been in better shape than most. "Have Leading Spacer Rownes report to me soonest."

"Sir." Devall did a smart about turn and left.

Siobhan glanced at her first officer, a smile playing on her lips. "Well, Mister Pushkin, maybe we have a solution to our problem after all. What do you think?"

"Don't know, sir. Unless she saw the incident, hearing a PO threaten a rating with counseling doesn't amount to much at a summary trial."

"We shall see." Siobhan's fertile mind was already toying with an idea. If it worked, she would make some progress toward resolving the morale problem.

*

"Sir," Lieutenant Devall reported a few minutes later, "Leading Spacer Rownes."

A strong, broad-faced woman wearing a clean but well-worn uniform marched into the room and stopped at attention three paces in front of the desk. She saluted crisply.

"Leading Spacer Yvonne Rownes reporting to the captain as ordered."

"At ease, spacer."

Rownes relaxed and adopted the 'at ease' position, rather than the more formal 'parade rest.' Her eyes dropped down and met Siobhan's with undisguised interest. The two women examined each other in silence for a few moments, and Dunmoore found herself in the unusual position of being evaluated by a rating.

Rownes exuded an almost palpable aura of self-confidence. She could well imagine that the other woman had weathered Forenza's period of command with her self-respect and sense of duty intact.

"You have information relating to the incident involving Able Spacer Vincenzo, Rownes?"

"Aye, sir. Me and Able Spacer Vincenzo are buddies," Banger said, establishing her interest in the matter up front. Siobhan nodded, understanding. The simple gesture seemed to satisfy the rating, and she continued, in a more forceful tone. "We and two other of my buddies were finishing lunch just before eight bells when PO Zavaleta came into the mess and told us to get a move on. Then he told Vincenzo that no matter what he did, he'd be reported as late on duty, and Zavaleta would take care of him personally, with a bit of counseling."

Siobhan did not speak, but her eyes held Rownes'.

"Then," Banger continued, "when Vincenzo left the mess, Zavaleta gave him an all mighty shove and promised him a little talk. Oh, and he also called Vincenzo a greaseball." Rownes fell silent, watching the captain for a reaction.

Siobhan sat back, studying the other woman. "Tell me," she finally said, "how do you think this will help Able Spacer Vincenzo? You did not witness the incident. All you saw was a petty officer going about his duty."

Rownes' face tightened, and she stiffened into the parade rest position, her eyes snapping up to stare over Siobhan's head.

"I'm sorry to have bothered you, sir," she spat out, anger working her jaw muscles.

"At ease, spacer," Siobhan snapped, standing up so that their heads were level. She caught Banger's stare and held it, reading resentment and contempt in the rating's eyes.

"What I need to know about this business is the truth." Siobhan's tone was harsh and biting. "So far, all I have is PO Zavaleta' declaration, your words hinting at friction between a non-com and a rating, and Vincenzo recognizing the veracity of the charges. With this information, all I can do is proceed with a summary trial. Now do you, or don't you have something that changes the circumstances of the incident?"

"The truth, sir?" Rownes replied bitterly. Behind Banger, Pushkin stiffened, ready to reprimand her for her insolent tone. Siobhan shook her head minutely, stilling the words forming in the first officer's mouth.

"Yes, the bloody truth, spacer. Something that seems to be in short supply aboard *Stingray.*"

"The truth, sir, is that Zavaleta is a fucking bully who's been beating the living shit out of a lot of people. And he ain't the only one doing it. Vincenzo's been his scapegoat ever since you came aboard, 'cause he wants to do his duty right, and Zavaleta wants to do what he's always done. Now, Vince is fucking scared shitless to tell anyone, 'cause he'll just get the crap kicked out of him again. That's the way it's been on this ship for a long time, and it ain't gonna change any time soon."

Unless Captain Dunmoore does something about it, Siobhan thought, understanding Rownes' unspoken words. The captain nodded.

"Fine, spacer. Strange as it may seem to you, I have no problems believing you."

Rownes started in surprise and looked searchingly at Dunmoore. A flash of hope crossed her face before she slipped back into naval formality.

"You and Vincenzo are buddies, right? Well then, the best thing you can do for your mate is to convince him to tell the real story. As for whatever lower deck consequences that may bring, I think it's past time this ship was cleaned up."

Rownes looked uncertain. "It'll be difficult, sir. Vince is scared, and to tell you the truth, so's everybody else." Then, resolution wiped the uncertainty away. There was something in Dunmoore's manner that showed the new captain meant business, and Banger desperately wanted to believe she would make things right again.

"I'll try, sir. The crap has got to stop."

"You do that, and report any problems to the cox'n or Mister Devall."

"Aye, aye, sir."

"Dismissed."

"Mister Pushkin, ask the cox'n to join us. We have a few things to discuss."

*

The sickbay was empty when Banger stepped in. Doc Luttrell was off watch, and the duty medic was cleaning out the operating theater, whistling as he worked. Vince lay on one of the beds, his face a mass of bruises. The monitor above the bed showed no immediate danger, but Rownes' gut clenched at the sight of her friend.

Gently, the gunner sat down on the neighboring bed and looked at Vincenzo, struggling to contain her rage. He must have sensed somebody's presence, even in his sleep, and his one good eye opened.

"Hey, Banger," he whispered, "what's happening."

"Lots, kid. Zavaleta really gave you a beating, didn't he?"

Vince tried to shrug, grimacing in pain. "Shit happens, eh."

"Not this kind of crap, Vince. I've been to see the captain, and told her Zavaleta' been on your case for a while, and that I think you got beat up by the bastard just for the hell of it."

"Aw," Vince coughed painfully, "why do you go do a thing like that? Now Zavaleta is going to go crazy."

"It's got to stop, Vince, before someone gets killed."

"Too late for that," the bosun's mate replied. "How do you want to make it stop, eh? Nobody saw what happened."

"Yeah, but the captain believes you got the shaft, buddy. Just tell her what happened."

"My word against the word of a petty officer? Do you think I'm that stupid?"

Banger hated doing this, but she could see Vincenzo was going to be intractable. "It's too late, Vince. You gotta talk. The captain knows and pretty soon Zavaleta, and his buddies will know. If Dunmoore doesn't get some reason to stop 'em, I'll be the next on Zavaleta' list, and he ain't stupid enough to take me on like he did you. More'n likely I'll fall down a maintenance shaft and break my neck."

"Shit!"

"Yeah, shit. C'mon, Vince."

He thought about it for a good long time. "Okay, Banger, I talk."

"I'll tell the cox'n. Hang tight, buddy." Rownes smiled at Vince, repressing an urge to squeeze his heavily bruised shoulder in reassurance. Then, she rose and left, feeling guilty at her successful blackmail, but relieved nonetheless that things were going to move.

Alone once more, Vincenzo stared at the bright ceiling, trying to calm the shiver of fear running through his abused body. He knew he was not a very courageous man, but Banger was right. It had to stop.

*

"Come."

Leading Spacer Jallaba stepped into Petty Officer Second Class Zavaleta' cabin, a grim look on his face.

"We got trouble, PO."

"Trouble?" Zavaleta laughed. It was an ugly sound from an ugly soul. He took another sip from his juice bulb, the orange pressings heavily laced with vodka, in violation of Captain Dunmoore's orders. "Anyone gives trouble, and I take care of him."

"Maybe not, PO." Jallaba leaned against the wall, wrinkling his nose at the sour smell of sweat and unwashed clothes that permeated the small compartment.

Zavaleta shared his bunk space with another petty officer, who was currently on duty. The latter's tiny private area was immaculately clean.

"Rownes spent some time in the captain's ready room an hour ago, and then she went to see Vincenzo in sick bay. You figure it out."

"Figure nothing, Jallaba," Zavaleta snorted. "The bitch was trying to get her little buddy outta the shit, but it won't work. Maybe I'll go have a talk with the greaseball, just to remind him where his best interests are. Then, during the night watch, perhaps Rownes has an accident, just to make sure everyone understands."

"Dangerous, PO. Rownes ain't a wimp."

"Fuck it. No one pisses around with me, and stoolies get special attention. In fact, I'll go see the little greaseball now." Zavaleta shrugged on his tunic and downed the rest of his drink. "You come with me, and stand watch at the sickbay door. Doc ought to be off duty right now, but the bitch could come back any moment. Fucking officers!"

Vincenzo was asleep when Zavaleta got there. The single medic on duty, a young able spacer on his first tour, came out of the pharmacist's cubby when he heard the door slide shut. Zavaleta looked at him with a sneer.

"Get lost, junior. Me and my man Vincenzo here have some business to discuss."

"Sorry, PO," the medic replied, scared of Zavaleta, but more scared of Luttrell's fury if he disobeyed her orders and let Zavaleta near Vincenzo. "Doctor's orders. No visitors."

"I said, fuck off, kid. Or do you want to join the greaseball in feather merchant's heaven?" Zavaleta smacked his right fist into his left palm.

The medic shook his head and backed into the cubby, intending to call Luttrell over the intercom the moment he was out of sight.

"Good lad," Zavaleta smiled. Then, he walked over to Vincenzo's bed and prodded the sleeping man with his finger. "Wake up greaseball, we gotta talk."

"Huh?" Vince blinked, still groggy from sleep. His disfigured nostrils twitched at the non-com's sour breath.

"A little birdie's told me you're going to tell the captain some things that'll make me look like a big bad wolf. You aren't gonna do that to your PO, now are you?"

"Piss-off, Zavaleta," Vincenzo rasped, "you beat the crap outta me because you get your jollies that way, and I won't let you get away with it this time."

Zavaleta snorted.

"You suddenly grow some *cojones*, greaseball? But hey, go stool to the captain, and I promise you what I'll give you later is gonna be a hundred times worse than what I gave you this morning. And just for good measure, your little friend Banger Rownes is gonna get the treatment too. Nobody fucks around with me; you ought to know that by now."

"Does that include the captain of this ship?" A hard female voice suddenly asked from the door to the operating theater. "Or do you confine your violence to those who can't fight back?"

Zavaleta whirled around, panic spreading across his face, and then utter fear. The sight was almost comical, and Vincenzo would regale the lower deck mess with stories of it for a long time. But give the bastard his due. A second or two later, Zavaleta snapped to attention, wiping all expression from his brutal features. Only his bloodshot eyes moved, taking in the captain, the cox'n, and the second officer in turn as the filed out of the operating theater.

"G'day, sir. I was just seeing how Able Spacer Vincenzo was doing, sir. After all, he is my responsibility."

"Spare me the hypocrisy, Zavaleta. Mister Drex, place PO Zavaleta under arrest and escort him to the brig."

"What charges, sir?" The second officer asked in a flat voice.

"Oh, we'll start with uttering threats. Then, I think, assaulting a subordinate, giving false testimony and," she smiled cruelly, "consuming alcohol, contrary to orders."

They had the satisfaction of seeing Zavaleta' look of wounded innocence collapse into an expression of utter terror. The last charge, that of consuming booze, had been a stab in the dark. Siobhan was pleased to see it hit home.

If nothing else, it would give the other assholes on board notice that very little escaped Captain Dunmoore.

"Take him away."

Out in the corridor, Jallaba was standing at attention between two burly bosun's mates, his face a mask of stone. He said nothing when Zavaleta looked at him as he marched by, led away by an infuriated bosun.

Guthren stepped up to Jallaba, his broad nose only centimeters from the other's face. "Now listen, and listen good maggot. Zavaleta is going down for what he did to Vincenzo. If you and the other maggots don't want to go down with him, I suggest you forget any notion of revenge and start doing your jobs by the fucking book. Is that understood?"

"Aye, aye, cox'n." Jallaba barked out.

Guthren smiled. "Carry on, then, and spread the new gospel according to Captain Dunmoore, and tell 'em those who won't convert better learn how to swim through vacuum." He nodded at the guards who released Jallaba.

Watching the retreating back of the bosun's mate, Guthren grinned to himself. Cap'n Dunmoore was something else. When she proposed they wait for Zavaleta to appear in the sickbay, he thought she was playing at cops and robbers, and would not get anything out of the effort. But she knew the stupid bastard would condemn himself out of his own mouth. The cox'n reached over to the nearest intercom panel.

"Bridge, this is Guthren. Call a chiefs' and petty officers' meeting in the mess in ten minutes. I want everyone there."

"Aye, aye, sir."

"Cox'n, out." Time to make like a disciple and spread the good news himself. A couple of petty officers were gonna have to watch their step real close. Bullshit time on *Stingray* was truly over!

Word spread through the frigate like wildfire, and when Siobhan came off watch, she noticed many crewmembers looking at her with renewed respect. The ugly mood was breaking. She still faced the unpleasant task of trying

Zavaleta, but if nothing else, it would be a good occasion to cement her hold on the ship.

*

"March in the accused."

"Sir." The cox'n opened the door to the passageway. "Charge parade, quick MARCH."

Petty Officer Zavaleta, in full dress uniform, minus beret, quick-stepped into the ready room, escorted by a gunnery PO of the same rank, also wearing a formal uniform, but with headdress.

"Charge parade, HALT. Right TURN."

Siobhan looked up from the sheaf of paper on her desk. The trial had lasted for over an hour, with witnesses, sworn depositions and the whole paraphernalia of a summary trial in deep space, in a time of war.

Ten minutes earlier, she had ordered Zavaleta marched out while she considered her verdict. Captains of warships on active duty had broad disciplinary and punishment powers, much more so in a war zone, and she had to use the occasion to pass a clear and unmistakable message.

Zavaleta literally smelled of fear, because he knew already what the minimum verdict would be and the resulting punishment. His escort's face was hard and unfeeling, the man chosen by Guthren because he disliked Zavaleta intensely.

No one in the room showed any signs of triumph or anger, only anticipation at seeing justice done. Commander Forenza had not used her powers of discipline for nearly all her term as captain of *Stingray*, and Zavaleta' trial had attracted considerable attention. No doubt several off duty crewmembers were finding reasons to be near the bridge, to spread the word about the outcome the moment Siobhan pronounced her verdict.

In the three days since the incident, morale had shown heartening signs of improvement, and that had been most evident in the performance she obtained from the crew during the last few drills.

Guthren had told her about the sermon he had laid on the chiefs and POs, putting the bullies on notice. He laughed when he described the way some of the non-coms had edged away from Zavaleta' friends, now that their power over the lower decks was being throttled. A few might give some problems, but the big cox'n would take care of them in a way befitting his job as chief of the frigate.

"Petty Officer Zavaleta, I have carefully considered the evidence given, and I must find as follows. Charge Number One, Article 129 of the Code of Naval Discipline, uttering threats: guilty. Charge Number Two, Article 120 of the Code of Naval Discipline, unlawful use of force: guilty." She could not find him guilty of the more serious charge of assaulting a subordinate, thanks to the lack of direct evidence, but unlawful use of force would do just fine. "And charge number three, Article 130 of the Code of Naval Discipline, conduct prejudicial in that you consumed alcohol while the ship was dry: guilty."

For a moment, Dunmoore thought Zavaleta was going to faint. And so he should, she repressed a cruel smile. His life would become a living hell until she found a way to transfer him.

"Before I pronounce sentence, I will ask your divisional officer for anything that would mitigate your sentence. Mister Drex?"

"Sir." The second officer came to attention, his face expressionless. "PO Zavaleta' performance of his duties has been satisfactory."

Siobhan raised her eyebrows in surprise. Damning with faint praise. The wretched bosun's mate deserved it, but usually a divisional officer made more of an effort than that. Drex was probably feeling the heat. Zavaleta had been one of his non-coms, and his long history of bullying was a direct indictment of Drex's leadership. After high hopes, the mustang was proving to be a disappointment.

"Very well. Petty Officer Zavaleta, I sentence you to a reduction in rank to able spacer," Zavaleta whimpered in despair, as the reduction would condemn him to life on the lower deck with the ratings he had tormented. "And you will serve thirty days of detention on board this ship, said detention to occur when you are off watch. March Able Spacer Zavaleta to the brig, cox'n."

"Sir." Guthren saluted. "Left TURN. Quick MARCH."

When Zavaleta and his escort were gone, Siobhan rose and stretched her long limbs. "He will be beached the moment we touch port again. In the meantime, cox'n, make sure nobody takes it out on the bastard's hide. There will be an end to the violence in this ship, period."

"Aye, aye, sir." He saluted and left.

Siobhan looked speculatively at the second officer.

"Tell me, Mister Drex, were you aware of what was going on in your department? This informal counseling bullshit, I gather, has been happening for a long time."

"No, sir." Drex's tone was somber, but his eyes refused to meet hers.

"I see." Siobhan wanted to scream 'bullshit' at him, but it would have been undignified. "I must say I'm disappointed in you. You were a chief petty officer, and chiefs are supposed to know everything that's happening on a ship. More than that, an officer must know what's going on in his division. In my opinion, you have been derelict in your duties. I could slap you with a report of shortcomings for this, but I shall let it slide," her tone hardened, "as long as there is no repeat performance. You will do your duty to the ship, the people under your care, and me or you will find yourself a new home. Understood?"

"Sir." Drex's face remained carved in granite. Not a hint of emotion crossed his eyes. For a brief moment, Siobhan found his lack of human reaction disturbing.

"Dismissed."

As Drex marched off stiffly, Kery appeared, fussing about to ensure Dunmoore signed all the necessary forms making Zavaleta' sentence legal. War had given a ship's captain greater powers, but it had not cut down on the mass of paperwork. By the time she thumb-printed the last pad, she felt the niggling desire to share her annoyance with the rest of the crew.

Siobhan rose, poked her head through the door to the bridge, and called out, "Officer of the watch, the fusion reactor has gone critical, shorting out the plasma conduits, the main gun capacitors, and life support."

Kowalski, who had the watch, turned around to glance at the captain, that damned ironic look still pasted all over her fine-featured face. She, like the other officers, was no longer surprised at Dunmoore's unannounced drills. It was slowly becoming a kind of competition, with the captain devising increasingly tougher situations, and the watch responding with equally increasing efficiency. If Kowalski realized that Dunmoore was manipulating them into playing her game, she gave no sign.

"Aye, aye, sir." The signals officer slapped the intercom on the chair's armrest. "All hands, this is the bridge, the fusion plant has gone critical. Damage control teams to engineering. Report on status of plasma conduits and gun capacitors." Kowalski looked back at Siobhan as the alarm sirens began to whoop loudly, and smiled. Then, she turned to the intercom again.

"This is a drill, I repeat, this is a drill. Do not prepare to jettison the fusion reactor."

Satisfied, Siobhan nodded and returned to the sanctity of her ready room, to chart the progress of the damage control teams on her master console. The buggers were indeed getting somewhere fast with all the remedial training. In the end, all this crew needed was a bit of attention and a lot of hard work.

Siobhan Dunmoore was giving them that, in spades.

— Eleven —

"Yard Master Hralk is nothing but an excrement sucking plaything of the spineless women who disgrace the robes of imperial admirals," Brakal snarled as he paced his small, dark cabin. He slammed his massive fist into the palm of his other hand, the sound of mailed leather striking mailed leather loud in the confines of the room.

"How dare he delay *Tol Vakash*'s refit even longer? Three weeks? Unacceptable, Jhar!"

"Agreed, but you can do little," Jhar replied, eerily calm in the midst of his commander's fury. The first officer was all too conscious of his role as sober second thought to Brakal's forceful personality. He had to make sure the Clan Lord of the Makkar did not let his ferocious disregard for danger take him into areas where even his finely honed tactical mind became useless. If Brakal vanished into the dungeons of the *Tai Kan*, how long before Sub-Commander Jhar and other low-born Warriors suffered the same fate. "If Hralk wishes to place self-preservation first, and give the flagship a new coat of paint, then we have no choice."

"There are always choices, Jhar," Brakal bellowed, "only death removes all options, and I am alive. Do not," he pointed a gloved finger at his first officer, "seek to placate me with your reassuring platitudes, this time, miscreant. I know only too well how you strive to manipulate me, but enough is enough. *Tol Vakash* is a warship, not an oversized yacht, and she is needed on the line. Bugger the flagship and all those who fornicate aboard her."

Brakal stabbed the intercom unit on the small, obsidian desk. "Have my shuttle ready to depart."

"*Kha*," the harsh voice of the duty officer replied. "Your shuttle is at your command."

Brakal turned to Jhar and grinned cruelly. "Yard Master Hralk will have an uninvited guest at his midday meal. Maybe I will find out what happens to all the fresh rations we never receive. And maybe Hralk will find a way to refit *Tol Vakash* much sooner. It is all a question of motivation, eh, Jhar?"

"Tread carefully, commander."

"I shall tread with as much caution as if I were a hunter entering a *kroorath*'s lair," Brakal's grin widened, uncovering sharp, yellowing teeth.

"That is what I fear, commander." Had Jhar been human, he would have sighed in exasperation. But being Shrehari, he merely growled. "Just remember that Hralk is not a mighty *kroorath* but a cowardly, venomous *yatakan*. Even if he is the whelp of a noble line."

Brakal laughed. "You insult the *yatakan* by comparing them to that inflated piece of toad shit. And anyway, the Gralik are not a noble line. Hralk's ancestors sold their women as whores for low caste dung-collectors. The shit still sticks to their heels."

*

Toralk flew his commander over to the massive orbital shipyard in silence, his wordless disapproval as clear as Jhar's openly voiced misgivings. Brakal, much admired for his battle prowess and leadership, was a mere infant in the murky world of political favors and constant hypocrisy. His brother Mharak had been trained for both war and politics, not the commander, and Brakal's inclination to charge into touchy situations had more than once given his close friends and retainers concern for their collective survival. That Brakal had survived so long was more a result of his popularity as a war hero than his standing as Clan Lord.

The loyal bodyguard and pilot did not deny Yard Master Hralk desperately needed a reminder that there was a war going on. He, like the others on *Tol Vakash,* wanted nothing more than to return to fighting the humans. But they wanted to do so under Brakal's orders. And the commander was about to charge into the slime of home world politics again.

The orbital shipyard hung before them like a fantastic construct from some ancient saga about a long lost civilization. A spider web of box-like struts radiated from a thick central core, each construct big enough to hold a battleship. Brakal snarled at the sight of an empty bay, vowing that it would soon house *Tol Vakash*.

"Unidentified shuttle, you are not cleared to approach the shipyard. Remove yourself from the security zone now, or face the consequences of your disobedience," a pompous, youthful voice ordered over the open frequency.

Toralk glanced questioningly at his commander. "Lord?"

"Stop calling me Lord," Brakal growled, "and open a visual link with that young puppy."

Moments later the dark, bony face of a pure race imperial officer appeared on the screen. A product of the hereditary Warrior caste and the Imperial Academy, the young officer nevertheless managed to appear stylish and soft, like most aristocratic whelps these days. He had probably never served a tour in the war zone, and if his sire's political connections held, would probably never do so and still enjoy the promotions *real* officers had to fight for.

"You will clear me for landing now, excrescence," Brakal replied, scowling, "or I will throttle you with your own intestines for your insolence."

The officer recognized the legendary Brakal, for his face changed from its arrogant mien to the expression of a polished courtier who knew his social and military rank.

"Many pardons, Lord Commander, I did not know your illustrious presence was aboard that insignificant shuttle."

Toralk snorted. The officer's statement was a bald-faced lie. The shuttle's transponder functioned flawlessly and identified the craft as Brakal's personal barge. A flash of annoyance crossed the officer's face when he realized the snort had come from a lowly enlisted spacer, but he kept his oily, insincere mask of abject civility. Brakal, however, was more vocal than his pilot.

"In that case, lieutenant, I suggest you kill your sensor technician, or better yet, hand him over to the *Tai Kan*, for his inefficiency is a danger to the Emperor."

"Indeed, Lord. I regret, however, that I cannot let you land without clearance from Commander Hralk."

"You *what*?" Brakal snarled. "How dare you forbid a Commander of the Deep Space Fleet from landing on an imperial station? Clear me now, turd."

The lieutenant visibly blanched at Brakal's fury. Fear of his own Yard Master warred with fear of the legendary Brakal. In the end, he did what home world maggots did best: he equivocated, with a keen eye to running for shelter beneath his superior's skirts.

"I shall advise Commander Hralk of your request, sir. In the meantime, may I offer you a landing berth on shuttle deck six?"

Brakal knew very well that deck six was the furthest from the yard's command center, the tradesman's entrance, so to speak. He stared at the lieutenant. "Shuttle deck one, insect, this instant, and I shall overlook your insubordinate behavior."

"Lord," the officer nodded, unable to find enough courage to stall the commander any further, no matter what Hralk had ordered. "You are cleared for shuttle deck one. Please commence your approach."

Brakal did not reply for a few moments. Then, he took pity on the lieutenant, for in granting the Lord of the Makkar a priority berth, he had assured himself of the ire of Hralk. In a low, dangerous voice, the commander said, "Take some advice, young puppy. Make the difference between a *kroorath* and a *yatakan*, and learn how to deal with each. Otherwise, though you may stay far from the honorable lines of battle, you will just as surely die."

With a savage gesture, he cut the link and sat back in his hard seat. Toralk needed no instructions to start his approach, though his scowl remained as dark as ever. The battle of wills between the impetuous Brakal and the politically wily Hralk had begun even before the two met face-to-face. It was not a good omen.

Toralk's control of the shuttle contrasted sharply with the mood of his passenger. His landing was so soft, the slight bump of struts meeting deck did not even register over the low hum of the thrusters. Stretching his large frame, Brakal climbed out of the small craft, nostrils filling with the scents of hot metal, ozone, and harsh chemicals.

He nodded once at Toralk and strode across the shuttle bay toward the sentry post guarding access to the station proper. At his approach, the young spacer standing watch snapped to attention and saluted.

"Your business, commander," he asked curtly.

"My business is with the Yard Master, the Honorable Hralk." The way Brakal said 'honorable' left no doubt of his low regard for the station commander. The spacer stared at Brakal for a few heartbeats, and then nodded, deciding it was better for his continuing health to let the visitor proceed without further stalling.

"As you wish, *Kha*. Pass."

Brakal gave the sentry a toothy grin and unerringly headed down the maze of passages toward the station's command center. Yard workers and officers saluted him as he strode by, their looks either curious or knowing as they recognized the Imperial Fleet's most aggressive and successful captain. When he entered the rarefied command levels, the decor changed from the austere, hard look common throughout the Fleet, to the kind of sickening luxury all too prevalent near the core of the Empire. Here, the war remained a distant business, one transacted by the uncouth, low caste Shrehari who manned the deep space vessels.

In the plush antechamber to Hralk's office, a young female, dressed to provide more stimulation than a deprived front-line spacer could handle, rose from behind an ornate wood desk and bowed briefly, giving him an uncluttered view of her charms.

"I am Borunna, aide to the Yard Master. How may I help the noble lord?" She eyed him warily.

Brakal considered her for a moment, surprised that Hralk was allowed a civilian secretary on a military station. She was undeniably attractive, with a full head of deep red hair, slanted eyes, and smooth skin, stretched tautly over the bony ridges of her face and shoulders. Her words had an exotic accent, and that, along with her unusual appearance, marked her as a mixed-blood, a product of the mating between a Shrehari and one of the subject races. An appealing combination in a private whore. Hralk deprived himself of little, the fat pig.

"Tell the honorable Commander Hralk that Brakal wishes to speak with him now."

"I regret, but Commander Hralk is in conference, and cannot be disturbed. Would you care to make an appointment?"

"I would care to see him now, Borunna." Brakal snarled and closed the space to the door in two steps. Just as he laid his hand on the door latch, he heard a rustling of silk behind him.

"Please, commander," the secretary said, courtly regret filling her voice as she pointed a nasty blaster at him, "I have orders to preserve the Honorable Hralk's privacy."

Brakal looked at her in astonishment for a few moments, then burst out laughing as he dropped his hand to his side. Borunna, thinking the moment passed, dropped the aim of her blaster to the floor as she smiled back. It was sufficient. In a flash, Brakal seized the woman, smelling her delightful perfume, and wrenched the weapon out of her delicate hand.

He held her warm body for longer than necessary, feeling arousal course through him. Then, the scourge of the Commonwealth Fleet released the half-caste secretary and gently pushed her into a waiting chair. He pocketed the gun.

Still smiling, Brakal opened the door to Hralk's office and walked in.

Yard Master Hralk, mouth full of bloody meat, fingers shiny with the juices of his midday meal, looked up in anger at the intrusion. The desk before him lay covered with silver dishes, each holding a delicacy whose aroma made Brakal's mouth water.

"Greetings, Hralk," he bellowed. "Kind of you to invite me to this feast."

Hralk, mouth full, could not reply without losing face, though his expression darkened almost comically. In three steps, Brakal reached the large desk and grabbed a handful of grapes. While Hralk convulsively swallowed his food, he popped the blue fruit into his mouth one by one, smiling at the fresh, tangy taste.

"We never get these delicacies out on the line, you know. But I am pleased to see you eat well. It aids the war effort immeasurably."

"Get out of here, Brakal," Hralk finally said, "or I will have my guards throw you out."

Brakal shook his head, grimacing. "It saddens me to receive such a cold welcome from a fellow officer. And here I thought you would invite me to partake in your meal, offer me your hospitality, as a visitor to your fief. I suppose the exigencies of war take precedence over our revered traditions."

The words and tone remained light, but the import of their significance was not lost on Hralk. Neither were the many meanings attached to them. Had Hralk possessed more courage, he would have chosen to take Brakal's comments as an insult and demanded reparation. But the plump, soft Yard Master, like so many of the home planet's nobility, feared the man who commanded such loyalty and respect among the Deep Space Fleet. It was a feeling that humiliated Hralk and made him lose face in front of himself and his ancestors.

Brusquely, he gestured at the dishes. "Eat then, Lord of the Makkar, and be damned."

Brakal smiled as he reached out for a leg of *geta*. "Your generosity does you honor, Hralk." He bit into the tender meat and growled. "Most excellent. I compliment you on your choice of cook. Unfortunately, we see little *geta* on the fighting ships."

He sat on a corner of the desk, his massive bulk dominating the sitting Yard Commander.

"You know, Hralk, I have always asked myself where those food requests we send go to. It seems the choicest rations never quite make it to our tenders when we are out on patrol. But as long as you eat well, I suppose..." He shrugged dismissively.

Hralk growled at the naked insult, but as before, chose not to take offense. "State your business," he said instead, "and be gone before I inform the Admiralty of your uncouth behavior."

"I quite agree," Brakal replied, around a mouthful of meat, "the air on a warship is much healthier than the rich environment of the shipyards, or the Admiralty for that matter. Tell me, Hralk, are you invited to the Emperor's levee in three days?"

The question was another deliberate insult and Hralk, to his credit, did not answer. Only admirals and Clan Lords attend the child-Emperor's levees, occasions that Brakal tried to avoid like the plague when he was on Shrehari Prime.

Hralk, on the other hand, though a noble, was neither clan lord nor admiral, and was shut out of the highest social functions of the home world. As a second son, he would probably never attend a levee, unless his elder brother died, which remained unlikely, as that worthy had decided to spend the war tending to the family estates.

"I apologize," Brakal continued, "I forgot your duties do not permit you to spend your time on frivolities. I, however, must be there. Not, as you may think, a pleasant way to spend one's time. But unavoidable, with the reception line and all. Ah, the reception line," Brakal took an absent bite from the drumstick, looking at the ceiling, "where the Regent asks all those annoying questions, such as how are you? How is your ship? When will you return to battle? You do well to avoid the levees, my friend. I, on the other hand, will have to tell the Regent that my ship is still awaiting repairs; that I cannot serve my Emperor by killing humans for many weeks yet. Quite embarrassing, you know. Then, the Regent will probably also ask why my ship awaits repairs for so long when there is an empty bay in the orbital shipyards."

Brakal glanced at Hralk out of the corner of his eyes as he kept on eating. He saw many thoughts flash across the fat officer's eyes, and was amused by the struggle between belief and disbelief in his face. For one living so close to the intrigues of the home world, Hralk was surprisingly transparent. But maybe that is what commended him to Trage and his cronies, for the post of Yard Master was an important one.

"I wonder," Brakal continued, fighting to keep amusement from his heavy-browed features. "Will Admiral Trage tell the Regent that the empty bay is for the flagship, which desperately needs a new coat of paint, or will he tell her that he knows not why it is empty while a famous warship awaits repairs? It could make for an entertaining evening. Are you a gambler, Hralk?"

"Damn you to hell, Brakal, you, and your low caste ways." The Yard Master's snarl was subdued as he swiveled his chair to look out at space through the porthole behind the desk.

"Low caste ways, Honorable Hralk?" Brakal asked softly, his words underscored by a subtle tone of menace.

Only too late did the Yard Master realize the magnitude of the insult he had given the most redoubtable fighter in the Fleet. A man who held his honor above all else.

Turning around in sudden fear, Hralk hastily said, "I apologize for those words, Lord of the Makkar. They were unworthy of you, me, and the Empire we serve as Warriors. The pressures of work, you know."

When Brakal chose not to reply, picking a ripe fruit instead from one of the silver plates and biting into it with a loud crunch, Hralk turned toward his computer console. He hemmed and hawed for a few moments.

"Ah, I have good news, commander. By re-arranging the schedule slightly, your ship can take the empty bay now, and the flagship will not be much delayed."

"Good news indeed, noble Hralk," Brakal's smile was chilling, as if to hammer home how close the Yard Master had come to a challenge of honor. "When can I dock my ship?"

"As soon as you wish."

"If you will give your people the order to receive her, I will call *Tol Vakash* now and have her dock within the hour."

Hralk nodded curtly, his ill manners returning now that the crux of peril had passed. He gave his orders and Brakal, to Jhar's astonishment, called the ship directly and gave the word to dock. It had been so easy; Brakal wondered why he had not done it earlier when Jhar had first announced there would be a delay. If this was an example of what passed for backroom dealing and intrigue on the home world, then he had nothing to fear. These soft turds were no match for Brakal's wits.

He stood and grinned at Hralk. "With my thanks, Yard Master. I shall now leave you to your meal."

Hralk grunted and waved him away, morose at losing this contest of wills. Outside, Brakal tossed the blaster back to Borunna and gave her his best leer. Then, he headed for the shuttle deck's observation platform, to see *Tol Vakash* dock. Word had already passed through the shipyard like wildfire, and Toralk looked at his lord with deep suspicion as the big officer stood by the large windows, an expression of satisfaction softening his harsh features.

"Success, Lord?"

"As you can see, Toralk," Brakal waved expansively at the sight of the big, gull-winged cruiser slowly sailing into the empty docking bay under Jhar's deft control. "One has but to know which buttons to push. Hralk was very cooperative."

Toralk grunted, wondering what new troubles his impulsive commander had called down on them all. Had he but known, his worries would have increased a hundred-fold, for Brakal had been all bluff, as Hralk would eventually find out, once *Tol Vakash* was safely docked and undergoing the needed repairs.

There was no levee in three days, and even if there had been, Brakal would not have attended. No one, least of all the Regent, would have noticed the absence. She was under the Council's soft thumb, some said in Trage's soft bed. And even if Brakal had attended, his words to the usually half-drunk Dowager Empress in a reception line would have been so much water flowing over worn stones. But as he had gambled, Hralk knew none of these things, being a younger son and shut out from the highest levels of the capital's social morass.

Thinking back at the ease with which he had frightened Hralk out of his vindictive little game, Brakal laughed softly. Toralk, who knew his Commander and Liege Lord's moods well, felt his worry increase. But he could not deny that whatever Brakal had done, it worked. Soon, *Tol Vakash* would return to the war, where only military skill counted, and the long arm of the *Tai Kan* remained feeble and ineffective.

Later that day, Brakal recounted to Jhar his conversation with Hralk, mirth shaking his great frame. Even the first officer had to admit his commander possessed more skill in dealing with scum than he previously believed. Yet his worrying nature would not find as much pleasure in the outcome.

"Commander," Jhar said, shaking his head, "you have made a very dangerous enemy. Hralk has lost face in such a way as to bear an eternal grudge. He will attempt revenge, now or later and he has too many friends to remain harmless."

Brakal snorted in derision. "Hralk is a spineless woman, from a family of shit-eating whores. He would never dare move against the Clan Lord of the Makkar. We are one of the oldest families in the Empire, and that still counts for something these days."

"Just take care, commander. Remember that the *yatakan* can be as deadly as the *kroorath*."

Brakal grunted, remembering his words to the young duty officer. "No matter, Jhar. Let us get this ship ready and return to where there is honor to be found, and may the seven *irathis* take Hralk and his ilk down to their fires of torment."

*

Jhar's words proved to be prophetic in a way Brakal had never imagined. Three days later, Admiral Trage summoned him planet side. The old commander-in-chief of the Imperial Fleet received him in the privacy of a disgustingly luxurious office suite, a mask of barely suppressed hatred distorting his desiccated features. He did not invite Brakal to sit, nor did he offer refreshments. Brakal took this abusive treatment in stride, keeping a sardonic expression on his dark lips as he stood stiffly in front of the platinum-trimmed desk, wondering how many vital ship systems could be built with the precious metal thus wasted on furniture.

"Brakal," the admiral rumbled, "the Council warned you to hear and obey, and cease doing things according to your whims. It appears that warning had no effect. The orderly running of the Imperial Fleet cannot account for ship commanders, no matter how noble, disrupting tight schedules and long laid plans. I tell you now, for the last time, obey your betters or suffer the consequences. Your rank does not give you leave to disregard orders as you please, and will not protect you from punishment."

Brakal smiled, knowing that Trage could not tear into him for his actions at the shipyard. Hralk's obstructionism was just as indefensible, and would create a strong wave of discontent among the Warriors by elevation who followed Brakal if the commander decided to spread the word that home world scum played petty games with those who fought and died for the honor of the Empire. Trage knew this also.

"You are amused, Commander Brakal?" The admiral asked sharply, a hint of menace in his matter-of-fact tone.

"I was merely thinking, Lord Admiral, that rotating senior officers to and from the war zone would avoid any future misunderstandings. Those who have experienced the exhilaration and fear of battle can make better decisions about the use of our Empire's resources in this struggle."

Trage stiffened as if slapped. The insult was veiled, but clear nonetheless. Most of the High Command had never served in battle, and neither had their sycophants here on the home world. That the Admiralty remained blind to the deepening divisions between the Deep Space Fleet and the rear echelon fornicators bode ill for the future of the war, as the minor dispute between Brakal and Hralk had shown.

"You walk dangerously, Brakal," Trage warned. "I shall not waste breath warning you again. Take your ship back to the line, and be careful. Clan Lords, even of the revered Makkar, are not immune to the displeasure of the Emperor."

Or the Council, Brakal silently completed the threat, since the child-Emperor and his Regent acted as the Council ordered. His father had already found out it was not an empty threat, though proof of Trage's involvement had never surfaced.

"You are dismissed, commander." Trage turned his attention to the stack of printouts on the desk.

Brakal saluted and turned on his heels, wondering about the admiral's real intentions, and what he had hoped to gain by this interview. That Hralk had complained, he did not doubt. The Yard Master could hardly confront Brakal in person. It would be an open acknowledgment of his loss of face, and could only, had Hralk been a man of courage and honor, end with a challenge. Instead, the fat turd had whined to Trage, and the demons knew which other powerful men in the capital, not realizing that his loss of face was thereby compounded. Even worse, Trage's mention of the incident showed the admiral had as little appreciation of a Warrior's honor as Hralk. But the powerful on Shrehari Prime were honorless turds from upstart Clans with no history. To them, it did not matter.

What did matter was Trage's warning. It lacked the subtlety of previous threats and Brakal realized that his position had shifted once again in the unending swamp of Shrehari politics, and not for the best.

The commander passed the sentry box outside the High Command palace, absently returning the salutes of the soldiers, and let his feet take him toward the lower town, his preferred shortcut to the spaceport.

If, he wondered, the poisonous toads cared so little about face, how much did they care about the feelings of the new Warriors? All those officers who had made loyalty to the Empire as much of a virtue as their contempt for the spineless Council members, represented a potent force, one which could bring about the collapse of the current power structure. All they needed was a leader and an excuse to rise and name a military dictator, a *Kho'sahra* who would clean out the filth of home world politics.

For the first time, it occurred to Brakal that maybe Trage and his cronies did realize this, and saw him as the greatest danger, as the one man who could unite the Deep Space Fleet and topple the Council. The man who would be *Kho'sahra*.

His victories, noble lineage, and unimpeachable sense of honor made him justly famous, as did his open disdain for the weaklings in the Admiralty. He commanded the undying loyalty of his crew, and if rumors were true, that of many raised to the Warrior caste on merit throughout the Fleet. Perhaps that was why the Council refused to let him fight in his successful manner, promote him to command a strike force, or give him the honors he had earned.

Brakal stopped, struck by the sudden light that illuminated the events of the last few months. He had been politically naïve and thereby missed too many chances to further the cause of the Empire in this endless war. He grinned at the revelation and then realized his instincts had brought him deep into the slums of the capital, where the stench of shit mixed with that of thousands of unwashed people, living topsy-turvy in crumbling ancient houses. Still, this smell was better than the stench of dishonor in Trage's office.

The stream of lower town beggars, pimps, merchants, whores and petty criminals flowed around him, all careful to stay out of arm's reach of the tall, powerful officer with the wicked dagger stuck into his sash. In the east, the red sun settled on the horizon, painting the rooftops of the city with great strokes of blood and illuminating the brooding imperial palace on the hilltop with an eerie glow.

Brakal took his bearings and set off through a narrow alley on his left, dodging the piles of rotting refuse and waste. His thoughts returned to the Council and their fears, and the commander's attention to his surroundings wavered for an instant. But that instant was enough.

A cloaked figure stepped out of the shadows and soundlessly barred his way, the gunmetal gray blade of a serrated knife flashing dully in the last rays of the sun. Brakal instinctively fell into a fighting stance, drawing his own dagger as his eyes probed the assassin, searching for an opening, while a single thought flashed through his mind: *Tai Kan*. Trage had decided to do away with him after all.

As the assassin came on, low and wary, like a professional, Brakal became aware of a second man behind him. The bastards knew his habit of taking the lower town route and had boxed him in. Brakal whirled to the side, trying to get his back against a wall so he could see both assailants, but his boot stepped into a squelching mess of shit, and he slipped backward, falling to the ground. The long, thin line of a weighted garrote flashed by his cheek and Brakal briefly thanked the gods for the pile of excrement in his path, for if he had not slipped, the razor thin wire would have wrapped around his throat, and he would have died.

Though by how much that had prolonged his life was debatable, because he was now as vulnerable as a child, sitting on his ass, with two professional killers silently closing in. Brakal had no hope of help from the slum dwellers. They knew better than to interfere with an assassination.

The one with the serrated knife drew back his arm, preparing to throw the wicked blade at Brakal while the other had gathered his garrote and swung its weighted end in an ever larger circle, ready to wrap it around the commander's neck and decapitate him. Brakal froze with indecision. He had but one knife, and one chance of killing one attacker. As soon as he committed himself, the other would strike.

Brakal snarled in defiance and yelled the Makkar battle cry as he pushed himself up for a lunge at the garrotter, gambling that he could come under the spinning wire and dispatch the assassin before the other could react.

At that moment, a blaster flashed brightly from the other end of the alley, and the garrotter's head exploded in a mess of blood, bone, and brain tissue. Surprised, Brakal turned on the other killer, but before either could move, the blaster spoke again, punching a smoking hole through the man's chest.

Brakal stood up straight, sheathed his knife, and watched his rescuer approach. He was a non-descript Shrehari without caste marks, a civilian whose face and eyes spoke of things no ordinary civilian should know. The commander's lips twisted in an ironic smile.

"Lower town is dangerous at night, Lord Commander," the man said, his blaster disappearing under his loose jacket. "You should use the military transport service."

Brakal shrugged. "Danger is the spice of existence. My thanks for your timely intervention."

The man nodded once. "You should not be troubled any more, Lord of the Makkar. Enjoy the evening." He turned away and vanished into the shadows.

Brakal's smile transformed into a feral grin as he brushed the filth off his uniform and stepped over the ruined bodies of his would-be assassins. His rescuer was *Tai Kan*, which could only mean the ambush was another of Trage's warnings, this one as clear and direct as possible: the Clan Lord of the Makkar could die the moment the Council decided his life was over.

Which meant they really did fear his power and influence within the Deep Space Fleet and had begun to fear it even before Brakal discovered it. The irony tickled the warship commander to the very core of his being.

So be it then. If Brakal had a power base to build on, and then build he would, for the Empire, and for the survival of the Clan Makkar. *Kho'sahra* Brakal. It had the ring of destiny. But first, he had to get his ship back to the line, where his supporters overwhelmed the carrion eaters of the Council.

— Twelve —

"Secure from general quarters, Mister Pushkin," Siobhan rose from the captain's chair and suppressed a yawn. "I think we've finally got all the drills straight."

"Aye, sir," Pushkin cracked a small grin. "By now, they can man all their stations sleepwalking."

Siobhan smiled wryly at her first officer. "I'd rather they did it wide awake, but you're right."

She had drilled the crew hard during the past week, and they had responded well. A steady hand at the helm and an end to the bullying had gone far in restoring the ship's efficiency. As the crippled steward at Starbase 31 said in what seemed a lifetime ago, *Stingray* had a decent crew beneath the lousy reputation.

"We shall see when we meet our first Shrehari," she continued. "There's no substitute for real-time experience."

"Aye," Pushkin nodded, the grin disappearing. "Anything else, captain?"

"No. Go rest."

Alone in her cabin, Siobhan sighed wearily and dropped into the padded chair behind the desk. Drilling a crew to a fine pitch was hard work, and she had not slept more than four hours in a row since Zavaleta's trial. But as she had said, their first space battle would tell whether the training had stuck.

Morale was improving along with the hard work, and she could sense the growing respect of the officers and crew for their new skipper. But as yet, the invisible barrier between her and the others remained as solid as before. The officers had not yet invited her to dine in the wardroom, nor did she feel confident enough to invite a few of them to join her in her quarters for a quiet meal. She lived in splendid isolation, and that seemed to suit the others just fine.

It all came down to trust, a concept the *Stingrays* had forgotten and did not appear inclined to relearn along with their duties. Too many unanswered questions remained to poison the atmosphere. The undercurrent of fear she had felt the first day still remained although its presence dimmed under the crew's better spirits.

Dunmoore did not have the time or energy to pursue the things that troubled her, but that did not stop them from bothering her during her precious few resting hours. As much as she wanted to ignore the past, it hung so heavily over the frigate that she knew she had to confront it sooner rather than later. If the present atmosphere did not change, the crew would never become a match for the best Shrehari crews, like Brakal's.

More than once, she had come close to confronting Pushkin, but always something held her back. And now that the first officer started showing signs of thawing, she did not want to destroy the precious rapport between them.

Shrugging, Dunmoore got a mug of coffee from the small urn behind her desk and opened her personal log for the daily entry. In a sense, Nosey Bertram had been right: the captain's primary concern was to turn this into an efficient ship with an equally skilled crew. The family feeling would come after if it ever did.

However, after a hard week of deep space maneuvers and drills, she was as confident as she could be that *Stingray* would not succumb to the first Shrehari raider they met. Though not in any way a capable ship, she was at least ready for most unpleasant surprises. Should they meet Brakal, or another commander of his caliber, it was a safe bet that they would not even have the chance to bring a limping wreck home. Fortunately, there was only one Brakal. For now.

Dunmoore stared absently at the old ship's clock, ticking away softly. A captain's personal log was anything but. If something went wrong, it along with the ship's logs would end up before a board of inquiry. Some things had to remain in the privacy of her thoughts.

"Bridge to captain."

She frowned at the interruption. The ship's clock had just rung seven bells in the evening watch, and it was high time for bed.

"Dunmoore."

"Sir, Lieutenant Kowalski. Sensors have picked up a contact traveling on a course parallel to the border. It doesn't read like a military vessel. The energy curves are too flat. But if it's a legitimate civilian, he's pretty far from the patrolled star lanes."

"Has he picked us up yet?"

"Probably not, sir. He's in hyperspace. His sensor is next to useless. We've got him at the outer limits of our range, which means he wouldn't be able to see us with civvie-grade stuff even if he was sublight."

"Any transponder signal?"

"No. But that's not unusual this close to the enemy."

"Agreed. Lay in an intercept course. When he emerges, we'll order him to heave to. It'll be a good occasion to practice boarding party procedures."

"Aye, aye, sir. What if he refuses to stop?"

"Then, in accordance with standing orders, we open fire."

All civilian spacers had been warned by the navy years ago to cooperate or suffer the consequences. If he was legitimate, he would content himself with some irritated grumbling. If he was not...

Dunmoore suppressed her desire to return to the bridge and take over. Kowalski needed the seasoning, and if she got into the habit of rushing up whenever something unusual happened, she would never get a moment of peace. More importantly, by letting Kowalski keep the con, it showed she trusted her officers. Maybe the example would inspire them to show some faith in their captain.

"Call me when we've intercepted him. Dunmoore, out."

For a fraction of a second, Siobhan saw Kowalski's surprised and delighted expression. Then, the screen turned to black, returning Captain Dunmoore to her splendid isolation. Seconds later, she felt the wrenching nausea of the jump as the frigate went FTL to intercept the other ship. Ten, then fifteen minutes passed without word, and the captain fretted, wondering whether Kowalski would botch the action. This was the first operation *Stingray*'s crew executed in real-time conditions under Dunmoore's command, and she wanted it to work well if only to raise the crew's self-confidence.

Then, unexpectedly, the battle stations siren broke a silence underscored only by the soft thrumming of the jump drives. Siobhan grinned with pleasure. Kowalski had not forgotten her standing orders. Normal wartime procedures required warships to go to general quarters when approaching an unidentified ship, but on *Stingray*, Forenza's incompetence had let the crew slip into laziness. As a consequence, Siobhan had to drum in her exacting standards. That at least had taken hold.

Quickly, Siobhan grabbed her emergency kit and left her cabin. Just as she stepped through the door, the nausea of emergence twisted her gut. She immediately went up to the bridge, satisfied at seeing the controlled rush of a crew that knew what it was doing. On the screen, a tactical display showed that the other vessel had emerged five hundred thousand kilometers ahead of the frigate.

Kowalski yielded the captain's chair and reported in a clipped voice. "They've identified themselves as the fast trader *Mykonos* out of Wyvern and claim their transponder is out of order." The signals officer's tone showed a healthy disbelief. "They've agreed to comply with our orders."

"Thank you. Helm, close the distance to one kilometer. Guns, keep 'em loaded and on *Mykonos* at all times. Scan for any signs of weaponry or unusual energy readings. Mister Kowalski, check this guy's registration in the database."

"Already done, sir. The hull number, name, and homeport match. He's legit."

Dunmoore felt disappointment. No excuse to board the trader and do a thorough search, unless the sensors revealed something strange. Though she had the right to board any non-military vessel she met in the war zone, civilian captains were quick to yell harassment when a search was unjustified, and admirals were unwilling to take too much heat from the media or politically connected shipping firms.

Out of the corner of her eye, she saw Lieutenant Shara enter the bridge and head for the navigation console. When she saw the ship on the screen and the name displayed by the tactical readout, her step faltered for a moment, and something indefinable flashed through her eyes. Then the sailing master took her station and busied herself. Shara's reaction had come and gone in a flash, and Dunmoore was sure no one else had seen it, but she knew, instinctively, that the sailing master recognized the trader.

"Mister Shara," she asked mildly, "does *Mykonos*, perchance, seem familiar to you?"

Shara's shoulders stiffened, but she shook her head. Without turning around, she replied, in her irritating voice, "No, sir. Never seen it before."

Quickly, the captain scanned the bridge, looking for some reaction from the others, but all were busy at their stations and gave no sign of having heard anything. She was aware that Pushkin had taken his place, waiting for orders.

"Right. Mister Kowalski, open a hailing frequency. I want to talk to their captain. Put it on screen."

A few seconds later, the bland, clean-shaved face of a man whose age could be anywhere between thirty and sixty appeared on the main screen. His dark hair was shot with gray and he had the lines and wrinkles of a lifetime spacer etched on his tanned face.

"I am Captain Augustus Slayton of *Mykonos*." The man's eyes watched her intently, but his expression remained neutral, emotionless. His voice was deep and rich.

"Dunmoore, Commonwealth Star Ship *Stingray*, 31st Battle Group."

"A bit out of your area," he replied in a smooth tone.

Siobhan raised an eyebrow in question. *A Trader who keeps track of warship assignments?*

Slayton saw her reaction and smiled. "I gather Captain Forenza has gone on to bigger and better things," he said matter-of-factly before she could respond.

Siobhan suddenly understood that Slayton was indulging in some gallows humor; that he knew of Helen Forenza's disgrace. Even more unusual.

"You are acquainted with my predecessor?"

"Out here, near the border, we traders get to know those who protect us. It's good policy for all concerned."

Siobhan grunted in reply, making it clear she did not care for his explanation.

"What are you doing so far from the patrolled star lanes?"

"A shortcut, captain," he shrugged as if it were unimportant. "Our cargoes tend to be time sensitive, and the less time in transit, the better the profit."

Siobhan pursed her lips. "Dangerous, Captain Slayton. I could just as well have been a Shrehari on a raiding mission."

"But you're not." He gave her a soothing smile.

She stared at Slayton in silence and decided she did not like him.

The devil take standard procedure, she thought. *I'll deal with the fallout later.*

"Captain Slayton, you won't object to my sending a boarding party to inspect your ship?"

"Is that really necessary, captain." He looked and sounded disappointed. "You and I have better things to do. I'll send you a copy of our cargo manifest, bill of lading, certification and anything else you want, and we can both be on our separate ways."

"I'll certainly require a copy of all your paperwork captain, but I will insist on inspecting your ship."

Slayton' eyes hardened, and his voice took on a sharp edge. "Captain Dunmoore, I have given you no reason for this kind of treatment. I'm sure Admiral Kaleri would not approve of your disrupting honest trade."

Again, his words seemed to convey a deeper meaning. The crew watched in silence waiting for the outcome of what was turning into a battle of wills. She restrained an impulse to glance around and gage the reaction of her officers.

"And equally, Admiral Kaleri would not wish me to pass lightly over my duties. Stand by to be boarded and inspected in accordance with applicable Commonwealth Naval Orders. You may, at your leisure, complain to the nearest authorities, *after* you have complied." Siobhan's voice carried a finality that dared him to argue. Slayton' face lost all expression and he nodded.

"All right, captain. Your game. We're standing by to receive your boarding party."

"*Stingray*, out." Kowalski cut the transmission on cue.

Pushkin looked expectantly at Siobhan, eyes narrowed. "Sir?"

"Assemble a boarding party, armed and armored. I'll be leading them personally."

The first officer's eyes widened in surprise and disapproval. Captains did not conduct their own boarding parties. But Pushkin held his peace in front of the others. He had learned that much by now.

"As to the composition," she continued, "I'll want one chief, make it the bosun herself, and experienced ratings from gunnery, engineering, security, and supply."

Pushkin seemed to consider her order for a moment, then nodded as he understood why Dunmoore wanted specialists along with the usual group of bosun's mates. The specialists would be better able to notice any unusual details pertaining to their areas of expertise. It was something Siobhan had learned from Captain Prighte. The war had spawned much illegal space travel and smugglers were learning from each encounter with patrolling warships.

Dunmoore thought for a moment. She wanted a group she could trust to act properly and report honestly what they saw.

"Make one of the gunners Leading Spacer Rownes," she said. The woman had struck her as trustworthy, plus she was a former merchant gunner, which meant she knew what to look for on a trader. Devall silently nodded his approval. "Anyone among the crew who's worked on the shadier side?"

"I think Nosey Bertram used to be a thief of sorts or a smuggler before the law caught up with him and offered jail or the navy, sir," Guthren said, turning in his seat. "He's a buddy of Rownes too."

"Okay, so much the better. Put Bertram on the list. I'll be in my ready room. Warn me when we're within shuttle range. You have the con, Mister Pushkin."

"Aye, aye, sir."

In the solitude of the ready room, Siobhan wondered about her impulse to break procedure and take the boarding party herself, instead of letting the second officer do it. There was only one answer. She did not trust Drex and had not since the Zavaleta incident.

Ten minutes later, in full armor with a pistol strapped to her hip, Siobhan Dunmoore joined the boarding party on the shuttle deck. She inspected them briefly. The nine spacers wore the same armor as their captain and carried short carbines, except for Chief Foste, who held a stubby, ancient, and very deadly scattergun in her gloved hands. They also carried handheld battlefield sensors on their utility belts. Whoever had put the party together had done her homework.

The faces peering at her through the open faceplates radiated excitement at the break in routine, and Siobhan recognized Able Spacer Vincenzo. His bruises were healing nicely. Beside him stood Banger Rownes, her comforting bulk looming large and dominating the small, weasel-faced engineer's mate on her left. The latter's name tape identified him as Bertram, and Siobhan could see how the weasel-face spacer had acquired his nickname. He had the shifty look of a professional criminal.

Beside Bertram was another gunner's mate, a young, pale, and slender woman with Slavic cheekbones and a nametape that identified her as Demianova. Next in line, the purser's mate, Leading Spacer Rajmurti, returned her gaze placidly, as if joining a boarding party was an everyday occurrence. The others were bosun's mates, from the security division.

Dunmoore stepped back and ordered them to stand at ease.

"We're going over to inspect *Mykonos*. There's nothing, in particular, I'm looking for, but she may not be what she seems. Keep your eyes open and your mouths shut. Use those sensors on your belts and record everything you can. Those who are specialists concentrate on your area of expertise and visit those parts of the ship that concern you. Always stay in pairs, one specialist, and one bosun's mate. Vincenzo, you're with me. Bosun, you're with Rajmurti. Take a long look at their cargo and don't let them talk you out of a close inspection."

Foste stepped forward. "Aye, aye, sir. If I may?" When Siobhan nodded, she turned toward the boarding party. "Trang, you're with Rownes, Gonzalez, with Bertram and Christiansen with Demianova."

"I'm not expecting any trouble," Siobhan continued, "so make sure your weapons are on safe. Do not use them unless threatened or on my orders. If anything strikes you as strange, wrong, or unusual, use secure comms to tell me. Make sure none of the *Mykonos* crew can overhear you. Questions? No?" She paused. "Okay, bosun, mount up."

The boarding party climbed into the tiny shuttle and strapped in. Siobhan went up front with the pilot, who, to her surprise, was none other than Lieutenant Kowalski. The signals officer gave her captain a grin and a thumbs up, and then raised the shuttle's ramp.

The radio crackled to life with Pushkin's voice. "Boarding party, this is the bridge. We're in position one kilometer off the target's starboard side. You may launch now."

"Bridge, Dunmoore here," Siobhan replied, "General Order Eighty-Eight is in force."

"Aye, aye, sir."

"Dunmoore, out."

Kowalski looked at Siobhan for a few seconds before lighting the thrusters. General Order Eighty-Eight meant that if *Mykonos* was not legit and took the boarding party hostage, *Stingray* was to disregard their presence on board and deal with the other ship in whatever manner the acting captain thought proper. If that meant blowing her up and thereby killing the boarding party, so be it. The navy did not deal with hostage takers.

The frigate's massive shuttle deck doors opened slowly, revealing the aft lower hull framed by the jump drive nacelles. A band of stars dusted the black velvet of space in the distance, the Milky Way in all its glory. Deftly, Kowalski raised the shuttle above the deck and inched her way through the energy field keeping in the shuttle bay's atmosphere. Dunmoore felt the small hairs on the back of her neck stand up under the charge of static energy. Then, they were through, floating in space.

Kowalski swept the shuttle around the upper hull, and Siobhan took a long look at her ship. For her age and the unhappiness within her, *Stingray* remained a beautiful frigate, a marvel of technology and ingenuity, and Siobhan felt strangely touched by the sight.

Then, the shuttle swung away, toward the small, toy-like ship in the distance. As they got closer, Siobhan, and indeed the entire boarding party stared at *Mykonos*, wondering what about her had made the captain order an inspection.

The trader was sleek, built for speed and maneuverability, not for bulk cargo. Her drive nacelles seemed strangely outsized for her hull, and she sported a large number of gun blisters. *Mykonos* appeared in good repair and well cared for. Better than most traders Siobhan had seen. At a glance, the captain decided it could take on a corvette-sized warship, and probably had the legs to run from anything bigger, like a frigate. Which means Slayton could have evaded *Stingray* successfully if he'd wanted to. Maybe he really had nothing to hide.

"Cor," a disbelieving voice said behind Dunmoore, "if that's an effing trader, I'm an effing admiral."

Siobhan turned around to face the speaker, Nosey Bertram. "What makes you say that, spacer?"

"Begging' yer pardon, cap'n, but I served on smugglers with less power and guns than that one."

"Which is why you got caught and ended up in the navy," Demianova tartly replied, to the general amusement of the party. Bertram made a face at his friend.

Siobhan smiled at the ribbing, surprised that Bertram was so free about his less than sterling past. But then, the lower deck probably knew all about his pre-navy days.

"I agree with Nosey, captain," Rownes calmly stated when the merriment died down. "I've served on many fast traders, and the ones with outsized engines and heavy armament usually carry cargo they don't want the Fleet to see. But then," she shrugged, "what with the war, civvie shippers could do worse than equip their barkies with powerful drives, so maybe it don't mean anything."

Siobhan nodded. "We'll have to see when we climb aboard. Like I said, keep your eyes and ears open. If she's a smuggler, then we've got ourselves a nice prize. A ship like that would probably be bought into the service."

Eyes lit up at the mention of prizes. Pay in the Fleet was good, better than in most merchant outfits, but the wartime navy had another perk that never failed to fire up a decent crew. All ships captured, whether enemy, smuggler or pirate, became prizes of the capturing ships, and when sold by the Admiralty or taken into service, the crew received prize money equivalent to the value of the ship and its cargo. Some ships were said to be doing very well in this war, and their crews, if they lived to see the end, would return to civilian life with full pockets.

Nosey Bertram grinned broadly. "That'll be one hell of a change, cap'n, an' I says it's about time, too. Ain't making the same kinda money no more since I volunteered for the navy." His wistful tone brought on another round of laughter, and for the first time since taking command, Dunmoore started to feel comfortable with her crew.

Moments later, *Stingray*'s shuttle eased onto the trader's shuttle deck and settled on the center mark between two modern, armed, and unmarked craft. Siobhan quietly pointed at them and then at Kowalski's scanner console. The signals officer nodded her understanding. Some traders liked to use armed shuttles when calling at dangerous ports beyond the Commonwealth, but these hardly looked like the surplus stuff civilians could buy cheaply.

Kowalski then gave them thumbs up, signaling that the static charge, picked up when crossing the energy barrier, had bled away, and it was safe to disembark. The ramp dropped, and Siobhan walked through the aft compartment to climb out first. Vincenzo immediately followed her, his carbine held at the ready.

Slayton met her at the foot of the ramp, unsmiling and tense. He did not offer to shake hands. In person, the trader captain was shorter than Siobhan expected, shorter than she was, but heavier.

"Captain Dunmoore," he nodded in greeting. "I'm flattered that you're leading the boarding party yourself. Any particular reason for that or your warlike get-up?" He pointed at the body armor covering Dunmoore's battledress.

Siobhan smiled tightly. "Let's just say I wanted to stretch my legs. As for the get-up, it's standard procedure. If the shuttle loses pressure during transit…"

Slayton raised his eyebrows. "Are your shuttles in that dangerous a condition? Maybe I could sell you some of mine," he offered, a faintly patronizing smile on his lips.

Siobhan pursed her lips tightly. "Why don't we get on with it?"

"Yes," Slayton sighed, "let's. I still think you're wasting your time, captain. In fact, I know you are."

"We'll just see, won't we? Please have someone conduct Chief Foste to your cargo holds, Spacer Bertram to engineering, Spacers Rownes and Demianova to your defensive systems. I'd like to tour your bridge and examine your permits and manifests."

Slayton lost his weary look and a hint of steel glinted in his dark eyes. "You seem to be well prepared, captain." He snapped his fingers over his shoulder and a bearded, thickset man, armed with a blaster, trotted up. "Targa, take the chief to the holds. Get Hicks to give the navy a tour of engineering and Mkila to give a tour of the defensive systems."

The hard-faced merchant spacer nodded, unhappy with his orders. "Aye, cap'n."

"Captain Dunmoore," Slayton gestured toward the open door leading to the ship, "before we visit, I'd like to have a private word with you."

"As you wish," Siobhan shrugged.

Slayton led her through narrow passages to his quarters. On the way, Siobhan's alert eyes took in the excellent state of the ship, better than what she expected of a cost-cutting merchant and the hard look of the crew they passed. All were armed.

The trader captain's quarters were small and sparsely furnished, but he had a small collection of antique, printed books lining a single shelf above the bunk. Siobhan recognized several of the Anglic titles and was amused to see a copy of Machiavelli's masterwork among them.

Slayton perched himself on a corner of the desk and sighed. "Quite frankly, captain, your insistence on inspecting the *Mykonos* is presenting me with some difficulties." He rubbed his jaw with a hand that literally dripped gold and precious stones. The jewelry looked like it would keep a four-star admiral in luxury for a year. "Not that I have anything to hide from the navy, but to avoid any misunderstandings, I'm afraid I'll have to breach security. Unfortunately, that means you, and I will probably suffer some consequences."

Dunmoore remained silent, eyes on Slayton.

"You see, Captain Dunmoore, this ship is under orders from the Special Security Branch." Slayton waited to see how the naval officer would react to this revelation.

The Special Security Branch, known as SSB, was the all-powerful civilian spy and secret police arm of the Commonwealth Secretary General. The organization had used the war to expand its reach and powers, and that brought it into frequent conflict with the military.

Dunmoore, like most line officers, knew little about the Service, except that it was dangerous, unaccountable and, if rumors were true, frequently screwed the Fleet in the pursuit of its own goals. SSB agents were said to have infiltrated just about every part of the armed forces.

She repressed a sudden shiver when the thought of SSB operatives among her crew crossed her mind. If any of the stories were true, crossing the SSB was equivalent to a one-way ticket to hell. There were rumors that many dissenters had disappeared since the start of the war, supposedly in protective custody of the security services.

Siobhan took a deep breath. "Do you have any proof, Captain Slayton? I'm sure you understand that your word means little to me at this point."

The civilian laughed harshly. "Come now, Captain Dunmoore. Do you really think I carry an SSB membership card around with me? The whole point of undercover work is keeping your true allegiance hidden."

"Then I'm afraid I shall have to treat you like any civilian vessel in a war zone, captain. Is there anything else you wish to tell me?"

Slayton shook his head. "No. I just thought you should know what you're getting into. It'll be your funeral."

The temperature in the cabin dropped by several degrees when Siobhan icily asked, "Is that a threat?"

"No, Captain Dunmoore. Merely a statement of fact." He stood up and walked around his desk to pull his ship's papers from a locked drawer. "Here is my registration, manifest, safety certification and the rest of it."

"Thank you." Siobhan took each printout and read it carefully. The documents appeared in order and authorized *Mykonos* to conduct trade throughout the sector. The manifest listed the cargo as high-tech medical apparatus and pharmaceutical supplies. When she was done, Siobhan gave the printouts back to Slayton.

"Your bridge, please."

Slayton nodded and led the way out of the cabin. Vincenzo, who had been standing guard outside, watched by a civilian spacer, fell into step beside Siobhan. When she looked at him, he grimaced quickly, clearly conveying that he did not like this ship and its crew much.

The bridge was well appointed and clean. Most of the consoles were nearly new and would not have been out of place on a warship. Siobhan recorded everything she saw in silence, watched by the civilians. Vincenzo nervously fingered his carbine and moved to stay between his captain and the *Mykonos* crew.

"Foste to Dunmoore," her helmet's comm unit crackled to life.

"Dunmoore."

"Captain, can you come down to the cargo hold? I think you should see this."

"On my way. Dunmoore, out." She turned to Slayton. "I'd like to see your hold now."

He raised his eyebrows and then shrugged. "As you wish."

Foste and Rajmurti waited just inside the door to the cavernous cargo hold in the center of the *Mykonos*' main hull, a pair of civilian spacers at their side. The trader crew was distinctly angry, but the bosun's scattergun, nonchalantly held in the crook of her arm, kept them from doing anything stupid.

"Report," Siobhan ordered as her people snapped to attention.

"The contents of the containers do not match the manifest or the markings," Foste replied, glancing briefly at Slayton.

"Explain."

"We took readings of the containers, sir. Rajmurti here has a pusser's special," she pointed at the supply tech's sensor, "and what he got doesn't match any medical kit or drugs known to the Commonwealth."

Siobhan turned to Slayton and arched an eyebrow. "Any explanations, captain?"

"Only what I've told you before, Dunmoore. Take heed and steer clear."

Slayton's look and his dropping Siobhan's formal title were not lost on her and the bosun. But if the trader cum agent thought he could discourage Dunmoore with veiled threats, he had not counted on her native bullheadedness.

"In the immortal words of an ancient sea-going captain," she replied through clenched teeth, "damn the torpedoes, full steam ahead. Open any container my bosun will indicate."

"You don't really want to do that, Dunmoore. The consequences could be worse."

"So could the consequences of disobeying me, *captain*. Under Emergency Regulations, you either do as I say, or I will impound this ship and all its contents. Needless to say, you'll be under arrest."

"Fine," Slayton replied angrily, "it's your bloody funeral Dunmoore. I'll need a certificate explaining why you broke the customs seals." He savagely nodded at one of his crewmembers. "Open the bloody container."

Foste pointed at a meter-high, blue crate. "The manifest records this thing as carrying an OR table with a full suite of medical monitors. I say it doesn't."

Under Captain Slayton' furious glare, the two spacers broke the crate's customs seals, undogged the lid and flipped it open with an angry shove. Rajmurti, who had remained silent until now, stepped up and peered into the crate, working his sensor.

"Strange," he said, "my readings are very clear now. The crate must be shielded."

Siobhan smirked at Slayton, defying him to explain that away. Shielded containers were legal only to transport radiation sensitive organics, not machinery which, by usual standards, had built-in shielding.

"Can I remove the packaging, sir?" Rajmurti asked. "I'd like to physically check something out."

"Go ahead."

With Foste's help, the purser's mate removed sheets of packing material and unceremoniously dumped them on the deck.

"So?" Siobhan asked expectantly.

"As I thought, sir," Rajmurti replied. "This is an antimatter/plasma flux regulator of the same type we took aboard *Stingray* before leaving port. The serial number is close enough to have come from the same lot. Whether it came from Starbase 31 or not, I can't tell without accessing the central supply database."

"Are these things available on the open market, Rajmurti?"

"No, sir. Not the babies with this serial number sequence. The civilian-use parts have different markings."

"Well, Captain Slayton," Siobhan crossed her arms and turned to look at the civilian with an evil smile, "can you tell me what you're doing with navy supplies, or shall I take you under arrest now and claim your ship as a prize?"

Behind her, Foste, Rajmurti, and Vincenzo shouldered their weapons and covered the two trader crewmembers with clear intent.

"Damn you, Dunmoore," Slayton snarled, "I told you what I was about, and this is part of it. My job is to deliver these parts to ships working for the same employer and who can't, for obvious reasons, take them on at a Government-controlled installation."

"Proof, captain, proof is what I need. Your word is meaningless under the circumstances."

His nostrils flared whitely as he breathed hard, struggling to control his fury. "Very well. Call your Battle Group commander. She'll verify me. But don't say I didn't warn you about the consequences. This will mean your command, if not your career, Dunmoore. And once you've done so, make sure you and your crew forget all about this, or I cannot guarantee your continued health."

Siobhan considered him for a few moments, debating whether to call Kaleri or end this farce now with an arrest. Then she shrugged. It did not cost anything to call, except the lag time between question and answer. Her career was on the skids anyway.

"*Stingray*, this is Dunmoore."

"Pushkin here, captain."

"Mister Pushkin, please contact Battle Group HQ and ask them to confirm the status of the *Mykonos* as an undercover auxiliary. Captain Slayton tells me Admiral Kaleri is aware of his activities."

"Aye, sir. Time lag will be twenty minutes each way. Are you staying there?"

"Might as well. Remember General Order Eighty-One. Dunmoore, out."

She turned to Slayton. "My first officer will confirm your story. Meanwhile, consider yourself detained. This hold is to be locked and sealed. Foste, Rajmurti, you'll stand guard on what could become evidence. Let's go to your quarters, captain."

This time, Vincenzo stood guard at an open door, a grim look on his face. Slayton recovered his early poise within a few minutes and offered Siobhan a cup of coffee, which she accepted if only to lower the tension. However, neither made any attempt at small talk and the time passed awkwardly.

About twenty minutes later, Bertram reappeared with his escort, quickly followed by the others. Siobhan glanced at them, about to ask for a report when her eyes met Bertram's and Rownes'. Their expressions silenced her questions before she could utter them. Clearly, they had information neither wanted to discuss in front of Slayton, or even over the radio. When they saw understanding in Dunmoore's face, they relaxed.

"Nothing to report, cap'n," Rownes shrugged. "They're well-armed, but I can't blame 'em."

"Same 'ere, sir," Nosey chimed in. "Engine room's clear."

"Right. We'll wait until we get word from Starbase 31 about this ship."

The spacers nodded and casually took up covering positions along the corridor outside the cabin, as if they were simply wandering around, bored by their jobs. Time began to weigh heavily on everybody except Slayton, who took down one of his books and started reading, completely ignoring the presence of the armed naval personnel. Siobhan had to admire his poise and began to wonder whether she had blundered badly. Her instincts said she had not, but why she felt that way, she could not tell.

When Pushkin's voice sounded in her ears, Captain Dunmoore nearly jumped out of her skin.

"We got our reply from Battle Group, sir."

"And?"

"The Commander 31st Battle Group orders you to cease interfering with the fast trader *Mykonos*, under the command of Augustus Slayton, forthwith and release her to her business. Nothing is to be removed from the ship, and all logs pertaining to the interception and inspection are to be purged. The crew of *Stingray* is ordered to forget this incident ever happened. And the captain of *Stingray* will explain her actions at the earliest opportunity."

Slayton had overheard the communication and smiled sickeningly.

"There, Captain Dunmoore, you see. I trust that satisfies you. If you'll vacate my ship, we'll be on our way. You've made me lose enough time as it is."

Siobhan felt wooden as anger and embarrassment numbed her. Without saying a word, she nodded curtly and turned to her boarding party, who had heard the first officer's message.

"Let's go."

"You know the way to the shuttle deck, Captain Dunmoore," Slayton said to her stiff back. "Have a good life and don't let the doorknob catch you in the ass on the way out."

Siobhan ignored the taunt and led a puzzled and angry boarding party to the shuttle. A few minutes later, they were free of the *Mykonos* and headed back to their frigate.

Chief Foste broke the silence first. "If I may ask, sir, what was all that about?"

Siobhan did not reply immediately. She was still busy swallowing her pride. Then, she said, "It appears we've intercepted and detained a ship sailing under SSB orders, and that she's legit in all respects."

To her surprise, Nosey Bertram snorted loudly. "Then they're recruitin' some damn strange folk, cap'n."

"How's that, Bertram?"

Rownes, who recognized the look on her friend's face, interjected, "Better order him to tell it straight, sir. Otherwise, he'll want to draw it out like a long fairy tale. Likes hearing the sound of his own voice, Nosey does."

The general laughter broke the tension, and even Siobhan felt herself relax. "Okay, Bertram, give it to me straight, without embellishments."

"Cor, sir, ya don't hafta believe everything ol' Banger here says." The little man put on a mock hurt face. Then, he suddenly became serious, more serious than the others had ever seen him. "T'ain't no secret I was doin' some bad stuff before the war, sir, so I met a lot of bad people on them smugglin' ships. Well, guess my surprise when I see an old mate of mine down in engineering. A villain like you wouldn't believe. He ain't recognized me at first, but then, he went all pale an' his eyes damn near popped outta his face. The bastard scrammed from the engine room real bleedin' fast. If the spooks at SSB really hired Velvet McCloud, then they's finally turned into legal pirates. McCloud ought to hang for what he's done in his life."

"Not like you, eh," Rownes commented, grinning. "You cute little choirboy."

"Why didn't you report that over the radio?" Siobhan asked. She frowned, wondering how important that piece of information was.

"Simple, cap'n," Nosey grinned. "Those fuckers were listening to us. They got a gimmick which cracks navy frequencies. We used to have one a bit like it when I was workin' with the wrong people. It's illegal as all damn hell. Idiots didn't think I'd know what it was when I see it."

Siobhan slowly nodded. The SSB would, of course, have access to all sorts of non-standard toys including stuff with which to spy on the navy. Even hiring an ex-smuggler was not too far-fetched. Nosey Bertram was proof of that, although he'd been broken out of his bad habits by boot camp and the Fleet School.

"So what else do you have to report?"

"Just that I think that barky's doin' some serious smuggling, or worse, cap'n," Nosey replied, a solemn look on his sharp features. "She's overpowered like all hell, could fuckin' outrun *Stingray* flat. An' she's got an engine room I could work in with me eyes closed, but she ain't a navy hull, that's for certain."

"Okay." Siobhan nodded. "Rownes?"

"Good, well-maintained guns which probably started life as naval weaponry, until they got rid of the serial numbers and dressed 'em up to look like civvie stuff. Fire control suite's top of the line, newer than ours."

Demianova nodded in agreement, "*Da*. She is over-gunned for her size too."

"Well," Siobhan shrugged, "I guess the *Mykonos* has a lot to hide, but if she's really SSB, she wouldn't be set up all that different. We have our orders."

Bertram snorted softly. "Begging' yer pardon, sir, she ain't a spook ship, even if every last crew member flashed me a cute badge tellin' they're special agents of the SecGen. I can tell when a barky's legit and when she's full of hogwash. That one there," he pointed his thumb at the rear of the shuttle, "is up to no good." He tapped his large nose. "I can smell it."

"I agree with Nosey, sir," Chief Foste said. "She doesn't feel right at all. Too bad we got orders to let her go. A little creative search and interrogation would have told us one hell of a different story. Even if the captain is SSB, his crew isn't. There are probably more than a few of them who are wanted by various jurisdictions, including the Fleet."

"Security woman's instinct, chief?" Siobhan asked.

"Aye, sir. I've learned to trust my gut over the years."

"So have I, chief, so have I. Still, it's strange..." Siobhan's eyes rested on the bare metal bulkhead as she paused.

"What is, sir?" Foste asked.

"Well, a lot of things chief. Our friend Slayton knows Commander Forenza and Admiral Kaleri for one. For another, his hold is probably filled to the rafters with naval supplies hidden inside shielded crates, supplies which could easily have come from Starbase 31's depot, judging by the serial numbers. Then, we have *Stingray,* which has been chronically short of parts and supplies for months, even though the tender should be bringing up a full stock and the base's depot is full. Tell me, Rajmurti, did you know PO Melchor well?"

All of a sudden, Siobhan sensed a curtain dropping between her and the others as if she's just stepped on forbidden ground. Their eyes refused to meet hers, and their faces turned to stone.

"No, sir," Rajmurti finally replied, staring at the deck. And that was the end of the discussion. A minute or so later, the shuttle settled down in the hangar, and they disembarked, the ratings and chief leaving Siobhan alone with Kowalski with such alacrity that she felt as if she was showing signs of the plague.

A searing sense of frustration filled her mouth with the taste of acid. She turned toward the cockpit, watching as Kowalski finished her post-flight checks and released the straps holding her in the seat.

When the signals officer got up, she noticed Dunmoore watching her with a cat's intensity, and a chill ran down her spine.

"Mister Kowalski, you're an observant type. Do you think we were had by *Mykonos*?" Siobhan's voice was soft, almost hypnotic.

Kowalski met her gaze and slowly nodded.

"Personally, I think it stinks to high heaven," Dunmoore said, "and I'm tired of getting jerked around. If I ask you to tell me what you know about events on this ship before my taking command, are you going to clam up or lie to me like the others?"

The signals officer did not move or speak for a long count. Then, she did something which surprised Siobhan and shook her to the core. She placed her index finger in front of her mouth, then raised her hand to her ear and cupped it, while pointing up at the ceiling with her other hand, in the universal sign of 'do not talk anymore, we're being overheard.' Then, she mouthed the letters S-S-B.

— Thirteen —

Jhar wrinkled his nose at his superior's appearance when the latter climbed out of his personal shuttle. Brakal's uniform was liberally smeared with traces of offal, mud, and waste, traces he was unable to remove before lifting off, and he exuded a distinctly rotten odor. But his eyes shone with the excitement of battle.

"Commander, have you been consorting with the lower orders of the city again?" Jhar asked in a voice full of rough humor. The refit progressed well, and he was in good spirits. "Your appearance suggests a roll in shit with a cheap whore."

"Hah," Brakal barked, grinning, "just the effects of a warning delivered to me, courtesy of Admiral Trage."

Jhar snorted. "I did not realize Trage's tongue was so filthy as to leave those putrid traces on your uniform, though it hardly surprises me. May I suggest disinfectant and decontamination before we all die of some repulsive disease?"

Brakal laughed heartily at the treasonous joke, though Toralk, securing the shuttle nearby, made a disgusted face. The Clan Lord of the Makkar took the incident far too lightly in Toralk's opinion. This attitude would one day spell his doom, and probably that of Clan Makkar. Too many jealous intriguers had thrown covetous eyes on the clan's lavish estates. It would merely take an imperial edict declaring the Makkar line extinct once Brakal passed on to join his ancestors, for he had no offspring or siblings who could lay legal claim to the title, only cousins. And they had no power or influence at Court.

"Trage would never dare face me as a man, Jhar," Brakal sneered good-naturedly. "No, this happened on my way back from the Admiralty."

"Let me guess: in the lower town. I told you that route was dangerous."

"Only when the *Tai Kan* is on the loose, Jhar." Brakal showed his teeth.

"When is the *Tai Kan* not on the loose, commander? So, the Council finally decided to send you to join your father."

"Not quite yet. It was a most instructive incident. A *Tai Kan* operative rescued me from two professional killers, also hired by the *Tai Kan*. He killed them both. A quite unmistakable warning."

"You are sure they were *Tai Kan* hirelings?"

"Oh yes, Jhar, entirely. And I am as sure they came courtesy of Trage."

"Could it not have been Hralk?"

"No. That excrement-eater does not have the connections or the power to make the *Tai Kan* waste two of their contract killers for a simple warning. It was Trage and the Council. They are still too frightened to kill me outright, but their courage seems to gain in strength every time I return to the surface."

"Only because you provoke them, commander," Jhar grumbled. "A little submission would go a long way to ensuring your survival."

"Piss on submission, Jhar. I would rather submit to a human female than let those incestuous fornicators lose the Empire by their stupidity and cowardice."

"Strong words, commander." Jhar frowned. "The *Tai Kan*'s spies will no doubt be happy to transmit them to the Council."

"Piss on the *Tai Kan* too for that matter, Jhar," Brakal growled, suddenly bereft of his earlier, fierce good humor. "They are as much part of the problem as the whores at the Admiralty. The humans will win this war if we do not adapt and overcome. And none of the blind fools down below seem to realize this. Bah! How long before we are ready to sail?"

"Two days, commander."

"Two days too much," Brakal grumbled as he strode off toward his quarters. He had opposed the war in the first place, and now he had to watch the slow erosion of the Imperial Fleet's fighting power and spirit. Maybe it would be better if he died in battle so that his line died out before it became stained with the dishonor of defeat.

Humans were hard to understand, but the last war should have taught the Empire at least one thing: the humans' one constant was their unpredictability. It was their greatest strength. That and the deceptive way in which their alien, chaotic political system seemed to signal weakness, when it hid cold, hard steel at the core. Like the first officer of the battleship that refused to die. Dunmoore. He rolled the unfamiliar name on his tongue, wondering whether she had achieved the honors denied to him.

A few more mad commanders like her, and the war was lost, for the Empire could not deal with such unbounded tactical insanity.

*

"Commander, a Lieutenant Khrada has come aboard. He carries orders from the Admiralty."

Brakal stabbed at the intercom irritably, his temper frayed by the endless paperwork necessary to release his ship from the Yard Master's protective embrace. Half the Fleet's problems in fighting this war, it seemed, stemmed from the mindless bureaucracy that stifled even the most determined officer.

"Deal with it, Jhar."

"I regret, commander, but he carries orders appointing him to *Tol Vakash*. He demands to see you."

Brakal sat up in surprise. A mere lieutenant demanding to see a starship commander? And with orders appointing him to a vessel that already carried a full complement of officers, handpicked to a man. Jhar's choice of words had been no accident. Khrada had to be a political officer, a uniformed *Tai Kan* man sent to watch over Brakal.

He slammed his fist on his desk in anger. Trage and the Council go too far.

"Send him to my quarters," he snarled, and then shut off the intercom with a savage gesture. Political officers were a nuisance at best and a danger to the ship at any time. So far, the Council had not dared to make the practice common among the Fleet, though it had forced them on the ground troops shortly after the start of the war.

Most were chosen for their loyalty to the current Council and its individual members, and not for their martial prowess, yet even the least qualified among them wore officer's rank and uniform and presumed to interfere in the running of a unit. But they could be fobbed off.

The really dangerous ones were those who had come to their appointment after serving in the Fleet. These knew enough to make any commander's life a misery and more often than not were officers too incompetent or venal to attain high rank through honest means. They worked out their bitterness and gnawing anger on those who won success.

The door chime buzzed angrily, and Brakal snapped, "Come."

It slid aside to reveal a powerfully built officer of middle age, wearing his hair in the Warrior caste fashion. He stepped through, his arrogant eyes taking in the spartan cabin and Brakal's dark face without emotion. He sat down, uninvited, his gestures and demeanor making a joke of his lowly rank and supposed deference to a starship commander. Brakal kept his temper in tight check and observed Khrada with hooded eyes, waiting for the man to speak first.

"Commander," Khrada nodded, finally acknowledging the occupant of the cabin and master of the cruiser *Tol Vakash*. His tone turned the word into a mockery of courtesy. Brakal knew Khrada was trying to provoke him and refused to rise to the bait.

"Lieutenant," Brakal replied in the same tone. "Your business on my ship?"

Khrada tossed a data wafer on the pile of printouts in front of Brakal. None of the cruiser's officers would have dared behave in such a manner, and the *Tai Kan* man knew it. His eyes glittered with a kind of sick anticipation.

Brakal's volatility and fierce temper were well known. A simple trap then, Brakal decided. He ignored the gesture.

"By order of the Admiralty, I am appointed as political officer on *Tol Vakash*, to promote the crew's loyalty to the Emperor and encourage their fighting spirit."

Brakal smiled dangerously, revealing sharp teeth.

"Really?" He asked with obvious disbelief. "I thought the *Tai Kan*'s function was to scare those who refused to lick the Council's collective bum so that it can hold complete control over the Fleet and indeed the Empire."

Khrada returned the smile, unconcerned, and shrugged. "As you wish, commander. I suggest you acquaint yourself with my credentials and my brief on board this vessel. You will find your life has taken a different turn." He made to rise when Brakal's voice lashed out and stopped him.

"You are not dismissed, lieutenant."

The political officer looked at Brakal with barely disguised amusement, but remained seated, waiting for the expected storm to break. Brakal's next words erased his smile.

"I do not give a whore's fart for your credentials or your brief, nor do I care who sent you here to spy on me. You have been appointed to my ship. Fine. But that means you will obey my orders at all times or suffer the consequences. If I have to kill you, I will do so with pleasure. At the slightest provocation. One less *Tai Kan* swine in the universe is a blessing of the ancestors. You may report my words to Admiral Trage, and you may also tell him that the Clan Lord of the Makkar is tiring of his games. He should take care to avoid angering the old Clans of pure lineage any further. The Regent will not permit him and the Council to jeopardize the Emperor's reign by provoking the nobility."

Khrada stared in disbelief at Brakal's open defiance and insults to the leader of the Council. Whatever he had expected, in his *Tai Kan* arrogance, this was not it.

"Close your mouth, lieutenant. You look like a backwater colonist seeing a *gan*-dancer for the first time. You are dismissed."

Brakal turned his attention to the printouts on the desk, ignoring the furious *Tai Kan* officer. Khrada was not used to this kind of contempt from line officers, and Brakal's reaction unbalanced him. Others usually showed fear at the appearance of a secret police officer, but on this ship, he had encountered nothing but amused contempt. After a few seconds, during which he closed his gaping mouth, Khrada rose and left the cabin, intending to report this conversation to his superiors at once.

Out in the corridor, he met a smirking Jhar, who blocked his way with an outstretched arm.

"One moment, *lieutenant*," Jhar drawled contemptuously. "Now that the commander has made his position clear, I wish to do the same."

"Get out of my way, *bechin*," Khrada snarled, calling Jhar by the dismissive title used for low caste workers, an explicit reference to his low caste birth.

"What did you call me?" Jhar asked dangerously, refusing to budge.

Khrada's lips curled back in a distorted grin, revealing rows of cracked, yellow teeth. "You may have been raised to the Warrior caste, Jhar, but you still carry the stench of a *bechin*. Take care who you challenge. You were born in shit, and have no family name to hide behind, like your precious commander."

Without warning, or telegraphing his intentions, Jhar lashed out at Khrada, his fist catching the bigger man in the lower abdomen like a meteorite strike. Unprepared for the assault, Khrada grunted as he bent over in pain, the air forced out of his lungs. But Jhar gave him no time to recover or even react. He jerked his knee into Khrada's face, connecting savagely with the other's jaw, while his joined hands slammed down on the back of the political officer's head. Khrada collapsed to the deck in an untidy heap, breathing with difficulty and grunting in blinding pain.

Jhar contemptuously kicked him. "You too should take care who you challenge, *lieutenant*. Those born *bechin* learn hand-to-hand combat the hard way, in the streets, not in some rich family's dojo. We learn to fear no one. I am second to Brakal on this ship, and you will obey me or die. I suggest you watch your step at all times because the *Tai Kan* is hated even more than the humans on *Tol Vakash*, and I would not feel any sorrow if you suddenly had a fatal accident."

"Oh," Jhar smiled as Khrada looked up at him, "you should know that we sail in two hours. No one is to leave the ship, or use the communications facilities, and that includes the Council's shit-eating spies. Should you try, the sentries at the airlock have orders to kill you. Your quarters are on deck three. Confine yourself to them until we have jumped."

Jhar turned and walked away, knowing that Khrada could not be allowed to live once *Tol Vakash* began the hunt. The man was much too dangerous to Brakal, and to the ship. Accidents happen in space. More *Tai Kan* died that way than through enemy action, and Khrada would not be the first on this ship. Clan Makkar's feud with the Imperial Council was as old as the war itself. If only the old Emperor had survived until his son's coming of age. But the brain tumor that killed him knew no cure on this side of the border. In medicine, if nothing else, the humans were well ahead of the Empire. But honor, carried by the nobility to a peak of stupidity, forbade asking the supposedly weak Commonwealth for assistance.

Weak! Jhar snorted as he remembered their last battle. If only the luxury-loving toads in the capital knew the difference between their moon dreams and reality. As soon as he reached the bridge, Jhar confirmed the sentries' orders and set about to release *Tol Vakash* from the stinking manure heap of the home world.

*

Brakal glanced at his timepiece and dropped the last printout with a satisfied grunt. He rose and adjusted his uniform, running a callused hand through his crest of hair. He touched his dagger, remembering Khrada's face on the security camera after Jhar taught him the reality of life aboard a Deep Space Fleet cruiser, and decided to take no chances with the *Tai Kan* spy. Until Khrada's real agenda became known, he had to be treated with as much caution as a female *yatakan* during mating season.

The commander opened an obsidian cabinet and drew out a black gun belt with a much-used blaster in a *kroorath* hide holster. Brakal had killed the animal that had provided the leather himself. He still remembered that hunt with great pleasure.

He fastened the belt around his waist, over the green sash, and checked the blaster's charge. Satisfied, Brakal rammed the big weapon back into the holster and left his cabin.

Tol Vakash's crewmembers were already at their stations and saluted as the commander strode by, a smile of joyous anticipation on his harsh features. They were as happy as he to sail again and leave Shrehari Prime in their wake. Though none, save Toralk, were family retainers of the Makkar, any visitor would have mistaken them as such, so intense was the gleam of loyal devotion and pride in their eyes. To most, Brakal represented the best of the Empire's old nobility: a Lord who upheld his honor in the traditional way, and who knew how to lead by example. One of only a few.

The door to the bridge opened at his approach, its lights already dimmed in preparation. Brakal's nostrils twitched with pleasure at the familiar scents of ozone, leather, and hot metal. His cruiser vibrated with energy, like a shackled running beast waiting for the long anticipated release.

Jhar rose to face Brakal and saluted. "*Tol Vakash* is at your command."

Brakal grinned and nodded, then looked at each of his bridge crew, in turn, reading joy at the imminent departure in their faces. He took his chair behind the center console and basked in the tension that permeated the ship. This was his way, his life: command of an imperial warship.

"Stations," Brakal suddenly barked, his grin spreading.

Like hounds released from the pen, the bridge crew stirred into action.

"Dockyard control, this is the imperial cruiser *Tol Vakash*. We will rejoin the Fleet now. Release moorings." Jhar's voice was as harsh as it was formal. He stood at Brakal's side, hands clasped in the small of his back.

"This is Dockyard control. Stand by." Muffled thuds reverberated throughout the hull. "*Tol Vakash*, you are free to join the hunt. Make the Empire proud of your name."

"Navigator, position and running lights on."

"*Kha.*"

"Commander, *Tol Vakash* floats free."

"Helm, thrusters one-half ahead," Brakal ordered, fingers gripping the arms of his chair with great strength as if he wanted to merge with the metal and synthetics of his starship.

"*Kha.*"

The quality of the vibrations changed minutely, but for Brakal, it made all the difference. His ship was now under way. On the screen, the forward view began to change as the confines of the yard slipped by.

Slowly, the matte gray hull of the large, sleek and deadly imperial cruiser slid out of the box-like structure of the dry dock, its aft thrusters glowing orange as they poured out massive amounts of energy. The coiled red dragon of the Fleet blazed on either side of her hull, flanked by the imperial cuneiform script identifying her as *Tol Vakash*, the Fast Death.

She was barely a year old, of the latest design and Brakal had taken her out of the slipway when she was new, with a handpicked crew transferred from his previous command. She overpowered all other imperial ships of the same class with her heavy guns and the powerful drives jutting out from the rear of her elongated, diamond-shaped hull. Shrehari shipwrights commonly built for function, not elegance, but in *Tol Vakash*, both had combined to create a vessel more beautiful than any other.

"We are free of the station," the helmsman reported.

"Your orders, commander?" Jhar formally asked.

"Change course to one-one-five-nine, at full sublight. Plot a jump to the Cimmeria Sector by the most direct route. Let us see if the humans still have the stomach to fight. Let us hunt."

Gun Master Urag, at his station on Brakal's left, grinned and saluted. "When we are finished with them, commander, they will no longer have the stomach to live."

A low growl, like a pack of hungry *krooraths* on the prowl, filled the bridge with its primal potency, raising the small hairs on the back of Brakal's neck with excitement.

*

"You have a plan, commander."

It was not a question but a statement of fact. Jhar knew Brakal too well. Brakal's eyes gleamed as he looked up from the naked blade of his finely crafted dagger.

"I have, Jhar." He glanced down at the knife again, then carefully sheathed it and stood up, pacing his cabin. "Admiral Trage wanted to tie me to the apron strings of an Assault Force, as a way of controlling me. None of the admirals would cooperate. They either fear I will show them for the fools they are, or they hate Trage as much as I and want me to roam free. Either way serves my plans. But my orders limit me to patrols within our space. Forays across into human space are expressly forbidden, on pain of standing judgment before the Council."

"And Khrada is here to see you keep to your orders, or failing that, witness your disobedience."

"No doubt. But there may be another reason. Fool though Trage may be, his mind is twisted and filled with dark corners where he schemes endlessly. The only thing I can safely assume is that the Council dearly wishes me to disappear. It can no longer tolerate a Deep Space Fleet officer showing the Empire where the Admiralty has erred and taken us into this grinding war of attrition instead of taking us to victory."

"If victory was ever possible."

"It was, at one point, Jhar. But we gave the humans time to regroup and learn, while we have not learned a single useful thing."

"So what will you do with Khrada?"

"At this time? Nothing. My imminent death is not wished by my enemies. They know I have too much support. Khrada will be watched of course, and kept out of the way, but his presence does not affect my plans."

"And they are?" Jhar asked, returning to his initial question.

"Simple," Brakal grinned. "As all good plans. If we cannot go to the enemy, we will let him come to us." At Jhar's apparent incomprehension, Brakal's smile widened.

"Think, Jhar. What have we learned from the humans?"

The first officer thought for a moment, and then slowly nodded. "You intend to wait for humans to cross into our space on a search and destroy patrol, and hunt them down."

"Yes. It may not be the best way, but until I am sure of things, I will observe the Council's strictures. Here is what we shall do." In short, spare sentences, Brakal outlined his plan, and when he was done, Jhar smiled, happy to see that his commander had recovered his fierce good humor and shed the depression that had dogged him since returning to the home world.

If *Tol Vakash* could not go out and hunt the humans on an equal footing, it could at least catch them at their own game, a game Brakal had taught his crew a long time ago. And it would serve just as well to cement Brakal's reputation among the Deep Space Fleet, as would a foray into the Commonwealth. The only dark spot on the horizon remained Khrada. Jhar asked the commander for permission to kill him now, but Brakal refused, grinning cruelly.

"In good time, Jhar, in good time. First, I want to know exactly why Trage thought he could put a highly visible spy on my ship and get away with it. Where is the turd now, by the way?"

"Restrained in his quarters. Under guard."

Brakal's thick eyebrows rose. "Drastic acts, my generally careful second."

Jhar grunted dismissively. "He has no functions and was in the way as we prepared to sail. It was a logical decision."

The commander laughed. "You see, Jhar, you are learning. Soon, you shall be able to scheme and cause trouble with the worst of the sycophants at the Emperor's court." He sobered abruptly. "Let him roam free now. But ensure he is watched at all times."

"If he wishes to communicate with his superiors?"

"Let him. I care little for his gossip." Brakal shrugged. "On second thought, record his transmissions, and set someone about finding the key to whatever code he uses. Khrada will expect this, and I do not want to disappoint him. Yet."

— Fourteen —

After Kowalski's caution, the signals officer had clammed up, making Siobhan understand that no member of her crew would speak the truth for fear of the unknown agent or agents. If she had told the truth, it confirmed the recent past held more, much more than just a string of disconnected incidents.

If Siobhan flushed out the SSB agent, her officers might be more inclined to speak, to tell her what had happened. But who could it be? Shara's pinched face flashed across her mind, but she discarded the thought almost immediately.

A good operative was inconspicuous, and the sailing master had been anything but, antagonizing just about everyone and sucking up to Forenza openly. And that showed the magnitude of her problem. With a crew of over two hundred, it could be anyone.

Stripping off the armor, Siobhan forced herself to think rationally. Electronic surveillance throughout the ship, if it existed, had to be monitored by someone who had access to ship's systems on a routine basis. She bit her lower lip in concentration. That left out many people but included just as many. Siobhan smiled grimly. She could get paranoid very easily under these circumstances. The intercom buzzed and interrupted her thoughts.

"Dunmoore."

"Pushkin, sir. Did you want to see the message from Battle Group?"

Siobhan paused, puzzled for a moment. "Which message?"

"The reply to our query on the *Mykonos*."

It could easily have waited until she was back on the bridge, and Siobhan was about to say so. Then, she slowly nodded. "Pipe it down to my terminal."

"Aye, aye, sir."

Pushkin's face disappeared, replaced by Admiral Kaleri's severe features. Siobhan had never met the commander of 31st Battle Group in person. The rear admiral had the elegant, aristocratic features of a wealthy Earther, a scion of the great families who controlled the Commonwealth. Her short hair had turned iron-gray and framed a lean, seamed face which made her appear older than her fifty years. Kaleri's piercing blue eyes stared out from the small screen, frozen by the paused recording. Siobhan touched a key.

"Captain Dunmoore," her accent was precise, clipped, but her voice flat. "You will cease interfering with the fast trader *Mykonos*, under the command of Augustus Slayton, forthwith and release her to her business. Nothing is to be removed from the ship, and all logs about the interception and inspection are to be purged. The crew of *Stingray* is ordered to forget this incident ever happened." Pushkin had relayed Kaleri's words verbatim, but he had not mentioned what followed. "I am disappointed that you failed to accept Captain Slayton's identification, which I am sure, he provided. Try to avoid making an ass of yourself and this Battle Group in the future. You're already treading a fine line. As you know, you are not my first, or even my last choice to command *Stingray*, and I will not tolerate any of your usual insubordinate or reckless acts. You have already made the one mistake I was prepared to allow you. Oh, and send me a full report explaining why you're not at your patrol station yet. Kaleri, out."

Dunmoore stared at the blank screen in angry surprise. Kaleri's orders were already hard to believe after what she saw aboard *Mykonos*, but the insulting admonishment was out of line. Flag officers, by custom, reprimanded the ship captains under their command in private and in person, not over an open frequency. So that was why

Pushkin felt she should see the message before returning to the bridge. It was probably all over the ship by now.

Humiliation blazed a hot trail across her face, and she cursed savagely until she had exhausted her inventory of swear words in several human and non-human languages.

She finished stripping off her armor, leaving the rigid shell pieces in a pile on her bed. Kery would come by later and square it away. Funny, Siobhan thought, how she had come to depend on the self-effacing clerk for the mundane things in her life: meals, cleaning her cabin, keeping the paperwork straight. And despite her earlier fears, Kery had not been set on by any other crewmember. In fact, she had become so inconspicuous as to have almost vanished from Dunmoore's perception.

She froze in her tracks. Kery. The clerk had access to just about anything on the ship, including the captain's personal things. No one questioned her right to be anywhere, and she had already acted out of character once, during her low-voiced argument with Shara, an officer who should know better than to take lip from a rating. Was that the real reason for Guthren's suggestion Dunmoore transfer Kery off *Stingray*? The chief had an uncanny instinct for trouble.

With an angry shrug, she adjusted her battledress and headed for the bridge, where Pushkin waited for further orders. Wordlessly, she slid into the captain's seat and stared at the view screen, the humiliation of Kaleri's message still all too vivid.

Pushkin must have noticed her stiffness, because he leaned over and, in a quiet voice said, "I'm the only one who saw the message unscrambled sir. I took the liberty of using your ready room."

Siobhan looked up at Pushkin in grateful surprise. Her angry features softened at the unexpected support from a man who had shown nothing but resentment since she came aboard.

"Thank you, Mister Pushkin," she replied softly. "That means a lot to me."

He shrugged, as if embarrassed and straightened up. "Your orders, captain?"

"Set a course for the Cimmeria Sector," Siobhan replied, the weight of her anger diminished by Pushkin's surprising show of loyalty. "I want to see if we can track down an imperial supply convoy and ruin its week. A bit of hit-and-run should get this ship back into the swing of things, wouldn't you say, Mister Pushkin?"

"Aye, sir," the first officer nodded, a crack of a smile softening his severe expression. "But the convoys travel deep in Shrehari territory, even to resupply the Cimmeria outposts. Picking them up on sensors will be tricky."

"Correct, Mister Pushkin." Siobhan now smiled openly. "For that reason, we won't restrain ourselves to the safe side of the line until we have a target." The others now listened to Dunmoore and the first officer with interest, and Siobhan met Kowalski's dark eyes. "Playing it safe doesn't yield results. Risks, calculated risks do. Just as long as you do it right. Don't you think so, Mister Kowalski?"

After a moment's hesitation, during which the signals officer tried to decipher Dunmoore's words for any hidden meanings, Kowalski nodded. "Aye, captain."

"Tell me, Mister Kowalski," Siobhan continued, her smile widening as her eyes narrowed, "as an electronics whiz, what do you know about electronic countermeasures?"

Again, she paused, and Siobhan could literally see the little gears turning in her head.

"Some, sir. Anything special in mind?"

"Let's discuss it some time when we're both off watch." Siobhan turned to Pushkin. "I think a few lightyears this side of the Cimmeria system ought to do for now. Somewhere near the spot *Victoria Regina* got plastered by Captain Brakal."

Did she see his face muscles tighten for a fraction of a second, or was it just her overheated imagination?

Pushkin nodded. "Aye, sir." He leaned over his console and tapped a few keys. "Navigation, plot course bearing one-four-five mark fifteen, emerging at grid Alpha Pictoris five-four-four-seven by eight-eight-one-zero by six-nine-two-two."

Shara repeated the figures in her nasal tone. "Course locked-in."

"Helm, engage."

*

Three days passed without Siobhan becoming any wiser to the ship's recent history. It frustrated her to no end, and she had developed half a dozen theories, each of them sounding like something out of a cheap novel. Fortunately, she had other things to occupy her mind. Matters of more immediate import, like the life and death jokes the gods played on spacers in a war zone.

The ship had reached the coordinates near where Brakal had ambushed *Victoria Regina* and had assumed a patrol route that took it deep into the war zone. So far, all was quiet on the Shrehari front.

To keep herself from going nuts at the thought of SSB spies, far-fetched conspiracies and the nearness of an enemy who could spell death for the inexperienced *Stingray* crew, she had begun to contemplate tactical simulations of various convoy-raiding scenarios.

Dunmoore found the intellectual stimulation relaxing, even though she usually fought her battles by instinct, not according to some set of formalized rules or in slavish adherence to doctrine. What she found even more stimulating were her discussions and wargaming with Pushkin. The first officer had a solid if conventional grasp of frigate tactics. It bode well for their patrol.

Her time with Pushkin also gave her another insight into the man. He obviously had all the grounding and abilities to fight a starship, and as he had proven over the last few weeks, knew how to administer and sail one. Yet he was older than Dunmoore and still had not taken the step to command his own vessel. These things happened in a large Fleet. Often, the difference between one officer taking the step and another, of equal ability remaining second fiddle was a matter of being at the right place at the right time, and catching an admiral's eye.

Siobhan had obtained her first command thanks to Admiral Nagira. He had been impressed by her sharp mind while she worked on his staff before the war. When the position of captain of an auxiliary scout opened up shortly before the Shrehari invasion, he had given her a chance.

Don Quixote had been a dream for a young and somewhat wild lieutenant with glory in her eyes. It did not last long. Within eight months, she lost the yearning for glory when the Imperial Forces all but destroyed her small command at the first battle of Cimmeria, killing or injuring half the crew.

Siobhan learned the hard way that wildness and dash had to be tempered by thoughtfulness and experience. Still, she emerged from the subsequent inquest with lieutenant commander's stripes on her shoulders because she had not sacrificed *Don Quixote* in vain. But she did not get another command immediately. Nagira decided that Dunmoore had to do some penance if only to hammer home the lessons she had learned. He appointed Siobhan to the *Sala-Ad-Din* as second officer to gain some more seasoning under experienced superiors. Adnan Prighte had been first officer and had fast become her close friend.

The thought of Prighte distracted her from the simulation, and she turned off the terminal with a sigh. Something perverse in her nature had pushed Siobhan to make the Cimmeria Sector her prime patrolling area, even though as an independent frigate, she had orders to roam a large slice of the line. The Shrehari occupied system had much to commend it to enterprising captains.

It was the Empire's main outpost in occupied space and received a steady stream of convoys to resupply the garrison and build up a forward support base for future thrusts. However, Siobhan doubted the Empire could regain enough momentum for another push into the Commonwealth against a ready if thinly stretched human Fleet.

She suspected her motives for choosing Cimmeria were more personal, the kind that responsible ship captains did not enjoy acknowledging.

The door chime sounded its muted call and, on Dunmoore's word, Kery trotted in carrying a supper tray. Its delicious aroma tickled Siobhan's nose, and her stomach rumbled loudly in response. Kery gave her a sly glance and Siobhan smiled back, embarrassed at her body's primitive reactions. But when the clerk turned away to leave, the smile vanished, replaced by a hard, speculative look as Siobhan stared at her retreating back.

Just as the door closed, the clerk turned her head. Their eyes met for a fraction of a second, but it was enough. Siobhan knew that Kery had seen her expression and come to the correct conclusion. An unpleasant metallic taste filled Siobhan's dry mouth while blood pounded loudly in her ears. If Kery was a spy, she now knew that Siobhan suspected her.

Suddenly, the hot meal in front of her seemed a lot less enticing.

As she ate, Siobhan felt the bulkheads close in on her. Tension made her neck ache, and she knew she had to move, get her mind on mundane things. Otherwise she would become too jumpy and nervous to give even a mediocre Shrehari commander a decent fight. An impromptu and informal inspection of the ship would do nicely.

Rising to adjust her uniform and slip on her gloves, Siobhan had an idea that made her smile. She would start with a visit to the Number Two portside one-oh-five gun turret, Banger Rownes' little world. She instinctively liked the burly ex-merchant spacer. Rownes projected an innate honesty and integrity that Siobhan found refreshing. And she was not afraid to speak her mind.

*

When Dunmoore reached the thick bulkhead protecting the ship's environmental integrity from the cold vacuum of space, the armored door to portside Number Two gun opened with a soft groan and a sucking noise, proving the turret had been depressurized moments before. She stopped near the hatch and waited. A few moments later, a pair of pressure-suited feet appeared on the ladder leading down from the turret housing proper. The gunner skipped the last few rungs and landed on the bare metal deck with a dull thud. The polarized helmet visor turned toward Captain Dunmoore, and the suit's occupant snapped to attention.

Before Siobhan could speak, another gunner, clad in a bigger, bulkier suit, climbed down the ladder and joined the first one. The new arrival nudged her companion and removed her helmet, revealing sweat-slicked, short brown hair.

"Captain," she nodded politely, standing at attention.

"How are you Rownes?"

Beside Banger, Demianova also removed her helmet and tucked it under her left arm.

"Fine, sir," Banger replied, her expression guarded.

"Practicing under emergency conditions?" Siobhan tried to project a relaxed demeanor, but the two gunners' faces remained bland.

"Aye, sir. Mister Devall has been running us through just about every simulation he could think of. Did us a lot of good." She pulled off a glove and ran her hand through her wet hair. "We worked for our pay today, and that's no error."

Siobhan nodded, smiling at Rownes' solemn, yet satisfied tone. She clearly enjoyed hard work. The captain was about to ask another question when the intercom beeped loudly in the turret housing.

"Devall to Rownes."

Banger glanced at the intercom and then back at the captain. Siobhan nodded to go ahead and answer. While Rownes went over, Siobhan examined Demianova. Her face was familiar now that she no longer wore a helmet.

Banger touched the intercom pad. "Rownes, sir."

"Start collecting your bets from your fellow gun captains, spacer. You got a perfect score on the last run, and you were the only gun team to make it. Congratulations."

"Thank you, sir."

"Don't thank me, Rownes, thank yourselves. You can stand down now. That was the last simulation for the day. If I call you to the guns again before tomorrow, it'll be to get a crack at a real, live Shrehari. Devall, out."

Though neither woman smiled, their eyes reflected the pride they felt receiving praise from their divisional officer. Siobhan was glad to see that, because it showed good morale. And it demonstrated that Devall was taking his duties to heart, drilling his gun crews on his own time. Rownes took her place at Demianova's side again. Siobhan looked the younger woman in the eyes. Now she remembered. Not much, only a vague picture of a ship that no longer existed.

"You served with me on the *Sala-Ad-Din* in sixty-two, didn't you? Lower main battery, junior gunner's mate on her virgin tour."

Demianova was both surprised and pleased that Dunmoore remembered her from their days on the ill-fated cruiser. The captain had been second officer then, the third-ranking officer on board, while Demmi was just an ordinary spacer on her first time out, assigned to the most menial job on the main guns.

"Da, Kapitan."

"At ease, both of you. How's the grub in the lower deck galley these days?"

Her unexpected question threw the two gunners momentarily off track. Then, Banger smiled for the first time. "Great, sir. Nicely varied menu too. Seems like the cooks found their cookbooks again."

Siobhan laughed at Rownes' knowing look. "Aye, so it appears. What say we take a tour of your gun?"

Rownes nodded and turned to climb back up the access ladder. Demianova politely deferred to the captain, letting Siobhan follow Banger. A hard metallic smell assailed Dunmoore's nostrils as she stepped off the ladder into the cramped turret, and she repressed a sneeze. Rownes saw her facial expression and grinned.

"We always get short-changed when we depressurize the turret."

"How's that?"

"We give 'em perfectly good air and get back this processed crap."

Siobhan smiled at the wry tone. A starship's emergency tanks always gave captured air an industrial tang, no matter how much the environmental scrubbing system tried to make it more palatable. In battle, most captains, including Siobhan, preferred to fight with the gun turrets and vulnerable outer compartments depressurized. It reduced the damage caused by direct hits and often let the individual guns keep on fighting. And it forced the crews to wear full pressure suits, which meant they would not give in to sloppiness and die at the slightest hull breach because of an imperfectly sealed helmet or glove joint.

Number Two portside turret housed twin one-hundred and five-millimeter plasma guns in a dome-like shell amidships on the upper side of the main hull. It could fire in a one-hundred and eighty-degree horizontal arc, covering the frigate from bow to stem, and in a ninety-degree vertical arc from just above the drive nacelles straight up.

On either side of the turret, between breech and bulkhead were acceleration seats and targeting consoles. During a controlled ship-to-ship engagement, the computer received its firing orders directly from the bridge. All the gunners had to do was make sure the gun did its job; the ammunition feed did not jam, and be ready to take direct control if the automated systems failed. Which they often did.

But the gunners really came into their own during a melee, when the battle was too fluid and the bridge too busy firing guided weapons for the system to work properly, especially in a target-rich environment.

Though more dangerous for the ship, gun captains loved melees. They had total control over their turrets and could engage any target at will within their arcs of fire. Even with the assistance of the computer, it was a job that demanded skill, dexterity, and quick thinking. Judging by Devall's message a moment ago, Rownes possessed all three.

"Your guns working fine, Rownes?"

"Oh aye, sir. I maintain 'em myself, and they're always ready to blast away at the fucking Imps. Though, to be honest," she scratched the top of her head, "there's a coupla parts close to needing replacement. Wear and tear, you see. This baby moves fast when it's tracking a target, and that's hard on them mechanical parts. I've had to do a few fixes myself with the old pieces to keep her going."

"Have you reported this to the gunnery officer?"

"Aye, sir. I did three months ago, and three months afore that. And when we were getting ready to sail this time. I got a few things from your raid of the Starbase stores," she grinned, "and put 'em in, but a lot is still back-ordered."

Siobhan frowned, leaning on the massive breech of the left tube. She crossed her arms below her breasts.

"You haven't been getting the parts from the tender runs?"

"Nope. Mister Devall made sure he checked whenever we got topped-up, but always lots of stuff missing. And not only for my little babies." Rownes patted the other tube possessively.

"Yes," Siobhan mused, locking eyes with Rownes. "A lot of strange things going on aboard *Stingray* under Commander Forenza."

Banger snorted. "You don't know the half of it, sir." Then, when she saw the curious look in Siobhan's eyes, her expression changed as she realized she had betrayed herself. Rownes glanced at Demianova, but she kept a stony face.

"Want to tell me about it, Rownes?" Siobhan softly asked. "I'm getting tired of living under the oath of silence. You're an old space hand; you know it's no way to run a ship in a war zone."

Again, Banger glanced at Demmi, but this time, the younger woman shrugged. Slowly, keeping hard eyes focused on the captain, Rownes shifted position to lean against the breech of the left-hand tube, facing Siobhan and crossed her arms. Then, she jerked her head at Demianova. "Close the access hatch, Demmi."

She complied silently and then resumed her place near the ladder.

"Okay, cap'n. You want to know what went on aboard the barky afore you took her, I'll tell you, 'cause you're right. Ain't no way to run a ship by treating the cap'n like a leper. And you did right by Vince, I mean Able Spacer

Vincenzo, and that means a lot to me. He's a good friend and a reliable mate."

Siobhan did not reply but kept her eyes locked with Banger's.

"You wanna know what life was like under Forenza, I'll tell you, cap'n. It sure as shit wasn't like life is supposed to be in the navy."

Rownes took a deep breath.

"Cap'n Forenza liked her ease and didn't like getting her hands dirty. She lived like a goddamned queen in her cabin, fucking just about any crewmember she got the hots for. And believe me, she got lots of hots. If you didn't want to do it, she threatened you. Some got scared, some didn't. Those who got scared, participated in some strange doin's, let me tell you. Oh yeah, cap'n," Rownes said, seeing the look of distaste on Siobhan's face, "ain't ever seen nothing like it, even on some of the less respectable ships I met in my tradin' days."

"I've been on this here ship for nearly two years," Banger continued, anger beginning to feed her words, "and in all that time, we must have run one battle drill a month, if that. And we haven't seen a bleeding Imp for over six months. You see, Cap'n Forenza was a fucking coward too, like most bullies. She got yellow whenever there was a toss-up in the wind. She also never made an inspection tour, never took a good look at the insides of her ship and at her crew, and never said a kind word to anyone. At least outside the bedroom, that is. Mister Pushkin was doing all the work and getting no credit for it. Hell, I even saw Forenza tear a strip off him in public once. Only officer the bitch got along with was Mister Shara. The others hated her guts."

Rownes shook her head in disgust.

"Hell, this fucking ship would have seen a mutiny last New Year's day if Forenza didn't have her little spies on the lower deck. But she was a great one for keeping people in line. Ruined a few careers I know of. She was a bully but went through with her threats. Connections, cap'n. Good ones. And there was nothing you could do about it. Forenza had her nose so deep up Admiral Kaleri's ass, she could get anything she wanted. A crew member transferred to a shit-hole outpost?" Rownes snapped her fingers. "Done. A crew member discharged 'cause he'd crossed her?" She snapped her fingers again. "Done, even though it was nothing but a pack of lies. Ain't no one who stood up to Forenza who got a fair shake."

"Even worse, cap'n," the ruddy-faced gunner paused and glanced at Demianova before continuing in a softer tone. "Four guys offed themselves on this ship in the last six months. Four. And every one of 'em 'cause they were caught in Forenza's hell. One of 'em, a kid officer called Rasheed, who couldn't have been a day over twenty-one, shot himself in the head 'cause Forenza was about to put him up on false charges. He knew the charges would stick and couldn't face the disgrace. Came from a poor colonist family. First one who passed through the Academy and became an officer. No, cap'n, I dunno why Forenza wanted to get rid of him, but the kid was a good sort. Would have made a decent gunnery officer."

Siobhan felt nauseous at Rownes' all too convincing tale. She had no problem believing the gunner. Forenza had tried to make her a victim long ago. Maybe there was a bit of exaggeration here and there, but not enough to make a difference.

"Do you know if there's any proof of all this, Rownes?"

The big gunner laughed without humor. "That's another thing Forenza was good at, cap'n, keeping her soft fingers clean. No evidence I know of. But there ain't a spacer on board who won't be able to tell the same tale or better. 'Specially the officers. But they're scared shitless. Like us."

"Why?"

"Like I told you, sir, the bitch had a knack for threatening people into doing what she wanted and making the threats stick. When she was relieved to face a Disciplinary Board, she made sure we knew what would happen if we talked too much. Which means she gets away with it."

"Maybe not this time, Rownes. Admiral Kaleri can't cover her any more."

Banger shook her head. "She's fireproof, cap'n. Believe me. Ain't no one who doesn't want to see her bite the dust, but it would hurt way too much."

Siobhan slowly nodded. It fit with the Forenza she remembered from the Academy. There too, her family connections and wealth had protected her from a well-deserved expulsion, while it nearly cut Siobhan's budding career short. Remembering those days still made Dunmoore's blood boil, and Rownes noticed her growing anger, mistaking it for outrage at the tale she just told.

"Dunno if it's worth keeping on about, cap'n. When someone's that fireproof, you just forget the past and pick up the pieces."

"Except that no one on this ship has forgotten the past, have they? Anyways, how will Vasser, Melchor and the others pick up the pieces?"

Rownes shrugged as a troubled look creased her face.

"Sorry, cap'n I can't help you there." She looked away, running her fingers absently over the tube of her gun.

"Why not, Rownes? You've told me more in the last five minutes than the rest of the crew combined in weeks. Why stop now?"

The gunner's eyes turned back to stare defiantly at Siobhan. "'Cause there's things it ain't worth your life to talk about. Those poor sods ain't ever coming back, but I'd like to retire in one piece, and so would everybody else."

"Why would you fear for your life if you discussed an accident with your captain aboard a starship deep in interstellar space?" Siobhan tried hard to keep a patient tone.

"You figure it out, sir."

Siobhan was about to press the point when the ship-wide comm came on.

"Captain to the bridge, I repeat, captain to the bridge."

She looked around for an intercom unit. Rownes helpfully pointed one out, relieved that the summons had cut the discussion short.

"Bridge, Dunmoore here."

Pushkin's face appeared, a grim smile transforming his strong features.

"We've got contact on the long-range scanner, sir, deep in occupied space, heading for Cimmeria at low velocity."

"A convoy?" Siobhan felt her anger melt away, replaced by the excitement of the hunt.

"I'd say so, sir. The gunner makes it seven ships in close formation."

"Hot damn," Dunmoore hit the bulkhead with her gloved fist. "Keep it on the scanner but don't move any closer. If they're at our outer range, we're beyond their range, so they don't know we're here yet. I want to keep it that way for now. I'll be on the bridge in a few minutes. Dunmoore, out."

She grinned at Rownes. "Looks like you'll get to shoot off your guns for real pretty soon, spacer."

"Aye, sir. 'Bout what I said earlier..." Banger did not smile back.

"It'll remain between us," Siobhan nodded, understanding the woman's caution.

"Thanks, sir, but that's not what I meant. Just be careful when you ask questions. Forenza still has a few ass-kissers on board, people who'll rat on you if you start getting too close to the truth. And not all of 'em are simple suck-ups either."

Siobhan remembered Kowalski's warning. "Oh, you mean SSB agents?" She asked nonchalantly.

"Aye, sir," Rownes looked at her with a faint air of wonder. "We got warned that the spooks are keeping a particular eye on this ship and that they're friendly with Admiral Kaleri like you saw with that smuggler a few days ago. In fact, Cap'n Forenza made sure word got around that the SSB will watch for us to remain real quiet. Especially about 'accidents' in cargo holds. Can't trust all of us, sir."

"Thanks for the fair warning, Rownes."

She shrugged. "Ain't nothing, sir. You're a good cap'n, and you deserve better'n what we gave so far. Don't worry, that imperial convoy's as good as destroyed. You just get my guns close enough."

Surprising herself, Siobhan reached out and grasped Rownes' armored shoulder. "I guess I'd better get to the bridge and bring this ship within range then, eh?"

With a quick wink at the gunners, she turned and slid down the ladder, her mind already pushing away Banger Rownes' revelations to concentrate on the coming chase. She would get one chance to maul the convoy. After that, every Shrehari in the area would be on her trail. Maybe even Brakal, if he was still around.

Back in the turret, Demianova eyed her friend in silence for a long time. Rownes stared sightlessly at the deck while she thought hard about what she had done.

"Tell me, Banger," Demmi finally asked, "was this wise of you to speak? Never has Captain Forenza lied when she threatened."

Rownes shrugged. "Dunno, kid. I figure the shit has to come out some day. Maybe I'm crazy, but I don't feel like running scared for the rest of my hitch. You know, I actually feel better now that I told some to Cap'n Dunmoore. She's a good skipper, has her heart and her guts all in the right place, and she hates Forenza like we do. If anyone's gonna break the curse, I guess she's the best bet."

"And what about the 'accident,' Banger? More like it can happen."

"If I'm right, our captain is gonna keep going until she finds out everything, and then, the SSB and Forenza and the rest of the scum, watch out."

"Why?"

"Because that's one hell of a dangerous lady when she's pissed-off, Demmi. You look at her eyes sometimes, and you'll see." Rownes chuckled. "Wait 'til the convoy feels our bite. Then you'll see just what kind of a captain we got."

Demmi shivered. "I hope to God you are right, Banger."

— Fifteen —

Word of contact with an imperial convoy had spread through the ship like wildfire. It was the first time in a long time that *Stingray* was actually preparing to pursue the enemy with the intention of destroying him. For many among the crew, it was a new feeling, the thrill of the hunt.

Older hands knew that stalking a convoy meant more than a sudden bout of excitement and blazing cannons. It involved extended periods of tense boredom while the captain maneuvered into position, waiting for the best moment to strike. That deep in enemy territory, they would get only one chance, and they had to make it count. But they felt the thrill nonetheless.

"Report," Dunmoore ordered as she strode onto the bridge, her hand forestalling Pushkin's call to attention. With the enemy in sight, she was not about to waste time on formalities. Pushkin rose from the command chair and stepped aside. He nodded at the tactical display on the main screen.

"The convoy is traveling FTL again, presumably after calibrating the drives and taking a navigational fix. There's no chance they'll detect us. We made out five transports of various types and two warships, probably light cruisers or heavy corvettes." His face was as somber as usual, but there was no mistaking the gleam in his eyes. Pushkin wanted this as much as the rest of the crew, a chance to redeem himself in the eyes of his captain, and in his own eyes. Whoever said there were no bad sailors, only bad captains, had it right on the money.

Siobhan sat down, gnawing at her lower lip, reminding herself that the Shrehari were predictable when you understood why.

"Where's the third escort?"

"Sir?" Pushkin seemed surprised at the question.

"The Shrehari work with a fixed set of tactical doctrines. Initiative below the level of assault force commander is discouraged. Imperial doctrine on convoys specifies three escorts: one in the lead, and two covering the transports from opposite sides, aft of the last ship, so they can bear down on any raider. It's an efficient tactic for the level of resources commonly assigned to escort duty, and would be more efficient if their captains were allowed to show anything like our level of initiative."

"With two escorts, the pattern is open, but not that much more vulnerable to a single raider." She stared at the tactical. "Replay the time before they went FTL."

"Sir." Devall nodded. The tactical display changed to show a series of wedge-shaped red outlines in formation, moving slowly against the simulated background. An ever-changing set of numbers below told off the distance from *Stingray,* the course of the convoy and its velocity.

"Huh," Siobhan grunted, her gloved hand absently tracing the scar on her jawline. "See, Mister Pushkin. One escort ahead, one offside and slightly aft of the transports, but between them and us. Where's the other one?"

"Beneath the convoy, just out of range of our sensors?" Devall ventured.

Dunmoore nodded. "Most likely."

"Are you sure, sir?" Pushkin sounded dubious.

"Unless the convoy commander is someone like Brakal, that's what it'll be. It's the Shrehari' greatest weakness. Their predictability. For now at least. But if they let captains like Brakal change their way of doing business is spreading within the Deep Space Fleet, we're in trouble."

"You'd think after five years they'd have learned something," Guthren grumbled from his helm seat.

"Some have, cox'n. But the Imperial Council is wary of anything that weakens its control over the Emperor's Armed Forces. Imaginative ship captains are seen as a threat, and threats to the Council usually find themselves victims of the *Tai Kan,* the imperial secret police. Under those circumstances, it's little wonder most imperial officers stick to orthodoxy, thankfully for us. But then there are always the mavericks who live under some kind of social or political protection."

Pushkin stared at her, quizzically. Siobhan smiled and winked.

"Know thine enemy, Mister Pushkin, and use his weaknesses against him. Sailing master, plot a micro jump to a position ten light-seconds this side of their jump point. Mister Devall, the moment we emerge, plot the convoy's course and feed it to navigation. As they teach at the Academy, to start an FTL stern chase, begin by aiming your ship precisely at the enemy's stern."

After weeks of exhaustion and frustration, Siobhan suddenly felt very pleased with the situation, relaxed and confident. She enjoyed the challenge of a successful battle run more than she remembered, and it energized her like a drug.

If I was a hunting dog, I swear I'd be quivering. Then again, I've been cursed for a bitch lately... She grinned at the thought.

"Why ten light-seconds off their jump point, captain?" Pushkin asked, genuinely curious. "It would be easier if we started the chase *at* the jump point."

"It would. But if one of the Empire's few lone wolves is shadowing the convoy, he'll be hoping for some foolhardy frigate to appear in his gun sights, and thus, he'll be watching the jump point. As we are not a reckless frigate," she grinned, "we will emerge far enough from it to have space room in case an enemy cruiser is waiting and still be able to follow the convoy with only one subsequent course correction."

Pushkin nodded, impressed by Siobhan's sharp thinking, and simultaneously disgusted at his own atrophied tactical senses. Two years under a cowardly captain had done much to quash what he had learned at the Academy and from serving under other commanders. He could do a lot worse than listen, watch and learn from Siobhan Dunmoore. She clearly was in her element and knew exactly what she was doing. It comforted Pushkin, but worried him too, for she also had the wild streak of a gambler and he did not have her confidence in the crew's ability to respond with split-second precision.

"Course laid in and ready, sir," Shara's nasal voice announced.

"Helm, stand by. Mister Pushkin, the hunt is on. Take the ship to general quarters."

"Aye, aye, sir. Mister Kowalski, sound general quarters."

Almost immediately, the screech of the siren filled the frigate with its grating sound.

"Mister Pushkin," Siobhan sat back in her chair and crossed her legs, the perfect image of nonchalance, "kill the transponder, and turn all running and navigation lights off."

Pushkin cocked an eyebrow in question. Whether *Stingray*'s lights and transponder were on or off would have no bearing on the enemy's ability to detect them. They did not intend to go to silent running, and the frigate's FTL bubble gave off a strong enough trace to act as a space beacon for any decently sensitive detection gear. Then, the first officer noticed the reaction of the bridge crew to Siobhan's words. He slowly nodded and gave the order, wondering how she managed to gage the crew's mood so accurately.

Siobhan however, felt slightly cheap for a few heartbeats. It was sheer manipulation, a play on the crew's perceptions. But Adnan had taught her to use everything she could to make her people fight better, by getting them to believe in themselves and their ship. It was irrational, but shutting off the lights made them feel the frigate had become dark and menacing like a deep space shark, or a submarine in ancient wet navy days.

She shrugged off the feeling and grinned at Pushkin. It was meant to be reassuring, but it merely reinforced his ambivalent fear that she could easily take *Stingray* to its doom. Or to a victory that would wipe the shame away.

Then, she squared herself in the chair. "Helm, engage."

Nausea gripped Siobhan, as it gripped the others, only to vanish a second or so later.

The FTL jump lasted just long enough to let the crew come to full battle stations. By the time the wrenching emergence nausea dissipated, the temporarily disoriented humans and computers were ready to fight. Though the precaution was sound, it turned out to have been wasted. There was no lurking imperial cruiser. But it only took one imprudent jump to end the battle run.

"Guns, put the convoy on tactical."

The Shrehari were ahead of *Stingray*, their signatures already fading as they sped away. The convoy icons merged on the screen, flickering as they moved beyond range. But two other symbols stood alone on either side of the transports, still within sensor range.

"There, Mister Pushkin, the third escort. It was indeed too distant for our instrumentation when we first sighted them. That's good. It means we're dealing with a conventional Shrehari commander, as I hoped." She smiled briefly.

"Mister Shara, plot a half light year jump to intersect their axis of travel. That ought to put us within stalking range by the time we re-emerge. From there, we can close in at FTL and use their drives' wake to mask our approach."

Moments later, "Course plotted and laid in, sir."

"Helm, engage."

Again, they felt the jump sickness hit and vanish. But this time, the wait until emergence would stretch to hours, not minutes. A stern chase was a long chase. The scanners lost all trace of the convoy, their range in the hyperspace bubble severely limited. Nor could they detect a vessel moving in normal space unless it was very close. For all practical purposes, *Stingray* was blind and deaf, while any enemy traveling in normal space nearby could track her and plan her death. It was an uncomfortable thought, this deep within Shrehari-controlled space, something one did not dwell on. Solitary ship missions always had a sharper edge of risk and higher levels of paranoia. The only alternative to compulsive nail biting was keeping busy.

"Mister Devall," she turned to the gunnery officer, "how good are your people at torpedo sniping?"

"Fair, sir. I put them through about three hundred simulations over the last week, and I estimate they could force a ship into normal space within three shots. But we would have to be incredibly lucky to cause any damage."

Which was what one could say about any average ship's torpedo gunners. A few captains pushed torpedo sniping to a fine art, but Siobhan had always believed them to be only a means to bring an enemy ship back into normal space, where she could use her guns and missiles to beat it into submission. But at three torpedoes a ship, she would burn up her stocks in no time. And the tender was not due for another two weeks. The thought reminded her of the many unanswered questions still hanging over them. Irritably, she pushed them back into a conveniently dark corner of her mind.

Siobhan suddenly realized she was a lot more nervous than she cared to admit. It would be her first solo fight from start to finish since she lost *Shenzen*. And back then, she had Ezekiel Holt and a familiar, happy, and well-trained crew to back her. Repressing a yawn, one of those sure signs of nervousness, she rose and casually adjusted her battledress tunic, feeling like an actress in a play. A very deadly play.

"I'll be in my ready room, Mister Pushkin." Siobhan kept her tone light, unconcerned as if this was an everyday cruise. "Unfortunately, paperwork will not outwait the war. If only someone found a practical way to strangle the Empire with all our red tape. Call me when we're ready to start the chase in earnest." She made it sound as if their initial moves were routine, not actually part of the hunt. Pushkin shot her another speculative look.

"Aye, aye, sir."

When the door closed behind her, Siobhan exhaled slowly, conscious of the curious glances that had followed her. The kind that wondered how the skipper could be so bloody cool and crack jokes when they were bearing down on a certain fight. She shook her head ruefully. Command was more often in the realm of the actor than anyone cared to admit. That was probably why they called it the *art* of leadership.

With a sigh, she dropped into the chair and switched on her terminal, calling up a list of the red tape rituals she had to perform to keep the tin gods at HQ happy. And this was before the battle. Siobhan did not even want to think of the paperwork waiting for her after the fight. If they made it that far.

*

The sleek, dark shape of the imperial cruiser *Tol Vakash* cut through hyperspace on a shallow approach to the Cimmeria Sector. It would not do to cross the invisible barrier between conquered space and the Commonwealth against orders. At least not yet, not while a *Tai Kan* officer watched. It would not do to make Trage's life too easy.

Over the last few days, Brakal and Jhar had come to the conclusion that Khrada was more than his putative rank indicated. And therefore much more dangerous. He displayed an intimate knowledge of starship operations, Fleet doctrine and of Brakal's career and family. Though the last two were expected of *Tai Kan* operatives, the first was unusual indeed.

Brakal had hoped to curb Khrada by playing on his *Tai Kan* ignorance of real life in the Deep Space Fleet. That hope had vanished, along with Jhar's confident plan of killing Khrada as soon as the cruiser reached the line. While the death of a *Tai Kan* lieutenant could be overlooked, even if he was sent on the Council's order, Khrada represented a deeper danger, one which his death on Brakal's ship would only worsen.

Surprising Brakal and Jhar too was Khrada's lack of involvement in the ship's affairs. He declined to meddle with the commander's exercise of his command, with life aboard the ship and did not comment on the often-treasonous jokes bandied about freely by the crew. Neither did Khrada show the usual crude disdain and suspicion toward Brakal's less than orthodox leadership style and his open study of anything human.

The *Tai Kan* officer quietly watched, took notes, and sent reports to his masters. Even the code he used proved childishly easy to crack as if Khrada wished it so.

His actions reminded Jhar of nothing so much as an investigator preparing a case for the Imperial Inquisitor, for Brakal's court-martial. The thought stunned him, for the Council had not shown much desire to adhere to the Codes of late, preferring the expediency of staged accidents and other forms of more or less subtle assassination.   But it made sense, in a perverse way. Killing Brakal would only fan the flames of discontent among Deep Space Fleet officers and among the Clan Lords opposed to the Council's dictatorship. Discrediting him, however, presented a pleasant alternative, especially if they could prove Brakal actually did disobey orders and conducted himself in a manner offensive to the Code. That would stay the hand of those who would be inclined to rise for a real martyr. A conviction would not carry with it the punishment of death, but simple dismissal from the Fleet would do just as well, followed, once the dust settled, by a well-crafted accident.

When Jhar presented his thoughts to his commander, Brakal laughed uproariously and slapped his first officer on the shoulder.

"You are definitely becoming a *hereditary* member of the Warrior caste, Jhar. Your ability to see through the webs of intrigue spun by the scum on the home world is nothing short of astonishing in someone who has not lived among them all his life. Yes, my friend, I fear you are right. I have come to the same conclusion. Khrada is here to build a case. The Council intends to use the Code against me because it fears to use its usual dishonorable methods." Brakal suddenly became serious as he turned to stare at the pseudo-view of space on the view screen in his cabin.

"Mind you, this new tactic of theirs is much more dangerous than any direct attack. I cannot, as an officer and Clan Lord, deny and evade any valid accusation under the Code. Even half-truths, dressed to resemble actual facts, are enough to stay those who would support me."

"What will you do?"

Brakal grimaced as if he had bitten on a sour *r'fit*. "What choice have I? Obey my orders and yet try to fight the humans as best I can. And leave Khrada to carry out his duties in peace. But I will not dishonor myself or this ship in any way. If that means I must face the Inquisitor upon our return, then so be it."

Jhar growled with displeasure. "If this is how the Empire wishes to function, then it deserves to submit to the humans."

Brakal laughed again, but this time, it was tinged with bitter irony. "Take care of your words, Jhar, lest you face the Inquisitor with me. For all the good it will do the Empire. We are losing this war, and the turds on Shrehari Prime cannot even see it." He turned around to face his first officer. "Be that as it may. We still have our duties. Find me a convoy I can shadow, and I guarantee a small victory for the Empire."

"Commander." Jhar nodded and left Brakal to his thoughts.

*

Two hours later, the commander joined his first officer on the bridge, observed as always by Khrada's sharp, unblinking eye.

"You have something, Jhar?"

"Yes. Convoy *Lhat-One-One* is proceeding to Cimmeria to reinforce the garrison. Its course brings it within striking range of the human patrols on the line. It is composed of five transports, two of which carry Regiments of Imperial Levies, and three *Kardan* class corvettes. The convoy left Garenga one week ago."

"Interesting, sub-commander," Khrada remarked from his vantage point near the security console. His words momentarily stilled Brakal and astonished the crew. He had not yet spoken on the bridge, and his words cut through the tense atmosphere. "Convoy information is highly classified, and not for dissemination to every patrol ship. How did you come across it?"

Jhar looked at Khrada with teeth bared in a parody of a grin. "A little *irag* whispered it in my ear, lieutenant."

"And does that *irag* have a name and rank, sub-commander?" Khrada's tone would have been insubordinate, had everybody accepted the fiction of his lowly rank. As it was, Jhar merely snorted.

"The *Tai Kan* will forgive me for doing my duty, lieutenant. Even you should appreciate the difficulties of protecting our operations with inadequate information."

"I see," Khrada replied, a vulpine grin creasing his bony features. With deliberation, he took his pad from his pocket and made a few notes for his periodic report to the home world. "It will not be difficult to ascertain the origin of the security breach."

Brakal, who had kept silent, letting his first officer show his confidence and power aboard *Tol Vakash*, now snarled.

"Stations!"

The crew stiffened and turned their attention back to their duties. Jhar and Khrada remained in their respective postures, staring each other down.

"Lieutenant Khrada, you will include, in your report, that the *Tai Kan*'s paranoid notions of security are helping the humans best us in this war." Brakal swiveled his chair to face the spy. "And, Khrada, if you actually claim such high knowledge of tactics and combat, you should know that keeping a convoy secret from our own forces will hamper any attempt to counter a human raid. Three corvettes will not prevent an enterprising human frigate captain from cutting out one, even two transports without suffering any damage. Not if that captain understands the Shrehari way of thinking. And more of the humans than you may think do understand us, while we make every effort to not understand them. You are dismissed, lieutenant."

Khrada's face had tightened in anger at the public rebuke, but he dared not challenge the commander on his own bridge. He saluted crisply, turned on his heels and left. Jhar's cruel grin followed him out but was cut short by Brakal's pre-occupied frown.

"Your orders, commander?" He asked.

"My orders are to shadow convoy *Lhat-One-One*, Jhar. No matter what the *Tai Kan*'s notions of security entail, my instinct tells me the humans will find it and strike."

"Maybe without the *Tai Kan*'s paranoia we can eventually win this war, commander," Jhar grumbled. "A pox on all spies, admirals, and politicians."

— Sixteen —

Siobhan shut off the terminal with a sigh and checked her timepiece. Another four hours before they emerged to pick up the convoy's trail. Time enough for some sleep. They would get precious little of it once the hunt was on in earnest. She rose and poked her head through the door to the bridge. Lighting was back to normal, now that the ship was in a sort of half-state between full battle stations and cruising stations. But from this state, *Stingray* would be combat-ready in less than a minute because the crew now lived at their posts. It was tiring and not a little unnerving, but there was no helping that. This deep in enemy territory, personal comfort took the backseat to survival. Any skilled Shrehari captain could creep up behind *Stingray* in hyperspace, masked by the frigate's own wake and take aim. Which was exactly the kind of tactic Siobhan intended to use on the convoy. A blind cat and mouse game at unimaginable speeds, in parallel universe bubbles where the normal laws of physics did not work.

Lieutenant Devall had the watch, and all was quiet. Siobhan quickly drew her head back into her ready room, lest Devall calls the bridge to attention, and took the other door to the passage. The ship was eerily quiet, except for the thrumming of the jump drives, a sound that soothed Siobhan's taut nerves. She met no one on her way to her quarters.

She was about to enter her cabin when, on an impulse, she turned around and stared at the door to Pushkin's quarters across the way. Siobhan had never entered them, as indeed she had never entered any of her officers' cabins. Without quite knowing why, she touched the call plate by

the door and waited. A few seconds later, the door opened
to a gruff voice.

When Pushkin caught sight of his captain, he tossed his
reader aside and rose. The first officer still wore his
battledress but had unfastened the tunic to let it hang
loosely. His emergency bag sat squarely on the small desk
by the bed, ready for action.

"Am I disturbing you, Mister Pushkin?"

"No, sir. What can I do for you?" His tone was polite,
though his eyes spoke of surprise at this unexpected
invasion of his privacy.

"May I come in?"

He waved his arm, clearly resigned at the interruption.
"Please, sir. This ship, including my cabin, is yours."

She considered him for a fraction of a second, and then
shook her head as she took a step back into the passage.
"I'm sorry for interrupting you. Maybe some other time."

Startling both Siobhan and himself, Pushkin held up a
hand. "My apologies, sir. Come in. This time, I mean it."
And he did, but for reasons he could not explain. Siobhan
Dunmoore had in turn, puzzled him, infuriated him,
confounded him, and made him reassess his most basic
assumptions. In short, he no longer knew where he stood
with her, and with his career. He did not much like the
feeling.

Siobhan cocked her head to one side, meeting his dark
eyes, but she entered the cabin and let the door close
behind her. It was small, smaller than Siobhan's, but
larger than the regular officers' quarters.

Pushkin's decoration tastes were as spartan as Siobhan's,
which, on second thought did not surprise her. The man
himself was spare and withdrawn. An officer's sword hung
on the wall, a few printed books occupied a shelf, and an
exquisite bonsai maple grew in a simple clay pot on the
desk. Those, along with a trio of holopics were the only
personal touches. Two of the pictures showed smiling
groups of people, one apparently Pushkin's family, while
the other was his Academy graduation class.

The third hologram held her eyes, and she examined it
with profound interest. It showed an ancient, gray

wooden building, a pagoda-like structure whose eaves jutted out to form stylized sea serpent heads, like those found on Viking ships. A modest cross adorned one of the many roofs. It was surrounded by a low fieldstone wall and a meadow covered with small yellow flowers. In the background, an immense blue sky seemed to go on forever. The building's simplicity and surroundings enchanted Siobhan, and she smiled.

"It's the church in my ancestral village back on Earth, sir," Pushkin softly explained, surprised by Dunmoore's delighted reaction and interest. "It's gone now, but legend has it that it was built by the Vikings who settled on the Volga more than a thousand years ago."

"You're a Christian?" She turned to face Pushkin, suddenly reminded that she knew almost nothing about the real man behind the bland personal file. He probably knew more about her.

"Yes, sir. But I guess I don't practice it much anymore. My mother always insisted on retaining the old traditions and upholding our family's faith." He shrugged absently, as if it was all in the past, long forgotten. "When she died, I gave up caring about God."

Siobhan glanced at the holo again, intrigued by Pushkin's reason for keeping it so prominently displayed, and by the unexpected, intimate turn of the conversation. She had no particular reason for visiting him. Now, it seemed a reason was emerging anyway: a chance to learn more about her closed, brooding first officer. She decided to make the most of it, opening herself as he had opened himself.

"I don't follow any particular religion myself or have any special beliefs. My family never has. I guess my father's only faith was money and fame." *Now why did I tell him this?* "My mother, if she believed in anything, never had the time to teach us." She fell silent and shrugged. Pushkin wordlessly offered her a seat.

"It's funny, though," she finally continued in a thoughtful tone, "but when I look out the porthole at the immensity and deadly beauty of the universe, of the stars, I can't help think that there must be a Higher Power somewhere who created it all. I can't explain it otherwise."

Pushkin chuckled. "You know, sir, I think you've just defined religion in its purest sense. Awe at what we can't explain."

Siobhan smiled. "Maybe I have. But maybe sometimes it would be better if I did believe in a particular philosophy. It might help me face life more easily."

Pushkin considered her reply. "It might. Or it might give you an out, something to follow blindly when another, more considered if less comfortable response would be better. Religion is a double-edged sword."

Siobhan sighed. "Quite. And so is command. We'll be fighting the Shrehari in less than a day."

"And it's about high time." His voice had an unusual undertone of relief.

She cocked an eyebrow. "I had the feeling you were dubious about this battle run."

Pushkin smiled tightly. "Not about the run, sir. But about the crew's ability to get it right. They haven't seen the whites of the enemy's eyes in a long time. And they've lost their faith. In themselves and in the ship."

"Have you?"

He grimaced, mentally taking a step toward the dark abyss that had beckoned him since Siobhan had entered his life. Toward the honesty his duties demanded, the honesty he had been unable to give her so far.

"I'm not sure anymore." His eyes slid away to the small holo of the church. "I thought so at one time. Now? I just don't know what kind of an officer I am, nor do I know what kind of a ship this is. I guess we'll find out soon enough."

"It may be too late by then," Siobhan replied in a whisper. "A crew that doesn't believe in itself or its ship cannot fight and survive for long. You're right, though, you don't know what you are, and neither do most of the people aboard. It shows. And if you don't know, you can't believe."

He did not reply or meet her gaze. His eyes remained fixed on the holo and the silence deepened, underscored only by the low hum of the ship driving headlong toward an imperial convoy.

When he looked back at Siobhan, she read pain and self-loathing in his eyes. The intensity of his gaze struck her like something physical, but she successfully repressed the urge to speak.

"You're right too, captain." His voice was hoarse, but his tone hard. "We, except a few select bastards, have lost our faith, thanks to that bitch Forenza." The depth of feeling in his words twisted Siobhan's guts. He laughed harshly, an ugly, tortured sound. "You wouldn't bloody believe what this ship was like before, thank God, the Admiralty had the courage to relieve her."

"I would," Siobhan quietly replied. "You see, I nearly lost my chance at a career thanks to Helen Forenza. And Leading Spacer Rownes has been telling me something of what life was like under her."

He stared at Siobhan for several heartbeats. Then looked away. "Whatever you think, whatever Rownes told you, it was a lot worse. And there was nothing I or anyone else could do. The hell-bitch had us all under her power, and we sacrificed our integrity and our honor just to survive, in the hopes that we could get away from this ship of the damned. God Almighty," he ran his trembling hand through his short hair, "I — I lost all the courage I thought I had. I hated myself for letting her go on, letting her get away with it all. But," he stared at Siobhan again, a wildness replacing the self-loathing in his eyes, "I desperately wanted to command my own ship one day, and crossing Forenza would have extinguished that hope forever. She broke more careers than the Disciplinary Board, for trivialities. I tried to keep things together as best I could, without hanging myself, but it wasn't enough. And I simply didn't have the guts to do more. There are many aboard this ship who hold me in contempt, and they're right to do so. *I* hold myself in contempt."

"When faced with Forenza's kind of evil," Siobhan said, once Pushkin had fallen silent, "all bets are off. I can't blame you for seeking to preserve yourself, and there's at least one solid crewmember who thinks you did your best."

"Rownes?"

Siobhan nodded. "What I said when I came aboard still holds. Everyone gets a clean slate. Otherwise, I'd only be compounding Forenza's unfairness. So far, I have no complaints, first officer. You know your job, and you do it well. Although," she smiled sadly, "you had to relearn some of it."

"Yeah." He rubbed his face with both hands and then looked at her. "Listen, captain, the shit isn't over yet. Forenza's hand still hangs over us."

Meaning you're still scared enough of her to keep quiet about something. "I figured that. With the kind of friends she has, she can make sure nothing about her indiscretions is ever heard about."

"Yeah, right again. And not only Forenza. She and Admiral Kaleri are asshole buddies. The admiral took good care of Forenza and is still watching her back now that she's facing the board."

"Why?"

A guarded look covered Pushkin's open gaze. "I'm not sure, sir. At least, I don't have any proof, only theories. But it's unhealthy to speak of them."

"Unhealthy like Vasser, Melchor, and Byrn found out?"

Pushkin slowly nodded. "That's what I think. They crossed some invisible line, speculated about things they should have left alone, and paid for it with their lives. But they're not the only ones who paid." When Siobhan raised her eyebrows in question, he continued. "We had four alleged suicides on this ship in the year preceding Forenza's departure. One ensign and three ratings."

"Alleged?" Siobhan frowned, remembering Rownes' words on the same subject.

"I don't know, sir. Really. She used them for her own ends, that much was generally known, but they had no reason to kill themselves. Maybe it's my paranoia, sir. God knows it was rampant before you got here. And still is, to some extent."

"A great extent, I think."

"Yes," Pushkin shook his head ruefully. "When you took command, we didn't know what we were in for. Forenza had warned us to forget the past entirely before she left, and Admiral Kaleri reinforced that message, not directly mind you, but clearly enough. I even thought for a while that you were Fleet Security, come to find out what *actually* happened, and dump the rest of us right into it."

Not only you, Gregor. Hell, that would explain everybody's caution and reticence. Siobhan frowned as something in his words tugged at a fleeting memory. He looked at her questioningly, and she shook her head.

"Just a thought about something I heard back at Starbase 31. I can't pin it down right now. Go on."

"Listen, captain, I freely admit I'm scared, too bloody scared to tell you what I think, what I pieced together. So are the others. I believe we trust you by now. At least I do. You've made us relearn what trust, honor and all the other qualities of a good officer are. But I don't think you can protect us, least of all from whoever is still watching us aboard this bloody ship."

"Who is doing the watching, Gregor?"

He flinched at the sound of his first name.

"I don't know."

"Someone hinted that the SSB had watchers aboard."

His head came up so fast Siobhan almost expected to hear his vertebrae crack.

"Good Lord, captain," he said in an anguished tone, "you place yourself in danger by even mentioning them."

Siobhan shrugged. "I've always believed that the best defense was a good offense. If I can find out who is a danger to this ship, and I must because it's my duty as captain, then I can neutralize them. The SSB aren't the bogeymen we make them out to be, especially not on a navy ship."

"You can't take the whole corrupt bunch on by yourself. Not if your own superiors are against you."

Siobhan smiled cruelly. "Who said anything about taking all of them on? What I want to do, no, make that must do, is clear the air on *Stingray*. And that's within the scope of my abilities. Whatever happens in deep space happens within the confines of the ship. By the time we're in physical contact with civilization again, it'll be too late for 'them' to do anything about it, and they'll simply cut their losses. That's the way these people work. But we have to return to civilization, and that means we have to win in the next few days."

"And to win, we have to make the crew believe again, feel secure on their ship," Pushkin completed the thought, slowly nodding. The fear still remained in his eyes, but a new, hard look of determination was gradually pushing it out.

He took a deep breath and then exhaled slowly.

"Okay, captain. I'm tired of being scared. If I hang, then so be it. At least I'll hang with a clean conscience."

For the next half-hour, Siobhan listened to her first officer, fascinated by his story, his theories, and suspicions. She did not interrupt him once, letting the flow of words come in a continuous stream. He proved to have a sharp, insightful mind, and the ability to analyze and form accurate theories with widely scattered bits of information. But what intrigued Siobhan most, was that his ideas matched hers with frightening precision.

When Pushkin finally ran out of words, he sat back and looked at Siobhan, his eyes steady, his jaw set.

"Well, what now, captain?"

She slowly shook her head. "I don't know, Gregor. I'll have to think about what you said, and what we do with it. In the meantime, speak to those crewmembers you trust, and tell them you told me, that I know. If nothing else, spreading the word may make people feel a bit better."

He nodded again.

"Don't worry," she gave him a tight smile, "we'll get this sorted out soon enough. Our duty to the ship demands it."

She rose, suppressed a yawn that had more to do with nervousness than fatigue and stretched her long arms in front of her.

"Time for a snooze, I think. Good night, Gregor."

*

Back in her cabin, Siobhan was too restless to sleep and paced the small room, lost in thought for a long time. Then, she checked the duty roster and smiled, her plan taking shape at last. She touched the intercom.

"Lieutenant Kowalski to the captain's quarters as soon as possible."

"Acknowledged, sir," the younger woman's voice replied a few seconds later. "I'll be there in a few minutes."

"Good. Dunmoore, out."

Siobhan did not have to wait long. Slightly out of breath, Kathryn Kowalski appeared at her door less than two minutes after the summons.

"Come in, lieutenant. Sit." Siobhan waved at a chair by the desk. "Have you given the matter of ECM some thought?"

"Yes, sir." She nodded, her eyes looking warily at the captain as if she was not sure of her ground. Then, with a mental shrug Kowalski dug into her bag and produced a handheld sensor, similar to the ones the boarding party had used to such good effect. Wordlessly, she placed it on the desk and touched a button. Nothing overt seemed to happen, but Kowalski glanced at the sensor's screen and nodded, apparently satisfied.

"I assumed, sir, that you wanted something to mask conversations inside the ship, rather than electronic countermeasures aimed at the Shrehari, who wouldn't fail to notice us in their space any way we put it."

Siobhan smiled with wry amusement. "You assumed correctly, Kathryn."

Kowalski grinned with apparent self-satisfaction and seemed to take the captain using her first name in stride. "Then, sir, what you have before you is a totally illegal, jury-rigged and impossible to duplicate full spectrum scrambler." At Siobhan's questioning gaze, she continued. "What I've done is modify the sensor's scanning emitter to produce an inaudible wave that conflicts with human speech sound waves as they're picked up by a listening device. The waves are scrambled out of all recognition. It's pretty crude and won't stand up to a sophisticated filtering program, but I damn well know we don't have such a program aboard. It's something the spooks use and guard pretty jealously. The scrambler is good for a radius of about two meters, which cover most of your day cabin."

"Well done, lieutenant. You have hidden talents begging to come out into the limelight."

Kowalski's smile became self-conscious, and she glanced away. "It's all a question of motivation, I guess."

"And getting at the watchers is good motivation?"

"Watchers? Oh, right. I did tell you to beware the SSB, didn't I?" The smile vanished, though the eyes remained on the ship's clock ticking away quietly on the shelf. Kowalski sighed. "Hell, they can't understand us so I might as well tell you. It's been itching to come out ever since I pegged you for a *real* captain and not another Forenza."

"You were, ah, wary." Somehow, the word 'scared' did not seem to fit Kowalski.

"Yes. I still am, but I can't keep this to myself any more. I want to have a normal career one day, and leave *Stingray* behind me. And the only way I can do that -"

"Is chase away the demons," Siobhan cut in. "It seems to be catching, thank God. First Rownes, then Mister Pushkin, now you." Kowalski's head came up at the first officer's name.

"Yes," Siobhan continued, "Mister Pushkin has made a clean breast of it." *Or at least as much as he could stomach in one session, which was still a lot.* "For pretty much the same reasons as you. But why don't you give me your version? Feel free to speculate."

Siobhan Dunmoore nodded grimly when Kowalski fell silent, after a long, almost confessional discourse. The stories matched, even though Kowalski's appraisal of Pushkin was not quite as flattering as Rownes'. While it still did not provide Siobhan with any proof, it reinforced some of her ideas.

The signals officer, however, seemed to feel none of the self-loathing and disgust that had filled Pushkin when he spoke about his role under Forenza. True, the first officer did bear more responsibility than Kowalski, but the young woman seemed to have a greater toughness, a better ability to absorb the shocks and keep her emotions under control. For the first time, Siobhan caught a glimpse of the fire and steel within her, and knew, if given half a chance, that Kathryn Kowalski would go far in the navy. She had an uncanny realism and a sense of proportion one usually expected in older, more experienced officers.

"Kathryn," Siobhan spoke softly, "as I told Mister Pushkin, I do not intend to leave matters as they are. But I've got to catch the watchers first, and get them out of the way before I can convince the crew that Forenza's long-distance hold on the ship is finally over."

And do a few other highly satisfying things too, come to think of it. Whoever said revenge was a dish best eaten cold didn't get it.

"I need your help to flush them out before they decide that I've become too much of a liability. And I need to do it within the next day because I could easily go the same route as Vasser and Melchor: have an accident. During a battle, that's pretty damn easy to arrange."

Kowalski nodded her understanding. When Siobhan described what she wanted, the signals officer smiled. "That might just work, sir."

Unfortunately, they did not get any further. Time had passed more quickly than Siobhan thought.

"Captain, officer of the watch here." Devall's lean face appeared on the screen. "We emerge at the convergence point in five minutes."

"Get the ship back to full battle stations. I'm on my way."

— Seventeen —

By the time Siobhan and Kowalski got to the bridge, the lighting had returned to battle red, and Devall reported the ship ready. The tension had risen to a fine pitch and Siobhan caught several crewmembers anxiously glancing at the countdown to emergence ticking away in the lower right corner of the screen. If an enemy had them pinned, he would strike in the seconds after they dropped back into normal space, when both humans and machines were disoriented by the brutal transition between universes.

Unconsciously, Siobhan braced herself in the chair as the final seconds flashed by. Then, the sickening nausea hit her like a sledgehammer, and her world became flawed, indistinct, and hazy. The sensation lasted the time of a few deep breaths, then the momentarily stunned crew recovered and plunged into a flurry of activity.

"Nothing within sensor range, save for the convoy, sir," Devall reported first.

"All systems green," Pushkin chimed in.

"Good. Sailing master, verify the convoy's course and plot a pursuit on their exact vector. Helm, get the FTL drives cycled and ready. Guns, get those torpedoes armed." Siobhan smiled cruelly. "Let's go draw first blood, people."

Maybe she could do nothing about her internal enemies for now, but she could release her pent-up frustration and anger at the Shrehari.

"Ready," the sailing master and cox'n announced almost simultaneously.

"Helm, engage."

Vision distorted as stomachs lurched in protest, and *Stingray* sped off in her own FTL bubble again, on the exact course taken by the slower convoy. This time, the wait would be much shorter, and maneuvering more delicate. Siobhan had to place her ship within striking range of the last transport in line but remain outside the sensor range of the two trailing escorts.

"Mister Shara, what's your estimate of time to intercept."

The thin lieutenant cocked her head to one side but did not turn to face Siobhan. Then, she said, "If they keep the same speed and don't emerge, one hour."

It tallied with Dunmoore's own gut feeling. "They won't emerge, Mister Shara, not unless they have a compelling reason."

"Sir?" Pushkin looked at the captain with a questioning frown.

"Standard Shrehari procedure, Mister Pushkin," Siobhan replied, smiling. "They emerge to recalibrate and change to a new tack every six hours. That means in two hours from now. We'll have them before then."

Unable to sit still this close to the fight and unwilling to appear antsy in front of the others, Siobhan rose. She looked unconcerned as she glanced around the bridge.

"I'll be in my ready room, Mister Pushkin. Mister Kowalski, as per our early conversation, if you could manage it within the next hour, I'd be grateful."

"Consider it done," the younger woman replied, nodding.

Pushkin gave them a questioning glance, but saw the warning in Dunmoore's eyes and understood this had to do with something other than the battle run. He held his peace.

Alone in the ready room, Siobhan steeled herself and sat down, drawing the computer terminal toward her. She opened her personal log and began typing in the routine daily entry. Then, she gathered her thoughts, forcefully pushing aside the coming battle, and set her trap.

I have learned, she wrote, *that my predecessor has been guilty of the most discreditable neglect of duty imaginable. According to the statements of two officers, one of whom quite senior, and one experienced rating, Helen Forenza has, while refusing to seek out and engage the enemy, alienated most of the crew, pitted the officers against each other and played favorites in a manner too disturbing to make public without sworn testimony to back it up.*

Fingers flying over the keyboard, Siobhan added all the details she knew, including Forenza's abuse of power, her threats, and the high rate of supposed suicide on the frigate.

This explains, in great part, the terrible state of the ship and the crew's nonexistent morale when I took command. Both have since improved, the state of the ship considerably, and the morale sufficiently to function. When we return to port, I hope to have learned more from my crew and gained enough of their trust that they will agree to testify against Commander Forenza at the Disciplinary Board hearing, if it isn't concluded by then. If it is and she's out of the navy, I'll at least try to have their statements read into the record.

The statements will also destroy Rear Admiral Kaleri's credibility since Forenza was a friend and trusted subordinate, by all accounts. The obvious excuse that Kaleri had no idea what went on aboard the ship during the time of Forenza's command won't wash, as that is also a clear admission of neglect of duty. In a just universe, Forenza and Kaleri should hang for their failure as officers and commanders. But there is more to Stingray's saga than just an incredibly incompetent captain, raised to the post by political patronage and protected by the ill-advised friendship of a flag officer. Both were also involved in something much worse.

Siobhan sat back, organizing her thoughts for the next part of her log entry, the one that would deal with speculation and theory, the one for which they had no proof, only circumstantial evidence. And very strong suspicions. Unexpectedly, her intercom buzzed. She swore at the interruption.

"Dunmoore."

"Pushkin, sir. The chief engineer reports a problem with the antimatter injection controllers."

"How serious?"

"According to Tiner, plenty. I'm in engineering right now, sir. Devall has the con," he added.

"On my way." Siobhan cut the transmission and cursed volubly. If they could not maintain FTL speed, their prey would slip away while they became a very vulnerable and isolated target far from the nearest naval unit. She glanced at her incomplete log entry and saved it before leaving the bridge deck for engineering, deep down in the frigate's hull. It would have to wait. As she stepped into the lift, Siobhan felt a change in the drives' vibrations, and she knew that Tiner was right. This was no ordinary malfunction.

The chief engineer and Pushkin met her by the bulkhead separating the engineering compartment from the rest of the ship. Under the circumstances, Siobhan dispensed with pleasantries. She nodded at Tiner.

"Report."

Tiner's face, for once, showed more worry than nervousness. "Both antimatter injection controllers are approaching the red zone. We've already got sparking in the starboard one, and I don't think I'll be able to hold them much longer. If we get a catastrophic failure..."

"Why the breakdown?" Siobhan struggled to hide her frustration, lest she flustered the chief engineer into agitated uselessness.

"I really have no idea, sir. The units are old but haven't reached end-of-life yet. As best I can tell is that the command circuits are failing under load."

"Including the redundancies?" Siobhan asked, incredulous.

Surprisingly it was Pushkin who replied. "Aye, captain. The design was never a great success. The primary and secondary circuits are too intimately linked. In most cases, primary failures spread rapidly to the secondary. We have to take the engines offline and pull the controllers."

"Damn! Okay." Siobhan turned to the nearest intercom panel. "Bridge, Dunmoore here. Cut out the jump drives, but continue on the same course at maximum sublight. We have some repairs to do."

"Aye, aye, sir," Devall replied promptly.

"And keep your eyes peeled for Imps," she added, unnecessarily, almost savagely. "Dunmoore out." A second or so later, they were gripped by emergence nausea.

"How are we set on spares?"

Pushkin grimaced. "One spare controller, sir. Just one. The damn things aren't supposed to fail in tandem."

"Did anyone tell *them* that?" Siobhan's lips thinned in frustration. "Unless your wizards can fix one of the two busted ones, we're essentially stuck behind enemy lines, Mister Tiner."

"I'm afraid so, captain." The chief engineer blinked nervously. "But we'll manage, I'm sure. Cannibalize one to fix the other."

"How long?"

"I'll put part of the team on installing the spare, and the rest on fixing one of the two damaged units. I'd say three hours."

Siobhan mentally calculated the range to the convoy and bit back a particularly juicy oath. They would probably lose it, but there was no helping that. She nodded curtly at the chief engineer.

"Better get going then. Coming Mister Pushkin?"

"Aye, sir."

Back in the passage beyond engineering's thick bulkheads, Pushkin surprised Siobhan by swearing softly.

"You know, captain, this is one of those times where I could actually start believing *Stingray* is a jinxed ship. We're within an hour of ambushing an unsuspecting convoy and zap! Both antimatter injection controllers crap out at the same time. It's like the universe is conspiring against us."

Siobhan grunted. "The universe or someone aboard the ship?"

"Sir?" Pushkin stopped and stared at Dunmoore.

She smiled bitterly. "Creeping paranoia, Gregor. My persecution complex has grown to the point where these mechanical failures look like a contrived and personal attack." But as she spoke, the idea seemed a lot less far-fetched than it sounded. Sure the frigate was old and had been poorly maintained for a long time. The amount of repairs engineering carried out watch after watch attested to that. But two critical failures at once did stretch credibility. Ships only carried one replacement injection controller, even if it used two at a time, one per drive because the chances of dual failure without warning were approximately one in several million.

"So what do we do if Tiner can't repair one of the two busted units?"

Siobhan shrugged. "Take the risk of an unbalanced FTL jump home, with only one drive. No tender or repair ship is going to come out to us here."

This time, it was Pushkin's turn to grunt, but he did not challenge her statement. Risky as an unbalanced jump was, remaining in Shrehari space was infinitely worse. Until Tiner pulled the units and checked them over, they could only wait, and hope. The first officer no longer even thought of resuming their pursuit. For him, the convoy had already slipped beyond sensor range and jumped on a new, unknown tack.

"Coming in for a coffee?"

Pushkin looked up and realized they were back on the bridge deck, level with the ready room door. He shrugged. "Sure. I have nothing better to do for the next while."

Siobhan gave him a tight, commiserating smile. "Then I suppose it'll be better if we both fret in private. Keeps the peasants quiet."

Pushkin snorted softly. "Ain't that the truth, captain?"

Sipping coffee in silence a few minutes later, Siobhan's mind returned to what she had termed her paranoia. She touched the intercom panel.

"Dunmoore to Tiner."

A male voice replied, "Engineering, Petty Officer Frelivo, captain. Mister Tiner is up to her ears in the injector housing. Can I help you?"

"Ask the chief engineer to examine both controllers carefully for signs of anything that would not be normal in this type of system failure."

"Aye, aye, sir," Frelivo acknowledged, though he sounded dubious. "Can I tell Mister Tiner exactly what you're looking for, sir? It might help."

"Not really, PO. I'm not an engineer. Just ask her to examine both controllers side by side. If there's something to be found, she'll know it when she sees it."

"It'll be done, sir."

"Dunmoore, out."

Pushkin stared at her over the rim of his mug, heavy eyebrows raised in question. Siobhan made a face and shrugged, feeling foolish now that she had given in to her latent paranoia.

They spent the next ten minutes in uneasy silence, neither wanting to speak, neither comfortable with the forced intimacy of the moment. Siobhan rationalized her tension and unease away by reminding herself that even though she and Pushkin were sitting on their thumbs, the crew would think the two had locked themselves away to plan and plot. It would do no harm to Pushkin's standing among the officers and non-coms.

Eventually, unable to stand the silence anymore, Siobhan began a surprisingly vigorous discussion on tactics with Pushkin, and the ice between them melted that much more. When he wanted to, the first officer came off as an intelligent, well-spoken man. Finally, though, the intercom chirped, and Tiner's voice came on, cutting short their light-hearted argument on the relative merits of retrograde sublight action.

"Go ahead," Siobhan replied, repressing the urge to jump down the intercom and shake information out of the chief engineer.

"I think I've found what you're looking for, sir." Siobhan's lean face flashed a look of pure triumph at Pushkin, her paranoia vindicated. "You might want to come down and see this yourself. It'll be easier to explain."

"We're on our way."

Dunmoore forced herself to keep a steady, unhurried pace as she led Pushkin back to engineering, but there was no mistaking the aura of impatience and anticipation that surrounded her. Tiner met them by the bulkhead and guided them straight to her office.

"So, Mister Tiner," the captain stared down at the shorter woman with a smile she hoped looked reassuring.

"Ah yes, sir. The controllers." Tiner touched the console beneath the large work screen. Two identical circuits materialized on the viewing surface. "These are micro-resolution scanner shots we took of the command circuits on both units. As you can see," she pointed at each in turn, "the burnout patterns are nearly identical."

"How nearly?"

"Ninety percent, sir."

Pushkin let out a low whistle. His primary training at the Academy had been in engineering, and he was a competent and knowledgeable generalist. Siobhan, who had taken only the required basics in ship's systems, glanced at her first officer and chief engineer in turn.

"I assume by your reactions that this is not supposed to happen."

"Damn right it isn't, captain." Pushkin looked at Tiner. "Sorry there, Anna. Go ahead."

The short woman nodded and turned back to the screen. "Two identical circuits burning out in nearly the same manner at the same time stretches the laws of probability by a quantum factor, captain. Unless they were manufactured with an identical flaw and have been subjected to exactly the same stresses. Now this type of injector control isn't exactly the best piece of kit the New Aberdeen shipyards have come up with, but they're not supposed to be failure-prone in a regular, identifiable manner. Otherwise, someone would have found out a long time ago, and fixed the problem."

"Correct, captain," Pushkin chimed in. "This kind of controller has been used on Type 203 frigates since the start, thirty plus years ago, more than enough time to find regular manufacturing defects. Though," he scratched the side of his head, "I don't suppose they make them anymore. We're the last Type 203 ship left in service." He shrugged, aware that his last comment was beside the point, although Tiner nodded vigorously.

"So you're convinced that this wasn't due to a built-in defect."

"No, sir." Tiner sounded as confident as Siobhan had ever heard her. "Can't be, even if there was a defect. Like I said, if they were built with a flaw and subjected to the same stresses, and the gods of engineering felt puckish, it might be possible."

Siobhan raised her eyebrows at the unexpected stab of humor.

"But," the chief engineer continued, "as it happens, the two units weren't subjected to the same stresses. I checked my personal logs, and we replaced the starboard unit thirteen months ago. The port unit dates back from before my time aboard."

"Thank God for your personal logs then, Mister Tiner," Siobhan smiled devilishly, "because they're probably the only recent maintenance records we have, thanks to whoever impounded all of *Stingray*'s official logs."

Tiner did not quite know how to interpret Captain Dunmoore's comment, so she remained silent, waiting for Siobhan's next question, one she had already anticipated.

"How, if we're looking for unnatural causes, could this have been perpetrated?"

"I've figured out seven different ways this could be done, sir. Do you want me to describe them?"

Siobhan shook her head. "The technical subtleties would probably be lost on me. Include your theories in your report. I'm sure Mister Pushkin will be delighted to explore them," she added grinning at the serious-faced first officer. "That being said, how difficult are they to carry out without anyone noticing, and who has the necessary expertise to do so?"

"Not very hard to carry out, I'm afraid, sir. That's one other reason why this design is obsolete. Anyone with a basic engineering diagnostics unit, wired to put out an energy pulse at a particular frequency, could weaken the circuits enough for them to fail after a specific interval. And most of my staff, at least the group five -qualified petty officers and above, would know how to rewire a diagnostics unit and how to damage sensitive circuits. Though I doubt a non-engineer would," she added.

"One final question. If I hadn't asked you to compare the damage on both units, would you have found out anyways?"

"Oh yes, captain. Definitely. Every time a major module fails, I run a full diagnostics check to record the reason for failure. It's one of the ways Naval Engineering monitors life expectancy and quality control problems. I would have noticed and told you either way because this is not normal."

"And everyone in your division knows this procedure?"

"Aye, sir."

Siobhan raised her head to stare at the circuits displayed on the screen, forehead creased and lips pursed in thought. The two other officers knew what the captain was thinking, and they could not make head or tails of it either. Finally, Siobhan shrugged and turned to face them.

"How long before failure do you think someone tampered with the controllers?"

"Hard to say, sir. Anywhere from fifteen minutes to four hours, depending on how much damage was initially caused."

"Okay. Mister Tiner, find out if any of your people have been near the controllers at any time within say, five hours before the things went pfft. Not as suspects, mind you, but to ask them if they noticed anything unusual. We'll consider suspects later."

"I understand, sir," she replied, nodding, though it was obvious she didn't put much faith into finding anything useful. She stuck her head out of the office door and yelled "Chief Weekes," at the top of her voice, punching through the loud drone of the power tools. Moments later, the chief petty officer third class who reigned over engineering appeared and Tiner passed on Siobhan's orders. He trotted off, shaking his heavy jowls in wonder.

"Now for the real question," Siobhan eyes locked with Tiner's. "How long before we can jump again?"

"The replacement unit is already in place portside and tests just fine. I have my best techs working on fixing one of the broken controllers, but I can't give you a definite time. It's a dangerous piece of kit to be tampering with, sir. Rebuilding a circuit from scratch is tough without the proper tools."

Pushkin snapped his fingers and then tapped the side of his nose, a slow grin spreading across his face.

"We'll lose the convoy if you try to do a full rebuild. How about bypassing the burned out parts directly. It'll still control the antimatter injectors well enough to get the starboard hyperdrive working before the Shrehari sail out of sensor range."

Tiner looked horrified at the suggestion. "That's bloody suicide, Mister Pushkin," she replied hotly, a professional engineer defending her turf from an amateur. "Without the circuit's hardwired protection, a bad hit by a Shrehari could cause catastrophic damage to the unit, and it'll be an even bet if the overload blows us first or if the static discharge from the controller makes us go up in flames of glory."

"Yes, but while we're running after the bastards, an operation that'll take several hours at this point, you can work on fixing the other broken unit properly, and we'll have it in place before the plasma starts flying in earnest."

"Mister Tiner," Siobhan's voice cut through what was about to shape up as a heated technical argument between the two officers. Their next words died unspoken. "Is Mister Pushkin right? Can you bypass the burned-out circuits and get this ship back into FTL flight?"

Grudgingly, she nodded. "Yes, but I strongly advise against it."

"Your advice is noted and understood, Mister Tiner. But we're not losing that convoy on account of some saboteur who doesn't look like he has all his marbles. Carry out the first officer's suggestion. The moment you've rebuilt the second unit, I promise we'll drop out of FTL, and you'll be able to install it correctly. We can't afford to sit here, vulnerable as we are, for the hours it'll take you to rebuild us a safe unit. A Shrehari patrol ship could find us at any time, and I'd rather have a dangerous controller that can do the job, than attempt an unbalanced emergency jump or even worse, see myself outmaneuvered in an uneven fight."

"Excuse me, sir," a gruff voice interrupted from the office door.

"Yes, chief," Tiner turned, unsuccessfully trying to mask her resentment at being overruled.

"Able Spacer Bertram here saw someone at the controllers in the hours before the failure."

"Send him in."

The weasel-faced rating stepped around the massive chief without waiting for further orders, and reported to the captain with all due naval protocol, even though he was in rumpled coveralls and had grease stains all the way up his bare arms.

"Able Spacer Bertram reportin' to the cap'n, sir."

"You saw someone at the controllers, Bertram?"

"Aye, cap'n. I did. 'Twas something like three hours before we dropped outta FTL. Petty Officer Hartalas ran a diagnostic check on the portside hyperdrive control systems. He had a handheld unit with him. Didn't think nothing of it at the time. Normal like."

"And it probably is, Bertram," Siobhan replied, unwilling to pin the blame on PO Hartalas before she had solid proof. "But maybe he noticed something that didn't strike him as abnormal at the time. Something which could help us further." Nosey Bertram looked dubious but knew better than to reply. "Thank you, Bertram."

"Sir." He did a precise about turn and marched out of the office.

"Chief," Siobhan turned her eyes on the big man, "ask Petty Officer Hartalas to report to me."

He frowned. "Hartalas is off watch right now, sir."

Siobhan repressed a surge of irritation. "Then track him down."

A few minutes later, the chief returned, an unhappy look on his face. "He ain't in his quarters, he ain't in engineering, no one's seen him for the last hour or so, and he ain't responding to ship-wide."

Siobhan nodded.

"Thank you, chief." She walked over to the intercom on Tiner's desk.

"Dunmoore to the second officer."

"Drex here," he promptly replied.

"Mister Drex, I need to speak with Petty Officer Hartalas but he can't be found in his quarters, at his duty station or anywhere else, and he's not responding to calls. I want you to find him for me and bring him to my ready room."

"Shall I place him under arrest?" Drex's more than obvious lack of curiosity annoyed Siobhan briefly. She expected her security officer to take a more personal interest in events aboard the ship.

"Only if necessary. I simply want to speak with him."

"Aye, aye, sir. I'm putting out a general search now."

"Dunmoore, out."

She turned, and her eyes met Pushkin's. In them, she read a reflection of her own mounting suspicions and that did not reassure her at all. Siobhan broke the contact first.

"Let's leave Mister Tiner and her people to their work, Mister Pushkin."

*

The stem to stern search did not take very long. Siobhan and Pushkin barely had five minutes to discuss events in the ready room, before Drex's flat voice issued from the intercom with the news Siobhan had been dreading.

"I'm on my way, Mister Drex. Don't touch anything until I get there."

"As you wish, captain."

Siobhan cut the connection and glanced at Pushkin, his face a mirror of her own grim expression. "You coming?"

Lieutenant Drex and a squad of armed bosun's mates waited for them on deck fifteen, the lowest of the main hull decks. It was a stark, bare environment of cold metal and humming machinery, far from the warmth of the crew decks. A lonely place too, especially with the broken body sprawled at the foot of an access ladder, its head at an odd angle from the body.

The smell of voided bowel and bladder assailed Siobhan's nose and brought back the painful memories of other deaths she had witnessed not too long ago, on another ship. Petty Officer Hartalas had been in his mid-thirties, young for a race whose lifespan now routinely exceeded a full century. There was a stunned, almost outraged look on his face as if he'd seen death in the moments before it struck. His open eyes seemed to stare accusingly at the bare ceiling.

Emotionlessly, Drex pointed up at the emergency access tube running between decks. "Petty Officer Hartalas must have slipped and fallen. His neck is broken. Died not too long ago. His body is still warm."

Siobhan saw the evidence, heard the words, but could not believe the second officer's cold-blooded conclusion. Her own words about coincidences rang through her mind.

"Or," she replied in a soft voice, "someone could have broken his neck for him and tossed him down the tube. It's just a bit too strange that the last man seen near the antimatter injectors ends up at the bottom of a ladder with his neck broken before we can speak to him."

Drex shrugged. "Maybe you are reading too much into both events, sir. This looks like an accident to me. Murder on a starship?"

His tone shifted subtly, hinting that Siobhan was speaking crazy talk. Or it could simply have been the captain's imagination. Ever since the Zavaleta incident, her opinion of the second officer had taken a turn for the worse, and the older man knew it. Sometimes, his cold, emotionless look made Siobhan feel guilty. It was irrational, but then, nobody had ever accused her of being sane.

"Maybe, Mister Drex. Still, I want the doctor to conduct an autopsy. Do a full investigation and scan of the area, including the access tube. Treat this as a suspicious death until you have evidence to the contrary."

"Aye, aye, sir." He seemed resigned.

"Engineering to captain," the nearest intercom panel blared, Tiner's words echoing through the deserted, bare corridor. Caught by death's silent fascination, the living started at the sudden, loud sound, some of them reaching for their blasters in reflex. Siobhan unsuccessfully repressed a shiver and walked over to the intercom.

"Dunmoore."

"We've bypassed the circuits on one of the damaged units and put it back in place. It appears to work, but I still want to run a few more tests, just to be sure."

"How long?"

"Ten minutes."

"You've got it, Mister Tiner. And well done. But we go FTL in ten minutes, not a second more. Dunmoore, out."

Siobhan glanced at Pushkin and smiled. "We won't lose the convoy, Gregor, and they won't miss their date with death." She turned to the second officer. "Carry on, Mister Drex. You'll have enough time to wrap up here before we get within shooting range of the Imperials. I may have told you this before, but I have a problem with coincidences. When I see more than two of them as closely connected as this, I either run or clear for action. In this case, I prefer the latter. Death always leaves a bad taste in my mouth."

"Sir," Drex nodded curtly, face as expressionless as always.

For a fleeting moment, Siobhan thought she caught a flash of something else. She shrugged mentally and headed toward the waiting lift, a pensive Pushkin on her heels. As the doors closed, she caught a last glimpse of Lieutenant Drex's spacers surrounding Petty Officer Hartalas' broken body. Murder or accident? Siobhan knew what she would bet on.

A brief glance at Pushkin's somber face told her she was not alone in placing her money on a cold-blooded assassination.

— Eighteen —

"Jump drives are online, sir," Devall reported, rising from the command chair as Dunmoore and Pushkin made their way to their stations. Relief was visible on most faces. Stuck in enemy space without FTL engines was a most uncomfortable situation, let alone the prospect of losing a rich prey and proving *Stingray*'s status as a jinxed ship beyond any doubt.

"Thank you," Siobhan smiled. It had taken Tiner somewhat less than the ten minutes she had given her. "Where's our convoy?"

Devall slid behind his console, letting his fingers dance on the control panel. A scaled tactical view appeared on the main screen. "Still within our sensor range," he reported. "They're currently moving at sublight, on the same heading as before. No changes in composition or deployment."

Siobhan glanced at a time readout and winked at Pushkin, who was studying her lean face with interest. Her predictions had turned out nearly spot-on. It had been six hours now since they started the chase, six hours since the convoy's last drop into normal space for calibration and tacking.

"Okay. Keep a close eye on them. The moment they jump, feed their new course to the sailing master. We'll move out when they do, when their scanners can't pick us up until we're about to put a thick, hot torpedo up their Shrehari asses."

Devall turned to look at Dunmoore with delighted surprise on his aristocratic face. Her words and the image they conveyed were highly unusual for a warship captain, trained to be serious, aloof, even dour, but Siobhan made

them sound like a darkly delicious battle call. Somehow
the young gunnery officer had never associated hard,
intense Siobhan Dunmoore with anything even remotely
sexual, but in this case, the image was all too vivid in his
imagination. He turned away quickly as he felt a flush of
red burn his cheeks.

"Aye, aye, sir."

Siobhan noticed his reaction and smiled, pleased with
herself. As long as the crew remained in high spirits, they
had a damn good chance of making this work. But then,
battle had always held an element of arousal for her. Why
shouldn't others feel that way?

"They've jumped without tacking, sir." Devall's voice
brought her back to the present.

"Have they?" Siobhan smiled wryly. "That sort of kills
my one-hundred percent prediction rate. I'll have to have
a word with the convoy leader. Preferably over a surrender
ceremony. His." Then, she became more serious. "We're
getting close enough to Cimmeria that he figures another
tack would just lengthen his journey. He has no way of
knowing someone's on his tail. Are we ready to follow,
Mister Shara?"

"Aye, sir."

Siobhan was about to order the helmsman to engage
when Devall bit off a curse.

"Anything the matter?" Siobhan asked, holding up her
hand to stop Guthren from anticipating the jump order.

He shook his head angrily. "I don't know, sir. For a
second or two, I could have sworn there was another ship,
deeper in enemy space, on an FTL convergence course
with the convoy. But the blip was so short, even the
recorder didn't get it. Either it's a sensor ghost or someone
so far away we got him when ionic interference dropped
low enough for a brief scan window."

"Or a cloud of ionized gas momentarily bounced his
signal to us. Either way, he's too distant to give us any
headaches just yet." Siobhan shrugged dismissively. "If
he's connected with the convoy, he'd be in closer. If not,
he won't know anything about it. The Shrehari are

sticklers for security." She dropped her hand. "Helm, engage."

*

Brakal paced his cabin, impatient to move within strike range of the convoy. This close to their destination, the convoy ship masters would be slacking off, tired after days of hard sailing toward the outpost. They relied too much on the local squadron to keep the area clear of enemy raiders. And yet it was the most vulnerable moment. No matter how much experienced officers tried to counter the inevitable decrease in vigilance, it happened. The better human starship captains knew it all too well.

They waited for the escorts to lose their high degree of alertness and then struck. Brakal grinned. On that, if nothing else, the Shrehari and humans resembled each other. He too had often taken advantage of a convoy's premature relaxation to strike.

Khrada, the *Tai Kan* spy, continued to hover behind him whenever he left his private quarters, taking notes, sending coded messages to the home world, smiling arrogantly, and hardly speaking. Brakal had to stop Jhar from killing him more than a dozen times. His loyal first officer reacted badly to every provocation, no matter how minor, Khrada offered. The spy enjoyed baiting him and felt immune to the violence carefully repressed in most fighting officers. One day he would surely know the peril he courted. By then, of course, the lesson would not be of much use, for Khrada would be dead.

Tol Vakash sailed on a converging course with the convoy, dropping out of hyperspace every two hours to scan for intruders. So far, none had been spotted, but Brakal knew that human scanners had greater range than his own and that a good human captain would wait at the outer limits of his detection range until the moment to strike. Until Brakal got closer, any lurking enemy had the advantage, provided he, *or she*, he mentally amended, remembering the flame-haired female called Dunmoore, knew how to fight.

Something instinctive, an ancient genetic hunter's feeling told him a human ship had spotted the convoy and was even now stalking it. He had not bothered explaining the feeling to Khrada. *Tai Kan* bastards knew nothing of the hunter. But Jhar and his other officers knew, and believed, as he did, that humans were somewhere out there, near, and waiting. The value of experience. Five long years' worth.

Still, Khrada waited like a bloody carrion eater. Maybe his behavior, his refusal to take up a predictable patrol route as ordered and his suborning Fleet Security to obtain classified information would be enough for the weak women on the Council to finally relieve him of his duties. Or maybe Khrada was waiting for a treasonable act to remove Brakal there and then, and take personal command of *Tol Vakash*. It had happened before.

For all they knew, the spy could, in reality, hold the rank of commander and carry full authority from Trage. In which case, Khrada might interpret a treasonable act according to his whim. Yet he had to give the bugger his due. He let every provocation slide off his back with the same sardonic, knowing smile. It all proved that while the spy was biding his time, his revenge would be worse for the waiting.

Brakal grunted. It was the Shrehari equivalent of a human sigh. As if the Deep Space Fleet had the time or the energy to waste on the idiotic ego maneuvers of those incompetent, overaged maggots at the Admiralty. The Empire was on the verge of losing this war, and all they could think about was silencing those who spoke the truth, trying to reverse the inevitable slide into abject defeat.

The intercom beeped rudely, pulling Brakal out of his dark thoughts. He had been wallowing so deeply in his anger and contempt for his superiors that he failed to notice his ship's return to real space. He turned around with a snarl and savagely hit the panel.

"Yes?"

The watch officer did not seem to notice his commander's irritable tone, or if he did, he wisely chose to ignore it. Brakal's crew knew all about his tempers and moods and believed it was part of his genius. His anger or joy, both equally intense, reassured them. Listlessness or dullness made them worry.

"A contact, commander."

Brakal's anger vanished in a flash, and a cruel smile twisted his lips as he furrowed his thick brows.

"Describe, Urag."

"It travels in hyperspace," Lieutenant Urag, gun master of *Tol Vakash* replied, "on the same course as the convoy, but at greater speed."

"Show me."

The screen sprang to life, displaying three green icons in a roughly triangular configuration. Script flashed beneath the icons, showing the relative distances between the convoy, *Tol Vakash,* and the unknown pursuer. On the scaled display, the imaginary line between hunter and convoy was visibly shorter than the line between *Tol Vakash* and the convoy. The intruder would reach them ahead of Brakal's cruiser, unless its captain did something stupid. Brakal swore in a low, guttural voice.

The thought that the unknown ship might be an imperial vessel did not even enter Brakal's mind. He knew instinctively that it was human, and that its captain knew what he was doing. All *Tol Vakash* could do was maintain an optimum convergence course, travel at maximum speed and hope to close the distance before the human escaped. Convoy losses were inevitable, but then, so was the Admiralty's stupidity and adherence to outdated doctrine.

Brakal had his own ideas on convoy practices, ideas that could go far to counter the humans' sneaky, and on the whole, admirable tactics. But they would not give him charge of a convoy, just as they would not now give him charge of an assault force.

Brakal studied the ever-changing figures and grunted. The race would be close, close enough that luck might just give him the additional push he needed to meet the human before he could harvest all of the hapless transports. Luck being, in Brakal's realistic belief framework, an uncharted ion storm, a mechanical failure on the enemy ship, or a

simple miscalculation by his adversary, the latter figuring
most prominently.

Praying to the ancestors was, as he knew, useless, no
matter what the zealots crowding around the infant
Emperor said. These days, such an opinion was best kept
to oneself. Some would be tempted to use it as a sign of
treason against the Emperor, and act accordingly.

At the rate at which the distance between the two ships
was closing, his unknown adversary would become aware
of his presence the next time he dropped back to normal
space for a spot check on the convoy. Maybe the added
factor of an approaching patrol ship would push the
human commander into acting with less than calm
deliberation.   Humans reacted to stress in strange
manners. Quite unpredictable. But they had learned only
too well that the Deep Space Fleet acted on predictable
lines. A weakness that had cost the Empire dearly.

"Urag."

"*Kha*?"

"Modify our course by one-tenth *rogath* and take us back
to FTL at maximum. Tell that lazy bastard of an engineer
to kick his engines until we can outrun even the fastest
courier. We have work to do."

"Your command." Urag cut the transmission but left the
tactical on screen. Moments later, Brakal felt the wrench
of the jump at his guts, and he grimaced. The tactical
display wavered for a fraction of a second, as the computer
replaced the real-time view by an estimate, now that the
scanners had become myopic again in the strangeness of
the FTL bubble.

Brakal touched the icon representing the enemy ship
with a gauntleted fingertip and smiled. "Who are you, my
adversary? Have we met before with honor, or are you so
new that you will not even afford me a decent fight?"

He laughed at his arrogant words for he knew too much
about humans to underestimate their ability.

His good humor had returned, now that a battle was in
the offing. Brakal only hoped that the human captain
would prove to be of cunning and resource, a match for his
ship and crew. And may the Great Demon rise from the

flames of the Deathworld and feast on the Council members' fat bodies.

Bah, Brakal thought, *the Demon would probably get ill eating Trage's black heart. Even he does not deserve such treatment.*

*

Hyperspace is a nuisance, Siobhan reflected, pacing her small ready room. A deaf and blind hunter pursuing a deaf and blind prey, under the excited gaze of deaf and blind spectators. Every time the frigate dropped back to normal space for a position fix, she lost ground, and if both hunter and prey dropped back at the same time, she would lose her advantage of surprise too. So Siobhan had chosen to barrel up the convoy's rear, trusting her gut instinct to keep *Stingray* on course and at the right speed to move into position, a feat which, privately, her officers believed impossible. But they had also thought that getting the ship back up to Navy standards was impossible. Yet Dunmoore had succeeded.

Few now dared meet her piercing eyes, sardonic smile, and sharp wit without the answers she demanded. Though Dunmoore did not believe in severe punishment for failures, like some captains in the Fleet, her cutting words, and stony gaze had as much effect, if not more, than any threat. And her words of praise, to the surprise of even the hardest cynics, touched them just as deeply.

Like all gossip, word had spread through the ship that Dunmoore knew what had been going on aboard the frigate under Commander Forenza. And that she intended to dig even deeper, being unbeholden to her predecessor's secretive protectors and to the Battle Group commander who had permitted Forenza's goings-on. It gave some heart, while it frightened others, for once everything became common knowledge, even the lowest spacer would be tarred by association, never mind that he or she had no choice in the matter, indeed had to tread softly to survive. But some began to consider seriously the option of coming forth with what they knew. Until that is, Petty Officer Hartalas mysteriously fell to his death.

It acted like a warning signal that the past remained all too present and that *Stingray* was not yet safe. Siobhan, of course, knew nothing of this, her mind totally focused on the coming battle. She had that ability. Most captains did. It was necessary, even essential. Unfortunately, it left matters, including the bait she planted in her logs, in suspense. Not for long, though.

"Sickbay to the captain," Luttrell's voice over the intercom snapped Siobhan out of her contemplation of the tactical subtleties of a backdoor assault. The doctor had avoided her since the uncomfortable meeting over Able Spacer Vincenzo's beating.

"Dunmoore."

"You wanted an autopsy on Hartalas."

"Yes." Siobhan's eyes narrowed in irritation, but she kept her voice calm and as friendly as she could manage. "What did you determine?"

"He died of a broken neck, captain. Death was instantaneous."

"Caused by the fall?"

"Oh, he fell all right." Silence.

Siobhan's lips thinned and she stared at the screen, with its ever-changing tactical display. A computer's best estimate. It only lacked the third icon, the one that completed the triangle. But traveling in hyperspace, they could not know of the unexpected addition to the chase.

"Did the fall kill him?" Siobhan finally asked. Silence again. She could literally picture Luttrell's shrug.

"Hard to say. His body's a mass of bruises, including several on the back of the head and neck. He took a tumble, but whether he was dead before, if that's what you're asking, or died when he hit the ground, I don't know. I'm not a pathologist. I've put him in stasis. You can have a specialist look at him when we return home."

It was clear that Luttrell was not about to advance a theory or discuss her gut feeling. Accidents happened on a starship. Fatal ones. And on a ship considered unlucky, three accidental deaths in two months would not arouse as much suspicion as, say, on a well-run flagship.

"Thank you, Doctor. Dunmoore, out."

Siobhan felt like punching the bulkhead, something that would have earned her a shattered hand, and probably an injection of some sedative or other while Pushkin and Luttrell discussed her mental state. If there was something funny about Hartalas' death, only Drex's investigation could find it now. And somehow, Siobhan doubted the second officer would come up with anything other than a verdict of accidental death. Just like Vasser and Melchor.

She glanced at the tactical display again. If the preprogrammed parameters held, she had another half-hour or so before the tricky part. Before she had to show her crew how it was done. With short, brisk movements, she sat in the chair behind her desk and pulled the terminal into a comfortable working position. Its screen came to life, and she entered her personal access code, opening her log.

The text she wrote a few hours ago scrolled before her eyes, stopping at the end of what she termed the facts column. A small, unobtrusive cursor blinked quietly just after the last period. Then, two more lines scrolled beneath the text and Siobhan stared, frowning. Kowalski's surveillance program was in place and had already fingered two unauthorized hackers, two members of her crew who read the log entry. The first name did not surprise Siobhan. She suspected for a while now that Kery's nervous diffidence was a sham. It made sense. The captain's clerk had the right kind of access and cover for unauthorized activities.

The second name, however, shocked her, and she slumped back in the chair, staring at the bulkhead, trying to digest this piece of information. It did not make sense and yet was all too plausible at the same time, but Siobhan just could not accept it. Something was very wrong. She knew it, felt it instinctively. Gregor Pushkin simply could not be one of 'them'.

And yet his name and access code flashed at the bottom of the screen, where Kowalski's program listed all those who had hacked their way into the captain's personal log, the only file in the computer restricted for anyone without her personal password.

Siobhan stood and stretched her tense muscles. Then, she pulled out her blaster, checked the charge, and placed it on the desk, within easy reach. What she intended to do now might not be the smartest move, especially not with the ship about to go into action, but she wanted to have it out, clear the air and make sure she did not have to worry about someone stabbing her in the back while she prepared to savage an enemy convoy. She stabbed the intercom.

"Kery, report to my ready room."

Moments later the door slid aside with a soft sigh, and the short, plump, and unassuming clerk stepped in. Her eyes registered Siobhan's hard look, the bright computer screen, and the blaster sitting on the desk by Dunmoore's right hand. Understanding lit her dark eyes, but she went through the motions anyway.

"Captain?"

"Sit." Siobhan pointed at a comfortable, deep chair by the closed porthole. It was big enough to swallow the little clerk and make getting up a more difficult proposition. Kery's expression, guarded as it was, betrayed her understanding of Dunmoore's choice. Yet she obeyed, aware of the nearness of violent death. Within the Service, Siobhan Dunmoore had been tagged as a hothead, an impulsive officer with a cruel streak of ruthlessness, one who would not hesitate to act directly and brutally if necessary. She was, in effect, a very dangerous and very loose cannon. As far as the Branch was concerned, of course. The navy had a somewhat different opinion, being mainly concerned with the destruction of the Imperial Deep Space Fleet, something for which Siobhan had proven ability.

"Tell me, Kery, will your superiors in the SSB miss you?"

The clerk-agent shrugged, having decided her game was up. It was bound to happen. No undercover agent could maintain the pretense forever and still do the work required by the spymasters on Earth.

Of course, spying on the Fleet was considerably less risky than other jobs, since the military took pride in its reputation for upholding the law and that law frowned on the unsanctioned execution of its servants, though it was something the SSB ignored routinely, in the name of national security. But Siobhan Dunmoore had a reputation and a loaded blaster.

"There's an old Earth saying, Kery, that curiosity killed the cat." As if to make her point, Dunmoore's hand briefly rested on her weapon, like a furtive caress.

Kery, unimpressed by old sayings stared at the captain impassively, determined to let her make all the moves. The silence deepened as the two women stared at each other.

"Surveillance program?" The question slipped out of Kery's mouth before she could stop herself. Curiosity indeed. Dunmoore nodded.

"Now what?" The clerk asked, her eyes leaving Siobhan's face in favor of the tactical display. They were very near the convoy now, and the captain did not have the luxury of playing a lengthy game of wits.

"I suppose you telling me what this is all about is out of the question."

Kery smiled. "I'm sure you can figure it out by yourself, captain. You'll understand that I cannot offer you any help. You have your rules, I have mine. And we both have another, common set of rules we are sworn to uphold."

"The SSB, sworn to anything other than their own ends?" Siobhan snorted with disbelief. "I could force you." She picked up the blaster and rested it on her thigh.

The spy shook her head. "Please don't try, captain. I'm conditioned against interrogation, and I'd rather not die quite yet. Anyway, the navy does not have the authority to question SSB officers. Your best move now is to hand me over to my Service. It would avoid any further unpleasantness."

Siobhan's lips twisted into a cruel, hard smile. "You know, Kery, if that's your real name, I don't give a rat's ass about whether I have authority or not. We're not even in the Commonwealth anymore, and the laws put out by our dear, corrupt government don't mean anything here. This is my ship, and I can do as I damn well please, especially with a spy. What proves to me you're with the SSB? You could just as well be in the Empire's pay, in which case I can execute you quite legally right now. Oh, I agree the Fleet won't be too happy if I splash your brains all over my ready room, but we're at war. Interrogation? I wouldn't dream of it. But you're not conditioned against fear, are you? As you said, you'd rather not die yet. Or are you really willing to die for whatever corrupt activities your service used this ship?"

Kery shrugged, trying to appear unconcerned, though Siobhan knew better. She had an almost animal ability to detect fear in others, and its smell surrounded the smaller woman. Dunmoore's reputation, for once, worked for her. Reckless, impulsive, a killer's instinct. All those words resonated through Kery's mind as she watched the captain stare at her like a wolf savoring the terror of a cornered prey. And the agent knew how easy it was to cover up a death in deep space, especially with the protection of a high-ranking admiral. Forenza had enjoyed Kaleri's patronage, misguided as it was, but Dunmoore reached even higher, and Admiral Nagira was one of the Fleet's rising stars, a man tapped as a future Grand Admiral.

"Let's start with the usual pleasantries, shall we?" Siobhan's predatory smile became even more pronounced. "Rank, name and serial number." When Kery did not reply, Dunmoore pointed the blaster at her. "C'mon, kiddo, don't piss me off."

Kery made a face. "Very well. But I assure you my superiors will not treat this lightly." Siobhan snorted at the threat. "My real name is Elidia Cayne, major in the SSB, serial number oh-one-five-eight-alpha-six."

Siobhan nodded, amusement twitching at her lips. "An officer no less. My, this operation of yours must have been profitable. What's the price for intermix controller modules on the black market these days?"

Her amusement grew as she saw the reaction in Kery/Cayne's face. *Bingo, you little bitch.*

"It must have been a lot to warrant the murder of four people. I suppose Vasser and Melchor stumbled onto something they shouldn't have, and poor Byrn was more thorough in investigating their deaths than he should have been. But sabotaging the ship, and then killing the man who did it seems to me a bit much. Congratulations, though, on making it look like an accident. You fooled the doctor."

A look of incomprehension flashed through Cayne's eyes, and Siobhan stopped all amusement vanishing.

"You're not responsible for Petty Officer Hartalas, are you?"

Which meant there was someone else aboard with a different mission, unconnected to the SSB, or at least operating in isolation from Major Cayne. And that someone wanted Siobhan to think it was Pushkin.

The spy, feeling Dunmoore shift onto unknown and untested ground, regained some of her composure. She let a small smile play on her full lips. "I'm sorry, captain. I don't know what you're talking about."

Siobhan nodded. "Maybe not. But you do have Vasser, Melchor, and Byrn on your conscience, or at least your service does. That's enough for a one-way ticket to a penal colony. But that's not my concern. I'll see that the Fleet does justice to your crimes after they blow your scheme wide open. I think I have enough now to point the investigators in the right direction, starting with the trader *Mykonos*."

The intercom buzzed, interrupting Siobhan.

"Captain, we're within the computer's estimated contact range."

"Thank you, Mister Pushkin. Please ask Mister Drex to join me in the ready room with a squad of bosun's mates."

Pushkin did not immediately respond, surprised by the request, but Dunmoore had trained her officers to respond promptly to orders. "Aye, aye, sir."

A few minutes later, Drex and four spacers showed up at her door, armed and armored, ready for battle. Able Spacer Vincenzo was one of them. He and the others stared uncomprehendingly at the scene before them. Only Drex showed no surprise.

"Sir?"

"Mister Drex, I'd like to introduce you to Major Elidia Cayne, of the Special Security Branch."

Siobhan waved at the seated woman, her words causing four jaws to drop in astonishment. Drex's was not among them. "You will take the major into your custody, strip her of her clothes, and scan her body for anything that might be used to commit suicide, then give her a pair of coveralls and confine her to a cell. You will treat her as an officer of a Commonwealth service at all times. No one is to speak to her without my permission, and that includes you."

Cayne looked at the captain with an ironic smile, but Siobhan ignored her. The coming battle made the spy very unimportant right now. Her brain had already shifted to the immediate problem.

Drex nodded briefly. "Sir."

"Take her away, then. And make it fast. We're about to get busy with our Shrehari friends."

The door to the bridge hissed open. "Captain." Pushkin poked his head into the room, eyes shining with excitement. "We have a contact."

"On my way. Mister Drex?"

The second officer stopped in his tracks and turned his head toward her. "Sir?"

"You won't have time to do a full search on the major. We're going to battle stations within the minute. Just shove her in a cell as is. If she wants to kill herself, let her. But if she tries to escape or do anything funny, shoot, and ask questions later."

"Aye, aye, sir. Get the prisoner moving, Vincenzo."

— Nineteen —

"Describe the contact."

Siobhan slipped into her chair, tense with the imminence of action. A typical question would have been 'where is the contact?' But in the other universe, 'where' did not actually exist, at least not in terms that could easily be grasped.

"We've picked up a strong wake to starboard of our line of travel."

Dunmoore nodded absently, listening to her instincts. Above, below and any other reference point was meaningless. One was either on another ship's line of travel or not. Thus, the question that bedeviled every warship captain stalking her prey was whether the wake belonged to the vulnerable target ship or an escort. Following another ship's precise line of travel was a matter of luck, not calculation, a blind man's game of tag. They could end up behind either, and tag the wrong one.

Statistics meant the chances of finding the right target were something like thirty percent, if one counted both escorts and the rear most transport, and there was no way of increasing the odds rationally. One wake looked exactly like another, a mere disturbance of the other universe's fabric. And that was all the sensors could tell, all they could see. Weapons officers in the convoy were, of course, just as blind. They kept security by watching the wake of the ship ahead. If it wavered or vanished, they knew they had a problem.

Siobhan came to a snap decision, as always going with the first gut feel she got, never stopping to think it out and let doubt cloud her professional instincts.

"Escort. Are we within their sensor area?"

"Doubtful, sir," Devall replied, sounding confident. "Their equipment's range is about eighty percent of ours, and we crept up slowly enough that we're probably still a good margin outside their range. The wake's strength isn't increasing, which means we're not getting any closer."

Siobhan smiled. "Excellent. We should track the target within a few minutes then."

"Mister Devall," she said after a few moments of silence, "fuel torpedoes and stand by to launch."

"Aye, aye, sir. Fueling one through four."

She nodded and let her eyes lose their focus again as she mentally reached out and tried to touch the target ship, feeling, as she often did, like a submarine skipper during Earth's Second World War. They too had fought on instinct and bits of hard data provided by inaccurate instruments in a little-understood environment. The fact that the only usable weapon in hyperspace was the inaccurate and expensive torpedo, essentially a large, unguided missile driven by a small jump engine, completed the analogy.

"Nearly there."   Siobhan's voice had a smoky, otherworldly tone.

Pushkin looked up from the console where he monitored the ship's systems and glanced at Dunmoore. She looked mesmerized as if lost in the unpredictable currents of the other universe. He felt a shiver run down his spine at the weird look on her face. The first officer had heard of captains who possessed an eerie sixth sense for finding the enemy in the murk of hyperspace, but this was the first time he saw one in action. No one knew whether it was an acquired or genetic talent, or whether it even existed.

"Contact!" Devall's usual reserve vanished in a surge of excitement. "Dead on track. You did it, skipper!"

Pushkin had been one of the doubters. No more. Siobhan Dunmoore had tracked down an enemy convoy, in the bubble universe, over a distance every tactics manual called impossible. The Shrehari were about to get a very unpleasant surprise rammed up their collective behinds.

So this is what it feels like to actually *hunt!* He marveled at the bloodthirstiness filling his heart.

*

"Scan." Jhar's order broke through the emergence disorientation, ringing loudly in the tight, bare confines of the bridge.

Wordlessly, the gun master bent over his console and let the sophisticated instrumentation expand its reach into the surrounding void. The minutes ticked by slowly as the computer analyzed and sifted through the cascade of information. Imperial ships were deadly killing machines, outmatching, gun for gun, and armor for armor their human equivalents. But in the area of sophisticated electronics, the upstart Commonwealth had everybody beat.

This time, however, the Shrehari designed and built scanners worked just beautifully, feeding the tactical processor with an image of events billions of kilometers away. The processor, in turn, compensated for the ever-present time lag and transformed the electronic bits of data into a simple and understandable format, projecting the result as a schematic.

Commander Brakal, Master of the imperial cruiser *Tol Vakash* swore like an ordinary peasant, drawing a hard look of disapproval from 'Lieutenant' Khrada. The tactical display no longer showed a rough triangle, with the convoy's ships at the apex, the human hunter at the square angle and Brakal's ship at the third corner. The eight imperial hyperspace bubble signatures had spawned a ninth. And *Tol Vakash* was too far away to do anything but watch in helpless rage. The report was already several *utras* old. Time lag was unforgiving and immutable.

"He chased through hyperspace for the whole distance since we spotted him," Jhar commented emotionlessly, though he felt rage mixed with awe, a most unusual sensation. "Only thus could he have closed the range so fast."

"Yes." Brakal stroked his chin, watching the screen through narrowed eyes, thinking hard. "A very good ship commander, that one. He will be a worthy adversary, one we will learn from." The admiration of one professional for another in his voice caused Khrada to frown. "The last ship of the convoy is lost, I fear. And no one but us and the human commander know it yet. Hah! And the senile toads in the Council refuse to believe me."

"Treasonous thoughts, commander?" Khrada's tone bordered on the threatening.

"Silence, excrescence," Brakal snapped, "or you will leave my bridge. This is a time for real Warriors, not home world lackeys who think eating the Council's turds will win this war. That," he pointed at the screen, his voice loud and hard, "is what will win the war for the humans, Khrada. Daring, initiative, and more courage than any of the lazy child fornicators at the Admiralty. We could do much worse than learn from them. We damned well have not learned from our own experience."

He fell silent, breathing hard, aware again that he had let his temper get the better of him. That outburst might just have cost him his career, if not his life. But frustration at being outmaneuvered, before the human commander even knew of his presence, had stripped Brakal of any remaining patience with the *Tai Kan* serpent.

He successfully repressed the desire to strangle Khrada, realizing his urge was unworthy, as his quarrel remained with Trage and his cronies, not their lackey, unpleasant as he may be. Not for the time being.

"Let us salvage what we can. Navigator, prepare a jump to the spot where the enemy will most likely emerge, and be fast about it. Helmsman, when you have the coordinates, engage without waiting for my order. With any luck, the human will take his time and linger around his prey until we arrive. Bah! If security had not forced me to wait until a friend gave me the convoy's course so I might protect it, we might have been close enough to take the bastard. Tell that to your masters, Khrada, and tell them the treason is not mine but theirs. I fight for the Emperor. All they do is obstruct me. Who is the real traitor then?"

Jhar growled but did not otherwise show his disapproval of his commander's reckless words. If not now, then the

Tai Kan would have found another time and reason to ensure Brakal's downfall. The Lord of Clan Makkar would never change, not to gain the approval of the Council or the infant Emperor himself. He knew his duty, treasured his honor, and commanded the loyalty of his crew. If only the Empire had more like him. The war would then be on a very different course. Brakal should be Admiral of the Deep Space Fleet and free to act as he wished. If they survived this tour, perhaps it would be time to count his support among the ship commanders and act.

Jump nausea gripped Jhar, rendering any further thought impossible.

*

Down in the blunt bows of the Commonwealth frigate *Stingray*, the two senior torpedo gunners waited patiently, tracking the target's wake on their fire control screens. Generally, the senior petty officer in charge of the torpedo room rotated her people through the firing chair to give them as much experience as possible. This time, however, she sat in the hot seat herself, with her most experienced rating acting as backup. Captain Dunmoore would get the best-goddamned torpedo shooting this ship could give.

Both gunners wore full armor, the better to survive should the frigate take a bad hit and the isolation it provided helped the petty officer concentrate. Below their feet, in individual tubes, the four ready torpedoes waited for the signal to launch.

They were huge, thick, and stupid weapons. Consisting mainly of a miniaturized jump drive topped by a small antimatter warhead, the torpedoes had no guidance system. Under the laws of hyperspace, they could only travel in the direction they were launched and therefore, anything more would have been useless. This did, however, make the gunners' job a most challenging one. Where the missile techs and regular gunners could use the computer to aim and shoot, the senior torpedo gunner had to go entirely on instinct, pointing the entire housing in the direction she thought was the right one.

On a warship, torpedo specialists were reckoned to be the best gunners in the business, and those who managed to beat the usual thirty percent success rate were minor legends in their own right.

Petty Officer Second Class Ashara Lako did not consider herself a legend, but she knew her business inside out, even if she had not practiced it much under Commander Forenza. This would be her first real shot in nearly a year, and she was nervous. Captain Dunmoore demanded high standards and Lako definitely did not want to disappoint her.

The armor's efficient environmental system kept her body's temperature steady, reclaimed her perspiration before it soaked her underclothes, and generally ensured her body's well-being. Still, Lako's palms felt moist and slippery inside the thick gloves, and the suit could not eliminate the butterflies in her stomach. It could, however, relieve the pressure she felt in her bladder, and she made full use of the built-in plumbing.

Lako glanced at her second, who monitored the 'fish', as torpedo gunners called their weapon for some obscure reason. His board remained green, showing that the antimatter warhead was stable, the jump drive warm, and the tube ready. On top of being enormous and dumb, the fish were sensitive things. The unstable antimatter fuel for both warhead and drive were injected at the last moment, and if any reading slipped outside the safety parameters, her assistant would eject the torpedoes from the ship without so much as a second thought. One of these buggers could blow the ship's bows off. Four exploding together did not bear thought.

The wake signature of the target was in range now. Lako gently nudged her joystick to the left and then up, feeling her way to a firing solution. Under her feet, the tube moved by millimeters, responding to the petty officer's slightest correction. As the range changed, she kept updating her aim, ready to fire on the captain's command. It would not be long now. Lako knew *Stingray* could not get too close.

"Torp, this is the bridge," Devall's voice startled Lako out of her intense concentration. "Do you have a firing solution?"

"Aye, sir," she replied through clenched teeth, her eyes still glued to the screen.

"Fire Tube One when you feel ready."

Lako was too caught up in the complicated process of maintaining a steady aim to grin at Devall's order. Some captains insisted the torpedo gunners fire the moment they gave the word. It did not make for a great hit ratio, but they never seemed to understand why. Dunmoore, on the other hand, was letting her choose the moment of firing, and Lako would make damn sure the captain's confidence was rewarded by, if she could manage it, a first round hit.

The petty officer's eyes narrowed to a slit, and she took one deep breath, releasing it halfway. Then, she pushed down on the firing button with her thumb, ejecting a torpedo from Tube One with a blast of compressed air.

The fish's signature wavered for a fraction of a second as it tried to return to normal space before its drive kicked in. But the miniature jump drive worked perfectly, as Lako had known it would. She had selected and checked out the four first torpedoes herself when they spotted the convoy hours ago. Her screen tracked the torpedo's tiny wake as it sped away from the frigate, heading straight toward the large, pulsing turbulence that marked the target.

*

On the bridge of the escort *Ptar Korsh*, the sub-gun master yawned loudly, exposing yellowing teeth in a leathery face, and absently scratched his crotch. He was a non-commissioned officer of the fourth level and had served aboard this vessel for a long time. The boredom of escort duty had long ago blunted his alertness, and he looked forward only to the pleasures of shore leave on the occupied world of Cimmeria. It was rumored that human females sold themselves to Imperials as whores. The petty officer was curious to discover this for himself, and maybe even try one of the soft-skinned creatures. He did not find humans attractive, preferring the females of his own species, but the exoticism of the idea appealed to him. And it was more than likely no Shrehari female on Cimmeria would even look at him, let alone cater to his needs.

The helmsman, as bored as the sub-gun master, made a snide remark about the latter's yawn and was rewarded by the amused growls of the others, including the officer of the watch. Grinning toothily, the sub-gun master replied with a jab of his own, which also drew the expected laughter. It lightened the atmosphere on the small, dark bridge and raised, if only momentarily, the crew's spirits.

Unfortunately, the exchange of rough wit also distracted the sub-gun master from his scanner, and he failed to notice the minuscule wake that had appeared on the tail of the last transport. The tracking computer might have reported it automatically, but other space was full of strange signatures and the sub-gun master had shut it off, preferring to rely on his own experience, which was considerable. If only, he thought later, he had repressed the yawn as he usually did in the presence of others.

*

Petty Officer Lako's aim proved truer than she dared even hope. The fish entered the broad area of turbulence created by the transport's drives and vanished from all screens. Its warhead, encountering the conditions specified by its program, armed itself and waited for the conditions to change again.

Back on *Stingray*, the crew waited for signs of detonation, none more so than Lako. She had a gut feeling about this one. On the frigate's bridge, Chief Petty Officer Guthren waited tensely for Siobhan's order to emerge, his right hand hovering over the drive cutout. His job now demanded a split-second reaction, to ensure they did not overshoot the target by more than a few hundred thousand kilometers when the torpedo forced it back into normal space.

Of course, the torpedo might be off by just a bit, enough to rattle the transport's crew, but not enough to collapse the hyperspace bubble. After that, they would have only a few seconds to attempt another shot before the enemy reacted because a torpedo explosion would reveal their presence to the trailing escorts. The energy surge of the antimatter warhead would register on sensors, no matter in what universe.

Petty Officer Lako knew this and prayed. She did not enjoy the idea of snap firing the next fish because its chances of hitting were considerably less, while the pressure would be much greater, not least the pressure she would place on herself.

The dumb torpedo's simple warhead registered the fact that it no longer swam in an area of turbulence. Had it possessed intelligence, it would have marveled at the skill and luck of its former controller. It entered the transport's bubble dead center between the two engine nacelles, five hundred meters aft of the main hull. Like clockwork, the detonator closed a simple circuit that collapsed the magnetic bottle holding the antimatter fuel. By the time the antimatter reacted with the matter containing it, the fish was a mere two hundred meters from the hull. It exploded with the force of several nuclear warheads and collapsed the jump bubble, sending a massive energy feedback through the drives' circuits. They fried to a crisp.

The explosion registered on the screens of *Stingray*, *Ptar Korsh* and of course, the transport itself. Only the frigate was ready to react and when the transport's wake vanished, Guthren cut out the hyperdrives before Siobhan even had time to complete her order. The crew of *Ptar Korsh* took several precious seconds to understand the situation and react appropriately, and by then, they had overshot both their wounded charge and the human ship by several million kilometers. The officer of the watch had no orders on how to react, knowing only that if the humans worked with more than one ship, returning to aid the already lost transport would open the convoy to another strike, so he kept on course until *Ptar Korsh*'s commander appeared. They lost precious time that they could never make up.

Sub-Commander Yorganth, master of the escort, correctly divining that the enemy ship worked alone, gave the order to emerge, come about, and engage the human. Only thus could he avoid the worst of the criticism which would befall him once the High Command analyzed this ambush. If he could destroy the human, his career would be safe. But Yorganth should not have worried so much about his future. It was already decided.

*

"Guns, shields up. Track the target. Helm, come about one-eighty, emergency turn." Siobhan sprang into action with a ferocity that belied her earlier, eerie calm. "Mister Devall, this may the best occasion we get for some individual gunnery practice. Mister Pushkin, give me a split screen display."

"Range to target four hundred thousand," Shara reported, grudging respect in her voice. It was as good a distance as any ship could hope to achieve, and Guthren grinned with satisfaction.

"Well done, cox'n," Siobhan replied with a nod in his direction. Guthren was not surprised that she took the time for praise when she had the situation to think about.

On screen, a small bright dot grew, transforming into the shape of a large, heavy cargo hauler, boxy and inelegant. Its hyperdrives crackled with blue energy, sparking and blackening where the highly charged circuits burned out, overloaded by the torpedo's kick. A shimmer of green wavered visibly in an elongated sphere around the hull as the ship's shields tried and failed to create a seamless defensive bubble.

"What a shot," Pushkin commented, shaking his head in disbelief. "The torpedo nearly did our jobs for us."

"Aye." Siobhan tapped the comms unit in her chair's padded arm. "Torpedo room, this is the captain. Judging by what I'm seeing, you've come as close to a first shot kill as I've ever seen with a fish. Well done."

"Thank you, sir," Lako's uncertain voice came back. She was still staring in awe at her small screen, not quite believing her aim had been so good. She gave a little prayer to her ancestors and tried to fix the moment in her mind's eye, knowing that such a lovely shot would likely never come her way again.

"You've just earned yourself a double tot, spacer. Dunmoore, out."

Lako glanced at her assistant, who pumped his gloved fist in the air, a grin of exultation transforming his usually dour face into a mask of pure pride. When she turned back to her screen, the petty officer realized her whole body was shaking with the release of tension. Her job was over, for now.

"Reload Tube One," she ordered.

*

On the bridge of the transport *Hurgan*, Lieutenant Verkont faced the worst nightmare of his admittedly dead-end career. Like a demon, the human frigate had appeared from nowhere to fire an other space missile that had nearly disabled his ship. Their gun master must be an evil magician. The *Hurgan* had lost all jump capability, so badly had the feedback-damaged its engines, and its stern was all but gone. The elderly lieutenant's crew of subject race levies performed well enough, but they were not fighters, and could not hide the terror they now felt at the sight of death on the main view screen. For death it would be. Though armed, the *Hurgan* could not, in his wildest fantasies, stand up to a human frigate. And his long-range scanners showed the escort too far away to reach him in time. He briefly cursed the slackness of the escort's gun master, but that changed nothing.

"Commander," the shaggy, ursine navigator turned around, eyes wide with fear, though he strived to perform like a true servant of the Empire, "our shields will not stand up to their fire." His growling voice held a note of finality. As it should.

Verkont nodded, his features composed and serene. His life may not have been glorious, but in death, at least, he would prove himself worthy of his ancestors. "Thank you, Trank. You have done well. All of you have done well. May your forefathers greet you with honor."

The shaggy Gardal nodded back, baring his teeth. Though his culture did not practice ancestor worship like the Overlords, preferring the gods of their natural world, he appreciated the regard implied by Verkont's words. The lieutenant was a respectful and honorable officer, better than many Overlords who openly despised the subject races.

"Tvant," Verkont turned to his Gardal first officer, "prepare to return fire. We will show the humans this ship serves the Emperor." His guns would be like pinpricks on a dragon, but the humans would know that even the Empire's lowliest ships had honor and spirit.

*

"Mister Guthren, we'll pass the transport on the starboard side, at a range of one-hundred kilometers, then come about on the port side, same range. Mister Devall, individual fire under control of the gun captains. No missiles."

"A bit close, if he chooses to self-destruct." Pushkin seemed dubious.

Siobhan smiled. "Imperial transports have no self-destruct mechanism. The High Command doesn't want to risk some glory seeking ship captain committing suicide and utterly destroying the precious cargo. They count on recovering some of it if something like us happens." *Know thine enemy, Gregor.*

"Captain," the gunnery chief raised his arm to attract her attention. He had taken over surveillance duties, to leave Devall free for the engagement. "One contact at sublight heading toward us at zero-seven-three mark one-five. I make it a Gecko-class corvette."

"One of the escorts." She nodded as if she had expected this. Which she did. Gecko-class corvettes did not pose a significant threat to a well-handled frigate unless commanded by an officer with Brakal's abilities. Fortunately, the Empire had managed to produce only one of those, and he commanded the Gorgon-class cruiser *Tol Vakash.*

"Time to intercept?"

"Ten minutes." But Chief Penzara was not finished yet. "Another contact FTL on a heading two-nine-five mark four-five."

This caught Siobhan's attention, though she took care to remain as unconcerned as before. A new player, not part of the convoy. A shadow? Unexpected, but of no immediate danger.

"Time to intercept?"

"Approximately fifteen minutes."

Pushkin and Devall looked at Dunmoore, expecting her to change tactics and destroy the transport as quickly as possible from a standoff position, the better to slip away before enemy warships arrived. But she only nodded, cool and composed. One target at a time.

"Put the contacts on tactical. When the guns bear, Mister Devall, your gun captains may open fire."

The first officer turned back to his console, worried. He knew she was giving the gunners a chance to draw first blood personally. It was good for morale and confidence, but she cut it close, too close for his comfort, and it broke all the rules of proper raiding: fast in, fast kill, fast out. Was Dunmoore succumbing to bravado? Pushkin realized he still knew very little about the captain. And what he knew did not seem to apply now that her blood was up.

Slowly, too slowly for the first officer, *Stingray* pulled abreast of the wounded transport and the main as well as the starboard guns opened fire in a measured and steady cadence. The transport replied feebly, its shots splashing on the frigate's energy shields like bugs on a windscreen. At first, the *Hurgan*'s dying shields dispersed *Stingray*'s shots, but each round hit the target precisely, and the weakened force field collapsed. The next rounds hit the hull with devastating effect, punching black holes through the armor. A salvo from the main two-oh-three millimeter turret destroyed the starboard hyperdrive in a shower of sparks and crackling energy, then the frigate was past.

Guthren brought her around the *Hurgan*'s stern, giving the humans a clear view of the torpedo's damage. Devall whistled softly. "That was damned good shooting indeed, captain. I didn't know Lako had it in her."

Their view of the transport flipped one-eighty degrees as Guthren turned the ship on its axis to give the portside guns a chance to engage on the undamaged side. Then, with the same slow precision, the frigate raked the transport again.

They would never know which shot finally ended the target practice. Suffice to say a heavy plasma round found its way through a hole burned into the main hull moments

304 No Honor in Death

before and hit the now unprotected fusion reactor sitting atop the cargo holds. Lieutenant Verkont and his Gardal bridge crew never felt the final explosion that tore apart their ship. A direct hit from the frigate's main gun had already sent them to oblivion.

The crew of Stingray watched Hurgan die in silence, aware that they had just condemned thirty-odd sentient beings to death. A chain of linked explosions ripped apart the transport's hull, spewing frozen atmospheric gases into space. Then, a bright flower of pure energy blotted out the ship as the antimatter fuel tanks blew. When the light faded, what had been a large, ungainly but serviceable transport was gone, replaced by an expanding cloud of wreckage.

The Stingrays felt none of the triumph they expected from their first victory in over a year. They were no longer used to dealing out violent death and the whole business had an unpleasant taste to it. Simply put, it had been too easy, like clubbing a baby seal to death. But it had been a kill, and it had value to the Commonwealth's war effort.

"Scratch one consignment of arms and equipment that'll never reach the imperial ground forces on Cimmeria," Siobhan commented coldly, aware of her crew's feelings. She had met the same attitude at the start of the war when computer simulations that hurt no one turned into bleak and deadly reality. She had not expected it in an experienced crew, though she should have. Killing was a habit that had to be fed regularly, or human scruples gained ascendancy. That, more than anything else, blunted a crew's edge in battle.

"It'll make re-taking the system that much easier for our Marine colleagues."

"That it will," Pushkin commented flatly.

Siobhan gave him a sharp look.

"This one was the easiest," she said. "The next will be more of a challenge."

"Next, sir?" Pushkin was surprised. He never considered that Siobhan would want to hang around, now that their advantage of surprise was blown. A quick kill and a quick run back to their side of the line seemed the sane course of action, and no one would fault them for it. After all, a kill was a kill, and they had damaged engine components.

"Do the unexpected, Mister Pushkin," Siobhan grinned cruelly. It was time to lay out the cold reality of war, and force them to acknowledge the true nature of their duties: to kill as many Shrehari as possible, before they killed more humans.

"I'm not finished with these bastards yet. Every transport we get weakens the Empire's position here just that much more, and we haven't even hit a troopship yet."

The first officer repressed a shudder at the thought of slaughtering a transport filled with hundreds, if not thousands of defenseless troops. Siobhan read his thoughts as they flashed across his face. Her voice hardened.

"Every imperial trooper we kill here will mean one less to kill our Marines later. They started this war. We'll finish it. Chief, range and bearing of the escort?"

"Same course as before. Intercept in three minutes."

"Mister Shara. Program a micro jump of three seconds on bearing two-five-three mark seven-five. Cox'n, the moment we emerge, take the ship around one-eighty degrees. Let's try something more challenging."

"Course laid in."

"Engage."

*

Sub-Commander Yorganth of *Ptar Korsh* watched the death of the *Hurgan* with rage, unable to accept his helplessness, knowing his life would be forfeit if the Fleet Commander chose to make an issue of his competence. He offered a pro forma prayer for the transport's dead crew, although his beliefs had been sorely tested of late.

His only chance remained in taking the offending human frigate. Yorganth recognized it as a Type 203, an old, outclassed model and he ordered his helmsman to push the corvette beyond the safe sublight speed limits. Then, to his even greater horror, the human jumped, escaping his stillborn attempt at revenge.

"His course?" He snapped at the gun master.

The younger officer glanced at his scanner and swore. Before Yorganth could reprimand him for using offensive language, his gun master blurted out the horrible truth about his situation.

"Commander, the human is behind us and closing in at maximum sublight!"

"Helm, emergency turn. Gharl, prepare to engage."

"He has launched missiles, commander."

"Argh!" Yorganth slammed his fists down on the arms of his chair. The human commander was an evil magician. "Defensive fire on the missiles. All spare power to shields."

*

"Birds away, captain."

Dunmoore nodded, bloodlust dancing in her eyes. She had surprised not only the enemy but also her own crew. The sharp turn right after emergence had strained the ship, but after hearing a battleship's dying creaks, Siobhan could easily ignore the feeble protestations of an undamaged and far more agile frigate. Not so her first officer, but then, his duty in battle was the health and continued functioning of the ship.

Four antiship missiles streaked toward the corvette. Though she doubted more than one would get through to damage the Shrehari's shields, the spread of birds kept his guns busy while she brought her frigate to the optimum firing range. She could have saturated his defenses with another spread of missiles, but she needed them for later. Siobhan had no intention of running for home even after she took care of this one. Four transports still sailed to Cimmeria, and she intended to bag them all.

"Mister Devall, centrally controlled salvo from all guns at my order."

"Aye, aye, sir." He touched his keyboard, slaving all weapons to his own fire control system. This was more to his liking: hit 'em hard, hit 'em fast and get 'em out of the way before another ship came within range.

On screen, the corvette grew at an alarming rate, both ships now closing with each other head-on. Guthren glanced back at Siobhan, a knowing look in his eyes. "We're on a collision course, sir."

Dunmoore smiled. "Excellent. Remember the last time you and I played chicken, cox'n?"

Guthren chuckled. "It's graven in my memory forever, skipper," he replied, his attention divided between the enemy and his captain. He did not share the crew's misgivings. After what he and Dunmoore had survived in *Don Quixote*, none of her tactics would faze him. He trusted her with his very existence.

Catching Pushkin's dubious stare, Dunmoore's smile turned into a vulpine grin. "Ask Mister Guthren about his hair-raising experiences during the first battle of Cimmeria, Mister Pushkin."

"Engaging our missiles," Devall reported. Streams of plasma tracked across the starlit background as the corvette's less able computer tried to nail the birds in mid-flight. One exploded with a brief flash of light, but the other three kept coming. The gunnery officer found himself holding his breath as if the missiles were an extension of himself.

"Got another one," he reported, feeling his heart beating wildly. The two remaining birds were getting closer to the target, and he mentally cheered them on, as if they were sprinters in an inter-Academy race.

The imperial ship's gunner fired without ceasing, but it was in vain. Both missiles struck *Ptar Korsh*'s bow shield, and the five-megaton nuclear warheads exploded simultaneously, bathing him in the glow of a thousand suns. *Stingray*'s scanners blanked out momentarily under the assault of radiation, but she remained on her collision course, Devall's hand hovering over the firing button.

*

The flash of both missiles exploding a hundred meters from *Ptar Korsh*'s hull overloaded the ship's cruder electronics and burned out the heavily shielded visual pickups. On the bridge, Yorganth and his officers were blinded by the flash in the fraction of a second before the screen went blank.

Genuine fear now possessed the sub-commander and panic threatened to choke him as his gun master reported the collapse of the bow shields. Yorganth blinked several times, willing his eyes to see clearly again, and in that time, the human frigate came within firing range, but he could not know that. He was blind until the backup systems came online.

When the screen lit up again, Yorganth faced his greatest nightmare. His entire bow was open to the enemy's guns, and these now winked brightly as they spewed round after round of destructive plasma.

"Helm, bring the ship to port. Gun master, open fire as you bear." Yorganth was pleased his voice remained strong and steady, hiding the fear he felt.

The helmsman moved too slowly, and the first salvo came through the hole created by the missiles, striking *Ptar Korsh*'s gray hull. Yorganth's ship shuddered under the impact, groaning with pain. A console flared as feedback from the plasma strike traveled down the shielded conduits and shorted out the bridge electronics. The sickening smell of burned polymers and plastics assailed Yorganth's nostrils. He suddenly knew he would explain himself to his ancestors and not his admiral.

*

"He's wide open," Devall's excited voice cut through the sounds of the straining ship. "His front shields are gone."

The gunnery officer hit the firing button, releasing the full weight of the frigate's broadside again.

Ptar Korsh's responding salvo, however, found fully charged and operational screens, and though the frigate's shields flared under the impact, none punched through

Siobhan, working only on instinct now, saw the hole created by the first lucky missile strike slowly slip away. "Guns, fire one missile down his throat. NOW!"

Instinctively, Devall's hand found the controls, and he released another bird at point-blank range. His mind caught up with him seconds later, but by then, Siobhan had already ordered the cox'n to shear off to starboard, abandoning the game of chicken just as the Shrehari began his turn. The two ships passed each other within spitting distance, each shuddering under the hammering of the other's guns.

Devall just had time to admire Dunmoore quick mind before the five-megaton warhead exploded on the corvette's main hull. The explosion, contained for the first second or so within the ship's remaining shields, cracked its armored hull as if it were an egg.

The Shrehari crewmen closest to the hull died first, flash fried inside their suits. On the bridge, Yorganth's mouth opened to speak, but whether it was for an order or a prayer, no one ever found out. The hull imploded under the pressure of the released energy, and then exploded outwards as the pressure of the contained atmosphere pushed at the broken seams. The magnetic bottles holding the corvette's antimatter fuel collapsed simultaneously, adding the propellant's immense power to the chaos.

Everything seemed frozen by the violence of *Ptar Korsh*'s death throes as if the *Stingray*s could not believe the rapid destruction they visited on the imperial ship. Siobhan, however, was in her element at last. She had not forgotten the other oncoming ship. The tactical display showed it emerging at the site of the *Hurgan*'s death. But the captain had already planned one step further.

"Mister Shara, lay in a course three-one-five, mark zero." To her credit, the sailing master responded as fast as she could. "Done, sir."

"Engage."

With a nauseating lurch, *Stingray* left the scene of the battle and vanished into hyperspace. The physical sensation jolted the others back to life, and they glanced around, uncertain of what their eyes had seen.

Siobhan smiled at them, though it was a chilling smile. "Scratch one corvette. Mister Kowalski, give me ship-wide."

"Stingrays, this is the captain. In the last ten minutes, you chalked up an imperial transport and a warship with barely a scratch on our hull. Well done. Well done, indeed. As far as I'm concerned, we have now proved that *Stingray* is far from being a jinx. This ship is as good as any in the Fleet, and we're just starting. Our raiding patrol is far from over, and you'll have more chances to prove your worth to the Fleet. For now, we will take a breather and let the Shrehari wonder about us. I'm proud of you this day. Keep it up. Dunmoore, out."

Pushkin looked at her curiously, as if coming out of a dream. "What now?"

"Now? We shake that other imperial warship, review the battle log, and take our next kill."

"Wouldn't it be more prudent to return to our patrol route? We've got two of them."

"That's the predictable move, Mister Pushkin. I don't like being predictable. No, we can still take out one or two more transports. Take a look at our course. We're heading deeper into the Empire. Our opponents would hardly expect that."

Her tone was utterly reasonable, matter-of-fact, but her eyes were very, very bright. Pushkin repressed a shiver. By his more sedate standards, Dunmoore was a madwoman, but one who could run circles around the opposition. Judging by the happy grins around the bridge, the crew had finally caught her madness and were willing to follow her wherever she took them.

*

Commander Brakal did not even feel the desire to curse as he looked at the expanding debris field which marked the graves of two imperial ships. He was too late, a first in his impressive career, and it was a feeling he did not like. The crew felt his mood and remained silent. Even the smirking Khrada held his peace before the deaths of over two hundred imperial spacers.

Although he knew it to be futile, he ordered a scan for survivors, on the off chance that one or two spacers had escaped in crew pods. Then, he turned his attention to the tactical screen which showed the retreating convoy and the fast vanishing human raider. He slowly stroked his jaw and thought carefully about his next move, noting, as Jhar did, that the enemy did not head for home, but deeper into imperial space. He was clearly not through yet, and that, if nothing else, presented the opportunity for revenge.

It would be an exciting chase and a long one too, if he judged his opponent right.

— Twenty —

Siobhan rose and stretched, repressing a groan. For the last three hours, *Stingray* had run deeper into imperial space, in the general direction of Cimmeria, and they finally completed the last of a series of quasi-random jumps to blur their trail. Hopefully, it would be enough to throw off the imperial patrol ship. Her crew needed a few hours rest, as did the ship. And she needed to think about a new plan to cut her next victim out of the convoy.

Dunmoore knew her first officer disapproved and would rather they ran for the line, standing on the two kills they already chalked up. But she would not let go. Frigates were supposed to find and engage the enemy to the utmost of their abilities, and that was exactly what she would do: fight until she was forced to withdraw. So far, the Shrehari response to her assaults had been less than forceful. That would change, of course, but not quite yet.

The convoy still registered on *Stingray*'s scanners, barely, but it sufficed. Of the other ship, they found no trace. Either they had outrun it, or its commander was lying doggo, waiting for her to reappear on his screens. Two could play this game, and it would give them the rest period they all needed. The convoy was not going anywhere other than Cimmeria, and this close, their options were limited enough. They would find them again when the time came.

"Mister Pushkin, dampen the reactors and go to electronic silence. Let's make like a space mushroom while we take a break, and see what happens out there." She smiled at the first officer. They were totally unlike each other, but in time, they could become a good team, his caution balancing her recklessness. Too bad he still held back. Hopefully it was more out of habit by now than out of genuine resentment. She had done all she could to get him onside.

"Aye, aye, sir."

"I'll be in my ready room."

Alone in her sanctuary, Siobhan slumped into the chair and sighed. The tension of the chase and the subsequent battle had taken a physical toll, and tired people make mistakes, as she proved to the Shrehari in a most devastating lesson. It would not do to fall into the same trap. Sure, the rest period would screw up her crew's momentum, but it was more important to soothe overworked reflexes and adrenal glands. To fully absorb the implications of what they had achieved.

Running silent, as it was commonly called, made the ship invisible to long-range sensors, and since space was one hell of a big place, the frigate should remain undetected. There was no way the enemy patrol ship could have followed them through the wild course changes they had made, and if she were in her opponent's boots, Siobhan would stick close to the convoy because it was the biggest honey pot in the sector. If she was lucky, the enemy commander lacked the necessary imagination and initiative and was now trying to run her down.

She sat up and pulled the computer terminal toward her. First, the damage reports. They were mercifully light. A few shorted-out systems and broken bones, as Pushkin had already told her. Nothing to make Luttrell and Tiner complain loudly. That too would change after the next engagement, which she knew would be much more challenging and probably deadly.

Then, while the memory of the fast battle remained fresh, Siobhan sketched a draft of her report to Battle Group. One Tuck-class transport and one Gecko-class corvette. Not bad for an afternoon's work. Not bad at all. She smiled at the names Naval Intelligence had chosen for the ship types. Their actual Shrehari class names were unpronounceable by human tongues.

Most important, however, her crew had been blooded. Many, like Pushkin, probably still harbored scruples about the swift and merciless death they dealt out to the Imperials, but their shells would harden with a few more engagements. If they could not hack the dirty work, after all that, then she would replace them at the end of the cruise. But the general atmosphere on the frigate was already a lot better as a result of the victories, easy as they had been. Which was all to the better. The next time would be much harder. Inflexible though they were, the Shrehari were certainly no fools.

*

Down in the lower deck mess hall, over a quick meal, the ratings swapped stories about the battle, especially the gunners, who compared shots. If Siobhan could have seen them, she would have smiled at their enthusiasm. But part of that was due to the ease of the fight, as Banger Rownes well knew. She took no pleasure in the kills, only quiet pride at a job well done.

"So whaddya think, Banger? We gonna go for some more Imps?" Nosey Bertram scratched his prominent proboscis, grinning slyly. "Cap'n sure as shit knows wot she's doin', eh!"

Rownes shrugged. "We surprised the buggers is all. Chief Penzara says we're still deep in enemy space, and the cap'n looks like she's gonna try the convoy again. But the next time it won't be so easy. They know we're here now. Hell, for all we know, we've got a bloody Imp cruiser on our tail. This ain't over yet by a long run."

The big gun captain's tone cut through the high spirits like a bucket of cold water. Confidence was a good thing, overconfidence was not. And the swift destruction of two unprepared enemy ships sure as shit wouldn't mean squat when they met a pissed-off imperial cruiser. Which they would, sooner or later.

Her friends fell silent and concentrated on eating the emergency rations served up by gloomy purser's mates. Electronic silence meant all unnecessary gear was shut down, including the galley. The food was not great, but they all developed a healthy appetite during the last few hours.

Vincenzo, unable to stand the silence any longer, switched to that favorite of all spacers, gossip. "I guess you have all heard," he said around a mouthful of soyburger, "Kery is in the brig."

"Yeah. Scuttlebutt says she's really an SSB spy." Banger was unmoved by the news.

Vince nodded vigorously.

"She is an officer, a major called Elidia Cayne. The captain asked her before we jumped the convoy. I saw them in her office, with the captain pointing an ugly blaster at the little *creatura*."

"No shit? I can just picture Dunmoore as a gunslinger, starin' down the filth." Nosey grinned. "A major, eh? She's more like a major pain in the ass, is Kery. What's the cap'n gonna do?"

"No idea, my friend. Regulations say we cannot interrogate her. I guess we hand her over to Naval Security when we reach the base. Mister Drex is keeping a close eye on her."

Nosey shuddered theatrically. "Be enough to spook me into talkin'. With his dead eyes and zombie stare. He's a queer one, your Mister Drex."

Vincenzo reflected on his friend's comment and decided not to tell how queer Drex's behavior actually had become in the last few days. The second officer frightened him enough, especially since they found Hartalas' body down on deck fifteen. Too much death on *Stingray* and all of it made up to look like accidents.

As if by telepathy, Nosey Bertram homed in on his thoughts. "Hey Vince, maybe now the cap'n can find out about the shit the old bitch Forenza was doin'. With the stoolie gone, no more danger to us."

"And what do we have?" Rownes scowled. "Gossip, rumors, and crap like that. If Cap'n Dunmoore wants to dig up old bones, then bully for her. We got a good ship now, with a good skipper and we got two kills to paint on our hull. Kery ain't alone in her business, and her sittin' in the brig don't make me feel much safer. What if there's another slag on board? What then?"

"What's with you, Banger?" Bertram looked at her with exaggerated astonishment. "You normally ain't like this."

She shrugged. "Listen, I told the cap'n about how the bitch ran this tub, that's all. It's enough to make her realize where we're coming from. The rest we can wipe from our memories, especially now that Kery's on her way out. That shit is over. We got a good thing going, let's not spoil it."

"Yeah, maybe you're right, Banger." Nosey sighed. "I still think them big crooks shouldn't get away with it."

"Only 'cause you're jealous, Nosey, 'cause you got caught. But what if we're right and they get caught? Judge can't make 'em join the navy like he did with you."

Banger's quip drew the expected round of laughter, and the mood lightened as the conversation steered toward safer waters. The gun captain did not like lying to her buddies. Well, it was not precisely a lie, but she knew things were not quite over yet, and it was best to remain quiet until the captain finished sweeping out the filth. She would have been surprised to know the quiet, thoughtful Vincenzo felt the same way, if not exactly for the same reasons.

*

"You do not pursue, commander?" Khrada's tone was silken, menacing, in a manner Brakal could not call insubordinate, or implying cowardice. Not quite. The *Tai Kan* officer knew how to skirt the limits of acceptable behavior with the flair of a consummate professional. But Brakal too was a consummate professional, and he would not have his judgment called into question on his own bridge.

"To what aim, lieutenant?" He asked, a malicious smile on his lips, as he pointed at the tactical display. "He is jumping around like a mad *loorak*. If I begin to follow, he will just vanish from view and bide his time. This one knows his craft. Sniffing up his arse like a filthy dog would be useless. Of course," he added, "*Tai Kan* training does emphasize sniffing, so your abysmal ignorance is natural. I excuse you."

The not so subtle insult flowed over Khrada like water over a snake, though Brakal thought he could detect a chink in his admirable patience. He briefly toyed with the idea of provoking *Tai Kan* into an open violation of discipline, something to give him cause for an arrest and formal charges, or a summary execution. But such behavior was not encompassed by his concept of personal honor, and he dropped the thought, pleasing as it appeared. The spy's cooperation would have been required in such a scheme, but there were always ways to push a man beyond the limits of his restraint.

"Jhar, take us near the convoy with quick, random jumps. Maybe we can tempt the human to move and thereby reappear on our screens. He will wish to take more victories, this one, and the glory that flows from success."

That had been four hours earlier. Now, *Tol Vakash* sailed in normal space a short jump behind the convoy. Brakal had alerted its commander to his presence, and though the man had not expressed his true feelings, the relief in his eyes had been plain for all to see.

Yet even with all the random jumps, Brakal was unable to lure the human commander from his hiding place. His signature, after slowly fading from view, was nonexistent. He ran silent, a human tactic Brakal knew very well. Imperial ships did not have the same uncanny ability to disappear in plain sight, their electronic shielding inadequate in the face of excellent human scanners. But he was there, somewhere, watching them. And his window of opportunity shrunk by the minute, as the convoy neared the Cimmeria system.

Soon, they would be in short jump range of the system's assault force, or rather would be if the senile idiot in command at Cimmeria would recall his ships from their flag waving patrol, as Brakal had urged. However news of his uncertain status had reached even this far out, and Admiral Kokurag refused to chance Trage's displeasure. It was just as well that the human did not know this, and would act as if the assault force was an immediate threat.

Or would he?

*

Lieutenant Commander Pushkin drew a mug of coffee from the thermos in the conference room, now set aside as rest area for the bridge crew. He added a packet of sugar and turned toward Chief Guthren, who was sprawled lazily on the padded bench that sat against the outer bulkhead.

The big non-com raised his cup in a salute. "Nothin' like a hot one, eh, Mister Pushkin? Too bad we can't add a splash. But then, the skipper needs my magic touch at the helm."

He grinned, pleased with his early performance on the bridge, but his eyes remained wary, searching Pushkin's face for signs of weakness. The first officer had cleaned up his act well enough since the skipper had taken over, but could he handle the stress of Cap'n Dunmoore's – unusual – tactics? He had looked worried enough at the time.

Pushkin sipped his coffee, a thoughtful frown on his face, eyes staring past the cox'n. Finally, he sat at the far end of the table and looked squarely at Guthren. "So what's the story, chief?"

"You mean playing chicken, sir?" Guthren's grin widened. When Pushkin nodded, the cox'n straightened, drained his mug, and took on a conspirator's guarded expression. Dunmoore would have recognized his look and groaned aloud. Guthren was a good storyteller, but he derived all too much enjoyment from the sound of his own voice.

"Picture this then, if you will, Mister Pushkin. It was the year 2460. The present war was all but a few months old, though Cimmeria, Mission, and Nabhka were already under the imperial thumb. The small auxiliary scout ship *Don Quixote*, all of two thousand tons of it and a thirty-strong crew, was leading Task Force Three-Alpha toward a clash of titans with an Imperial Fleet. Now *Don Quixote* was a fast, well-armed ex-smuggler, bought into the Fleet before the war and given to one Lieutenant Siobhan Dunmoore, skipper. Her cox'n, then a petty officer first class, was yours truly. In the months before the battle, *Don Quixote* and its commander had made quite a name for themselves in one crazy stunt after another. For instance, and I'll save that story for another day, our esteemed captain took personal control of the helm and weapons, and flew the scout ship like an attack fighter right through the imperial beachhead on Cimmeria, under the astonished eyes of the 2nd Battalion, 18th Marines, then fighting for their lives. But as I said, that's for another time. We were discussing games of chicken, weren't we, Mister Pushkin."

Guthren gave the first officer his most avuncular smile.

"Smart scouts as we were, we ferreted out the Shrehari Fleet heading on its way to cause mischief to Dordogne and led Task Force 3A across their hawse. The battle was one hell of a spectacle, sir, ships everywhere, shooting plasma, popping off missiles," Guthren's hands moved above the table, conjuring the picture of a mighty space battle between behemoths.

"Accounting for the fact that we were just a small scout, we sat on the sidelines, half of us watching for a second Shrehari force coming to flank us, the other half watching the fight of the century. Then, near us, the frigate *Barracuda* gets into real trouble. She has two Hades-class cruisers going at her and no help in sight. So the skipper, tired of sitting on her thumbs and seeing a opportunity to help – fact is," Guthren grinned wickedly, "her best friend was gunnery officer on the *Barracuda* – blindsided one of the Imperials with our popguns, drawing him off long enough so the *Barracuda* could send the other to join his ancestors. We gave the bastard a hard time, but he rattled us bad enough to leave us drifting, all power gone. Seeing that we were out of the fight, the Imp left us for dead and turned back to the *Barracuda*. Cap'n Dunmoore's friend must have been a good gunner, cause he got that one too."

"So there we were, dead in space, no power, no shields, and no guns. We were drifting on our last course, and everybody was ignoring us in the heat of battle. We were just another large piece of junk. Our first officer was down and as officers, it was just Cap'n Dunmoore and a terrified ensign not a year out of the Academy down in the engine room. Well, between the two of them, and the best machinists I've known, they got the sublight drives back on, the shields back up and the guns online. The jump drives were shot, and there was nothing we could do about that. So the cap'n and Mister Brocard, the engineering ensign, hatched a little plan to use our antimatter fuel in a most imaginative fashion. Like I said, *Don Quixote* was a well-built ex-smuggler, and she could do things no honest navy ship could," his grin returned, "for instance eject the fuel still in its magnetic bottle, like a big fucking bomb."

"By that time, we'd drifted right into the middle of the fight and our ships were getting a fearful drubbing. It looked like the Imperials might just chase us home with our tails between our legs. The moment our power and our systems came back online, I turned to look at the skipper and ask her where she wanted to go, like back to the edge of the battle maybe. But she grinned as if she was having the time of her life and said, 'cox'n, see that big mother of a flagship ahead. What say we give him a surprise?' Now the idea was crazy. A tiny scout ship going up against a massive imperial flagship. Sort of like David and Goliath, or, like the skipper put it a moment later, like Don Quixote tilting against a windmill. I don't know, but her madness infected all of us in the time it took to breathe a few times."

Guthren shook his head, still feeling the emotions of that moment, five years ago.

"We upped shields, deployed guns and opened missile launchers. Then, with all running lights on and us singing *Man of La Mancha*, we charged the *Gur Varig*, flagship of the 4th Imperial Deep Space Fleet. Buddies of mine who were there on other ships said everything stopped the moment they realized that a tiny scout was taking on the mighty ship. They thought we were fucking nuts. I guess we were at that. Even the crew of the *Gur Varig* thought we were nuts because they just looked at us come, popguns blazing, missiles burning space ahead of us. They tried a few shots, more for fun than anything else. Still shook us bad, but we got close enough to their shields. I don't know who was more surprised that we got that close, them or us. Anyways, at the last moment, the skipper has me shear off just as she dumps the antimatter bottle on the flagship. It hit the shields and collapsed."

Guthren stared at Pushkin, a strange fire in his eyes as if the chief was back aboard *Don Quixote.*

"You ever see the reaction when a full load of antimatter fuel intersects a power shield, sir? We just about didn't see it either. Fucking Imp shields overloaded and broke down in a fraction of a second, but the reaction was far from over. It just kept on going, eating up the outer hull. The *Gar Varig* started breaking up in front of both fleets, destroyed by a little scout under the command of a crazy lieutenant. We were tossed around by the ship's death throes. Damn near got wiped out ourselves, but Cap'n Dunmoore has the devil's own luck." Pushkin could read the evident admiration in Guthren's eyes. The cox'n stood up and stretched his stout frame.

"Anyways, with the destruction of their flagship, the fuckers didn't know which way was up anymore and pulled out, so that was the end of the battle. The *Barracuda* found us drifting among the wreckage, more wreck than ship ourselves, and threw us a tow. Towed us all the way back to Dordogne, as a matter of fact. Admiral was so impressed that he decided we should lead Task Force 3A from the emergence point in Dordogne system to Starbase 30. We patched up our sublight drive during the jump and painted an almighty imperial dragon on our hull, a kill mark, and then we cast off the tow a few million klicks out. The old *Don Quixote* rode for the last time." There was genuine emotion in his voice now. "We got permission for a fly-by and a full reception when we docked." Guthren shook his head again.

"Those were times, Mister Pushkin, those were times. Aboard the little *Don Quixote*, tilting at every goddamn imperial windmill. Anyways, since then, nothing our very own Dona Quixote does surprises me anymore."

"Yeah," he smiled at Pushkin's expression, "that's what we used to call her, Dona Quixote. She and the Don would have made quite a pair. Both as crazy as loons. You mark my words, Mister Pushkin; she'll cover us with glory on this one too. Any skipper who can beat a flagship with a scout can do just about anything." He winked, "including playing a good game of chicken with any bastard who gets too close."

Then, without a further word, Guthren left a thoughtful first officer alone in the conference room, happy that he had finally been able to tell the story and let the buggers on this tub know their skipper was one of the best there ever was. And that they were damned lucky to have her.

*

"Interesting." Siobhan steepled her fingers. The passive receptors, less accurate and suffering more from time lag than the active scanners, had recorded *Tol Vakash*'s random gyrations as it moved up to the reorganized convoy.

Chief Penzara was playing the battle log for the captain's benefit now, adding a few comments culled from the depth of his experience.

"A Shrehari commander who thinks. I could almost believe it's Brakal or one of his apprentices. See how he vanishes from view here," she pointed at the timeline display, "and here, going silent and listening, instead of bulling his way in our last known direction. Can we get a make on the ship?"

Penzara shrugged, a grimace creasing his weathered features.

"It's pretty indistinct, cap'n, but I give it a good chance of being a Gorgon-class cruiser. The electronic signature is close, and the Gorgons are the most common rated ships in their navy."

Tol Vakash was a Gorgon-class cruiser. By Commonwealth standards, Gorgons were closer in size to heavy frigates but they still packed a mean punch, as she remembered.

Siobhan knew it was wishful thinking to imagine the chase ship being *Tol Vakash*. Revenge was not only a dish best eaten cold, but it was also a dish rarely eaten. The Gorgon was the most common patrol type in the Imperial Deep Space Fleet and a very successful design by their standards. The chief could be wrong, and it could be something like the larger and deadlier Basilisk-class cruiser, though the Imps usually kept those in heavy assault forces, not on detached duty. Siobhan liked enemies who followed their own rules closely. It meant she could throw away her rulebook and confuse the hell out of them.

"He's placed himself in a good strike position. If he coordinates jumps with the convoy, one or the other will be able to keep watch in normal space. Except," she smiled knowingly, "the convoy commander will want to get to Cimmeria quickly and won't be under the orders of the Gorgon commander, so we'll get a few brief windows to maneuver in close. Look at the trace: no inter-ship coordination. The convoy's keeping the same jump-rest-jump pattern as before. We just have to time our jumps well."

"Pretty difficult, sir," Pushkin commented pessimistically. "The Gorgon's been moving randomly enough to make any hidden approach impossible to time well. He's made jumps as short as fifteen minutes and as long as seventy-two. God knows what that's doing to his drives."

"There's nothing scientific about this, Mister Pushkin. Gut instinct is the only way to go. Risky, sure, but it's just as risky for him to move toward us as soon as we pop up on his scanners. He'll be guessing too, remember that. And the one who makes the least mistakes will take the prize." She looked at the time display and rose. "Let's go look for our window of opportunity."

Penzara and Pushkin followed her out on the bridge. The varsity team was back at its stations after a short rest and Siobhan's instincts told her it was time to move on. Or, she suspected, she was simply impatient to get back to the fray before the odds increased with the arrival of the Cimmeria Assault Force. Was she really out to earn her ship glory, she wondered, or were the ghosts of her past driving her headlong into a situation she might not be able to handle? She shrugged it off.

"Status."

"The convoy is still moving FTL, sir," Devall reported. "The other ship is still tooling along at sublight."

"Looking for us, no doubt." Siobhan relieved Shara, who had the watch, and slipped into her seat. "Wondering how long we're going to wait. In this, we have some advantage. He has to react to our moves. As long as we keep the initiative."

A soft beep caused the gunnery officer to glance at his screen. "He's jumped, sir."

"Time to go, people. Mister Shara, make our course one-nine-seven mark three-one, ten-minute jump at max. Mister Pushkin, up systems."

"Laid in."

"Ready."

"Engage." Nausea gripped them and vanished. "Mister Pushkin, the moment we emerge, rig for silent running. We're going to take this slow and careful."

Pushkin raised his eyebrows. Pushing the jump drives to max sure as hell was not slow in his book. Too much of that would bring complaints from the chief engineer and with good reason. *Stingray*'s older engines had a definite limit on high-speed sailing. But Siobhan Dunmoore had a hard gleam in her eyes.

*

"Active scan."

"On screen, sir."

"Still moving on exactly the same headings. Good. Chances are he hasn't emerged and still hasn't had an opportunity to pick us up. Go silent."

The minutes ticked by slowly as they waited for the Shrehari to go sublight for a scan. He did, ten minutes after *Stingray*, and came up with a blank. The convoy remained in its bubble, confirming Siobhan's suspicions that the cruiser's commander could not work out a mutual search-jump-search arrangement with the convoy commander. Too bad for them. He jumped again and so did the frigate, slowly overhauling the line of transports.

"The convoy's due to emerge soon," Siobhan said, three hours of tense hide and seek later. "He has to tack at least once before making a beeline to Cimmeria. My guess is the Gorgon's skipper will use the time to move nearer. He's lost some ground and knows our strike window is closing." Siobhan studied the display in silence for several minutes. She picked a point on the convoy's course and pointed it out to Shara.

"This is his optimum tacking point, both for time and fuel consumption. How long is a redline jump from here to there?"

"*Redline*?" Shara and Pushkin turned to her at the same time. Redlining the engines was a definite no-no, forbidden except in cases of extreme emergency. It reduced the life span of the drives considerably, and on an older ship like *Stingray*, had a chance of burning them out.

"I don't recommend it, sir." Pushkin frowned. "We've already had enough troubles."

"They'll take it this once. How long, Mister Shara?" The sailing master queried her navigation computer.

"Six minutes."

"Our friend's still FTL?"

"Aye, sir," Penzara replied. "Has been for eleven minutes now."

"And the convoy?"

"Going on five hours and fifty-one minutes."

Silence enfolded the bridge as Siobhan pondered her next move. If the convoy commander held to his standard pattern, something a human would never do after an attack, he was due to emerge in nine minutes, at the optimum tacking point for a home run to Cimmeria.

"Mister Shara, lay in a course for the point I've indicated –"

"Cap'n, the Gorgon's emerged." Chief Penzara's warning cut off all conversation. "And he's damned close."

"We're as silent as we can be, sir." Pushkin forestalled Dunmoore's question.

"Okay, everybody, make like you're a bunch of mushrooms." Siobhan's quip drew the expected chuckles, releasing some of the sudden tension.

"Just as long as the bastard ain't out to pick mushrooms for his admiral's salad." Chief Penzara growled in a low voice as if his words could carry across the void.

"His scanner just passed over us."

"Any bounce back?"

"Probably some. Hopefully, he'll think it's a sensor ghost or a cloud of ionized gases."

*

Tol Vakash's gun master grunted at the scanner readout, stroking his short chin beard. He could have sworn... Just to be on the safe side, he swept the area again, but this time nothing.

Lieutenant Urag was a good gunner but lacked the imagination of a superlative weapons officer. In the time between sweeps, the human frigate had moved, hurtling through space at constant speed, like any natural object, for nothing in the universe was ever at rest. The movement changed the angle she presented to *Tol Vakash* and this time, the bounce back was scattered enough to escape the less capable Shrehari scanners.

"Something, Urag?" Jhar asked, alert as ever to the mood of the crew. It was one of the qualities that had attracted Brakal's attention and subsequently, his patronage.

"A faint reflection, sub-commander. I swept again and nothing."

"Sensor ghost," Jhar growled, "or a cloud of gas."

Brakal, sitting back in his chair looking as relaxed as a lord on his estate does, smiled. "Maybe not. If the human is running silent, we would get such a ghost. Plot the 'sensor ghost' on screen."

A green icon winked to life on the tactical display. Jhar frowned, doubtful. "Much closer than expected. If that ship is a Type 203, he has good engines."

"Or a shrewd and reckless commander," Brakal replied, a calculating look transforming his face. "The speed is possible. And with good discipline, a human ship can vanish against the background radiation."

"Then why no ghost on the second sweep?"

"Because he is no longer in the same spot, and does not present the same aspect. Then again," Brakal continued, toying with his gun master and first officer, "it could simply be a cloud of gas. Navigator, we will shorten our course to run on the convoy's flank as it changes direction.

Let us see what we can scare up by opening the window a crack."

"A trap, commander?"

"No. This one seems too canny for a trap. Bait perhaps."

*

"He's on a new course, cutting across our front."

"Avoiding the convoy's dog leg." Siobhan nodded knowingly.

"In a hurry, sir?" Pushkin looked at the tactical display, frowning.

"No," Dunmoore grinned devilishly, enjoying this contest of wits. "He's giving us a go at the convoy."

"A trap?" Pushkin looked alarmed.

She shook her head. "Not exactly. He knows we won't make it easy for him, so he's hoping we'll use this unexpected window of opportunity to strike, revealing ourselves at the same time. Then, he'll swoop in."

"Do we take it?"

"Oh yes, we do. But on our own terms. He's probably planning on the basis of our known speed, so we'll simply make him eat his assumptions."

"Redlining the engines."

"Yup. Give him a real shock when he finds us buggering his precious convoy behind his back." The crude simile drew barely suppressed chortles. Siobhan's manic mood was beginning to infect the others. "Course ready and laid in, Mister Shara?"

"Aye, sir."

"Up systems, Mister Pushkin. Cox'n, engage."

The jump, though short, proved to be uncomfortable, most of all for Gregor Pushkin. *Stingray* clearly did not enjoy Dunmoore's breach of engineering regulations and proved it by protesting under the strain. Tiner called up to complain, but the first officer, to his credit, quietly told her to shut up and carry on. Dunmoore had earned at least that much loyalty from him. To be honest, the element of risk, the gamble, stirred something within him, and he discovered he wanted to see this through. So, by the looks of the others, did they.

Siobhan glanced at the computer-generated estimate on the tactical schematic, excitement pounding through her veins. If she pulled this off... With a bit of luck and a sound knowledge of the Shrehari' ways. She could not ask for a better intercept solution than this. All those hours of maneuvering, of creeping closer, would pay off soon.

One minute to go and the icons on the display began separating, spreading out under the tense stares of the crew. Pushkin realized he was gripping his chair's arms with bone-breaking force and willed himself to relax. His heart felt like it was about to burst under the adrenaline rush. He briefly wondered if he would have been able to withstand the even greater pressure of *Don Quixote*'s reckless charge.

Siobhan's breathing had become heavy, deep, her pale face flushed. Perspiration gathered on her upper lip. She glanced at Pushkin, who read in her eyes an almost unbearable tension.

"Everything's ready," he said in reply to her unspoken question.

"Good." Her voice had reacquired that smoky, hoarse quality which sounded so eerie to the usually staid first officer. "Primary target is the trailing Gecko-class, Mister Devall. No screwing around this time. Pound him hard."

"Aye, aye, sir."

"Here we go," Guthren rumbled, hand closing down on the cutoff switch.

*

Through the haze of emergence nausea, Lieutenant Trevane Devall saw a sight he would never have dared dream of, a once in a lifetime event. *Stingray* emerged in an unremarkable area of space, a short distance from the outer rim of the Cimmeria system. It was, however, the same area the convoy commander had chosen for his final tacking maneuver, as Captain Siobhan Dunmoore had predicted with uncanny accuracy.

Within seconds of the frigate's return to this universe, the imperial ships materialized across her bows, almost within touching distance. Ripples of the trans universe movement struck *Stingray*, so close was she. And athwart the convoy's line of travel too, able to engage the entire line with nearly all her guns.

"My God," Pushkin whispered in the incredulous silence. "Guthren was right. You have the devil's luck, captain." The awe on his face was almost comical.

Siobhan smiled beatifically, looking at the culmination of her professional expertise. "Oh, I don't know about the devil, Mister Pushkin. Though that's where those bastards are going. What d'you say to a target-rich environment, Mister Devall?"

"Good morning an' how are you?" The lieutenant turned toward her, a broad grin transforming his aloof, arrogant features into those of a child in a candy store. He felt giddy with exhilaration.

"Indeed." Then, her voice lost its dreamy edge. "Engage the trailing transport with a full spread of missiles, then the same on the escort. Give him too many targets and watch him go. Cox'n, head straight for the Gecko at half speed. Mister Pushkin, full energy to the forward shield."

"First salvo of birds away." Then, "Second salvo away."

Siobhan stared hungrily at her two victims, ignoring Devall.

How the hell do the girls in Fleet Intel come up with those ridiculous class names anyways? Loon-class troopship?

*

On the narrow bridge of *Ptar Vanak*, Sub-Commander Reyvtal could not absorb the evidence provided by his own eyes. That thrice damned human frigate had appeared, as if by magic, on his port side just as he and his charges were at their most vulnerable. And now, the bastard had fired a full spread of the blasted nuclear ship-killing missiles, an astonishing profligacy, one which would overwhelm his gunners.

His crew still struggled to sort themselves out amidst the nerve-rending screech of the battle siren.

Reyvtal gave orders to wear ship and meet the raider head-on. Then, the two flights of missiles split, half kept on course toward him, a number he could handle, but the other four headed straight for the troopship *Mentara*, which carried the twelve-hundred strong *Ashari* Regiment to Cimmeria. His gut clenched with horror when he realized he could not both beat off the missiles headed for him and protect the troopship at the same time. Either his ship or the troopship was doomed, for *Mentara* could not defend itself adequately.

Reyvtal swallowed with difficulty. The legendary Brakal and his *Tol Vakash* still rode the currents of other space, unaware of this disaster, and *Ptar Brokat*, in its lead position, would never make it back in time.

"Gun master!"

"*Kha*?"

"Make your priority target the four human missiles heading for *Mentara*. And put every bit of energy you can on the port and bow shields."

The gun master nodded, knowing Reyvtal had probably signed their death warrant. But an escort was supposed to protect its charges, at the risk of its own survival if need be. The commander of *Ptar Vanak* was acting in the only way he could: with honor.

"Open fire. Frekat, send out a general distress signal."

*

Not that far away, by interstellar standards, *Tol Vakash* dropped out of hyperspace to see if the human had taken the bait and broken cover. What they saw surpassed Brakal's wildest expectations. His massive fist hammered down on the arm of the commander's chair as rage mixed with admiration.

"By all the demons, he has outmaneuvered *me*, Brakal of Clan Makkar!"

"But how is that possible? The frigate does not have the speed."

Jhar sounded beside himself with anger. Behind Brakal, Khrada smirked with barely suppressed glee at the great commander's mistake, one which would cost many Shrehari lives, and Jhar reached for his blaster instinctively to wipe the *Tai Kan* spy's face off the universe.

"Peace, Jhar." Brakal raised his hand, checking the first officer's instinctive draw. "It can, if the human commander wishes it so. But the cost is significant and he has damaged his engines with that dash of speed. We have him now. Helm?"

"Course laid in and ready, *kha*."

"Go, then. It is time we spoil the raider's amusement with some serious fighting. Oh, but what daring, eh, Jhar? Few humans can claim to outwit me. In fact, I remember only one, the fire-haired female –"

"Dunmoore." Jhar replied flatly, mangling the unfamiliar name. He and his commander looked at each other. The latter's eyebrows went up in amusement.

"Could it be, Jhar? A fitting foe then, if it is her. I look forward to meeting the human gun to gun."

"Make sure you win, commander," Khrada hissed, annoyed now by his open admiration of the humans, something which offended his racial sense of superiority. "Else you will be looking forward to meeting the Council in disgrace. Your arrogant overconfidence is costing the Empire dearly. You should have remained nearer the convoy."

"Hah," Brakal laughed humorlessly, turning his chair to face Khrada. He made an obscenely dismissive gesture with his right hand, a clear signal that the word games had finally ended. "You cannot have it both ways, *Tai Kan* cretin. First, you do not want me to shadow this convoy, now you blame me for its peril at the hands of a rogue human raider. Were I not here now, the human would have already snapped up the transports one by one. If you and your moronic ilk have not found understanding yet, you never will. The humans know the art of war intimately and have the courage to try new and dangerous tactics, while we wallow in doctrine under the nonexistent leadership of congenital idiots. At least I am learning from them, which is more honorable than ignoring the evidence of one's own eyes."

"Jhar, place Lieutenant Khrada under close arrest. I tire of his peasant manners and abysmal stupidity. You may report what you wish to your superiors, Khrada. It will not change the course of this war, except perhaps making it even less favorable to the Empire."

A pair of brawny security ratings appeared at Jhar's silent summons and escorted Khrada to his quarters. The *Tai Kan* officer did not protest his treatment, lest he lose face in front of Brakal's crew of uncouth low caste scum. But his eyes promised revenge, something that Jhar noted. The first officer resolved to take care of Khrada once the human ship had been blown to atoms.

*

On the troopship *Mentara*, the commanding officer of the *Ashari* Regiment watched the fast-approaching missiles with sick fascination. The escort's cannons tried valiantly to hit them, as did the transport's little popguns, but the gunners lacked skill and good targeting computers to have much success. One exploded in an ephemeral flower of energy. A lucky hit. The others simply kept coming. Leader-of-a-Thousand Oragit knew the troopship's shields could not survive a direct hit by a nuclear warhead.

A stupid waste, he thought, disgusted. His regiment had trained hard. His soldiers expected to die on the field of battle on some human world, fighting humans. Now, they would all perish, killed by a stupid missile, and the honor of leading Imperial Forces in the upcoming operation would go to others. The *Ashari* Regiment would no longer exist to claim its share of glory.

Strangely, he felt no fear. Just a lassitude, a fatalism in the face of certain death. Terror at a fate one could not change was for weaklings and humans. Except that the humans on the raiding frigate were anything but weak.

Another missile disappeared, and a small part of him began to hope for survival. No sentient being wished to die, not even Shrehari raised from birth to consider death for the Empire a noble and honorable end. Behind Oragit, his staff stood still, as if rooted to the spot, watching the same screen and, he hoped, thinking the same thoughts. Oragit turned around and looked at each of his officers, in turn, nodding his farewell. He did not see the third missile blink out in a brief burst, nor did he see the last one strike *Mentara*'s shields with all the force of its five-megaton nuclear warhead.

Within a fraction of a second, the force field protecting the troopship fought the released energy and lost. The port shield collapsed, letting the residual force of the explosion splash the unarmored hull.

With all its industrial strength geared to produce fighting ships, the Empire chose to commandeer civilian vessels for its troop transport tasks instead of building their own, and they sadly lacked the integral hard protection of the former. Sub-Commander Pagrat, Master of *Mentara* briefly cursed his superiors for their stupidity as the flash of the nuclear detonation blinded him and his men. He had little time to think of anything else.

Mentara's entire port side buckled and burst open at the seams, exposing its many decks. Air, subjected to the eternal cold of space, crystallized in an expanding cloud, while living bodies burst under the sudden decompression. Over half of Oragit's men died in the first five seconds, including himself and his staff. The rest died when the troopship's ruined systems failed spectacularly, breaking apart the already torn wreck.

*

On *Ptar Vanak,* Sub-Commander Reyvtal, freed of his responsibility for *Mentara* shut out the horror of over twelve-hundred useless, honorless deaths and turned all his rage toward the oncoming frigate. The helmsman had completed his turn and the corvette now faced the enemy head-on. All available energy was concentrated on the bow shield, to the point of dropping the side and aft screen sections. At least, if the missiles broke through, the force field's remaining sections would not reflect all of the energy of the blast onto the hull.

One of the missiles, its homing system obviously defective, veered off to lose itself in interstellar space. A lucky gunner got the second, and then the third. Reyvtal wanted to crow with pleasure, for now, he stood a fighting chance, the better to hold the humans' attention while his colleague and Brakal approached to deal this raider a death blow.

He ordered a shutdown of all tracking systems and visual pickups. Just in time, as it turned out. The corvette shuddered under the detonation of the warhead, but the reinforced bow shield held, barely. Reyvtal counted to five. Then, "All systems on, redistribute shield energy to normal configuration."

The first of the frigate's salvos was on its way.

*

The loud, bloodthirsty cheers at the destruction of the troopship faded under Siobhan's sharp orders. Ahead, the corvette had taken up her challenge and appeared intent on evening the score. When the single surviving missile exploded on its bow, Siobhan was in position and ready to follow up with her two punch routine.

"Fire as you bear, Mister Devall. His shields won't hold for long."

"Incoming," Chief Penzara warned moments after the gunnery officer loosed his first salvo.

"For what we are about to receive," the cox'n intoned with mock somberness, "may the Lord make us truly thankful."

"I'd rather thank him for what the enemy is about to receive, Mister Guthren," Siobhan replied. "Change course to mark one-four-oh and increase speed to full. We'll pass beneath him. Continue firing, Mister Devall. I expect his shields to die by the time we rake his belly. Then it'll simply be a matter of slicing him open."

Stingray shuddered with *Ptar Vanak*'s full broadside as energies clashed on the frigate's shield barrier. Shimmering green flickered visibly while the power feedback whined audibly over the bridge's speakers.

"Holding," Pushkin reported, "but weakened. We can take several more before it gets critical."

"Shit!"

"What is it, chief?" Siobhan's head snapped around.

"The Gorgon-class is coming up fast. Still FTL but we'll have her on our backs within minutes."

"Okay, we've been blown. Let's finish this one fast before we get buggered. Mister Devall, drop two mines with proximity fuses now, while we're still on his opposing vector."

"Mines?"

"Do it," Dunmoore snapped irritably.

The gunnery officer shrugged and ordered the automatic mine dispenser to eject two small proximity mines. Using them in a running battle was unusual. Most ships carried them to use as nuisance weapons along known star lanes, or in orbit around interdicted planets. But shooting them across an enemy's bow?

The two opposing warships neared each other at high speed, firing almost continuously, and the small mines, barely two meters across, escaped the Shrehari's notice entirely. When *Stingray* was ten kilometers away, the mines' onboard computers armed themselves and began seeking for a target.

Sub-Commander Reyvtal and his ship fought courageously until the very end. The corvette and *Stingray* passed each other at point-blank range, with the frigate raking the other ship from below. This close, the contest became utterly unfair for the weaker Shrehari ship. Its design was more suited to peacetime anti-piracy than a head-on fight with a human frigate. His shields failed with a jarring flash of green and *Stingray*'s gunners began tearing up his gray underside with concentrated bursts of plasma. Then, as fast as they came together, the ships separated. Devall kept firing with all guns that could bear directly aft.

Less than two minutes after the nuclear missile exploded against her bow shield, the now unprotected and badly mauled *Ptar Vanak* came within range of the smart mines, still ignorant of their existence. Reyvtal was too busy planning his next and probably last run at the frigate to think of such an underhanded trick. But the mines' onboard computers calculated the corvette's expected course and, as one, fired their small attitudinal jets. Unshielded ship and nuclear mines intersected at a given point in space.

The mines exploded two hundred meters from the still intact bow of the corvette. For a fraction of a second, the ship's forward movement was checked by the force of the simultaneous blasts. On *Stingray*'s automatic battle recorder, played in slow motion, it later appeared as if the corvette had hit an invisible wall. Then, it disintegrated.

Reyvtal's last feeling in this life was one of complete outrage.

*

"The Gorgon's now at one-hundred thousand kays off our port quarter, sir. And the last Gecko-class is also on his way." Chief Penzara could not repress a note of worry in his tone. *Stingray* had not come out of her fight with the Gecko-class totally unharmed and two enemy ships at once could be too much.

"He's hailing us, sir." Kowalski was astonished beyond anything she had experienced in her short career.

"Brakal." The word came out as a whisper. It could only be him. No other Shrehari had his gall or his cunning. She raised her hand, palm outwards. "No reply. Mister Shara, put a schematic of Cimmeria on screen, with current planetary positions."

Pushkin gasped, divining her intentions. "Shouldn't we run for the border now, captain? We've four kills. Surely that's enough."

Siobhan shook her head, lips compressed into a thin line. "That's Brakal out there. He'll cut us off because he expects us to head back toward the line. Remember, always do the unexpected."

"But the in-system assault force —"

"Is somewhere else, or it would be within range by now." Siobhan's eyes locked with Pushkin's. Her cold determination silenced him, while at the same time, it gave rise to a new and more chilling suspicion. With Brakal's arrival, it had become personal for the captain.

"We'll get home, have no fear, Mister Pushkin. I have the measure of this one," she said in a tone low enough to reach his ears only.

"System on screen."

Siobhan broke eye contact, her mind shifting back into the calculating gambler's mode that had brought her so far.

"Mister Shara, make a course for the sixth planet, have us emerge as close as possible consistent with emergency safety rules. We're going to hide in his magnetic field."

"The Shrehari is hailing again, sir. He identifies himself as Commander Brakal of *Tol Vakash*."

Siobhan flashed an I-told-you-so smile at Pushkin.

"Mister Kowalski, pass my compliments to Commander Brakal and tell him Captain Dunmoore is too busy right now to renew the acquaintance. I prefer to wait until it's time to discuss his surrender. Guns, time to firing range?"

"Thirty seconds."

"Course laid in, sir."

"Guns, the moment he's in range, loose off a general salvo. Cox'n stand by to jump on my order."

*

"She said *what*?" Brakal roared with laughter at Dunmoore's impudence. "Oh, this will be interesting. I had not hoped for a rematch so soon. Gun master, prepare to open fire. Navigator, she will no doubt attempt to flee back toward her lines. Four kills in one stalk are enough glory for anyone. Be prepared to pursue. Oh, and Jhar, tell the convoy commander to take himself and his ships away from here. This is now my fight, and I do not wish to see any transports come to harm under the crossfire."

"In range, *kha*," the gun master barked. Then, "She fires!"

"By all means, return the courtesy, Urag." Brakal sounded as if this were merely a sports match between competing ship's companies.

*

"We hit him," Devall exulted. "His shields just took a beating."

"Still holding, though," Penzara's gloomier voice cut off the less experienced lieutenant. "He's replying."

Moments later, *Stingray* shook under the force of a full burst, and Siobhan's memories of her last encounter with *Tol Vakash* returned in full force, momentarily overwhelming her reckless determination. "Stand by to jump. One last salvo, Mister Devall."

"Number six shield has collapsed, sir," Pushkin announced. Lights flickered as the ship groaned in pain at the direct strikes. "Port power coupling is down. Rerouting through the secondary. We have casualties."

"Guns, fire! Cox'n, engage."

*

"Quick, plot her course," Brakal shouted over the din of *Stingray*'s parting salvo as it broke through the defensive energy field and licked the armored hull, leaving black marks around ragged shot holes. "And prepare to pursue."

"Course plotted, *kha*." The Navigator sounded uncertain.

Brakal frowned. "On screen." Had he been human, the commander would have done a double take. As it was, Jhar noticed his surprise clearly enough.

"Commander?"

"The hell-bitch is headed for Cimmeria! What unbelievable gall. She is not content with four victories and wants more. Or," his eyes took on a calculating look, "she seeks to draw me into a trap of her own devising."

"Revenge?"

"Oh yes, Jhar, she would be the kind to seek it. But one who is fixed on vengeance often fails to think clearly. Inform the master of the convoy that I now take command and that we will proceed under my sailing orders."

Jhar complied. "He refuses, *kha*. Apparently, he does not recognize your authority."

"Inform him he is under arrest and tell his second to take charge of the ship. Advise every shipmaster in the convoy that I will kill anyone who refuses my orders. This is no longer a game. We will sail with the convoy and make sure Dunmoore's plans fail."

— Twenty-One —

"Sir, I must advise you I do not agree with your plan of action."

Siobhan sat back, fatigue lining her face. Pushkin stood formally in front of the desk, body stiff, hands joined in the small of the back. Devall had the con, and she had stood the crew down for another dearly needed rest period. All of the crew that is, but the two unfortunate gunners who died in Brakal's last salvo.

Dunmoore studied her first officer's closed expression. If only she had a plan of action he could disagree with. Once more, she had acted on instinct, without entirely thinking through or rationalizing her decisions. But the reason for her orders, now that she had time to think beyond the immediate, came quickly enough. Whether they would satisfy the cautious first officer, she did not know.

"Brakal has an edge on us. He hasn't pushed his drives as we have. That means if we had tried an end run for home, he would have overtaken us. There's nowhere to hide between here and there. Going to silent running when he has your course plotted doesn't quite make it either. The Cimmeria system, however, has some splendid hiding spots, where we can lay low for a long time before they find us. I've operated here before."

"So the cox'n told me. But Brakal will know where we're headed," Pushkin protested.

"Obviously. Brakal is anything but stupid." Siobhan rubbed her eyes, willing her first officer to understand. "He'll also know we can hide with ease whereas he'd have a hell of a time finding us. My guess is failing a clear fix on us, he'll stick with the convoy until they slip into orbit

338

under the station's guns. That gives us our window of opportunity to get away and shake off any pursuit."

Pushkin looked skeptical. With reason. Siobhan sighed.

"Okay, Gregor. I admit that if I get an opening to kick Brakal's ass or kill another transport, I'll take it. That's our job in this war. Find and destroy the enemy."

"And get your revenge on Brakal for *Victoria Regina*." It was not a question, but a flat statement.

"Dammit, Gregor, that was unfair. And insubordinate." Siobhan stood up and turned away to study the holo print behind her desk. It was a reproduction of an eighteenth-century painting depicting a naval battle at a place called Camperdown. From the looks of it, those sailing ship captains would have had little doubts about the right course of action. Close with the enemy and destroy him. Who won at Camperdown? Siobhan could not remember ever hearing the battle mentioned in her history classes back at the Academy.

In what she hoped was a gentle tone, she asked, "Has Helen Forenza actually taken all the fire out of your belly? This is war, man. And Brakal is the most dangerous player on the other team. Yes I want to take him out, and yes I'd like to avenge the crew he killed on my old ship, but first and foremost, it's my duty to eliminate the one man who is finding a way out of this stalemate for his side." She fell silent for several heartbeats and turned back to look at Pushkin.

"Okay," she admitted, "so those thoughts, those rationalizations are a bit mixed up in my mind right now, but I know what I'm doing is right. We'll never make it home unless we get Brakal off our tail. This guy is good, very good. He took out a freaking battleship! If I let him, he'll swallow up this old frigate for lunch."

"But he's got his weaknesses, Gregor," she continued through a clenched jaw, "and if someone had answered our distress calls, *Victoria Regina* would have won, Brakal would have been defeated. Two hundred men and women might not have died, and we wouldn't be in this damned pickle right now."

Suddenly, the first officer looked away, shame transforming his face.

"I wanted to," he finally said after a long pause, his voice a mere whisper. "But Forenza wouldn't hear of it."

Shocked by the unexpected admission, Siobhan's next words died before they passed her lips. She wanted to question him, satisfy her burning curiosity but the intercom interrupted her.

"Dunmoore."

"Second officer here, sir. I think you should come down to the brig. Major Cayne wishes to speak with you."

Siobhan glanced at Pushkin in surprise. "On my way, Mister Drex. Dunmoore, out. Gregor, brief the senior officers, please. It may help alleviate their fears about my sanity." *Or it may confirm that I'm stark raving mad.* She smiled wearily at him and walked out of the ready room, wondering what the SSB officer wanted.

She made her way through the ship, returning the smiling salutes of passing crewmembers. Whatever doubts Pushkin may have, it did not appear the crew shared them. They seemed proud of their accomplishments and were ready for more. The door to the security division opened obediently at her approach, and she walked in.

Lieutenant Drex sat behind his desk. He did not rise at her approach but instead touched a control panel. The door closed behind Siobhan and locked with an audible snick. She looked at Drex curiously, suddenly sensing that something was very wrong. The second officer was alone in a room that should have contained at least a pair of bosun's mates on duty.

"You said Cayne wished to speak with me."

He glanced at her with his hard, lifeless eyes and nodded. At his touch, a cell door opened. Siobhan took a step forward and saw Major Cayne's dead body sprawled on the metal deck in a pool of blood. She turned around to face Drex, incomprehension and anger twisting her face, and found herself looking into the barrel of a service issue blaster.

"What the hell is the meaning of this, Mister Drex?" She snarled.

"Drop your weapon on the floor, please sir, and no sudden movements." Drex's voice was flat, toneless, like that of a man in a trance. Siobhan made no move to comply. "I can make this very painful for you, captain. Please drop your gun."

The dead look in his eyes slowly faded as she tried to stare him down, replaced by the frightening spark of a madman. Siobhan repressed a shiver. And Pushkin thought *she* was crazy. He couldn't simply be planning to kill her just like that, could he?

"What's this about, Drex?"

"The gun, captain."

"Very well." Slowly, Siobhan reached down into the holster and pulled out the blaster with her forefinger and thumb, and carefully deposited it at her feet.

"Kick it over." Keeping his weapon aimed steadily at her, Drex squatted to pick the captain's gun up and shoved it in his trousers' cargo pocket. "Into the cell, sir. Move."

"Why kill Cayne?"

Drex stared at her in silence for a few moments, his head cocked to one side like a bird. A very sick bird, Siobhan thought flippantly. This guy was one-hundred percent nuts.

"It's like this, you see, captain," Drex smiled bleakly. "Major Cayne wanted to speak with you. I let you in her cell, and when my back was turned, she jumped you, took your blaster, and killed you, before I could react. I then shot her."

"That's bloody insane, Drex," Siobhan exploded. "Who the hell's going to believe it?"

The man shrugged as if he did not care. Which he did not. "What people think is immaterial. The fact that Cayne was SSB will make the story believable. If need be, I too shall die before anyone can find proof of the truth. Then, no one can do her harm."

Siobhan frowned, several pieces of *Stingray*'s puzzle falling into place. But she did not yet see the outline of a picture. "Why these murders, Drex?"

342   No Honor in Death

"To protect her!" He was becoming agitated. "Protect her from zealous nobodies like you. If you had left well enough alone and concentrated on running this ship, none of this would have happened."

"If I'm to die, Mister Drex, shouldn't I at least know why?" Her voice was soft, soothing, belying the fear that wormed through her gut.

Unexpectedly, he laughed. "Just like in bad novels, captain? The villain reveals all to his victim, then finds the tables turned and is condemned out of his own mouth. No. Get into the cell."

Siobhan did not move, her mind clicking pieces together at the speed of light. If only she could figure out the identity of the woman he was protecting, then maybe she would understand, and find a way out of this awful, deadly mess. It could not be Forenza. Helen was unable to command such loyalty in anyone. Those who followed her did so out of fear or greed. Then it hit her. Of course. "It's a shame that a mustang with your abilities resorts to murder. It would surely pain the captain who made you an officer. Who was it again? Ah yes, the skipper of the *Baikal*. Captain -" She frowned, and then stabbed in the dark. "Kaleri, wasn't it?"

"Damn you for a snoop, Dunmoore," he shouted. "I won't let you bring her down with your meddling."

Shit! She nearly hit herself. *He's the other one who read my private log entry.*

"You have Mister Pushkin's access code, don't you?" His eyes registered surprise, but he did not deny her accusation. "You read my personal logs and found out that I suspected Kaleri of being involved in some unsavory business with Forenza. And now you're trying to cover for her out of some misguided loyalty. It won't work, Drex. Too many people know things or suspect. If I die here, the chain of investigation is going is sure as hell going to end in Kaleri's lap anyway. Think about it."

Drex smiled cruelly. "I don't think so. This ship may well not make it back home, captain. And then who is left to tell? I don't mind dying for her, not after what she did for me."

He's nuts, absolutely and utterly crazy. "You made Hartalas sabotage the controllers, so we'd be a sitting duck for the enemy. And then killed him to cover up your tracks." The second officer still did not deny her words. "What did you have on him to make the man sabotage his own ship?"

Drex smiled chillingly. "When you're in charge of security on a starship, captain, you find out many things. Hartalas was indiscreet and lived with a guilty conscience. Mind you, he did not suffer. I snapped his neck before tossing him down the tube."

"So that's two murders you own up to. How about Vasser and Melchor?"

"Not my work. Ask the bitch in there." He waved his gun at the open cell. "Or rather ask her superiors. For my money, she did it herself, with Forenza's connivance. The SSB sent her on board to watch over their investment, seeing as how they considered Forenza a risk to their operation."

"So what's Admiral Kaleri's role in this?"

Drex tsked, a mysterious smile narrowing his eyes. "Ah, captain, remember what I said. I have already told you too much." The grin vanished. "Now get into the cell. I can shoot you where you stand, but it will be just that much messier."

"How'd you expect to keep *Stingray* from returning home?" Siobhan was desperate to keep him talking.

"With you gone, captain, I do not think this ship stands a chance against a foe like Brakal. *Mister* Pushkin cannot hack this kind of work, you know. And if by miracle, he pulls it off, there are other ways."

I would not write Pushkin off yet, if I were you, crazy man, Siobhan thought, casting around for another line of conversation that would prolong her life. Drex was becoming edgy. A small tic started pulling at his left cheek.

"Did Forenza know you were keeping an eye on her for Admiral Kaleri?" Siobhan was careful to use Kaleri's rank. No telling how his insane loyalty would make him react to the slightest sign of disrespect.

"Oh yes." Drex clearly relished the memory of his position vis-à-vis Forenza. "The admiral did not trust Forenza one bit and made sure she knew it. Forenza was merely a tool for the admiral. She would never have condescended to call that useless and depraved bitch a friend." Genuine loathing twisted his face.

Interesting. So Kaleri gave Helen her command for a distinct purpose because the good Admiral knew Forenza's vices and had a way of controlling her through them. But why?

"I suppose Forenza made some profit out of the venture?"

Drex laughed. "Yes, she benefited from the power and prestige of commanding a starship and the knowledge that she would not be court-martialed for her behavior. I suppose she made some financial gain on the side too. Commander Forenza is a foolish woman."

Siobhan snorted. "Don't I know it? That must have been one hell of a business proposition to make the admiral take Forenza on as a frigate captain."

"Ah no, Captain Dunmoore, you will not get anything more out of me, though I must admire your interrogation skills. You would have made a perfect security officer."

She shrugged. *Keep him talking.* "I took counterintelligence training as a young officer if you must know."

Drex's face lit up with alarm at her statement. "So that's why Admiral Nagira kept this ship's company together even though Admiral Kaleri wanted to disperse it, now that — never mind. You," he pointed accusingly at her, "were sent on board to gather evidence by Naval Security."

He looked distinctly worried now. Siobhan, after a moment's surprise, pressed her unexpected advantage.

"I wasn't kidding when I said you could kill me without stopping the investigation. Now you know why," she bluffed, hoping to gain some advantage over him. *Could the bastard be right? Nagira can be a real sneaky prick when his dander's up.*

"Black marketeering with naval supplies in wartime is a hanging offense, Drex. You didn't think security wouldn't tumble to Admiral Kaleri's little scam, did you?"

"How did they find out," he hissed. Then, "The tender captain! He betrayed the admiral. He was always the weak link."

Bingo, Siobhan thought as another piece fell into place. *Except my newfound knowledge won't do anyone a damn bit of good if I die here.*

Suddenly, there was a loud click behind her and the door to the passageway opened, revealing a short, tubby figure in battle armor minus the helmet. Drex instinctively turned his blaster on the newcomer and pressed the trigger. Siobhan jumped at the second officer without thinking, just as Able Spacer Guido Vincenzo fired his carbine. His aim proved truer than Drex's, whose shot grazed Vincenzo's head, leaving a strip of charred, stinking hair in its wake.

The second officer's unprotected chest erupted in a gout of overheated blood and flesh as the plasma round punched through the skin and flash-broiled his insides. Siobhan's flying tackle caught him at the knees, but he was already dead. Drex keeled over wetly, showering gore all over the stunned captain.

For what seemed an eternity, everybody was frozen in place. Then, Banger Rownes pushed past a stunned Vincenzo, whose face already showed shock at his first kill, and knelt at the captain's side.

"I'm all right, Rownes," Siobhan pushed herself up. Then she realized, for the first time, that she was covered with the remains of Drex's innards. That, and the stench overwhelmed her stoic resolve, and she vomited in disgust. Vincenzo, nauseated by what he had done, no matter how good the cause, followed her lead.

"How..." Siobhan asked between heaves.

"How're we here? Hang on, skipper. Nosey, drop that toolbox and fetch the Doc, and warn Mister Pushkin."

"No," Siobhan raised a hand covered in dark, sticky blood. "Not the doctor. I'm all right. I just need to clean this off me."

"Go, Nosey. Do it. There a fucking showers in this brig, Vince?" The big gun captain demanded, taking charge of the situation.

"Yeah," Vincenzo gasped, still feeling sick every time he breathed in the stench of death. "Behind that door."

"Cap'n, I'll tell you while you clean off. C'mon. Vince, get some of your mates down here to do whatever investigation you guys do, and clear this," she kicked at Drex's body, "up."

Siobhan could not get into the brig's open shower fast enough. She stripped off her clothes with trembling hands, part of it horror, part of it a reaction to her close brush with death at the hands of a madman. One of her own officers. Except that he was never her officer. He was Kaleri's. *Had been Kaleri's,* she corrected herself.

Rownes picked up Siobhan's clothes and stuffed them into the brig's sonic cleaner. She glanced at the captain's naked body under the running water and read her history in those white scars. Rownes liked her skippers to be tough.

Deep space was a hard place that demanded hard people. Dunmoore looked to be about as tough an officer as Banger had ever seen. The gunner was glad she had been able to help save her life. Not the pleasure that any reasonable person feels at saving a life, but particularly happy because Dunmoore was something special.

"You ready for the story, sir?"

"Go ahead."

"After we stood down, Drex sent everybody out of the brig area, saying he'd stand this watch himself. Now Vince, I mean Able Spacer Vincenzo, thought there's been something funny with Drex for a while, especially since PO Hartalas had his 'accident.' He figured Drex's offer to stand watch was unusual. So Vince keeps an eye on the brig and sees you go in. He tries the door and finds it locked from the inside, with Drex's own pass codes. So he comes to get Nosey Bertram, who's got a talent for locks, to open the door."

"Hold on," Siobhan interrupted Rownes, "why didn't he go to the first officer with this?"

"You never know which side the officers are on, cap'n. Not on this boat." Banger replied, shrugging as if Drex's actions proved her words. "Anyway, he feels he owes you something personal since you took his word against Zavaleta's. I was with Nosey when Vince came running down and joined the rescue party. Nosey did the lock and the rest you know."

"Looks like I owe you guys my life. Drex was about to shoot me and blame it on Major Cayne."

"Cayne? Oh, right, Kery. Yeah. He did for her, didn't he? But hell, cap'n what we've done is natural. You take care of us, so we take care of you. Simple."

Rownes' matter-of-fact summation touched Siobhan deeply, and she stopped scrubbing to look at her. "Thank you for my life, Rownes." The big woman looked away, embarrassed.

The moment was shattered when Pushkin burst into the brig washroom, out of breath. "Are you all right, captain? Bertram said Lieutenant Drex was about to kill you."

The look of incredulity on his face was too much for Siobhan's raw nerves. She leaned against the bulkhead and burst into laughter.

"I'm okay," she finally managed to reply, between outbursts. "Thanks to some incredibly loyal spacers, eh, Rownes."

"Sir," she murmured, avoiding Pushkin's curious eyes.

As if the release of emotion had wiped away the last of her terror, Siobhan became all business again. Disregarding her nudity in front of her first officer, her ship's surgeon, who arrived on the instant, and any number of ratings, she rattled off orders.

"Mister Pushkin, place Cayne's and Drex's bodies in stasis. Secure Drex's gun as evidence, then take depositions from Rownes and her crew. Have someone clean up the deck. I want a department head meeting in one hour. We have a lot to discuss, I think, and not much else to do for a few hours, until we're deep in the Cimmeria system."

*

"Captain on deck."

The assembled department heads rose to attention as Captain Dunmoore strode into the small conference room.

"Sit down," she snapped. "By now, you should all know what happened down in security an hour ago. If you don't, then you have no business as an officer on my ship." Dunmoore looked at the assembled officers, each in turn. "How many of you knew, or suspected Lieutenant Drex was in Admiral Kaleri's pocket? That he was a bloody madman? How many of you knew about the black marketeering with Fleet supplies this ship was doing? How many knew Kery was really an SSB officer?" When no one replied, she smiled cruelly.

"As I thought. Timid to the last. Well, either you're feeding me fucking bullshit, or you're so bloody incompetent, you aren't even aware of what's going on around you!"

"It took weeks," she continued savagely, "before someone was willing to tell me how Commander Forenza ran this ship and explain why morale was the pits. And what I heard sure as hell won't match the depositions you gave for the Disciplinary Board. No, I didn't read them, but it doesn't take a genius to figure it out. This puts you all in the uncomfortable position of having perjured yourselves. A court-martial offense, people, and the end of your careers." No one met her eyes.

"I thought that in time, once I'd gained your trust, you would do me the courtesy of telling the truth. Mind you, I didn't think the truth would be so deplorable. An incompetent predecessor, I can handle. A bloody conspiracy, I can't. I no longer have time to wait for you people to find your courage and remember where your duty lies. Therefore, it stops now."

"No more bullshit, no more lying, no more evasions. I nearly died an hour ago at the hands of a nutcase. Had I known the truth, that could have been avoided. Major Cayne's death could have been avoided. Drex's death could have been avoided. Had I known the truth, Drex would not have turned PO Hartalas into a saboteur and we'd be out of here, having destroyed the convoy before Brakal joined it. Hartalas would still be alive, as would the two gunners who died in the last engagement, as would the spacers who will die before we make it back home. How many more deaths are on your collective conscience? The cost of not doing your duty is too high for anyone to accept. Think about it."

"Permission to speak, captain?" Luttrell asked, her face a rigid mask.

"By all means. Just make sure you don't feed me crap this time." Her tone stung Luttrell. "You, of all people, a draftee doctor, should have known better."

"It's easy for you to speak like this, captain, but you don't know the hell we've been living in. How would you react if your skipper threatened to have you struck from the medical profession if you testified against her? She had the means to do it, too. The bitch gave us ample proof of that. And with her working for Admiral Kaleri, we had no way out, nowhere to turn. Think about that, captain."

Siobhan's nostrils flared whitely.

"A load of crap, that's what your rationalization is, Doctor. If it were up to me, I'd have your license removed right now, for lack of ethics. Tell, me how many autopsies did you fudge for Forenza?" She saw her comment hit home and smiled with cruel satisfaction.

"Think of the people who have died on this ship because no officer aboard had the guts to do something about the rot. You," she swept the table with her extended forefinger, "are all accessories to murder, because you didn't act, because you kept silent, even once the immediate peril to your precious careers was over. Well, I don't think like that. I still believe in personal duty and honor. I intend to nail Forenza's ass to the wall for what she did. I will also make sure Kaleri answers for her actions in front of a general court-martial, exposing the corruption in all its glory. Her family connections and wealth won't mean a damn!"

"We're fighting a bloody war out here, and we have a duty to the Commonwealth that goes beyond any obligation to our own persons. You people will assist me in this by telling me everything, swearing whatever deposition I ask and anything else, or so help me, what I will do to your careers will be much worse than anything Forenza or Kaleri have threatened. Doctor, I can make Forenza's threat of barring you from medical practice true in a way that makes it both open and untainted by any sign of corruption. By a court-martial that will see you disgraced forever in the eyes of your profession. The same goes for the rest of you. I'd rather have your cooperation because you've proven to me you were capable people and because I believe you can redeem yourselves in the eyes of the Fleet, and in your own."

"What happens when we admit to perjury by submitting new testimony to the Disciplinary Board?" Luttrell asked hotly. "We'll still go down. Not good enough, captain."

"Oh? I don't see you have much of a choice. Cooperate, and I'll see you're cleared. Otherwise, the only way out is to kill me right now. And even that won't save you for very long, assuming you succeed." The thought of murdering her appalled the assembled officers. Siobhan remembered Drex's words and the revelation that had struck her earlier.

"Navy Command is already aware of the shenanigans going on aboard this ship. Admiral Nagira, as we speak, is working to root out the corruption. All he needs is proof to bring down Kaleri. My disappearance or even your lack of cooperation won't stop anything. It'll only make things worse."

With sudden force, Siobhan slammed her fists down on the table and leaned toward them.

"Make your choice, people. The truth or you can kiss any hopes of a decent life goodbye."

"If we even get home," Shara said, in a stage whisper.

"Oh, we will, lieutenant, make no mistake." Shara quailed under Dunmoore's hard stare and looked down at the scarred tabletop. "I know how Helen Forenza ran her ship, and a simple, amended deposition from each of you will ensure she gets the dishonorable discharge she deserves. I'll make sure Admiral Nagira overlooks your initial testimony due to extenuating circumstances."

Pushkin, who had remained silent and contemplative all along, unexpectedly rose and nodded, every inch the first officer.

"Sir. You'll have them within the hour." He looked at each of the officers in turn. "That, ladies and gents, is a bloody order. You know the price of disobedience. Make sure you don't suffer it. I'll be reviewing your depositions personally so I encourage you to be thorough and accurate. God help you if they're not." He nodded at Siobhan again and sat. "Sir."

"Thank you, Mister Pushkin. I'm pleased to see that my confidence in you is not misplaced. That takes care of Helen Forenza. But we're not through yet. Not by a long shot."

"Mister Rossum, this ship has been short of just about everything ever since Commander Forenza took over, right?" The plump purser nodded, mopping his shiny forehead with the ever-present white handkerchief. "We never got a full load from the tender either, did we?"

"No, sir."

"Anyone care to venture an explanation why?"

*

Siobhan watched her officers file out of the conference room, subdued and silent.

"What now, sir?" Pushkin remained alone with her, looking as thoughtful as ever, wondering how to come to terms with his role as first officer under Commander Forenza, both officially and personally.

Dunmoore's public affirmation of confidence heartened him, but it would take time before he would be able to look at his reflection without a measure of contempt. And deservedly so. But Dunmoore's magic had worked on him as it had on the others.

Pushkin's catharsis had started earlier, and he had watched the others while they spoke. It had been for them, excepting Shara, an epiphany, a kind of professional rebirth. Faced with the ugly truth, they looked to Siobhan for guidance. She had given it to them by reminding them of the tenets of their oath.

*

"First, Mister Devall takes over as second officer. His junior will take the gunnery post. I believe Sub-Lieutenant Amiri is capable enough."

"Aye, sir. I think so too."

"Then," Siobhan continued, feeling drained after the emotionally charged meeting and her earlier brush with death, "change the warhead on one of the ready torpedoes for a log buoy system. Feed all the depositions into the ship's log. That way, if we don't make it, at least the torpedo will get back to our side with all the information." He nodded, taking notes on his personal computer.

"Finally, a question, Gregor." He looked up, into her weary, lined face and intense eyes. "What happened on the day *Victoria Regina* got ambushed? I'm curious, not out for retribution. The time for that has passed."

He glanced away and stared at the far bulkhead for a few moments, not because of any reluctance to speak. That had vanished in the last few hours. But he wanted to gather his thoughts, remember the day in question and his own role in the disgraceful events.

"Commander Forenza arranged for an unscheduled meeting with the tender, right after a coded message from Admiral Kaleri. God knows why. There was a lot of that in my time here. Hush-hush stuff that only Forenza and her familiars like Kery knew about. For a long time, I believed she was engaged in special covert duties, not corruption. Mind you, it was a good cover, especially with Kery-the-spook hovering in the background."

"You knew about Kery being SSB?"

"A few of us did. Forenza let it slip one day when I was pressing her on something I didn't like. As I said, we had an unscheduled resupply. Forenza always handled the paperwork and dealt with the tender captain herself so I had no idea what was really going on that day, like all the other times. Probably just more of the same. Except that time, there was another ship with the tender. Forenza said it was an undercover SSB ship and –"

"The *Mykonos*, right."

"Yeah." Pushkin nodded. "It didn't have that name then, but it was the same one. We docked with the tender, which had already docked with the spook tub, and Forenza went on board. The distress call came in at that moment. I relayed it to 31st Battle Group and 3rd Fleet, and then tried to get Forenza to return. But she ignored me."

Siobhan suddenly grinned as she realized something Pushkin apparently had not noticed.

"Tell me, Gregor, did it ever occur to you that you're responsible for Forenza getting fired?"

"Huh?" He looked at her with dumb surprise.

"Very eloquent response, Mister Pushkin," Siobhan replied dryly. "You relayed the distress signal to 3rd Fleet, right?" He nodded. "Did you tell Forenza you did that?"

"No." He slowly exhaled, frowning.

"Think about it, Gregor. You told 3rd Fleet about *Victoria Regina* getting clobbered. By doing that, you also gave them your position, which was close enough to the action for a quick helping hand. They obviously expected you to offer support in accordance with standing orders. When Forenza didn't act on the signal, Admiral Nagira had the perfect excuse to relieve her over Kaleri's objections. He probably had his jaundiced eye on her already at the time, even if it was only for gross misconduct. Now, would she have moved had she known you signaled 3rd Fleet?"

He shrugged, uncertain.

"It doesn't matter. Whether you forgot to tell her by accident, or your subconscious directed your actions that day, you're the one responsible for her relief." *And my arrival as pinch hitter slash detective. Oh, Nagira, you rotten prick!*

Pushkin looked at her, pleased with the idea. "I hadn't thought of it, sir."

Siobhan laughed. "I know, Gregor. You should see the shit-eating grin on your face. Taking the logic a bit further, I guess I have you to thank for my appointment as skipper of *Stingray*." She made a wry face. "In any case, Gregor, I absolve you of any responsibility for that day and take back the nasty comments I made."

He shrugged, embarrassment flushing his cheeks. "No need to, sir. I deserved the tongue lashing for that and many other things."

"Oh, maybe. Maybe not." She slapped him on the shoulder. "C'mon Number One. Let's go see how the ship's holding together."

Gregor Pushkin followed her out of the conference room, smiling like a little boy in a candy store. She had called him 'Number One.' For some strange reason, the familiarity and confidence the nickname implied made him feel better than he had for a long time. Now, he really knew why Ezekiel Holt felt so strongly about Siobhan Dunmoore. It gave him an unexpected feeling of kinship with the crippled officer, like belonging to a select club.

The club of those who had fallen under Captain Siobhan Dunmoore's spell.

— Twenty-Two —

"Captain on the bridge."

Siobhan took her seat from Pushkin. Ten minutes to emergence and endgame in the enemy-occupied Cimmeria system. She did not feel anything beyond a certain fatalism as if her actions, from the start, had been programmed to bring them here and now, across Brakal's hawse. Not many shared her calm acceptance, and nervous glances followed her every movement, trying to divine the future she held in her scarred hands. Siobhan had seen battle and death close up more often than most. *Victoria Regina* had taken her dying blows only a few months ago, nearby. She had also lived her greatest moments of glory aboard *Don Quixote* on and near Cimmeria, five years ago. A lifetime of war.

"Battle stations, if you please, Number One."

"Sir."

The crew of the Beta watch noticed her use of the familiar nickname. News of the last few hours had rapidly spread through *Stingray*, and a sense of normalcy was setting in, a sense they could begin to trust each other and their officers again. Siobhan enjoyed the subtle feeling of a crew coming together. It was happening just in time too.

Maybe she should thank Lieutenant Drex's shade for that. United and no longer plagued by the secrecy surrounding the past, they had a much better chance of surviving the immediate future, though the full responsibility for that still sat squarely on Dunmoore's shoulders. She had plunged headlong into battle, counting coup after coup, and her native pride and stubbornness would not let her stop now. The ship's name and her own would be cleared once and for all. Even if it killed them.

Within minutes, the Alpha watch, what Siobhan called her varsity team, took their stations.

The officers and non-coms had a new spring in their step, even though their tired faces were studiously expressionless, hiding any worries and misgivings they felt. They would see this through, if only to atone for their previous actions, and give Dunmoore their very best.

The flow of people ceased yet Lieutenant Shara shined by her absence. Young Ensign Sanghvi still held the sailing master's post. Dunmoore frowned. Shara might be contemptible as an officer, but she knew her job as navigator, and her skills would be much needed.

"Where is Lieutenant Shara, Number One?"

"I don't know, sir." Pushkin paged her, but without success. The minutes to emergence ticked by, and still no sailing master.

"Send a security detail to her quarters," Siobhan ordered, sensing that something was very wrong. The answer was not long in coming. Lieutenant Devall, newly elevated to second officer, and proud of it, reported in person.

"I am sorry, sir. Lieutenant Shara is incapacitated." He lowered his voice so only Siobhan could hear. "Dead drunk, sir. She downed a fifth of whiskey. I have the doctor in her quarters right now. Shara may have alcohol poisoning, but she'll live to feel the hangover." There was no sympathy in Devall's voice.

"Well done. Thank you, Mister Devall. You may carry on."

A strange silence enveloped the bridge. Siobhan sat back thoughtfully. She felt little surprise at Shara's reaction. The sailing master knew her role in Helen Forenza's schemes did not stand the same scrutiny as the others'. Her career would end with little honor once they returned to base. Shara's behavior toward the captain and her peers had ensured no one would speak up in her defense. But in truth, she was another victim. If only of her weaknesses. Had she possessed a stronger character, she might have kept free of the taint she now bore.

"Ensign Sanghvi," she met the young man's nervous eyes with a smile, "it appears you are now *Stingray*'s acting sailing master." *Why is it that the junior navigator on a starship always ends up being a shavetail on his first tour*? But Siobhan knew the answer to that one. She too had been the junior navigator on her first starship assignment. It was a demanding job but had no real leadership responsibilities, perfect to give a novice some time to find his footing in new surroundings. And to develop four-dimensional, multi universe thinking in young, malleable minds, preparing them for the demands of warship command.

"Yes, sir." He sounded embarrassed, and more than a little scared of his captain.

"Just relax and think things through, ensign. I know you can handle the job. You can count on the first officer and myself to back you up."

"Sir." Sanghvi nodded and swallowed, his prominent adam's apple bobbing like a buoy in a storm. Then, bravely, he said, "I'll do my best, sir."

"I know," Siobhan smiled again, and Pushkin could see her magic work on the young man. Amazing how people responded to her, now that they could look her in the face without embarrassment. Some might curse her for driving them hard, but they respected her all the more for it.

Sanghvi turned toward his console and ran a full, by-the-book pre-emergence check. It steadied his nerves. When the ensign glanced at the helmsman on his right, Chief Guthren smiled back reassuringly, almost fatherly.

"Set and ready, sir. Five minutes to go."

"How close to the planet will we emerge, Mister Sanghvi?" Siobhan already knew the answer, but it was a good question to get the kid thinking about his new job. Sailing masters had to stay one or two moves ahead of the ship, to better plot a route through navigational hazards and enemy obstacles.

"Two light minutes, sir," he replied after a short pause during which he queried the computer. "It's a little close but still within the bounds of emergency jump procedures." He sounded like a navigation manual, but at least it proved he knew the theory of his business. That was a good start.

"Okay. Now, the moment we're back in normal space, take the ship on a direct course to the planet's north magnetic pole. We'll duck under the magnetic belt and go silent. No one will find us there."

"And then, sir?" Pushkin asked for the benefit of the others.

"Then," Siobhan grinned in that chilling way she had, "we wait for the opportunity to sail by. I can't bring myself to leave this enchanting place without kicking sand in Brakal's face one last time."

*

The gas giant's strong magnetic field played havoc with electronic gear, and even the heavily shielded scanners suffered from random flickering. But it hid the frigate from anything the Shrehari had.

During the short dash to the planet, Chief Penzara had pinpointed the convoy's position and declared the humans to have at least half an hour, if not more, breathing space before it too dropped back to this universe. No other enemy contacts appeared on screen, however, and that worried Siobhan. The Cimmeria system had some ships permanently stationed there to defend it against marauding humans. By all rights, it should be vectoring on the convoy's planned course, to ensure *Stingray* caused no more damage. There was a time when Siobhan had played many a cat and mouse game with the Cimmeria Assault Force before the stalemate eroded the fighting edge of both humans and Shrehari.

"He's emerged!" Penzara suddenly announced. The tactical display on the main screen flickered and then stabilized with the convoy's new position. "A bit early if you ask me, sir. He could've gone on for another few minutes."

"Brakal's looking for us. He's nervous about the idea of an in-system ambush." *Does he know the system as well as I do?* Siobhan rubbed the scar on her jawline, a gesture Pushkin had begun to recognize as deep concentration.

"He won't see us here, though," Pushkin noted.

"I'm not even sure if he'll look or think about looking. Shrehari don't use planetary magnetic fields for camouflage. Their electronics have less shielding than ours and become practically useless. Shrehari captains get nervous when they can't see, hear, or operate their defensive screens. Plot their expected course, chief."

"A straight line for Cimmeria. Not terribly imaginative, sir," Penzara said. The crew did not yet know what Dunmoore intended, but they were sure it did not involve heading for home without a farewell attack.

"No, but quick. He's less vulnerable on a direct course in normal space. Remember, he still outguns us. Mister Sanghvi, what is the closest we can jump to hyperspace near this planet and not tear the ship apart?"

"Ten planetary diameters, sir. But it's not recommended due to stress on the hull and the drives." Sanghvi sounded almost comically earnest and self-conscious. But that was understandable. He was one of the most junior officers on board while the sailing master was usually a very senior and experienced lieutenant.

"Our drives have already suffered from that redlined jump," Pushkin reminded her, realizing what Siobhan was thinking.

"True, Number One. But they'll take a little more. Mister Guthren, the moment the convoy drops below our horizon, edge the ship to the opposite side of the planet. By the way, what's this stink-ball's name again?" *As if I didn't remember.*

"XP-2513, sir," Sanghvi helpfully supplied.

"Thank you. Once we have XP-2513 between us and the convoy, Mister Sanghvi, you will plot a micro jump to intercept the convoy just about," she pointed at the tactical display, "here. On emergence, Mister Amiri, fire off two missiles at the center transport but concentrate your guns on *Tol Vakash*. I don't intend to hang around, so Mister Sanghvi, you'll have to plot another micro jump to the edge of the outer asteroid belt, between planets five and four, the moment you have a fix. This one will be strictly hit-and-run. The faster, the better."

"To prove we can do it?" Pushkin asked softly, so only Siobhan could hear. His voice held a hint of reproach.

"That, and to give Brakal another bloody nose, Gregor. I still have a score to even up with him. Anyway," she raised her tone, a knowing smile on her thin lips, "how can I resist such a perfect target?"

"He's below our horizon, sir."

"Thanks, chief. Mister Guthren, take us out of here." She smiled mischievously at the cox'n. "Dona Quixote rides again." *And you thought I did not know my old nickname.*

Guthren began to chuckle uncontrollably.

*

"Nothing, commander. It is as if she has vanished, or never came here. Maybe she changed course while we were in hyperspace and is even now running for her side of the line."

Brakal grunted, stroking his chin. "Maybe, Urag. But Dunmoore has a fire in her soul. I ask myself, would I run or attempt another ambush, were I in her place? And my answer is always the same: ambush."

"Even with four kills?" Jhar asked.

"Even with ten, my friend," Brakal grinned, "as long as I see a chance for more. No, Dunmoore must be in-system somewhere, biding her time."

"Then she must believe herself a magician. She cannot approach us without being seen from afar. This is hopeless for her." Jhar sounded unconvinced by his own words. Strange how the thought of a female warship commander came naturally to him now. How good would trained Shrehari females be at the art of war? Certainly they were fierce enough and cunning enough when necessary. Then, the thought of several females on board his ship, to be fought over by the males, to excite lusts best reserved for battle, made him shudder. How do humans do it?

"Huh." The commander stared at the empty tactical display on a side-screen. "Offhand I can think of several things she might wish to attempt. But none that could ensure her the surprise she needs for success."

"The asteroid belt would seem to me a good place," Urag ventured.

"Indeed," Brakal was pleased to see his officers really *think* about this. "It offers concealment, cover, and protection. But the convoy will not pass closely enough for a successful ambush. Even the convoy commander is not that stupid. Still..." He turned his gaze on the slowly moving star field displayed on the main view screen.

Urag's console blipped, and the gun master turned toward his instruments. "Commander a contact."

Brakal came to life. "Identify and place on screen. It must be her!"

"Too late." Urag's tone rose to communicate something of the urgency he suddenly felt. "She has emerged ahead of us and launched two missiles on the troopship *Vannatikar* at point-blank range. She fires on us."

The placid star field vanished to show the angry shape of the human frigate. It was broadside to *Tol Vakash* and its guns winked brightly, spewing plasma at the imperial cruiser. A blinding explosion momentarily blotted out the cruiser's visual receptors.

"The *Vannatikar* is gone, commander," Urag announced angrily. "With the twelve-hundred soldiers of the *Altukaras* Regiment."

"Open fire, Urag. Helm, increase speed to intercept. She will not escape us this time." *Tol Vakash* shook under the weight of *Stingray*'s full broadside. "You are mine, Dunmoore."

Moments later, Brakal had the satisfaction of seeing his return fire splash on her shields and eat through the force screen, blackening the hull below with the appetite of voracious energy.

*

"Starboard shield down, a direct hit on turret three."

"Come about ninety degrees port, keep engaging. Mister Sanghvi, do you have a jump solution?"

"Not yet, sir. Still working." Beads of sweat stood out on the young officer's smooth forehead.

The quick destruction of the second troopship had raised a cheer throughout the frigate, but the momentary joy was giving way to grim determination in the face of the imperial cruiser coming at them with guns blazing. Each massive plasma round strained the already damaged shields and shook the stressed hull, forcing a whining feedback through sensitive electronic circuits. Already, casevac teams from the medical section were plying their trade.

"Jump solution sir!" Sanghvi's voice sounded unnaturally high and youthful to his own ears.

"Helm, engage."

*

"Gone, by the demons!" Urag swore, his last salvo rippling through emptiness, where seconds earlier there had been an enemy warship. "Tracking through hyperspace."

"The convoy commander wishes a word with you," Jhar overrode the gun master. His tone told Brakal that the call should be ignored.

"Deal with him, Jhar. As soon as we have a fix on her course, the convoy commander can take what is left of his ships to hell, for all I care. My interest lies with Dunmoore."

"Course fixed, commander," Urag announced, as if on cue. "She is headed for the outer asteroid belt."

"Hah!" Brakal slapped his chair's right arm. "We have her now! My compliments to the convoy commander, Jhar. Advise him to head straight for Cimmeria at best speed. We shall punish the humans for their insolence."

"The ship has emerged, and is entering the asteroid field."

"Helm, take us to her."

Brakal let a smile of bloody anticipation play on his lips. Jhar sensed the chase had passed beyond a simple contest between professionals. Dunmoore had outwitted Brakal once too often, and the strong-willed commander had taken it very personally.

She had obliterated five ships in two days, a disaster the Council would find difficult to explain to the child-emperor, and his Regent, especially since the origins of the debacle lay in Trage's incompetent handling of the Fleet, and his refusal to study the humans in order to defeat them. The tactics Dunmoore had employed were simply beyond the understanding of those old fools at the Admiralty. Now too, though it hurt Jhar to admit it, they appeared beyond Brakal's experience and understanding of this particular human.

Brakal's well-intentioned intrusion into what was by decree of the Admiralty none of his business would only give Trage a perfect scapegoat to cover his failings. It would have been better if the commander had proceeded to his hunting grounds and ignored the convoy. Thus, even its total destruction could not have been, by any stretch, laid at his feet. But it was too late now.

Of five transports and three escorts, only two of the former and one of the latter remained. The convoy commander would pay for his failure, of course, even though he was clearly outmatched by the humans' cunning. Regrettably, so would Brakal and his followers, and that presented a greater peril to the Empire than the wasteful destruction of two imperial regiments.

Death in battle with Dunmoore might be the only honorable way out for us. Even if we destroy her, the Tai Kan *will just as surely destroy us.*

From his seat, Brakal could not see these thoughts cross his second's face. Had he seen them, he would not have understood Jhar's gloomy outlook on the future. The commander had but one objective right: destroy the woman who had outsmarted him, and prove that he was still the Scourge of the Fleet.

*

"He's on our tail, sir."

Siobhan smiled. "Still reacting, is he. Good."

"Surely you do not intend to try the convoy again?"

"Have no fear, Number One. The convoy is safe. We took from it what was necessary: the two troopships. No, now I intend to lead Brakal a merry chase through the asteroid field. The advantage of his greater weight of guns is more than balanced by our better agility among the debris. We still have a brace of missiles left, our main guns, and a couple of mines. All we need is a disabling shot, and we're home free."

Pushkin's expression proved him to be less than sanguine about their chances. But his job was to provide a foil for his commander, play the devil's advocate, and ensure she did not plunge headlong into assured destruction.

"Consider this, Gregor; Brakal has repeatedly been stung by us. We took five ships under his nose. If I'm right, he's pissed-off at us by now, and angry commanders make mistakes."

"Are you angry, captain?" Pushkin softly asked.

"No. Interested by his reactions, but not angry. Brakal's tactical sense is good, especially for a product of the Shrehari Imperial Academy, and he has learned much from studying us. That's what makes him such a danger. But there's still one thing he hasn't cottoned to yet. Any idea what that is, Gregor?"

"Not offhand, captain."

"No, maybe not. It took me until now to figure it out myself. Brakal's thinking of our ship in terms of his own. He's not thinking of the differences, the relative advantages, and disadvantages, and how to use them to best effect. In fact, I do believe he's applying his cruiser's limitations to *Stingray*. That's where I'll get him."

Pushkin digested her statement in silence, wondering whether he would ever make good frigate captain material if he could not match Dunmoore's sharp, deductive mind. A touch of the old bitterness threatened to surface. It showed in his eyes.

"Don't worry," Siobhan said, pitching her voice so only Pushkin heard. "It takes a long time before you get the feel of this stuff. I've had the advantage of two previous independent commands, a hell of a good teacher and an insatiable appetite for reading." *And a bit of an ego,* she mentally added.

In silence, the two officers watched the main screen as Chief Guthren, a look of intense concentration on his face, steered the ship among the huge, dark rocks and planetoids, deeper into the asteroid field.

"We've lost contact, sir," Penzara reported.

"Keep a good lookout, chief. We're going to maneuver into a good ambush spot, but it'll only work if we remain hidden by the asteroids."

"Aye, aye, sir."

"Mister Guthren, forty-five degrees to starboard, down twenty. Place us in the shadow of the kidney shaped rock off our starboard bow, about one kilometer from the surface. When we're there, match its velocity and hold relative position. Mister Pushkin, we'll go silent then."

*

"She has vanished among the rocks, commander."

"Hmm." Brakal rubbed his jaw, a signal to Jhar that he was beginning to feel the strain. "Take us to her last known position. Urag, keep a sharp lookout. She is waiting for us somewhere in there."

And she has the advantage, Jhar bleakly realized. As she's had all along. It was a new feeling for Jhar and the other officers, one they did not enjoy.

The asteroids stopped moving on the screen, as *Tol Vakash*'s steering thrusters slowed the cruiser to the velocity of the orbiting debris. Human mining colonies once dotted the area, but they had been destroyed during the invasion. The Empire had not seen any profit in reopening them. Just as the Empire saw no advantage in studying the enemy.

Blind fools run it, Jhar reflected with disgust. But were it run by better men, this war would never have happened.

"Nothing, commander." Urag's tone spoke of disgust masking a growing sense of worry. Though his loyalty to Brakal remained undimmed, he wondered whether the commander had finally met his match.

So it is to be a fog and night battle, Brakal smiled, oblivious to his gun master's doubts. *Two opponents stumbling blindly among massive obstacles, moving on instinct, on the abilities of their respective commanders. A real test of skill.*

"Helm, vertical movement, ten *vraksash*, then match velocities with the nearby asteroids to bring us to a relative stop. She waits for us. Near, very near."

*

"He should be at our last known position just about now." Siobhan's eyes had lost focus as she let her instincts reach out for Brakal. "Cox'n, pivot the ship one-hundred degrees port, facing the asteroid." Then, "Thrusters, positive zee. Take us slowly over the horizon."

Ahead, close enough to touch, the dark, pitted surface of the moonlet passed by as the ship rose out of the shadow. Pushkin suddenly remembered Dunmoore's tolerance for useless maneuvering when the tugs released them aft of Starbase 31. Now, he could see why she had acted as she did. Dunmoore wanted to know how deft a touch the cox'n could bring to the massive warship's helm. With only one kilometer separating them from the rough surface of the asteroid, they needed better than average steering.

"Guns, stand by for full broadside." The captain's voice had acquired that chilling tone again. Pushkin suddenly knew the enemy would appear in their sights over the asteroid's short, jagged horizon.

"Cox'n, reduce the rate of climb, stand by thrusters for negative zee. All available power to bow shields."

When it came, it was as unexpected for everyone except Dunmoore. "Contact! One-hundred kays off the starboard bow."

"FIRE!" The ship vibrated under the pressure of her own broadside. "Cox'n, negative zee, ninety degrees to port."

Guthren responded quickly, but not fast enough to avoid *Tol Vakash*'s return fire, even though Gun Master Urag had been a few seconds slower than Lieutenant Amiri, his opposite number. *Stingray* groaned under the impact of plasma. Then, the two ships lost sight of each other again.

"Cox'n, asteroid thirty degrees off our port bow, at fifty-thousand kays. Slip under it, then come to starboard."

*

For the next half-hour, *Stingray* led a merry chase through the dense debris field, dodging asteroids and Brakal's guns. Twice, however, the wily Shrehari had scored painful hits on the frigate's stern and the casualty list aboard *Stingray* lengthened, as did the repair list Tiner and her engineers faced. Amiri's gunners had replied shot for shot, but the two ships were never in contact long enough to evaluate the damage.

The tension on *Stingray* was almost too painful to endure, and Chief Guthren bore the brunt of it. He perspired freely now, grunting every now and then as he threaded a way between the massive, jagged rocks, avoiding collisions by the minute. Siobhan, like any good chess player, tried to stay a few moves ahead, but all too often, she had to rely on her poker player's skills and make snap decisions without knowing what perils lay on the new tack.

Brakal, smarting from his inability to take the initiative, was gaining a new appreciation for the old frigate's agility and her helmsman's skill. He began to realize the scope of his misjudgment as Dunmoore slipped from his grasp time after time, forcing him to sail the cruiser to the limits of its maneuverability. If only the Cimmeria Assault Force were nearby. With two or three ships, he could cut the humans off and destroy them. Alone, it was like hunting the laughing *jakarl* and the thought that Dunmoore was thumbing her nose at him did little to calm his temper.

This was not the kind of neat, well-planned, and forcefully executed attack he had grown used to carrying out with success. Every hit from the frigate's guns was another painful reminder of Dunmoore's superior cunning. No one dared exercise his wit on *Tol Vakash*'s bridge anymore. The game had become much too dangerous and, Jhar knew, much too frustrating for a crew used to victory.

Gun Master Urag fired repeatedly missed the frigate as it dodged behind an asteroid, a fraction of a second too fast for the Shrehari's reactions.

But the game could not last. In the end, *Stingray* would suffer defeat from a stern chase. She simply did not have the weight of guns. And the Cimmeria ships might appear at any moment, spelling the frigate's doom. Of course, the humans might take the cruiser down with them, but that was small comfort to the crew.

*

On *Stingray*'s bridge, the officers, non-coms, and ratings worked their stations and waited with growing unease for their captain to act, to spring some surprise on the pursuing cruiser, something that would allow them to run for safety. But Siobhan, eyes narrowed in concentration, plotted a route ever deeper into the densest part of the asteroid field, increasing their peril from a slight miscalculation by the tiring cox'n.

She was looking for that elusive volume of rock-filled space where the frigate's greater agility would change from mere advantage to overwhelming superiority. It was all they had.

A tight, tunnel-like path between slowly spinning rocks opened to port as they passed a large planetoid. It was what Siobhan had been looking for. She almost sighed with relief.

"Eighty degrees to port. Take us through that corridor, Mister Guthren, nice and slow." Someone gasped in dismay at the order, for their path seemed too narrow, too dangerous even for a helmsman of proven ability, especially at speed. "Mister Amiri, prepare to drop two mines. Flash-sensing fuses."

"Ready." The ship passed the mouth of the narrows.

"Now."

"Mines away."

"Good. Prepare the last two missiles' warheads for independent wait-and-search. We'll launch them at the other end of this."

Understanding lit up in Pushkin's drawn face, and Siobhan grinned wickedly at him, winking.

*

"You do not propose to follow, commander?" Jhar was aghast. The enemy's radiation trail led straight through a perilous jumble of broken stones and jagged planetary fragments. "It is too narrow."

"And risk losing her? Reduce speed and follow the trail, helmsman." In his passion for victory, Brakal was giving less thought to his enemy's cunning and more to a headlong pursuit. Matched with his volatile temper, it produced a dangerous mix. Had Dunmoore not goaded him so, things might have been different, but staring professional ruin in the face, Brakal wanted her blood.

"Commander, I am picking up faint electronic signals ahead."

Brakal's eyes widened as he suddenly understood. "Mines," he shouted, "Helm, reverse course!"

But it was too late. The mines, set to explode the moment they sensed a starship's mass, went off in a blinding double flash. Unlike those armed with proximity fuses, these mines did not propel themselves closer to the target before exploding. It permitted them to remain undetected longer, though the damage they caused was less, but Siobhan had not expected them to cause fatal harm to *Tol Vakash*.

The energy backwash released by the twin nuclear blasts struck the cruiser's bow shield with enough force to throw the moving ship off course. It slewed around and came perilously close to an asteroid on its starboard quarter. Only the helmsman's quick reactions saved *Tol Vakash* from a catastrophic collision. Brakal fumed at the unexpected, and to his mind, cowardly assault. He ordered his ship to plunge through the narrows, determined to end Dunmoore's insulting dance once and for all. As Siobhan Dunmoore, captain of the Commonwealth frigate *Stingray* had told her first officer, angry commanders make mistakes, and Brakal began piling them on.

Tol Vakash emerged from the narrow corridor through the swirling asteroids at a higher speed than it should have, and the gun master initially missed the two nuclear-tipped missiles waiting for a target their programming could recognize. By the time Urag picked them up on his sensors, both birds had fired their engines and were accelerating at several thousand kilometers a second. An alert gunner engaged them, scoring one kill. But the other struck the cruiser's starboard shield with the full force of its warhead. The cruiser shuddered and groaned, as energy fought energy, washing back through thousands of badly shielded circuits. Consoles erupted in showers of sparks. The helmsman fought for control of his ship and Jhar, without looking at the incoming reports knew they had been severely damaged.

*

"He's found our little gifts, sir," Chief Penzara reported, grinning. "I hope he gets indigestion."

Siobhan smiled back but knew it was far from over. A Gorgon-class cruiser was a lot harder to kill than either a transport or a corvette. Brakal would be hot on their trail in no time at all. And they would be easy to find. *Stingray*, damaged in too many places, leaked enough radiation to leave a trail a blind sensor operator could spot.

A large planetoid, the largest so far, loomed ahead. "Cox'n take us down to that thing's surface at, oh, ten kilometers altitude." She was out of missiles, nearly out of mines and by all appearances, out of the best area of concealment. Time to change tactics again.

"There's enough residual gravity to stress the hull, sir," Pushkin warned.

"Noted, Number One, noted. In you go, Mister Guthren."

Stingray overflew a pockmarked surface replete with jagged, broken mountain spines, the result of the forces that tore the original planet apart, eons ago. A huge shadow loomed ahead. "Slow to one-tenth. Prepare to match velocities and come to a relative stop."

Moments later they hung over a bottomless abyss, more than a kilometer wide and long enough to lose its ends out of sight. Torn, irregular edges hid the canyon until the last moment. Perfect. "Mister Guthren, this will do nicely. Rotate one-eighty degrees, raise the bow twenty degrees, and lower us into the crack. Mister Pushkin, deploy a passive probe to the crest ahead. Guns, be prepared for a point-blank broadside at my command."

*

"We have lost jump ability, commander," Jhar reported, "as well as three gun emplacements to starboard."

"Casualties?"

"Fourteen dead, twelve wounded."

It was a heavy toll from a single strike, another of Dunmoore's cowardly acts. Like the mines, the layback missiles reeked of dishonor to Brakal's aroused passions. Any ability he possessed to calmly evaluate her actions as the goads they really were, had long since vanished in a primal Shrehari haze of aggression. It was the ultimate irony that Brakal had succumbed to the weakness he so abhorred in his peers.

Alone among the officers, Jhar kept a measure of restraint and self-control and saw with growing horror the trap into which Brakal sailed, damning his enemy and ignoring her true intentions. But the commander was now deaf to his advice, as he always was when blood clashed with thought.

"You have her trail, Urag?"

"Yes, commander. On screen."

"Helm, accelerate!"

*

"The probe has him, sir." Chief Penzara announced. "He's losing altitude. Probably following our trail, curious about why we're running so close to the surface."

"Curiosity killed the cat, or in this case the Shrehari," Siobhan smiled hungrily.

"Nearing, still at the same speed. On our horizon in sixty seconds."

Lieutenant Amiri's hand hovered over the firing button, his guns aimed at the spot over the crest where his computer predicted *Tol Vakash* would appear.

"Helm, thrusters, positive zee, slowly. Engage." Siobhan did not want to be boxed in by the canyon. She intended to emerge almost face-to-face with Brakal and surprise the pants off him. With excruciating caution, the frigate rose from her deep, dark hiding spot.

"There he is!"

"FIRE!"

Plasma lanced out of all guns, tearing at *Tol Vakash*'s underside like a serrated knife. His shields glowed with crackling energy and then collapsed, opening his gray hull to the full punishment of *Stingray*'s broadside. The humans saw Brakal's cruiser stagger under the onslaught, but to his gunners' credit, they returned what fire they could. It was enough to punch through the nearly motionless frigate's screens and wreak havoc on her physical envelope.

Stingray shuddered down to her very keel. Power surged and flickered, changing the battle red to full darkness and back again. Panels came loose as sparks flew from overloaded circuits. A thin, acrid haze of smoke began to fill the bridge while the distressing sounds of a wounded ship filled their ears. The image of the dying *Victoria Regina* flashed before Siobhan's eyes. It was so vivid she shuddered, a part of her praying she had not condemned her ship to death through sheer hubris. Then, reality returned as Guthren took the initiative and raised the ship out of the chasm to give them maneuvering room.

Tol Vakash was fleeing over the horizon, severely damaged and in need of emergency repairs before she could face the frigate again. This and more flashed through Siobhan's mind as she ordered the pursuit, hunter and hunted exchanging places.

"Captain," Pushkin's shout broke through her trance, "engineering reports the jump drive controllers offline. We have no jump capacity. And the sublight drive reads amber. It could go at any minute."

"Damn. How long to repair the FTL?"

"Unknown. They're still dealing with more immediate damage in life support. We took it pretty bad just now."

"So did they. Even worse than us no doubt. Casualties?"

"Yes. I don't have a firm count yet."

"Thank you. Mister Guthren, get on their trail. Now we have no choice but to finish Brakal before he turns around and does the same to us."

Like two punch-drunk boxers in the last round of an evenly matched fight, the two ships staggered around the planetoid, each seeking to finish off the other, one to regain his honor, the other to buy time for an escape. The end, when it came, was as unexpected as a knockout punch.

*

"Captain!" Lieutenant Amiri shouted. "There he is."

Like a wraith, *Tol Vakash*'s damaged hull rose in their sights. Brakal had turned his cruiser about to give the frigate a deathblow and had achieved at least partial surprise. He opened fire, his guns winking like obscene eyes. Dunmoore ordered return fire in the same instant, and both ships hit each other at the same time. Except now, the earlier damage the humans had caused gave them the edge.

Shields collapsed on both the cruiser and the frigate in an orgy of released energies, exposing the hulls to the backwash of the first salvo, and the death-dealing punch of the next one.

"We're wide open, cap'n." Pushkin's voice was loud, urgent and, he had to admit to himself, frightened.

She ignored him. "Fire again, Mister Amiri."

"Capacitors aren't ready yet, sir."

"Flood 'em."

"They'll burn out!"

"Just do it. *Now!*" Siobhan did not give a damn for the restrictions that limited their rate of fire to the regenerating rate of the capacitors. Flooding them with sudden energy would cause damage, but she knew, if they did not shoot first, it would be immaterial. *Tol Vakash* would win.

"Firing."

One after the other, a dozen heavy plasma rounds hit the cruiser's gray hull, eating through the metal with incredible energy, turning the once proud ship into a wreck. Clouds of crystallized gases erupted from the punctures as it began to drift away, all steering gone.

"She's lost power," Chief Penzara announced in an awed tone of voice. He turned to look at the captain. "We won, sir."

"Not quite," Lieutenant Amiri interrupted. "I'm picking up three contacts headed in from Cimmeria. ETA ten minutes."

— Twenty-Three —

Brakal slumped in his chair, unable to understand how his ship, the proud *Tol Vakash*, could be sitting helplessly under the human frigate's guns, how Dunmoore had outfought him with greater cunning and ability.

Around him, the cruiser groaned in its death throes, multiple fires sending smoke through all compartments. He had no power, no engines, no shields, nothing. The great Brakal had lost, actually lost, for the first time in his life. It was not a sensation he liked. As with those who grow too mighty, the fall from grace was a shock too great to bear.

"Your orders, commander?" Gun Master Urag coughed, his throat seared by the acrid fumes that turned the ruined bridge into a vision of hell. Death hung a few kilometers off their bow in the form of a powered and armed Commonwealth warship, a bird of prey gathering itself for the final, violent strike.

"Huh?" Brakal shook himself. "Orders? Jhar, status report." When he got no answer, the Shrehari turned toward his friend and first officer.

The loyal and able Jhar lay on the deck, in a pool of his own blood. He was as dead as could be, decapitated by a section of torn bulkhead. Brakal fought down the bile of despair and horror. His mind tried frantically to determine how they had been brought to this state, but dismay robbed the Scourge of the Fleet of his customary ebullience and decisiveness.

Gun Master Urag watched him with growing sadness, seeing the destruction of a once mighty and respected commander, knowing this defeat meant the end for them all. Brakal had embodied the future of the Imperial Navy's officer corps, and thereby the future of the Empire itself. That future now seemed a chimera, a mirage on a hot day in Makkar County.

"Commander, we are dead in space, living off our batteries."

"And the humans?" The powerful voice was reduced to a whisper of disbelief.

"Damaged, but still powered up, though they leak radiation from many sources. Their primary drives may be inoperative. Their guns, however, show no sign of being anything but operational. One more salvo and we are finished."

Of course, Urag could not know *Stingray* had lost the use of its main guns thanks to Siobhan's emergency firing order. The frigate could no more destroy them than they could destroy it.

"We have already lost pressure on half the decks and our casualties..." Urag did not complete the sentence. He did not have to. One glance around the bridge gave a clear enough picture of the devastation elsewhere. *Tol Vakash* was finished.

Brakal sank back in his chair, brooding. But his dark mood stirred something hard within him, something that would not give the human total victory. His eyes narrowed, reflecting the light of an electric fire, and Urag almost believed the old commander was back, that the initial confusion and shock had worn off. That belief crystallized when Brakal grinned savagely and stood up.

"Call the human. I wish to speak to Dunmoore."

*

"Captain, *Tol Vakash* is hailing. Brakal wants to talk to you."

Siobhan glanced at the signals officer in surprise, momentarily abandoning all thoughts of her next move. "On screen, Mister Kowalski." Her eyes met Pushkin's. He merely shrugged, mystified.

The view screen crackled and fizzed for a few seconds, as the damaged systems bypassed burned out circuits and fought to complete the connection. Then, the face that had haunted her nightmares since Adnan Prighte's death glared down at her.

Instinctively, Siobhan rose, adjusting her tunic. She felt a shiver of... Fear? Recognition? Sympathy? *Respect*? Brakal's face no longer showed the calm, calculating look she remembered. He seemed exhausted, desperate. Defeated. The roles had been reversed.

Strangely, Siobhan could find no pleasure in it, like the student who finally defeats her *sensei*, her master, and finds herself utterly alone.

Siobhan nodded. "Commander. You have fought well. It was an honor to meet you again in battle."

"And you," he growled, his Anglic guttural and harsh. "You are a witch, Dunmoore."

Some would make that 'bitch', Brakal, Siobhan thought, suddenly feeling light-headed. She acknowledged the backhanded compliment with another nod.

"I have a good crew, commander."

Brakal grunted. "I knew, the last time we met, that you were a true Warrior, with cunning and ability. But I did not then know how much of one you are. It does not please me to be helpless under your guns, but knowing your valor makes the humiliation more bearable. Few in either of our fleets could have accomplished what you did."

Suddenly, a harsh, hate-filled shout in the imperial tongue interrupted Brakal. Siobhan could not understand what was said, but she knew it was not congratulatory. The enraged face of a Shrehari officer briefly appeared on screen snarling, as he reached out for Brakal. Appalled, the humans watched as Brakal drew an impossibly big blaster from a hip holster and fired at Khrada, killing him. The act seemed to give the commander some pleasure for his face looked less despairing as he turned back.

"Forgive me, Dunmoore. A minor disagreement with an official my government has seen fit to place on my ship. I had confined him, but it appears he managed to escape during the battle. He will no longer trouble me."

Siobhan smiled, aware of his comment's full meaning. The man had been *Tai Kan*, secret police, the Shrehari equivalent to the SSB. "We sometimes have those too,

Brakal. They are better dead than alive, for all the harm they do."

"Agreed, Dunmoore." The small smile of mutual understanding vanished as his face turned to stone. "You realize I cannot let you take my ship. I will, therefore, activate the self-destruct mechanism the moment we end this communication."

"Why warn me of this? You could destroy us quickly with the explosion and turn our victory into defeat."

"Because you have earned the right to know, Dunmoore and the right to attempt your escape. I make war honorably, not like my government."

Siobhan felt a sudden chill. *Stingray* was well within the destructive range of an exploding Gorgon-class, and more damaged than Brakal apparently realized. She could no more take *Tol Vakash* than he could take *Stingray*. But she could not tell him that, in an oblique plea to stop the self-destruct. It would not have been honorable.

"Then I wish you the same you wished Captain Prighte not too long ago. *Harkash nedrin rakati,* Brakal." Perfect accent, Brakal thought, as she raised her fist in the Shrehari salute. "Your name shall be remembered and honored. Fighting you has been an experience."

Brakal nodded formally, an indefinable expression in his dark eyes. He raised his hand, and the transmission died.

"Mister Guthren, take us out of here at best speed." Siobhan's voice held a tone of urgency she had never used before. Real despair flared in her guts for the first time since Adnan Prighte's death. "We have to be out of his self-destruct radius within a minute."

"We have thrusters only, sir," the cox'n replied, fighting his fear as he turned to face his captain. "The sublight and hyperdrives are offline."

"Then move out on thrusters, best speed." Siobhan tapped the intercom. "Engineering, this is the captain. We need sublight drives online within sixty seconds, or we won't need them at all."

"Chief Weekes here, sir, Mister Tiner is already on it. I'll tell her about the deadline. Out."

With sickening slowness, the frigate backed away from the wrecked cruiser. All eyes watched it recede on the main screen, convinced they were going to die, yet still holding on to the hope that they would get the sublight engines online in time.

"We're not going to make it, are we," Pushkin murmured, to no one in particular. "And with the approaching Cimmeria-based ships, we're caught between the unmoving object and the irresistible force."

"The devil and the deep blue sea, if you want to get nautical, Number One," Siobhan replied, her mental countdown twisting her guts with anxiety. Brakal's final revenge: make the humans know they would die, and let them fret in the short minute before oblivion. "Launch the log buoy torpedo, Mister Amiri."

"Sorry, sir, the launchers took a bad hit. We can't launch anything."

"Damn!"

"We're still within the deadly radius, sir," Chief Penzara said as if the sight of the motionless *Tol Vakash* did not speak for itself.

"Well, sir," Pushkin took a deep breath. "It's been a blast. At least *Stingray* will have gone down with its reputation restored. Pity only we know about it."

"It is, isn't it," Siobhan smiled ironically. She had extracted her revenge and given her crew their pride again. But in so doing, she had overreached, and now, they would all pay for it.

"Shit!"

"What is it cox'n?"

"For a moment, I could have sworn the sublight engines were back online. Wishful thinking, probably." Then, "No! Hot damn! We have sublight power."

"Take us out, cox'n!"

"Are we going to outrun his blast wave?"

"Let's hope so, Number One."

"We've been spotted by the incoming ships," Chief Penzara announced. "Changing course to intercept. One Gorgon-class and two Geckos."

"Here comes the deep blue sea..." Pushkin muttered.

"Plot intercept." Siobhan took only a few seconds to study the tactical schematic. "Dammit, we're going to need FTL capability to outrun them. They'll cut us off otherwise. What are the chances of two miracles in five minutes? Mister Guthren, how full is our sublight engine power?"

"Entirely full, sir."

"Okay." She stood up clasping her hands in the small of her back. Siobhan's voice held a frantic note of urgency as her mouth struggled to keep up with her mind. "We'll have to break a few rules again. If we accelerate to relativistic speed, they won't be able to intercept, and we'll outrun their plasma."

"She's blocked at point two cee, sir. Command doesn't like relativistic travel," Pushkin reminded her. "Plays havoc with the orderly running of the fleets."

Siobhan leaned over Guthren's massive shoulder. "Cox'n, input access code Dunmoore Alpha-Two-Zero-Nine-Zero-One. Release restrictions."

"Done, sir."

"Let's go!"

The ship groaned under the thrust, but slowly accelerated beyond the maximum sublight speed prescribed by both the Commonwealth and the Imperial Deep Space Fleet.

A streak of unstoppable mass, *Stingray* passed within fifty thousand kilometers of the astonished Shrehari and left them far in her wake. Though they could outrun her in hyperspace, they could not bring her to battle. She was simply accelerating too fast in this universe.

*

"They've given up the pursuit," Penzara finally announced.

"Smarter than the brutes look," Pushkin commented.

"Yes, but we'll have to maintain current acceleration until we're beyond their tracking devices. Otherwise they'll only jump after us." Siobhan returned to her seat. "Chief Penzara, has *Tol Vakash* exploded yet?"

"Checking. No." He sounded confused as he turned to look at Siobhan. She glanced at the timepiece.

Suddenly she understood and began laughing until tears flowed down her cheeks. All the tension, the fear and the anxiety of the last few hours flowed out.

They had done it: racked up one hell of a score sheet, fought the Scourge of the Fleet, *and* survived. But the wily Brakal also survived to fight another day. The others looked at her, puzzled, wondering whether she had finally lost her mind. Then, Gregor Pushkin's eyes lit up with understanding, and he chuckled in counterpoint to Siobhan's uninhibited laughter.

"Oh the bastard," she said between outbursts, "he took a leaf out of my own book and threw it back at me. Out-bluffed me completely." When she sobered, she said, "In a way, I'm glad he didn't blow himself up."

"Yeah, you got to respect a guy like that," Pushkin added, to her surprise. "What did you do to teach him the art of bluffing, sir?"

"A long story, Gregor, one that's best told over a long meal and some good wine. We're safe, and that's the essential." She tapped the intercom. "Engineering, this is the captain. Well done, Mister Tiner. You saved the ship."

"Chief Weekes here," a somber, sad voice replied. "Lieutenant Commander Tiner died when the engines came back online. She was in the port plasma flux tube for an emergency jump start." His words took a few moments to sink in as total silence descended on the bridge.

"You mean she deliberately sacrificed herself?" Siobhan nearly choked on the question, unable to picture the nervous little engineer stepping into the tube and assured death.

"Aye, sir. There was no other way to do it. We don't have any engineering 'bots. Battle Group didn't issue them."

Probably because Kaleri sold them off, Siobhan thought angrily. *One more victim to her corruption and greed. No, not just one more...* "But we have both engines running. What about the starboard one."

"That was Able Spacer Bertram, sir. Volunteered."

Siobhan felt like she had been punched in the gut. She had developed an affectionate respect for the weasel-faced engineer's mate. "Nosey?"

"Yeah, cap'n. Nosey Bertram." There was a catch in Weekes's throat. The little guy was popular in engineering. Had been popular.

"Thank you. Captain, out." She sat back, a dull ache growing in her gut.

"Mister Kowalski, give me ship-wide." The signals officer made a thumbs up gesture. "Stingrays, this is the captain." Siobhan was pleased that her voice remained firm. "You'll be glad to know it's over for now. We're on our way home with six kills to our credit. We still have a lot to do before we can consider ourselves safe, but I don't think we'll be seeing the enemy again for a while. I'm very proud of you, of what you've achieved. No one in the Fleet can call this ship a jinx ever again, and that's thanks to you."

She wanted to say so much more, apologize to those who died or even now lay in sickbay with unspeakable injuries, but she found she could not. The crew did not want to hear any of that anyway. They wanted to hear they had done well, were safe and on their way home. The rest would just have been empty words, meaningless.

"Dunmoore, out. You have the bridge, Mister Pushkin."

"Sir." He saw the deep fatigue in her eyes. Reckless and hotheaded, maybe, but also deeply feeling.

Instead of going to her ready room, Dunmoore headed out the main door and down a few decks to sickbay. Pushkin could deal with the ship's needs. She had a much harder task: face the men and women who whose suffering she had caused. It was something the captain could not delegate, ever. No matter how she felt.

*

Brakal stood by a porthole, looking out at the nameless planetoid that had witnessed his defeat. Behind him, the bodies of his friends, and of the *Tai Kan* spy, cooled as *Tol Vakash* waited for a tow from the Cimmeria squadron ships. His cruiser was finished, he knew that. The High Command would order its destruction. But he did not want to die yet.

Brakal found he did not believe in his culture's notion of honorable death. Not when the Empire was heading for disaster under the leadership of incompetents like Trage.

It was more honorable and harder to live, to face the charges of the Council, and fight back if only to make the Empire's peril clear. When a human captain, a female at that, could wipe out a convoy and a cruiser with an old, outdated frigate, general defeat was very near indeed.

More importantly, he refused to give Trage the satisfaction of an easy passing, one he could use to his own ends. Oh, the wily old admiral would certainly have made Brakal a martyr, to better control his followers in the Deep Space Fleet, but underneath it all, Trage would have consolidated his hold on the Empire. And the Makkar family estates would have fallen into the hands of court sycophants who sucked up to the turds on the Council and leeched the Empire's lifeblood away.

Those events could still happen, but their passing was not assured. Not while Brakal still breathed. Khrada no longer lived to spread his poison, thank the ancestors, and his death could not be blamed on the commander. The spy had attacked him first.

And what dishonor was there in losing to a capable foe? He had learned much from her this time again and felt a faint glow of pleasure at using the same kind of deception on her as she had used on him. The next time, if there was one, Brakal would know how to toy with his opponent and make him believe what he wanted. As Dunmoore had done.

Never again would Brakal limit his thinking to the fixed parameters of so-called normality. If it is even remotely possible, consider it. And most of all continue to study everything about your enemy so you know what she *really* can or cannot do.

"Commander." Urag's voice broke Brakal from his thoughts. The gun master was now first officer of *Tol Vakash*, a post he would not hold for long, but one he would honor by carrying out his duties to his utmost. Jhar's memory demanded as much. "The *Tol Hrakan* is ready to take us in tow."

*

"Come."

Pushkin poked his head through the door, to a background of relieved cheers and backslapping. "We've just passed back into Commonwealth space, sir."

Siobhan paused her log recorder and smiled. "You may place the crew at cruising stations, Number One, and have the purser break-out a double tot for everyone. I think it's time we spliced the main brace. They've earned it."

"Aye, sir," Pushkin grinned. "I'd say they've earned several double tots, but we wouldn't want to be charged with sailing a starship under the influence."

"Indeed not, Gregor."

The first officer winked and disappeared.

Siobhan looked at her terminal again and sighed. Her official reports were already in Admiral Nagira's hands, along with the depositions of her officers, the casualty lists, and an advisory that *Stingray* was holding together with baling wire and duct tape.

They received a laconic reply ordering them to head for Starbase 31 at best speed commensurate with the safety of the ship. No word on the other business, nor a peep of congratulations. The frigate could be returning from a milk run to Earth for all the reaction from 3rd Fleet HQ. Except it was a trip made with only one jump drive, creating a dangerously unbalanced bubble. But there was no helping that.

The acting chief engineer and his crew had performed miracles in getting even one drive up and running. Whether it was in spite of Tiner's death or because of it, Siobhan did not know. She thought she had the woman pegged for one thing, and then Tiner went and did something utterly heroic to save the ship. Siobhan touched the record button.

"I've put Lieutenant Commander Tiner and Able Spacer Bertram up for a posthumous Commonwealth Medal of Honor, though I suspect they'll get the Distinguished Service Cross instead, which is no less than they deserve, the bloody brave fools. We're sailing short-handed now. Casualties were heavy, especially fatalities, and I'll be expanding the commendations list over the next few days."

As I write the letters to the next of kin. Again.

Siobhan paused the recorder and let her eyes lose focus as she thought of the rows of coffins down in cargo hold five. Twenty-nine dead, not counting those killed before the battle, like Drex, Cayne, or Hartalas. At least they were beyond pain. Even worse were the injured, overflowing the ship's sickbay. She had visited them daily since escaping from the Cimmeria system, not only out of a sense of duty as captain, but to remind herself of the horrors her orders had put those spacers through.

A few, those she knew personally, gave her exceptionally sharp pangs of guilt and compassion, like Able Spacer Demianova, who got severely burned when a Shrehari plasma shot ate through the armor of her gun turret. She was lucky to be alive, mainly thanks to Rownes' quick actions, but she would need months in a naval hospital for a full recovery. And even then, Demianova would forever bear the heavy scars of Dunmoore's grab for glory.

The wounded shamed Siobhan with their cheerful pride, and it was apparent none of them bore her a grudge or blamed her. Somehow, in a twisted way, Siobhan would have been able to handle their reproach better than their lack of it.

"It is an entirely different crew I bring back than the one I left with," she continued. "The old steward at Starbase 31 was right. They're good 'uns. Damn good 'uns. I'm proud as hell to claim them as *my* crew. They've come together marvelously with the shared experience of battle, and as we've found out, with the common experience of losing a week of our lives in the mad dash for the line at relativistic velocities. It's sad, therefore, that we won't be together for much longer. I can't see Command willing to sink millions into refitting a frigate slated for the knackers' yard. My engineers and technicians are doing amazing work repairing everything they can. But it won't change the fact *Stingray* is obsolete. One thing she isn't, and nobody will call her that again, is a jinx. Which, I guess, means I'm not a jinx skipper either, especially since I'm actually bringing her home and will see her decommissioned. A first for me." Siobhan smiled ironically at her reflection in the computer screen.

"As for Admiral Kaleri, Commander Forenza and everybody else involved in the SSB scheme, I'll just have to see what Admiral Nagira makes of my reports and my officers' depositions. We still don't know every detail and what we don't know can be used against any accusations. It is possible that this could still come to naught, and damage us personally. Lord knows what kind of protection Kaleri can call on, or whether Nagira will even believe my accusations against a rear admiral. I hope our success on the battlefield will lend us more credibility than we would have had before sailing."

The door chime buzzed, interrupting Siobhan's train of thought. "Come."

Able Spacer Vincenzo stepped in from the corridor, carrying a tray of food. Siobhan smiled and cleared her desktop for her supper. "Thanks, Vincenzo. I hadn't realized how hungry I was."

"So I figured, *capitano*. You do not take good care of yourself." He sounded reproachful, like a fussing mother.

"How's Demianova?"

He shrugged. "So-so. She does not like spending her days in bed and complains incessantly. But it is a brave face. She hurts much. Here you go, *capitano*. A good fresh linguini with clams and wine sauce. All you need is a good bottle of Valpolicella. Bon appetite."

Vincenzo left her to the delicious smelling meal. The bosun's mate had inexplicably, after the battle, turned up as her personal steward, clerk, and all-around aide. Siobhan had not dared ask whether he had volunteered or been assigned. She certainly did not request a replacement for Kery, knowing the spacer she took for her own business would be sorely missed in his division. But apparently, Vincenzo worked for her on top of his regular, if somewhat lightened duties. One thing was for sure. The menu had been very Italian since then, and tasty. At least the cooks had relearned their trade along with everybody else.

*

Later that evening, Pushkin appeared at her door, looking as tired as Siobhan felt. Everybody looked that way, with the strain of getting home on one drive, keeping the ship together, and coping with the battle's injuries.

"You said you had a particular task once we emerged for a course check before the final jump."

"Right." She had nearly forgotten. Thank God she had Pushkin around to keep things on an even keel. He was proving to be one hell of a first officer; almost Ezekiel Holt's equal, although he lacked the quirky spirit that made Ezekiel unique. But he had his own qualities, which Siobhan was learning to appreciate. "We have to paint six red dragons on the superstructure, to make sure everybody knows we bagged six imperial ships on this patrol. I hope we have red paint aboard."

Pushkin grinned. "I believe we do, skipper. Too bad we can't also tie a broom to the commo array."

Siobhan shrugged. "Wouldn't mean all that much. Any idiot who meets two or three small enemy ships on his cruise and kills them can tie a 'clean-sweep' broom to the array. Six kills and an escape from the better part of an imperial squadron, now that's noteworthy."

"Aye." Pushkin became thoughtful. "What do you think will happen when we dock, skipper?"

"No idea, Gregor." She let her eyes drift to the holo print across from her desk. "It all depends on Admiral Nagira. Either he sweeps everything under the table, or has me taken into custody as a nut case or brings Kaleri and the others up on charges. I thought I knew him, but right now, I don't know how he'll move. This is just too big, too dirty for any predictions."

"It sucks, doesn't it, skipper?"

"Big time, Number One. I could sure use a beer right now."

"That's what I came for, sir. Since you ordered the tot, I figure we're no longer dry?"

"I suppose." She smiled wryly, remembering the crew's reaction when she declared the ship dry even before they left port.

"Good. On behalf of the wardroom, I'd like to invite you for a drink and some snacks with your officers."

Siobhan's sudden smile of delight was dazzling, wiping away all of the accumulated fatigue.

"I'd be honored, Number One, honored indeed. When?"

"How about now?" His eyes twinkled. "They're waiting for you with a couple of cold ones. Maybe you could tell us about the time you taught Brakal how to bluff."

"With pleasure, Gregor. Lead on."

*

"We're in parking orbit, captain."

"On my way, Number One." Siobhan rose and straightened her tunic. It was over. Starbase 31 hung a kilometer off the starboard bow, holding their futures within its shiny white hull. She would once again be a captain without a ship. And her crew? It did not seem fair to disperse them to new postings just after they had proven their worth. But the ship and its crew had suffered almost too much to carry on.

The exhausted and subdued ship's surgeon had released almost half of the wounded back to light duties, but the rest would need base hospital attention. Some, like Demianova, were in for a lengthy stay. Two waited in stasis, their bodies too badly damaged for even Luttrell's skills. Hopefully, the specialists could revive them. Otherwise, Siobhan would have two more letters to write.

Their unbalanced jumps had further aggravated the damage to the engines and hull. Some privately considered it a miracle that they made it home unassisted. But make it they did. A few hours earlier, *Stingray* had slowly and carefully dumped her remaining antimatter fuel, giving birth to bright tail not unlike that of a comet as the antimatter molecules, pushed away from the ship by a magnetic funnel, reacted with the sparse matter present in interplanetary space. Maybe someone on the planet below had seen them in the night sky and wondered which ship returned home too damaged to dock with full tanks. If anyone still cared after five years of war.

*

"Any instructions from spacedock control?" Siobhan slipped into the command chair, still warm from Pushkin's occupation.

No Honor in Death

"None. They told us to stand by."

"Strange." Siobhan shrugged. A few minutes wait would not change a blessed thing now. Still, damaged ships had priority docking.

"Sir, I'm getting a number of small contacts aft," Chief Penzara reported, puzzlement creasing his weathered face. "Looks like two squadrons of fighters. They're headed our way, no mistake."

"On screen."

Pushkin whistled at the sight. The two groups of twelve sleek spacecraft in close formation were things of beauty. Obviously, the double-seaters were part of the base's defense wing, back from some training mission. Then again, maybe not. They decelerated to match *Stingray*'s velocity and took a position level with the frigate, one squadron on either side, a few hundred meters out. An escort? Siobhan was about to speak when the radio came to life.

"*Stingray*, this is space dock control. You are cleared to dock under your own power at docking port one. Welcome home."

Guthren turned around to stare uncomprehendingly at Dunmoore. Ships were rarely permitted to dock without the assistance of tugs and docking port one was the highest, the best, the one closest to the station's habitat levels. The one usually reserved for ships that distinguished themselves.

"*Stingray*, this is Rapier-One," an unknown voice chimed in behind the spacedock controller. "Your escorts, the 301st and 302nd Defense Squadrons, are in place and ready at your command. And may I say it's an honor for us, sir."

"Thank you, Rapier-One," Siobhan replied, somewhat bemused at the turn of events. "It appears all is forgiven, people," she said to the bridge crew at large, undefined emotions chasing each other across her eyes. Permission to dock unaided was an honor in itself, sometimes given to ships that had distinguished themselves on a patrol. But a two squadron escort on top of that?

The same realization spread among the crew, leaving smiles of disbelief and then pride in its wake. Siobhan was aware she wore a silly, girlish grin, but did not care.

"Mister Pushkin, please inform the crew that we will dock with a fighter escort. Tell 'em to look out the window and enjoy the sights. They've earned it."

"Mister Guthren," she squared her shoulders and sat up straight. "Aft thrusters, five seconds burn at half power. Take us in."

"Aye, aye, *sir*!"

"Number One, deploy the battle flag and our commissioning streamer and set the navigation strobes to three short and one long blinks. Oh, and Mister Pushkin, make sure the running lights are on our kill marks so everyone can see. We're coming home in style."

Slowly, majestuously, the missile frigate *Stingray* closed the distance to the gaping space dock doors, navigation strobes blinking the Morse code for the letter V, for victory, stiff flag, and streamer stretching out from the commo array and the six red dragons marking her kills brightly illuminated.

But the lights also illuminated the heavy battle damage, the black scars, gaping holes and twisted turrets. She had paid for the kill marks dearly.

The space doors grew on screen until they blanked out even the station's hull. After a wing-wagging salute and message from Rapier-One, the 301st and 302nd Defense Squadrons peeled off to port and starboard, their ceremonial mission completed. Siobhan did not know what kind of a sight her ship made for onlookers, whether she looked like a truly heroic survivor, or simply like a pathetic wreck. But then, she had other thoughts to occupy her bemused mind.

"Cox'n, forward thrusters, four-second burn. Engage."

The frigate's forward motion slowed to a crawl as she crossed the threshold into the cavernous space dock. Four other ships were at anchor, their hulls brightly illuminated for the occasion. Ahead, on the opposite end of the docking area, a giant screen, used to transmit visual docking instructions flashed the words 'Welcome home, Stingray.'

"Cor," Chief Penzara whispered in awe, "will you bleedin' look at that." All of the windows overlooking the space dock were black with people, station personnel watching *Stingray* come in. "Looks like they turned out the bleedin' garrison for us."

"Cox'n, full stop." They were level with docking port one. "Mister Pushkin, activate tractor beam to settle us in."

"In position," he reported a few moments later.

"Drop anchor," Siobhan joked, smiling. She suspected she knew what was about to happen next. The docking clamps latched on to *Stingray* with a loud thud. At that moment, a military band, the music retransmitted over the open frequency, broke into a jaunty naval tune.

"Commonwealth Star Ship *Stingray*," a deep, commanding voice cut through the music. It took Siobhan a few heartbeats to recognize it as Nagira's. "From the Commander, Commonwealth Navy, you have been awarded the Commonwealth Unit Citation for valor. Congratulations. I am proud to have you under my command."

Then, Nagira snapped out an order that was not directed at the frigate. "Third Fleet will man the yards!"

Commander Siobhan Dunmoore, captain of the frigate *Stingray,* felt a shiver course down her spine as emotion welled up uncontrollably. Manning the yards, an ancient tradition to salute valor, was a rare honor in this day and age. Nagira was really pulling out all the stops. She rose, straightened her uniform, and came to attention. Pushkin motioned the others to follow suit until everyone aboard the ship stood stiffly facing view screens and portholes.

"Three cheers for *Stingray*. Hip, hip, hip!"

"Hurrah," a storm of voices replied as the small figures in the windows doffed their berets and waved them above their heads.

"Hip, hip, hip!"

"Hurrah."

The huge space dock screen went blank and then came back to life to display a giant silver stingray, coiled to attack. Below, one by one, six red dragons, brothers to those painted on the frigate's hull, popped into view and began flashing.

"Hip, hip, hip!"

"Hurrah."

As the last cry faded into the flourish of drums, bugles, and bagpipes, Siobhan felt her eyes fill with tears of pride. And she was not alone. Pushkin's brief, whispered comment spoke volumes.

"My God!"

The band segued into the Commonwealth anthem and then faded away as the onlookers returned to their stations. *Stingray*'s glorious return was over. But her crew would remember it for the rest of their lives.

"Secure ship, Number One. We have a lot to do."

"Sir," Kowalski interrupted. "Message from control. Admiral Nagira will board *Stingray* in five minutes."

"Shit," Siobhan swore. They were in no state to receive a three-star admiral.

Pushkin and Guthren glanced at each other, the latter nodding. Then Pushkin raised his hand, palm outwards. "No worry, skipper. You have time to change into dress uniform. We'll take care of everything else. Admiral Nagira will be received with full honors."

Siobhan grinned, blinking back another surge of feeling. *Damn shame this ship is going to the knackers!*

A further surprise awaited her in her cabin. Vincenzo, already in full dress, had laid out her uniform and waited to help her change. Four minutes later, Siobhan was on her way to the main airlock, moving amidst grinning spacers busily carrying out the first officer's orders.

Life aboard *Stingray* would go on, admiral's visit or no admiral's visit.

A quarter guard, under Lieutenant Devall's orders, was already lined up by the airlock. Their immaculate dress uniforms, gleaming weapons, and shiny boots would have put the SecGen's guards to shame.

On either side of the armored door itself, Chief Foste and five bosun's mates also turned out in perfect uniforms, waited to pipe the admiral aboard with their silver calls.

At some unheard signal, Foste touched the airlock's control panel, and the heavy door slid out of the way, opening up on the short tube connecting the ship to the base. On the station side of the tube, sentries, two of *Stingray*'s spacers, snapped to attention and presented arms in unison as Admiral Nagira strode by, returning the salute. Siobhan could not have asked for a smarter reception.

The bosun and her mates raised their calls to their lips, wetting them in preparation.

The admiral was alone, without a staff officer or flag lieutenant, which was as unusual as his unexpected and rather inconvenient visit, even if it was an honor for the ship.

"Guard, atten-SHUN!"

Then, as one, the bosun's calls twittered, welcoming the commander of the 3rd Fleet aboard the frigate *Stingray*.

— Twenty-Four —

"Very impressive, captain," Nagira smiled as Siobhan led him off after he had inspected the quarter guard. "I am happy to see such a smart, proud crew." His eyes twinkled with more than just pleasure and Siobhan knew it had been a test, something to show him how well she had turned the crew around, how much they cared about making their captain and ship look good. She had passed the test and felt like thumbing her nose at him.

"Your quarters, I think." Nagira nodded toward the main lift. "We have much to discuss, captain. Your first officer is more than able to handle this ship alone for a while."

"As you wish, sir." He would see something of a mess, but there was no helping that. He had not given her time to prepare for his visit. Deliberately.

The door to Siobhan's cabin opened with a whisper at their approach. She should not have worried about anything. Vincenzo, in full dress uniform, was standing beside the desk, a steward's white cloth over his left forearm. The cabin would have done a boot camp drill sergeant proud, with not an item out of place or a speck of dust to mar its perfection.

A gleaming coffee pot and delicate china cups from the wardroom waited on the desk. Half-hidden behind the pot, Siobhan saw a dark green bottle of Dordogne brandy, one of Helen Forenza's private stock, now the property of the ship.

Nagira glanced around, his eyes missing nothing, and then examined the ramrod straight bosun's mate. Vincenzo met Nagira's gaze with calm confidence. The admiral nodded, as if satisfied, and turned his attention to the bookshelf with its antique ship's clock. As if on cue, it rang eight bells, four in the afternoon.

Siobhan gave Vincenzo a grateful look, which he returned with a sheepish smile and a shrug.

"Coffee, sir?" She asked.

"Oh, aye, captain. And a splash of that reactor coolant you have masquerading as brandy. The sun is over the yardarm somewhere in the universe, eh?" He turned around and smiled as Vincenzo poured with a steady hand. When the young man had served the two officers, he glanced questioningly at his captain.

"Thank you, Vincenzo. We'll be all right for now." Siobhan smiled warmly, conscious again of the man's touching display of loyalty.

"Yes," Nagira chimed in, "that was well done, spacer. My thanks."

Their eyes followed him out of the cabin, and the door closed behind his retreating back. Somehow, Siobhan knew he would be waiting just outside, ready for anything.

Nagira sipped his brandy-laced coffee and sighed. "The Dunmoore magic is alive and well, I see."

"Sir?" Siobhan still felt adrift, her mind a few steps behind Nagira.

"Your crew. You have charmed them into eating out of your hand, that much is obvious, Siobhan. I am glad. I had feared you no longer possessed the spark that gives you your extraordinary character, the one that attracts spacers like moths to a flame. You have an exceptional crew, Siobhan, and they a fine commander. Your actions will have laid the silly stories about the jinxed ship to rest at last."

"Hence, the triumphant return," Siobhan replied tartly.

Nagira smiled. "For that reason and many others. But mainly because you and your crew deserved every moment of it. You no doubt think I invited myself aboard your ship so shortly after docking as a kind of test. Oh, do not deny it, Siobhan. It is written all over your face. But you should know by now I never do things for only one reason. I also wished to speak to you before you saw anybody else."

A sudden darkness descended on Siobhan. "My report."

The admiral nodded. "Your report. In two words: well done. My faith in you is stronger than ever, though I knew from the start I had made the right choice."

Siobhan's cheeks colored. He watched her in silence, dark eyes narrowed with suppressed amusement.

"I knew it," she replied with asperity. "Sir, with all due respect, you're a bastard! You set me up to do your dirty work."

"Peace, Siobhan." He raised his left hand, palm outwards. "As I said, I never do things for only one reason. It is wasteful." He took another sip. "I was once a frigate captain, long ago. Does that surprise you? It was the best period in my career, one which I would relive with joy. Do you know which ship that was?"

Sudden insight struck Siobhan like a fist in the gut. She nodded weakly.

"*Stingray.*"

"Just so. This was once my cabin. I was its first occupant. The first in a long line of captains, good, bad, or indifferent." He glanced around. "She had a fine name in those days and scored many victories. I would have been much saddened if she was to go into history in disgrace, which is what Admiral Kaleri wanted, to cover herself. It would also have been a shame to lose such an excellent crew in the midst of such a bitter and endless war. So you see, I had three reasons to give you command of this ship, even if it will not be for a very long time. Knowing you, I had confidence that you would do all three things with the same stubborn, reckless energy you have displayed ever since I took you on my staff, years ago." He bowed his head at her with surprising humility. "I am grateful, captain. *Domo arigato.*"

"You — you're welcome, sir." Siobhan was flustered, an unusual sensation. But the expression in Nagira's eyes had struck a deep chord within her.

"Now, I will complete the story, so that you may appreciate the value of your contribution to resolving this sordid affair. You may share what I will say with your officers and crew, but they must keep the details to themselves." He held out his cup for a refill and settled back in the chair, eyes drifting to the porthole, and the brilliantly lit space dock beyond.

"You know that the SSB and the Fleet have been at each other's throats for a long time. It is a power game, to decide who will carry greater weight in the Commonwealth's affairs. With its political support and direct relationship with the Secretary General, the SSB was winning the game, working toward the kind of state that appeals to politicians unwilling to face the electorate every few years."

"Then the Empire invaded," Siobhan, murmured.

"Just so. All of a sudden, the SSB found itself with fewer friends. It failed to predict the invasion, a mistake we did not make, in great part thanks to smart, bold officers like you." Siobhan blushed at the unexpected compliment. Those heady days on Admiral Nagira's Fleet staff seemed so long ago. "For five years now, the navy has held the ear and purse strings of the mighty, to the SSB's detriment. Our less than friendly spies found themselves in the frustrating situation of lacking funds just at the time when Commonwealth society was vulnerable to greater secret police — shall we say — intervention. This, of course, we realized rather quickly and kept a careful watch to counter any moves that could affect the war effort adversely."

"The SSB wouldn't endanger the war effort for their own advancement, surely?" Siobhan sounded indignant, just like the young, brash lieutenant of five years ago who had attracted Nagira's notice.

"Oh, but they would, Siobhan. That is the tragedy of human stupidity. I imagine watching the SSB has become a full-time occupation for Naval Security and counterintelligence. A waste of people, but there you have it. In any case, about a year ago, one bright CI officer discovered a certain number of minor, but to his mind significant discrepancies in the 31st Battle Group's affairs. He built a good case but unfortunately based on the fragile foundations of speculation. Still, it was enough to convince his superiors to investigate further. He was sent as staff officer to Starbase 31, where he quietly began to dig up disturbing facts."

Another flash of insight hit Siobhan, though, after a few moments' thought, the conclusion she reached seemed all too appropriate. "Lieutenant Commander Holt was that officer."

"Correct. A fine man, with a mind to rival yours. He first discovered that Admiral Kaleri was shielding a most incompetent starship commander from general scrutiny, leaving her to destroy a perfectly good crew with her stupidity. Kaleri was no fool and had to be doing this for a reason. But she had surrounded herself with people she could trust, and who would protect her out of sheer loyalty."

"Like Drex, her former cox'n."

Nagira nodded. "Indeed. As you divined, she placed him aboard *Stingray* because Kaleri did not trust Forenza. Your predecessor was merely a convenient and pliable tool, never a friend and never to be trusted."

"But why? That's the one thing I've never understood."

"I am coming to that. Some bright SSB thinker formulated a plan to generate revenues by stealing from the navy and cast about for a suitable means to enact it. Just about that time, Admiral Kaleri's family, the once rich Kaleris of TransCom Enterprises, teetered on the edge of financial ruin thanks to some underhanded and illegal dealings that had gone wrong. On Earth, losing one's wealth is the worst social crime imaginable. It threw the family, including the admiral into despair. She, of course, had her career and a fine one at that. When all is said and done, Mila Kaleri was a superior officer who could well have succeeded me, had she not strayed from the path of honor. But her upbringing defined her place in life through family wealth, and not individual achievement. Most sad. SSB, being the swine they are, approached Kaleri, and proposed she help them fulfill their plans, for a sizable profit. I like to imagine she wrestled with her conscience before accepting, but we shall never know. Yes, I liked her, once."

"You keep talking of her in the past tense, sir."

Nagira's lips tightened. "When I received your report and confirmed its contents, I came to Starbase 31

398 No Honor in Death

unannounced on a fast courier. Admiral Kaleri heard of my arrival, and I assume the cause of my visit, two hours before we docked. I have a leak on my staff, but that is my problem. When I arrived, her flag lieutenant found her sitting at her desk, in full dress uniform with sword, a blaster in her right hand and the top of her skull splattered all over the bay windows."

"Suicide?" Siobhan did not know how to feel about Kaleri escaping justice if justice would ever have been served.

"No doubt at all. A note in her own handwriting apologized for her fall from grace." Nagira seemed disturbed and Siobhan knew he had seen the body himself. "In the end, the thought of facing the consequences of a scheme that had escaped her control left her no way out." He sighed. "It was the only way she could see to redeem at least part of herself. As I said, she was a good officer. Under different circumstances, you would have enjoyed serving under her."

"So the SSB convinced her to hand over parts and supplies for a cut of the profits, hiding the peculation behind *Stingray*'s books, courtesy of a compliant commander."

"Oh yes. Your ship was only one part of the equation, and I suspect only one funnel if the most important of them. Of course, we needed proof and had to discover how it was done. That is where you came in. I must confess it was a matter of serendipity more than calculation. Kaleri was protecting Forenza as best she could, hiding her misdeeds, but I fear the relationship became strained. At first, Kaleri believed she could control Forenza by giving her the command she should never have held and warning her of its loss should she not cooperate. But as the scheme went into full swing, Forenza held her own threats over Kaleri's head. Your predecessor was a cunning, if an utterly stupid woman, prey to her sensuality and perversions, both physical and moral. With the SSB and Kaleri both providing independent agents to control her, it worked long enough to net a fortune. With the demands of the war, starship parts, fuel, ammunition and other supplies are worth a fortune to smugglers, neutrals, and probably even Shrehari outside their navy's supply chain. The figures your friend Holt has amassed indicate the SSB's net profits surpassed the gross domestic product of a fair sized planet. Thus, I suspect Forenza would have met with an unfortunate accident at the slightest sign of betraying Kaleri."

"Instead, crew members died." Siobhan let her bitterness show.

"Unfortunate. We can only speculate, the principals being unreachable by now."

"Yes, but our speculation would be so close to the mark to make no bloody difference. Hell, the scheme couldn't work forever. All it took was a keen purser's mate to wonder why the captain handled bills of lading whenever they were resupplied by tender. Most likely, he got hold of the camouflage manifest, the one for the Fleet with a full consignment and realized it listed a lot more than what they really got. He paid for his curiosity with his life. I'd say Forenza did it to make sure she would keep her twisted little kingdom. She sure as hell didn't need the money."

Nagira nodded. "As you say. Though her means of keeping the crew from uniting against her were sufficient, even if they were discreditable."

"Yes, fear. It permeated the ship when I came on board. She really kept them down, damn her soul to hell." She glanced away, fighting to swallow her rage.

"But she made one mistake which destroyed everything. I was searching for a way to remove her from *Stingray* so that we might break the conspiracy. Forenza handed it to me on a silver platter and even Kaleri could not object."

"*Victoria Regina*'s call for assistance."

"Thanks to Lieutenant Commander Pushkin's retransmission, we had evidence to show Forenza had the time and means to render assistance, but failed to do so. Cowardice in the face of the enemy. It was enough for me. Mila Kaleri acquiesced and recommended I advance *Stingray*'s decommissioning by several months and disperse the crew. It was an attempt to protect herself. She let Forenza hang out to dry, though by what threats did she buy her silence, we shall never know. Then, you brought *Victoria Regina* home, and I knew you were the one to set things right again."

"Yes, and the good admiral tried her damnest to see me discredited."

"Desperate measures, Siobhan. Kaleri knew why I sent you to command *Stingray.* I can only assume that stronger measures, such as ensuring the ship's total loss, were beyond what remained of her honor, thankfully. The SSB was the greatest danger, but it appears their agent, Major Cayne, waited too long to act. Again, thankfully. Their scheme is over now. The tender and its crew are in custody and will be facing serious charges. I have no doubt some will turn and provide enough evidence to satisfy the Judge Advocate General. Unfortunately, the SSB ship which acted as receiver of the stolen goods has vanished."

"The *Mykonos?*"

"Yes, that was its name at the time of your interception, though by now, both her name and that of her skipper have changed, as will her appearance. You must have given them serious pangs of fear when you held her under your guns. But there was little you could do at the time."

"My actions with the *Mykonos* did give my crew an indication I was not part of the scheme and was serious in my intention to find answers. Some knew what she was, having seen her before." She gazed thoughtfully at the softly ticking clock. "In that, if nothing else, the smuggler served our purposes."

"Indeed. Well, that completes the tale I think, sordid as it was. It has cost the lives of good people, but at least you salvaged your crew, gave them back their pride, and wiped the stain of Helen Forenza's command. No doubt some other dashing frigate captain will attempt to break your kill record, but it will be safe for a long time to come. And you have the citation."

"What about Forenza?"

"The Disciplinary Board met, considered the available testimony, suffered the pressures of a politically connected family, and recommended she simply be retired from the Service. Which I endorsed, being unable to do more. She is a civilian now, beyond the reach of a court-martial. Or rather was a civilian. Ex-Commander Forenza died in a traffic accident on her second day back on Earth." From the expression in Nagira's eyes, he did not believe it was an accident.

"Who drove the hover car? Counterintelligence or SSB?"

"That too, we will never know."

"So what happens now?"

"Your crew is safe, sheltered from any accusations of perjury or participation in the misdeeds of your predecessor. There is a movement afoot to quash this story because of the bad publicity and effect on morale, not least civilian morale. We still have a war to prosecute. I find myself agreeing with the idea. The principal actors are all dead, the others are beyond our reach, and your ship is now a heroic figure in the public eye."

With mixed feelings, Siobhan shrugged. Her desire for revenge, for seeing Kaleri and Forenza face a firing squad had died along with them. She had her ship and crew. It was probably best to leave it at that. As Nagira said, they still had a war to prosecute. Which brought up the most important question.

"What about *Stingray*?" Siobhan feared the answer, just as much as she needed to hear it, and know their collective future.

"She will be decommissioned," he held up his hand, "in due course. At this stage, the Fleet cannot afford to retire ships without an immediate replacement at hand. Your ship will be the last of the Type 203s to go, but not yet. You will get a limited refit, enough to permit you to carry out internal security duties although I fear she will never sail the line again. Still, there are enough pirates, smugglers, and imperial infiltrators to give you a hot time, and you will free a less damaged ship for patrol duties in the war zone." He studied her face for a few moments.

"This pleases you. You expected to lose her right now. I understand perfectly. Enjoy your time aboard *Stingray*. She's an elegant lady, worthy of another fine lady. After her?" He shrugged. "We shall see."

Nagira rose and carefully replaced the coffee cup on the waiting tray. "I would ask you for a tour of the ship, but you have too much to do, and I fear the memories would not place me in a happy frame of mind. This, believe it or not, is the finest time of your career. Command of a frigate is many times better than an admiral's desk on some Starbase."

"Oh," he stopped and turned around to face her, "Lieutenant Commander Holt gives you his best. Unfortunately, he is no longer here to greet you personally. The moment your report reached my desk, his superiors in counterintelligence thought it best to remove him from Starbase 31, for his own safety. Lieutenant Drex was not the only one to owe his advancement to Admiral Kaleri, and apparently, he was feeling some adverse pressure from several senior staff officers, including Flag Captain Jadin, who will find his next posting less to his liking, let alone the fact that he will never be promoted again."

Siobhan's face must have registered surprise, for he continued. "I said the story would be quashed, not that the Fleet would let all those connected continue to live in peace. We will take care of them. The 31st Battle Group is about to experience a rare shake-up. Though that will not concern you once this base has repaired your ship. You are, as of now, assigned to the 39th Battle Group, based at Isabella Colony. Rear Admiral Quintana is a harsh taskmaster, but he is also a most remarkable commander. You will find your time under him interesting, to say the least." An impish smile briefly crossed Nagira's wizened features. "I hope you will also make *his* time interesting."

*

Siobhan saw Vice-Admiral Nagira over the side to the trill of the bosun's pipes and the stamp of the quarter guard presenting arms. Then, she was once more the sole master aboard *Stingray*. Her ship. At least for a while.

Lieutenant Commander Pushkin stepped into the airlock as the guard headed back to their quarters, to change into work uniform. "We'll be warped to the dry dock within the hour, sir. I've been assured that our refit will be reasonably fast, then we can be quit of this place. Though internal security duties?" He shrugged. "I guess it's better than the knackers' yard." He touched the bare bulkhead with surprising tenderness. "It's strange how much this old lady's grown on me in the last while. I'd have been sorry to see her go just when she got her reputation back."

"I entirely agree, Number One," Siobhan smiled. "We have an excellent ship and a great crew. Let's keep it that way for a little bit longer, eh."

"Aye, aye, sir." Gregor Pushkin smiled back, and for the first time, Siobhan no longer detected even the faintest hint of bitterness in his eyes. "So what did the admiral have to say?"

"Ah," Siobhan grinned impishly, feeling free for the first time in a long time, "that's another story which requires an attentive audience over a brace of cold beers."

Pushkin snapped his fingers, pretending to suddenly remember something. "I nearly forgot, skipper," he twisted his lips in a wry grin, "the wardroom would like to extend a permanent invitation for you to eat and relax with your officers, starting with," he glanced at his timepiece, "right now, it being supper time. We promise to let you eat before we ask you to tell tall tales for your meal."

She laughed. "Lead on, then, Number One. I find my appetite and thirst have become overwhelming."

Siobhan Dunmoore touched the bulkhead in passing, a warm glow of pleasure relaxing her tired sinews. Her ship.

Damn right she is!

About the Author

Eric Thomson is the pen name of a retired Canadian soldier who spent more time in uniform than he expected, both in the Regular Army and the Army Reserve. He spent his Regular Army career in the Infantry and his Reserve service in the Armoured Corps.

Eric has been a voracious reader of science fiction, military fiction, and history all his life. Several years ago, he put fingers to keyboard and started writing his own military sci-fi, with a definite space opera slant, using many of his own experiences as a soldier for inspiration.

When he's not writing fiction, Eric indulges in his other passions: photography, hiking, and scuba diving, all of which he shares with his wife.

Join Eric Thomson at http://www.thomsonfiction.ca/ Where you'll find news about upcoming books and more information about the universe in which his heroes fight for humanity's survival.

Read his blog at
https://ericthomsonblog.wordpress.com

If you enjoyed this book, please consider leaving a review with your favorite online retailer to help others discover it.

Also by Eric Thomson

Siobhan Dunmoore

No Honor in Death (Siobhan Dunmoore Book 1)
The Path of Duty (Siobhan Dunmoore Book 2)
Like Stars in Heaven (Siobhan Dunmoore Book 3)
Victory's Bright Dawn (Siobhan Dunmoore Book 4)
Without Mercy (Siobhan Dunmoore Book 5)
When the Guns Roar (Siobhan Dunmoore Book 6)

Decker's War

Death Comes But Once (Decker's War Book 1)
Cold Comfort (Decker's War Book 2)
Fatal Blade (Decker's War Book 3)
Howling Stars (Decker's War Book 4)
Black Sword (Decker's War Book 5)
No Remorse (Decker's War Book 6)
Hard Strike (Decker's War Book 7)

Quis Custodiet

The Warrior's Knife (Quis Custodiet Nº 1)

Ashes of Empire

Imperial Sunset (Ashes of Empire #1)
Imperial Twilight (Ashes of Empire #2)

Ghost Squadron

We Dare (Ghost Squadron No. 1)